Welcome to the world of St. Piran's Hospital

Next to the rugged shores of Penhally Bay lies the picturesque Cornish town of St. Piran, where you'll find a bustling hospital famed for the dedication, talent and passion of its staff—on and off the wards!

Under the warmth of the Cornish sun, Italian doctors, heart surgeons and playboy princes discover that romance blossoms in the most unlikely of places...

You'll also meet the devilishly handsome Dr. Josh O'Hara and the beautiful, fragile Megan Phillips...and discover the secret that tore these star-crossed lovers apart.

Turn the page to step into St. Piran's—
where every drama has a dreamy doctor...
and a happy ending.

Dear Reader,

Many years ago I was lucky enough to visit Cornwall, and I absolutely loved it.

The contrast between the sandy coves and the coast, where the surf crashes onto wild rocks. The stretches of rugged farmland and the villages with gorgeous old cottages. The Cornish cream teas...mmm.

I've always wanted to go back, and the invitation to be part of the St. Piran's Hospital series was irresistible. Not only could I revisit—at least in my imagination—the physical setting, I could get to know the people I'd already enjoyed meeting in Penhally a whole lot better.

Best of all, I got a really tortured hero. i've never had one quite as dark as my Luke, but it was amazingly easy to fall in love with him. Just as Anna does.

I hope you do, too.

Happy reading!

Love

Alison

ST. PIRAN'S: THE BROODING HEART SURGEON

Alison Roberts

HARLEQUIN®

entertain, enrich, inspire™

Recycling programs
for this product may
not exist in your area.

ISBN-13: 978-0-373-06855-5

ST. PIRAN'S: THE BROODING HEART SURGEON

First North American Publication 2012

Recent titles by Alison Roberts

THE NIGHT BEFORE CHRISTMAS

THE HONOURABLE MAVERICK

THE MARRY-ME WISH

NURSE, NANNY...BRIDE!

**These books are also available in ebook format from
www.Harlequin.com**

CHAPTER ONE

IF LOOKS could kill, Luke Davenport would be a dead man.

Dr Anna Bartlett had finally deigned to join him in Theatre for her assigned job of assisting him in a potentially complicated procedure, and she was clearly less than impressed that he had decided to go ahead without her.

Sure, he'd received a message while reviewing his patient's notes that she was caught up in the emergency department of St Piran's hospital with a chest trauma case requiring a thoracotomy and would therefore be late, but what had she expected? That he would delay the case until she arrived? This patient had already had to wait longer than he should have for his surgery. In any case, if the patient in Emergency survived the aggressive procedure to try and stabilise him, Dr Bartlett would be the only person available to take them to another theatre and that left Luke in precisely the same place—having to find someone else to assist him in surgery. Thankfully, this wasn't that difficult given the talented staff this hospital could boast, and paediatric cardiac surgeon James Alexander had been available and only too willing to assist the returning head of department.

James had joined the staff in the eighteen months Luke had been away. He was not only settled in the area but married to Charlotte, a senior registrar in the cardiology department. Just one of a countless number of changes. So many it was hard for Luke to imagine he'd once been a part of all this. It was frightening how one's world could change in a heartbeat.

Like Luke's had done when the news of his younger brother's death had rocked the seemingly solid foundations of his life and prompted the radical decision to join a military medical unit. Nothing would ever be the same and yet here he was, trying to pick up the pieces of his old life.

If it felt wrong to him, it was no wonder

he was an unwelcome disturbance in Anna Bartlett's world. She'd had enough time to become part of this medical community. To stake a claim and make this department her own. Maybe that was the real reason for the resentment he could detect. That he was in charge again.

It would be a bit of a blow to anyone's ego, wouldn't it, being bumped from a position as top dog? Everybody had known that his replacement was temporary but nobody had expected him to return so abruptly. Maybe Anna had secretly thought he might never return from Iraq. To add insult to injury, it wasn't the first time Luke had taken the position from her. He'd been the winner three years ago when he'd been chosen over her for the prestigious role of head of St Piran's specialist heart surgery unit.

Yes. That could well explain the death glare he'd caught from over the top of the mask as Anna had finally entered the theatre. She stood outside the cluster of staff around the operating table now, gowned and masked, her gloved hands held carefully away from her body. Taller than average, he noted in that split second of noticing her arrival, and her eyes were green. Very cool right now because she was displeased and that made them seem hard—like uncut emeralds. Unusual enough to make a lasting impression. As did her body language. The way she was standing so absolutely still. It advertised the kind of attention to detail, like not contaminating anything, that came from being not only well trained but highly disciplined.

He'd heard that about her from James as they'd scrubbed in together. That his missing assistant was skilled and meticulous. Uncompromising. Single because she chose to be. Or maybe no man could compete with a job that someone lived and breathed to the exclusion of anything else.

'She's good,' James had added. 'Very good. You'll be pleased she's taken on the job of Assistant Head of Surgery. With the reputation she's built here, she could have gone anywhere she chose.'

James obviously respected Dr Bartlett but he'd also said he didn't really know her. Not on a personal level. The way his sentence had trailed off in a puzzled tone had suggested that maybe she didn't have a personal level.

It was James who acknowledged her presence now, however.

'Anna! That was quick.' He gave his colleague a closer glance and frowned. 'No go, huh?'

'No.' The word was crisp. The attempt to save someone in the emergency department had failed. That was that. An unsuccessful case. Time to move on to the next. 'Want me to take over?'

'If that's all right with Luke. I am rather late to start my ward round now and I've got my own theatre slot this afternoon.' James sealed another small blood vessel with the diathermy rod and then looked up at the surgeon across the table. 'Luke? Have you met Anna already?'

'No.' His response was as curt as Anna's verdict on her emergency case had been.

He carried on with the long, vertical incision he was making in his patient's chest, not looking up until James moved in to control the bleeding.

She was standing closer to the table now. A

mask covered the lower half of her face and a disposable hat hid her hair and ears. All he could see were those green eyes and for a split second the accusation in them hit home.

Yesterday he had been supposed to meet the woman who'd looked after his job for eighteen months, but there'd been that hassle at his house with a burst pipe and there had been no water supply. There'd been a problem getting power reconnected as well, after such a long period of being empty, so he'd had no way of recharging the battery for his mobile phone when it had died. The hassles had underscored the fact that he wasn't exactly thrilled to be back here anyway and... and she hadn't waited for him, had she? He'd been less than an hour late but she had gone home and hadn't left any message other than the theatre list for this morning.

And now she was glaring at him as if accepting her belated assistance for this surgery was only the first challenge he had coming his way. Well, she could take her attitude and deal with it on her own time.

'If you plan to assist,' he said curtly, 'now's the time to start. I don't like my surgeries being disrupted and I'd prefer to start the way I mean to go on.'

A tense silence fell around them as James stepped back and Anna smoothly took his place. The familiar ache in Luke's leg kicked up a notch but that only served to increase his focus. He turned his head to the scrub nurse hovering over the trolley beside him.

'Sternal saw, thanks.'

The nurse jumped at his tone and handed him the requested item with commendable speed. Then the whine of the saw cut into the silence he could still feel around him. Luke concentrated on splitting the bone beneath his hands. For a short time at least, he had no need—or inclination—to look at the woman now opposite him.

So this was Luke Davenport.

The war hero she'd been hearing so much about in the last few days. Too much. As if it hadn't been bad enough to have her position as head of department cut short, no one hesitated in rubbing salt in the wound by telling her how marvellous Luke was. What a great surgeon. And soldier. How he'd single-hand-

edly saved everybody he had been with when
they had come under attack, dragging them
from a burning vehicle despite his own badly
broken leg and then providing emergency care
that had kept them alive until help arrived.

She could believe it. One glance from a pair
of the most piercing blue eyes Anna had ever
seen and she knew she was meeting someone
just as ambitious and determined as she was
herself. Two horizontal frown lines at the top
of his nose, between dark eyebrows, added to
the intensity of the glance and made her catch
her breath. To have him treating her like a
junior fresh out of medical school might be
unacceptable but it wasn't totally surprising.
This man had seen and dealt with things she
couldn't begin to imagine experiencing.

'An honourable discharge from the army,'
someone had said. 'He's up for a medal.'

St Piran's was so lucky he had come back.
The hospital, the patients, the whole damn
community was feeling lucky. Anna had
had to hide disappointment strong enough to
morph very easily into burning resentment.
Had to try and smile and pretend she felt

lucky that she was being given the opportunity to be the hero's assistant from now on.

No wonder the guy was so full of himself he hadn't even bothered to come and introduce himself yesterday. She'd given him the courtesy of sending an apology for being late for this theatre case and look at his response! He didn't like his surgeries being disrupted. The voice had been deep and the words clipped. This was a man who was not only used to giving orders, he expected them to be obeyed.

Anna's spirits—already well dampened by the unsuccessful struggle to save a life in Emergency—slipped a little further. The only way through this, as she'd discovered with any previous difficult episode in life, was to focus on her work to the exclusion of anything else.

It wasn't hard. 'Good grief,' she couldn't help but comment when the rib spreaders were locked into position and the target of this surgery was exposed. 'Look at that.'

The sac of membrane enclosing the heart had calcified and become a thick, white casing—a kind of scar from the inflammation a virus had caused and so solid it was preventing the heart from beating effectively. Luke was about to perform a pericardectomy and peel this hard layer away from the heart tissue. A tricky, fiddly procedure that Anna had studied but never performed herself.

She would have been happy enough to do the surgery if a better option hadn't been available, but she would definitely have preferred to have the patient on bypass and a still heart to work with. Luke was sparing this man the additional risk of being on a heart-lung machine. He was going to do the procedure with the heart moving beneath his scalpel.

'Your investigations showed the extent of the calcification.' Luke sounded mildly surprised by her exclamation of astonishment. 'Right-sided filling was poor and the stroke volume was abysmal. It's a wonder he's been able to function at all.'

'The first sign that it was anything serious only came when he collapsed at work three weeks ago.'

Anna watched as Luke used a scalpel to cut through the hard, white tissue, his hand large enough to make the small instrument almost invisible. She could see how much pressure he was needing to apply but how careful and controlled that pressure was. He needed to open the scarred tissue but not penetrate the heart beneath.

His response of a grunt to her statement could have actually been satisfaction at the gleam of healthy, pink tissue revealed, but Anna caught something that seemed more like a reprimand that it had taken that long to diagnose the condition correctly and arrange livesaving treatment.

The criticism was unfair. This patient, Colin Herbert, had avoided even going to his GP for years, putting his shortness of breath down to being unfit and his tiredness to the broken nights of helping to parent two young children. Even initial investigations hadn't pointed to a cardiac cause for these symptoms in the thirty-seven-year-old. It had taken a CT scan and then cardiac catheterisation to reveal the rare condition, and that had left Anna having to decide whether to attempt an unfamiliar surgery herself or refer Colin to someone more experienced.

The news of Luke Davenport's return had made it worthwhile delaying the surgery for just a little longer. If Colin could stay in St Piran's, close to his family and friends, it would probably speed his recovery. It would certainly make this period far less stressful for his wife and children.

Luke had now begun peeling the pericardium away from the heart muscle. The anaesthetist, amongst others, was peering into the wound with fascination.

'Looks like plastic,' one of them commented.

Another grunt came from the surgeon and then silence fell in the theatre again. His requests for instruments or responses to updates on monitoring were curt. He barely acknowledged Anna's assistance. Surgery with this man was never going to be a relaxed affair, then. Not that he shouldn't be concentrating fiercely on the task at hand, but that had never stopped Anna from involving her colleagues. Testing their knowledge and sharing her own. Discussing problems and allowing contributions to any trouble-shooting needed. The way mentors had done with her in the past.

Being Mr Davenport's assistant might be

like treading water as far as her career was concerned. Demoted to second best but only allowed to learn anything new by observation. Anna could feel the frustration creeping in already. She might well have to bite the bullet and start fighting for the chance to prove herself elsewhere. Having to apply for sought-after positions where most of the applicants, as well as those making the final choice, were male. Skilled, powerful, alpha men like the one working opposite her right now. Men who needed a lot of convincing that a woman was capable of being their equal.

But even as Anna felt the tightening knot of a tension she'd been aware of for her entire career in medicine, something else was pushing into her awareness. The skill Luke was demonstrating here told her that, merely through observation, she could learn from him. His timing was exquisite as he allowed the heart to beat and squeeze out blood, then advancing his scalpel to free the casing a little further in each fraction of time when the heart was filling again and, therefore, still enough to be safe.

* * *

The equipment and the technician needed to put the patient on bypass were standing by. Peeling the pericardium from the back of the heart would be the most difficult part of this procedure and Luke was keeping the option of using cardiac bypass available.

He would prefer not to, however, and so far things were going smoothly. The staff were more than competent and he had no complaints about Dr Bartlett's assistance. She was good. Somehow she had instantly tuned in with how he worked, and it was like having an extra pair of his own hands in action. Smaller hands, of course. More nimble ones. It was quite possible that Anna would be better suited to continue this when he got to the tight patches around the back.

The thought was embryonic. Barely registered, in fact, because Luke was so focused on what he was doing. Anna had the edge of the hardened pericardium caught in a pair of forceps, holding it up and helping to peel it away as he cut carefully beneath it.

He was using the scalpel with absolute precision. Tiny cuts as close to the hard casing as possible. There was less than a millimetre of space to work in. Luke was vaguely aware that the atmosphere around him was tense and that he could change it by relaxing a little and talking more, but he had no desire to do that.

He was being watched in this, his first surgery on returning to his role as head of department for cardiac surgery. Being watched and judged. They were wondering if his experience in the army had changed him—as a surgeon or as a person.

Of course it had. He had honed skills and one of them was the ability to focus no matter what kind of distractions were around. What anyone else, including Anna—no, especially Anna—might be thinking of him was irrelevant. What mattered here was a good outcome for his patient. His focus was on that scalpel. Right on its tip, which was the only part of the blade he was using.

The blood seemed to come from nowhere. There'd been small bleeders up to now that Anna had dealt with but this was a sudden gush that drowned his scalpel, washed over the fingertips of his gloves and began to form a pool. The beat of the heart made it appear briefly and then the blood washed over it again, totally obscuring his vision.

Red.

So red.

And warm. He could feel it on his fingers. Sticky life blood, ebbing rapidly from where it was supposed to be.

Someone was dying.

He could hear their screams. He could hear the sound of gunfire, too, and smell something burning.

He had to do something.

But he couldn't move.

Anna saw the moment the small artery got nicked by the tip of the scalpel. It needed more than diathermy. Clamping and tying it off shouldn't present more than a momentary delay. She picked up a clamp, ready to hand it to Luke, already eyeing up the suture material he would need.

But he didn't request the clamp. The hand that was holding the scalpel was as still as stone. Frozen.

And then the surgeon looked up, straight at her, and Anna's own heart missed a beat. He was looking at her but he was seeing something very different. Something that had absolutely nothing to do with this room or this patient or the surgery he was in the middle of performing.

He was seeing something…terrifying?

Her heart missed only a single beat. With the next one she was moving smoothly. Using the clamp in her hand and then a suture. To those around them, it would look as though Luke had silently requested her control of the nuisance bleeding. Given his virtually silent technique up until now, it wouldn't have surprised anyone. But Anna had been the only one to see the look in his eyes. Had felt the way he had frozen, and it had quite possibly been the most disturbing moment she had ever encountered in Theatre.

It took only moments to deal with the artery and a nurse used suction to clear the operating field again. Anna heard Luke's indrawn breath and looked up to see the way he blinked with such deliberation it gave the impression of a switch being flicked off. And then normal service was resumed. The surgery carried on as though nothing awkward had happened.

But something had changed. Maybe it was an acknowledgment of the way Anna had rescued the situation. Or maybe it was the beginning of the kind of bond that could weld a tight team together.

'If I tilt the heart,' Luke said quietly a short time later, 'you're in a much better position to deal with that patch at the back. Are you happy with what you've seen of the technique?'

'Yes.' The increase in her own heart rate wasn't trepidation. It was far more like excitement. The challenge of trying something new. The idea that she might be on a new journey to learn skills that nobody else could teach so well. There was something like relief mixed in there as well because her future here at St Piran's looked a little less bleak. There was even a letting go of a little of that resentment towards the man who had reclaimed his job. The job she had desperately wanted to keep.

Thank goodness her hand was steady as she took hold of the scalpel. Even better was

Luke's quiet praise as he watched what she was doing.

'That's excellent. Keep going. The more of this we can remove, the better the outlook for this patient will be.'

By the time the surgery was complete, the outlook was good and Luke finally stood back from the table and stripped off his gloves, thanking everyone for their contribution to the successful procedure. As he turned to leave, he tugged at his mask, breaking the strings that held it in place, and for the first time Anna saw more than those intensely blue eyes.

She saw a rugged, unsmiling face, with deep furrows from his nose to the corners of a mouth wide enough to balance the size of his nose. He wasn't what you'd call classically good-looking but it was hard to look away. The raw, unpolished masculinity was compelling. Those frown lines were still there at the top of his nose so maybe they were a permanent feature. When Luke started tugging off his bloodstained gown as he neared the swing doors of the theatre, Anna saw the lean muscles of deeply tanned arms. She could have sworn that those doors opened of their own accord, which was impossible but there was something about the commanding height and the way this man moved that made the notion perfectly feasible.

Luke Davenport was a soldier as much as—or possibly more than—he was a surgeon.

Every female in the room was watching as he made his exit, no doubt equally impressed, but Anna knew she would be the only one who found the image conflicting. Downright confusing, really.

Yes, Luke had lived up to his reputation as a gifted surgeon and he was apparently prepared to let her close enough to absorb valuable new skills but...what the heck had happened back when that bleeding had occurred?

Was Luke even aware of the way he had zoned out like that? He certainly hadn't acknowledged her contribution to the situation. He'd been injured during his time on the front line. An injury that was serious enough to prevent his return to his army position. Maybe he'd received wounds to more than his leg? A head injury perhaps that had left him with a form of epilepsy? Absence seizures where the sufferer was unaware of their surroundings and could freeze for up to a minute or so would explain it, but if that was the case, there was no way he should be still holding a scalpel.

That explanation didn't seem plausible, however. A seizure would have someone looking blank and Luke hadn't looked blank at all. He'd looked... *Haunted* was the word that sprang to mind. As though he'd been sucked into a flashback that he hadn't been able to escape from. This seemed far more likely but no less excusable.

What if he'd been close to the pulmonary artery? Or, worse, the aorta? Even a few seconds of delayed response in trying to control the kind of bleeding those vessels were capable of producing could have been disastrous. What really bothered Anna was knowing that she was probably the only person who had noticed the incident, which meant that saying anything might be seen as a form of professional sour grapes. Revenge, even, for the reprimand she'd received because of her late arrival for the case. Everyone knew that she'd missed out on the job as departmental head when she'd first applied. Now they'd be watching to see how she was handling her new role. To make an accusation that could have major repercussions on Luke's career within the first few hours of them working together was unthinkable.

There was only one person who might accept and understand her concerns. The same person who could provide an explanation that could possibly negate the need to take it any further. If nothing else, Luke deserved the courtesy of direct communication but it was also a conversation that needed to happen in private.

Right now her focus had to remain with their patient as he went into Recovery and was then settled into the intensive care unit for monitoring and post-surgical care. She had surgery she was due to perform with a registrar to remove sternal wires from a patient who'd had heart surgery a long time ago but was continuing to suffer pain that was probably a reaction to the foreign material in her body. The procedure wouldn't take too long and she'd planned to use her lunch break after that to talk to Luke and suggest a detailed ward round to bring him up to speed with all the cardiac inpatients.

Maybe she'd better use that time for something rather more personal. To make a judgment call on the integrity of the man she had to be able to trust if she was going to work with him at all. For some reason, the prospect of getting that close to Luke Davenport was more intimidating than anything Anna could remember facing.

She needed to think of it as nothing more than a new professional challenge. Backing away or trying to make it easier was not an acceptable option. She'd take it face on. Anna gave a decisive nod as she followed Colin's bed out of Theatre. She actually found herself almost smiling, having made the decision to confront Luke. If the situation had been reversed she had no doubts at all that Luke would be addressing the issue. He would probably have done so on the spot, with no thought of sparing her the humiliation of an audience.

Maybe this was a subtle opportunity to demonstrate not only her ability to do the job he had reclaimed but that her way of doing it might be better.

The prospect of the private interview with Mr Davenport was no longer simply intimidating.

It was…exhilarating.

CHAPTER TWO

THE need to escape was overwhelming.

And impossible.

Having ripped off the theatre scrubs, Luke had gone straight to the showers in the changing room but he couldn't wash away the aftermath of those few seconds in the middle of Colin Herbert's surgery. Turning the water to lukewarm hadn't brought its recent comfort of familiarity. Even the icy cold blast he finished with couldn't shock it out of his head the way it could chase nightmares away.

His clothes felt wrong, too. His trousers and an open-necked shirt felt too smooth against skin used to the thick fabric of camouflage overalls. At least he didn't have to knot a tie around his neck, like tying a bow on a pretty parcel. How ridiculous would that seem when he would far rather be fastening the Velcro straps of a Kevlar bulletproof vest over his shoulders. Feeling the weight of the armour plating and the bulkiness of pockets stuffed with whatever he might need at a moment's notice.

He felt too light as he strode out of the theatre suite without a backward glance. Almost as though he was floating.

Lost.

The corridors were full of people going about their business, but it was all so slow. There was no sense of urgency as beds and wheelchairs were propelled to new destinations or staff moved from one task to another. They had time to stop and chat to each other. He saw people smiling and even heard laughter at one point. Someone said hello to him and Luke managed to smile back, but the facial contortion felt grim.

He didn't belong here any more. This was a joke that wasn't the least bit funny. Like the whole of civilian life. It was a game. A pretence. Meaningless.

Going outside was better. A brisk walk around the sprawling, modern structure that was busy St Piran's hospital. A helicopter was coming in to land, no doubt bringing a trauma patient to the emergency department. Luke's eyes narrowed as he watched it intently and soaked in the sound of its rotors. If anything was likely to give him a flashback, surely that was?

It wasn't going to happen. He knew that because he was aware of the potential and he was focused. In control. The way he should have been for every second of that surgery. He kept watching anyway. Testing himself, until the helicopter took off again and disappeared into the distance.

A tempting distance. He could start walking again and just keep going. Stride down the cobbled streets of this picturesque market town until he got to the harbour. Or, better yet, a stretch of beach where he could push himself with the added difficulty of walking in sand. Or hurl himself into the surf with its magic, albeit temporary, ability to numb his body and brain and wash everything away. An effect a thousand times better than a cold shower.

But this was early December. It was freezing and his wetsuit was hanging to dry on his back porch after his early swim that morning. His leg hurt, too, thanks to standing so still for so long in Theatre. And he was here because he had a job to do. A job he had been lucky to be able to come back to. An anchor. Something to build on and the only thing he had, really. Given time, this might start making sense again, giving him the bonus of feeling like he was doing something worthwhile even, though after this morning that goal seemed further away than ever.

At least the patient who had been unfortunate enough to be his first case back here was doing well.

It was nearly an hour later that Luke arrived in the intensive care unit and Colin was awake, though very drowsy. A nurse was by his side and she smiled warmly at the surgeon.

'I've been hearing all about the surgery,' she said to him. 'I wish I could have seen it. I hear you did an amazing job.'

Luke made a noncommittal sound without looking away from the monitor screen giving detailed recordings of what was happening inside Colin's heart thanks to the catheter that had been positioned at the very end of the surgery.

Surgery that could have been a total disaster.

An amazing job? He didn't think so.

The nurse was still hovering. He heard the intake of her breath. She was about to say something else. Possibly another admiring comment. Luke shifted his gaze to give her what he hoped would be a quelling glance. Sure enough, her mouth snapped shut, a flush of colour stained her cheeks and she turned to fiddle with an IV port on her patient's arm.

Colin's eyes flickered open. He saw the surgeon standing beside his bed and smiled weakly.

'I'm still here,' he said, his voice slightly raspy. 'Thanks, Doc.'

Luke returned the smile. 'You're doing fine. We'll keep an eye on you in here for a bit and there's a few tests we need to run later today, but we'll get you onto the ward as soon as possible. Do you have anything you want to ask me about?'

Colin's head moved in a slow shake. 'I think my wife's asked everything already.

Dr Bartlett seems to know what she's talking about. I'm still a bit groggy to take it in but I'm alive and that's what matters.' He smiled again, his relief obvious.

'I'll be back later. I can talk to you and your wife then.'

'Dr Bartlett said how well things had gone. What a great job you did.'

'Oh?' That surprised him. Or did Anna not worry about embellishing the truth when it came to reassuring her post-operative patients?

'The wife's just gone to find my mum downstairs and look after the kids so Mum can come in for a visit. Hey, did I say thanks?'

'You did.'

Luke knew he sounded brusque. He didn't need the nurse to give a look vaguely reminiscent of the glare he'd seen more than once in Theatre from Anna. Did she know? Had word spread that his new colleague had had to leap in and prevent the error he'd made during surgery becoming a potential catastrophe?

'Where is Dr Bartlett?' he asked the nurse as he signed off a new addition to the drug chart and prepared to leave the intensive care unit. 'I need to have a word with her.'

'Back in Theatre, I expect.'

Of course she was. He'd seen the case listed on the whiteboard in the theatre suite. A sternal wire removal. In the same theatre Colin had been in. With the same theatre staff, presumably. Would Anna be checking whether anyone else had noticed the incident and could back up her report on the concerns she now had about the abilities of the returning head of department?

She hadn't said anything at the time. Hadn't even sent a significant glance in his direction, but that said something in itself, didn't it? She hadn't bothered to hide what she thought of him returning to take her job in those early glares. It suggested that she was weighing the implications. Making sure she used the ammunition he had handed her to best effect by choosing the best time and place.

Dammit! How the hell had it happened? He was well used to the nightmares, but to have a flashback like that happen during the day? In the middle of surgery? It was appalling. He wasn't quite sure of how long he had lost his focus but he had no doubts about what could have happened if there hadn't been someone as quick as Anna on the other side of that table.

It wouldn't happen again. He'd lost focus because that had been his first slot back in a civilian theatre. His concentration had been too much on a procedure that couldn't have been more different to the kind of work in an Iraqi field hospital or, more particularly, as a member of the medical emergency response team on a mission on the front line. It had been slow and fiddly compared to the aggressive, lifesaving measures of treating major trauma under circumstances as tough as they got. It had been a mental ambush, triggered by the unexpected amount of blood he'd seen, or the way it had pooled, maybe.

Whatever. It wouldn't happen again because he'd be ready for it and wasn't going to allow a loss of control. Luke was perfectly confident of his ability to do just that.

But would Anna believe it?

A pair of green eyes came to mind. Framed by dark lashes that were unadorned by any mascara. Angry eyes. Accusing and assessing at the same time. What would they be like, softened by trust?

Even more compelling, no doubt, but Luke had to wonder if he would ever witness such a change.

Winning Anna's trust was not even the priority it probably should be because this underlying tension…this waiting for something potentially unpleasant to happen, was oddly welcome. It made him feel a little more alive than he had ever felt since he'd been shipped home.

He was there, in the hospital canteen. Sitting alone near a window.

Brooding was the word that sprang to Anna's mind. Hunched over a plate of food he appeared to be toying with rather than eating. The big room was well populated and noisy. Was that why the table with its single occupant seemed to stand out like a beacon? Or was her glance drawn there like a magnet because so many other people were eyeing the newcomer and probably talking about him?

She could understand not wanting to be in there and either listening to or being the object of the kind of speculation and gossip rife in any group of people as large as the St Piran's staff was, but why on earth hadn't he done what she almost always did—buy a sandwich and some fruit to take back to the privacy of an office?

Was he hoping for company? There must be so many people there who knew him but there was a hierarchy involved and maybe there weren't any of his peers around. Anna found herself hoping that by the time she got to the end of this long queue someone would have joined Luke. That way, she wouldn't need to feel guilty about not doing so.

Not that she didn't want the chance to talk to him, but this was hardly the place to have the kind of conversation she had in mind, and the idea of making small talk with this man was not appealing. It would be dishonest, in a way, when they both knew what needed to be discussed—the kind of game-playing Anna had never had the slightest inclination to indulge in. Besides, Luke was making himself look so very unapproachable. Self-contained and cool. If he knew and agreed with all the praise going on behind his back, his self-image would have to be more than a little in-flated. Maybe his own company was enough?

Like Anna, Luke had changed out of his scrubs and was dressed neatly. Profession-ally. Anna slid her tray along the metal bars in front of the food cabinets and found herself running her hand down the side of her close-fitting skirt to make sure it wasn't creased. And then touching her hair to ensure that no tendrils had escaped the sleek knot at the back of her neck. She could do professional, too. Better than anybody, which was no surprise given the amount of practice she'd had.

'Anna… Hi!'

A new burst of hungry staff members was milling behind her, settling into the queue. The greeting had come from Charlotte Alexander, one of St Piran's cardiology staff members, who was behind a couple of nurses who'd stopped to stare into a chilled cabinet containing rolls of sushi.

If Anna made personal friendships among her colleagues, which she didn't, Charlotte would have been at the top of her list. While their relationship was friendly, it was still as professional as Anna could keep it. Even now, when the loose top Charlotte was wearing reminded her that she'd noticed the obvious increase in weight a week or two ago and it had occurred to her that Charlotte could well be pregnant, she wasn't about to ask such a personal question.

Girl stuff, like heart-to-hearts or sharing secrets and especially wedding or baby talk, was never going to happen. They were in the same category as frilly clothes or loose hair or make-up. Badges of femininity. Barriers to acceptance as an equal in a male-dominated profession. How did women like Charlotte manage it? Looking and dressing in a way that accentuated their best features but still having the respect of both colleagues and patients?

It made Anna feel like she had some kind of split personality, but it was so engrained now it was getting hard to know whether it was the Anna at home or the Dr Anna Bartlett at work that was the real her. The only thing she could be sure of was that never the twain could meet.

But sometimes…like right now…it struck Anna that her work persona was simply armour. Concealing anything feminine and vulnerable. Giving her focus and strength. Her gaze strayed of its own accord back to the solitary figure of Luke Davenport. What was it about him that made her even more aware that she didn't look as feminine or, God help her, attractive as she could? Just as well her work persona was so firmly engrained. If armour was what it was, she might need its protection more than ever.

Charlotte had been held up too long. She moved around the nurses who couldn't decide between the teriyaki chicken or smoked salmon.

'Hi.' She smiled at Anna. 'How's it going?'

'Very good. Theatre's over for today and both patients are doing well. I just took the sternal wires out of your Violet Perry. I'm sure the irritation will be gone and she'll be pain-free in no time.'

'That's great.' Charlotte was peering into the sandwich cabinet. 'Hmm. Chicken and Camembert sounds nice. Or turkey and cranberry. No…we'll be sick of that soon. Have you seen how many Christmas decorations are up already?'

'Mmm. Way too soon, in my opinion.' Anna found the seasonal celebrations at work disquieting. Too much of a bridge to personal lives.

'Ham salad,' Charlotte decided, reaching for one of the triangular plastic boxes. 'Oh… weren't you in Theatre with Davenport this morning? Doing Colin Herbert's pericardectomy?'

'Yes.' Again, Anna's gaze strayed towards Luke.

'How did it go?'

For a split second Anna considered confiding in Charlotte. Telling her all about how Luke had frozen and she'd had to take over the surgery. If she did, she'd be taking a step she could never undo. Charlotte would tell her husband, James, and the snowball effect might sweep them all into places they would rather not go. This man was going to be her professional partner from now on. They would be working closely together. Closer than she was with Charlotte or James or any of the other cardiology or cardiac surgery staff. She and Luke would share duties in Theatre, on ward rounds, during outpatient clinics.

As though he sensed her stare, Luke raised his head to look up. Straight at Anna. Just for a heartbeat she held his gaze and tried to analyse what she could feel in that connection.

Maybe he wasn't bad tempered and brooding, she decided as she looked swiftly away. Strangely, for that moment in time, it had looked more like something deeper. Possibly even unhappiness? What reason could he have?

He had been forced to leave the army early due to his injury, hadn't he? Perhaps Luke didn't want to be here just as much as Anna didn't want him to be.

She looked away but not before she felt an odd squeeze beneath her ribs. She knew what it was like to feel unhappy.

Lonely.

Did she really have to kick someone who might already be down? Maybe she was overreacting. She had stepped in so fast, after all. If he'd been about to move at the same time it wouldn't have been such a big deal at all. Not that she'd had the impression he would have moved that fast, but it wouldn't hurt to think about things a little longer.

'It was amazing,' she heard herself telling Charlotte, absently picking up a pack of chicken sandwiches. 'I've never seen a technique quite that precise. I got to do a patch behind the left ventricle and it wasn't easy.'

'Wish I could have seen it,' Charlotte sighed. 'Did you know he'd ordered the observation deck closed?'

Her disappointment was clear. It was an opportunity to express caution about the man's personality or even say something negative. Curiously, Anna felt the need to defend Luke.

'I guess you wouldn't want too many people watching when you're doing your first case after a long time away.'

'I guess. How's Colin doing now?'

'Really good. We might be able to move him to the ward later today. Tomorrow, anyway, if he stays this stable. We should be well past the danger period for complications from acute dilation of cardiac chambers but his heart's still got to get used to dealing with much more of a blood flow.'

'I'll get up to see him this afternoon. Here's hoping the surgery report won't be far away. I'll be very interested to read it.'

So would Anna, but her agreement was silent. If she'd voiced it, her tone might have suggested that there would be more to read about than Charlotte might expect. They were getting near the cashiers' part of the counter now and she turned her attention to the baskets of fruit. An apple, she decided. The nice-looking green one on the top of the second basket.

The crash that came from somewhere in the kitchens behind the food counters was astonishingly loud. Metallic. Jarring enough for every head in the cafeteria to swivel sharply in that direction and for conversation to cease abruptly.

And in that second or two of startled silence a scream rang out. And then a cry for help.

Jaws dropped as staff members looked at each other as though trying to confirm the reality of what was happening. Anna heard Charlotte's gasp behind her but she was watching something else. Weirdly, her instinct had been to look away from the source of the sound so she had seen the first movement in the crowd. A reaction time so fast it was hard to process.

Luke Davenport was on his feet. His chair tipped backwards and he pushed at the table in front of him rather than stepping around it. The table also tipped, the tray sliding off to send china and cutlery crashing to the floor but Luke didn't even spare it a glance. He was heading straight for the kitchen.

Access was blocked by the tall, glass-fronted cabinets apart from the space where Anna was, beside the tills and the fruit baskets. There was a flap in the counter beside the last till where kitchen staff could go in and out with the trolleys of used dishes but Luke didn't bother to stop and lift it. Or maybe he didn't see it. He swept the baskets clear to send apples and oranges bouncing around the feet of those still standing motionless and then he vaulted the space, making the action seem effortless.

Kitchen staff were backing away hurriedly, but not quickly enough for Luke.

'Move!' he barked. 'Clear the way. What's happened?'

'Over here,' someone shouted. 'Oh, my God... I think he's dead.'

Luke took several steps forward. Between the tills, Anna could see the blue uniforms of kitchen staff moving. Clearing a space near the stoves in front of which a large man in a white jacket lay very still.

Luke took in the scene. He turned his head with a single, rapid motion.

'Anna!' he shouted. 'Get in here. I need you.'

Someone had raised the flap now but, if they hadn't, it occurred to Anna that she might have tried to leap over it, too. Luke needed her?

The man was obviously one of the chefs. His white hat had come off when he'd collapsed and was lying amongst the pots and pans of an overturned rack.

Luke kicked one of them aside as Anna raced into the kitchen. 'Get rid of those,' he ordered. 'Someone help me turn him. Did anyone see what happened?'

'He just fell,' a frightened woman offered. 'One minute he was cleaning down the cooker and then he toppled sideways.'

'What's his name?'

'Roger.'

The man had been rolled onto his back now. Luke gripped his shoulder and shook it firmly, hunched down so that he could lean close and shout.

'Roger? Can you hear me? Open your eyes!'

He barely waited for the response that didn't come. His hands on Roger's chin and forehead, he tilted the head back to open his airway.

'Does anyone know him?' he demanded. 'Medical history?'

'He takes pills,' someone said. 'For his blood pressure, I think.'

'No, it's his heart,' another voice added.

The few seconds that Luke had kept his fingertips on the side of Roger's neck and his cheek close to his face had been enough to let him know that there was no pulse or respiration to be felt or seen. Anna crouched on the other side of the collapsed man as Luke raised his fist and brought it down squarely in the centre of the man's chest. A precordial thump that was unlikely to be successful but was worth a try.

Ready to start CPR, Anna was thinking fast, compiling a mental list of what they would need. Luke was way ahead of her.

'Get a crash trolley in here. Find a cardiac arrest button. Send for someone in ED or wherever's closest. Anna, start compressions.' He looked up at the silent, horrified onlookers. 'Move!'

They backed away. Anna heard someone yelling into the canteen for the cardiac arrest button to be pushed. If there wasn't one in there, it wouldn't be too far away. She positioned her hands, locked her elbows and started pushing on Roger's chest. He was a big man and it was hard work to compress the sternum enough to be effective.

Ten…twenty…thirty compressions. At least someone would arrive with a bag-mask unit very soon so she didn't have to worry about the implications of unprotected mouth-to-mouth respirations on a stranger.

The faint possibility of contracting something like hepatitis didn't seem to occur to Luke. Or it didn't bother him.

'Hold it,' he ordered Anna, pinching Roger's nose and tilting his head back as he spoke.

Then he sealed the man's mouth with his own. One slow breath…and then another.

Anna started compressions again, the image of Luke's lips pressed to someone's face emblazoned in her mind. The kiss of life… She'd seen it before, though it was a rarity in a medical setting. Was that why it was so disturbing this time? Shocking, in fact. She had to concentrate on her silent counting until it was time to warn Luke.

'Twenty-seven, twenty-eight, twenty-nine, thirty…'

By the time they had completed another set of compressions and breaths, there were new voices nearby and the rattle of a trolley.

'Crash team,' someone announced. 'We'll take over now.'

'I've got it, thanks,' Luke growled.

'But it's what we—'

'We just need the gear,' the surgeon interrupted. 'And some assistance.'

Anna could feel the resentment at not being allowed to do what they thought they had been summoned for, but a life pack was lifted from the trolley and put on the floor along with an IV roll, a bag mask and a portable oxygen tank.

She carried on with the chest compressions, pausing only to let Luke rip the chef's jacket and the singlet underneath open to expose the chest and stick the pads in place. On direction, one of the doctors in the crash team secured his airway and attached oxygen to the bag mask, holding it in place until Anna paused again.

Could she ask to hand over compressions to someone else? This was enough of a physical effort to make her aware of perspiration dampening her shirt. No, she wouldn't ask. She was with Luke on this.

He had been the one to respond and identify the crisis, which made this man his patient until he chose to hand him over. And he'd asked for Anna's help. Roger was their patient and they could do this as well, probably better, than the junior doctors assigned to crash-team duties for the day.

'Stop compressions.' Luke was watching the screen of the life pack, waiting for a readable trace to appear. 'V fib,' he announced moments later. 'Charging to three hundred joules. Everyone stand clear.'

The junior doctors inched back, exchanging glances.

'Who is this guy?' Anna heard one of them ask another.

'Luke Davenport,' came the response. 'You know, the surgeon who's just got back from Iraq?'

'Oh...'

In the short space of time it had taken for three stacked shocks to be delivered, the atmosphere in this inner circle around the victim changed. The crash team, who had been busy resenting not being allowed to showcase their skills in managing an arrest, suddenly couldn't do enough to help their leader.

'Do you want an intubation kit, Mr Davenport?'

'Shall I draw up some adrenaline? Atropine?'

'Here's a sixteen-gauge cannula. And a flush.'

'Dr Bartlett? Do you need a break?'

Anna sat back on her heels, nodding. There was plenty of scientific evidence that compressions became less effective after two minutes unless someone else took a turn. She didn't move far away, however. She watched, totally amazed by the speed at which Luke worked. And she noticed things she hadn't noticed before.

Like the streaks of grey in his short brown hair. They had to be premature because she knew he was only a few years older than her and couldn't have hit forty quite yet. He had such neat fingernails too and his hands looked so different without gloves. Far more masculine, which made their speed and cleverness more impressive as he gained intravenous access and secured the line.

His brain was working just as fast. He seemed to be able to think of everything at once and keep tabs on what everybody was doing, but most of all, Anna was caught by the way he'd taken a trolley of equipment and a group of young medics who hadn't been thrilled not to be allowed to take over and forged them into a team that was now working under difficult conditions as well as they could have in a resuscitation bay in Emergency.

It was a team that had achieved success even before Luke had made a move to secure Roger's airway with an endotracheal tube. When the static cleared from the next, single shock delivered, the flat line suddenly gave a blip. And then another...

'Sinus rhythm,' one of the crash team said triumphantly. 'Yes.'

'Have we got a stretcher?' Luke still hadn't relaxed. 'Let's get this man into the ED. Or CCU.'

Charlotte had edged her way to the back of the kitchen. 'Great job, Mr Davenport. Would you like to hand over now?'

'Call me Luke,' he said, still watching the monitor. The rhythm was picking up steadily and Roger was taking his own breaths now. The chef's eyes flickered and he groaned loudly.

And, finally, Anna saw the grim lines of Luke's face soften a little. He leaned down and gripped Roger's shoulder again with his hand——the way he had when he'd first begun this resuscitation effort. He didn't shake it this time. This was a reassuring touch.

'Just relax,' he told Roger. 'We're looking after you. Everything's all right.'

He looked up at Charlotte and gave a nod to indicate transfer of responsibility. Charlotte moved closer to talk to him, but as she moved, Luke shifted his gaze to Anna.

And something inside her tightened and then melted.

From the moment this incident had started—from when she'd heard the scream and seen Luke's instantaneous response, she'd been aware of his total command of the situation. Of his faultless performance and ability to absorb additional resources and personnel and then…right at the end…an indication that he really cared about this patient.

An impressive mix. If his glance had been in any way smug, it could have driven Anna into a defensive corner she might never have emerged from, but there was no hint of smugness. No self-satisfaction even. The fraction of time he held her gaze sent a message that was more like, We did it. This time, at least.

The triumph that was there was on the patient's behalf. Behind that was the acknowledgment of defeat in other cases and the sadness that they couldn't always win. Shining over both impressions was a kind of promise. A determination to always fight the odds and do the best possible job.

It sucked her right in.

She could work with this man. Could respect him. Like him.

More than that, in fact, judging by the odd ripple of sensation that caressed her spine and sent tingles through the rest of her body.

Dear Lord, she was attracted to him? No wonder she'd been so aware of her own appearance when she'd been standing in line with Charlotte. It explained a lot but it was a reaction that had to be crushed instantly. Allowing something that personal to threaten a professional relationship would be the ultimate play on femininity.

The reason women couldn't be seen as equals in this arena was largely because of the perception that they allowed emotion to cloud their judgment. Or, worse, they put a priority on relationships and undermined their careers by taking time off to have babies.

Not Anna Bartlett. It wasn't on any agenda she'd ever had.

Luke's return and—worse—his attractiveness were roadblocks. Ones she could detour around, which would see her working somewhere else, or deal with if the pull to stay put was strong enough. Either way, getting even remotely close to Luke Davenport would be a mistake.

It was Anna who broke the eye contact.

And turned away.

CHAPTER THREE

THE crisis over, Luke found he couldn't drag his eyes away from Anna.

Not that he hadn't spotted her the moment she'd walked into the canteen. He'd taken a good look then because he hadn't been sure it was her. Something about the height and body shape of the woman had seemed familiar but he'd only seen her eyes before this so it could have been anybody.

Just an attractive female member of staff. A senior member, obviously, because of the way she held herself. The way she moved with the confidence of someone who knew she was very good at what she did. And maybe he recognised something in the way this woman was dressed. Power dressing, really, with that pencil skirt and neat shirt. She probably had a matching jacket that would make the outfit the female equivalent of a man's suit. And what was that horrible thing she'd done to her hair? It was all scraped back into a round thing that made her look like a cartoon version of a librarian or frumpy secretary. All she needed was some thick-rimmed spectacles to complete the picture.

When her head had turned to scan the room, he hadn't needed to be close enough to see the colour of her eyes to recognise that this was, indeed, Anna Bartlett. While she wasn't radiating resentment right now, there was an air of containment about her that suggested she didn't change her mind easily. A reserve that could well morph into an arctic-type chill when she saw him. A woman that knew her own mind and woe betide anyone that got in her way. Like him.

Luke almost sighed as he dropped his gaze back to a meal he wasn't particularly interested in. He wasn't enjoying this lunchtime experience much at all, in fact. He knew that many of the people around had to be talking about him. Gossiping. The happy chatter and laughter going on around him, even the smell of abundant, hot food all seemed irrelevant. Superficial.

The crash and then the scream had been real, though. He'd reacted on autopilot. He wasn't sure what had made him demand Anna as an assistant. Possibly because she had been the only staff member nearby that he could call by name. Or maybe it was the memory of how well they had worked together in Theatre only a short time ago.

It had been a good choice. The crisis had been dealt with and a life had been saved and it had only been then, when it was virtually done and dusted and he was handing his patient into the care of a new team, that Luke had allowed anything else to enter his head. It was then that he'd had his first close-up look at Dr Bartlett and he'd had the curious impression that he'd been looking at something he wasn't supposed to be seeing.

No wonder! The cool professional he'd seen queuing for her lunch was absent. This woman, standing in the canteen kitchen with a creased skirt and a shirt that had come untucked on one side, was...wrong, somehow. Even more disconcerting was that a thick lock

of dark blonde hair had escaped the bun thing
and lay against a long, pale neck.

Her cheeks were flushed. From the exer-
tion and stress of doing CPR or was she embarrassed at being dishevelled? Even her eyes
looked different. Enlarged pupils made them
seem softer. Warmer.

Good grief…she was rather lovely.

Any impression of warmth vanished, however, as Luke stared at her, unable to drag his
gaze away.

And then she dismissed him! Simply turned
on her heel and walked away.

How rude. No genuine warmth there, then.
Anna Bartlett was clearly a career woman
through and through, and she probably saw
him as nothing less than an obstacle in her
scramble to the top of that ladder. Any hope
that she might discuss this morning's incident
with him before reporting it to a higher au-
thority faded and disappeared.

Charlotte, the cardiologist, was saying
something to him, he realised. Something
about whether he'd like to come with them
to the emergency department to see what the
investigations Roger needed would reveal.

'Yes,' he said. 'Please.'

'You'll remember Ben Carter?'

'Of course.'

'And have you met Josh O'Hara? No, you wouldn't have. He joined the A and E staff while you were away.'

Luke kept up with the pace set by the people pushing the stretcher, heading away from the canteen and any areas that his assistant was likely to be heading for.

He'd see Anna again soon enough. Doing a ward round later today or perhaps in the departmental meeting scheduled for early tomorrow morning. Given how he felt about her in the wake of that dismissal, it might even be too soon.

The aura of the war hero already surrounding the return of Luke Davenport to St Piran's had evolved into something far more tangible by the time Anna was halfway through her ward round later that afternoon.

He had become a living legend.

Thanks to the crowd in the canteen at the time, accounts of the incident would have spread like wildfire and reached every corner of this institution in no time flat. Spilling into ears eager for the smallest details.

The junior nursing staff on the cardiology ward were discussing it when Anna paused outside the central station to collect some patient notes she needed.

'It was like something in the movies,' someone was saying in awed tones. 'He just pushed everything off the counter and jumped over it.'

'I heard he did mouth-to-mouth without even using a face shield.'

'Yeah…'

'Is the guy still alive?'

'Apparently he's in the cath lab right now. He'll probably get admitted in here or CCU when they're finished.'

'Do you think Mr Davenport will come down with him?'

'Ooh…I hope so.'

The giggling from the young nurses was irritating. Anna decided it was because her own participation in the incident had been totally eclipsed by the actions of St Piran's new superhero. Except that she couldn't convince herself to be that petty. The irritation was really there because part of her was as star-struck as everyone else seemed to be. The man was intriguing. Compelling. Apparently trustworthy. And that was disturbing because Anna felt that she knew something about him that no one else knew. Or would believe.

If she wanted to discuss her concerns with someone, the obvious choice would be Albert White, the CEO of St Piran's. He would listen to any concerns she might have about Luke's abilities. He might even believe her and, if he did, he might set some kind of probationary programme in place. Things like that did not remain confidential. Eventually, it would leak. Given his performance in the canteen and new status amongst the staff, nobody else would believe Anna.

She might find herself more alone than she'd ever been in her struggle to break through the glass ceiling of her gender. It could affect how well she was able to do her own job. She stood to lose the trust and possibly even the co-operation of the people she worked with and teamwork was vital in this line of work.

Tread carefully, she reminded herself, even

when her demotion from being team leader had been rubbed in when a flurry of activity had heralded the new arrival in the coronary care unit adjacent to the ward and more than the necessary staff numbers flocked to greet both the patient and the new head of department.

Roger the chef was made comfortable and wired up so that every beat of his heart could be monitored, the trace and its extra information like blood pressure and the level of oxygen in his blood appearing on one of the screens flanking the central nurses' station. It was there that Luke caught up with Anna.

'He needs urgent revascularisation,' he informed her. 'I'm hoping you can fit him in on your list for tomorrow.'

Anna closed her eyes for a split second as she groaned inwardly. She opened them to find herself under intense scrutiny.

'Is that a problem?' Luke asked. 'You don't have any elective patients on the list?'

'I do, but I've just been talking to a Mrs Melton and reassuring her. She's stable but has severe triple vessel disease. This is her third admission for surgery because she's been bumped off the list for urgent cases on the last two occasions.'

'Has she had a major infarct? An arrest?'

'No.'

'Come and look at Roger's films and then we can discuss it. Have you got viewing facilities in your office?'

She did, but Anna was aware of a strong reluctance to take Luke there. She had chosen not to take over his office in his absence and her space was relatively small. It was also the most personal space she had here at work.

She was already a little too aware of this man. His size and reputation and…and whatever it was that was exerting a tugging sensation on something emotional. Not to mention the danger that frisson of potential attraction had represented. She didn't want him invading a personal space. Not yet. Not until she felt a lot more confident in her interactions with him and that wasn't going to be until she'd resolved the dilemma she was in.

'The seminar room's closer. Where we hold the departmental meetings.'

'Of course. Have you got the time now?'

'Yes. I've finished the ward round.'

The round Luke had been supposed to join her for, but if he noticed any reprimand in her dry tone he gave no indication of it. He led the way down the corridor, his pace fast enough to keep Anna a half step behind. The hint of asymmetry in the way he moved had become a noticeable limp by the time they reached the lifts but Luke didn't pause. He pushed open the fire-stop doors and headed up the stairs.

Commenting on something as personal, not to mention physical, as the aftermath of his injury seemed inappropriate. In the same ball park as asking Charlotte if she was pregnant, and this wasn't remotely like the far more social setting of the hospital canteen with its 'time out' from work atmosphere. This was work and Luke's focus was entirely professional. He had no difficulty using the computerised system to bring the images from the catheter laboratory onto the large screen in the meeting room.

'As you can see, there's a seventy to eighty per cent stenosis on the left anterior descending and diffuse disease over a significant segment of the vessel. And that's not all. There's a critical stenosis in the circumflex. Here... see?'

'Yes.' Anna watched and listened. It was quite obvious that Roger was in more urgent need of surgery than her Mrs Melton. As the head of department, Luke would have been within his rights to simply order her to juggle lists but instead he was taking the time to put all the information in front of her, presumably with the intention of giving her the opportunity to make the call.

Exactly the way they should be interacting as colleagues. There was every reason to take a moment to admire the way he was dealing with the situation but there really shouldn't have been any space in Anna's head to be so aware of the way Luke moved his hands as he spoke. Of how elegant those movements were for those large hands with their clever, tapered fingers.

It was quite reasonable to appreciate the way he spoke so clearly too and the transparent speed with which his mind worked, but that didn't excuse the enjoyment Anna found she was getting from the timbre of that deep voice. She brushed off the visceral reactions. So he was intelligent and articulate. She should have expected nothing else in someone who had beaten her in a job application.

But perhaps that underlying awareness of him as a person and not simply a surgeon made her more aware of his physical issues. When they had finished coming to a mutually agreeable compromise on theatre lists, which would see Mrs Melton staying on as an inpatient until her surgery could be scheduled, Luke stood up. His face was grim and he blinked with slow deliberation, as though he was in pain but determined to ignore it. Or switch it off. The action took Anna straight back to their time in Theatre that morning and she knew she couldn't avoid broaching the subject.

'How's your leg?' she found herself asking. 'I understand you suffered a fairly serious injury?'

'I survived.' Luke's tone told her it wasn't a welcome subject for discussion. 'It's improving all the time.' His stare was expressionless. 'Why do you ask?'

Anna had to fight back the urge to apologise for asking a personal question. His eyes were so blue. So intense. No way could she simply dismiss that sharp squeezing sensation occurring deep in her belly. It might have been a very long time since she'd experienced a shaft of desire but it was all too easy to recognise. She looked away.

'I've taken on a position as your assistant. If you have problems that I could help with, please don't hesitate to tell me.'

Luke made an incredulous sound, as though Anna would be incapable of giving him any assistance. That she had no idea what she was talking about. The sound rankled. She looked up to meet his gaze again.

'If, for example, you find it hard to stay on your feet for a long theatre session.'

A corner of his mouth lifted. Just a fraction. A sardonic twist but enough of a curl for Anna to realise she had yet to see Luke smile. He certainly wasn't about to now. His expression was anything but friendly or relaxed. Her heart skipped a beat and then sped up but it was too late to swallow any words that had been spoken and try to get back onto safe ground.

* * *

She had seen his pain when Luke knew how good he was at hiding it, and it seemed like he was exposing a physical flaw. Almost as bad as that loss of focus in Theatre that morning had been. Anna had been the only person to pick up on that, as well.

He'd barely met the woman and yet it felt like she was inside a very personal space. As for offering to help with his problems. Ha! She didn't know anything.

No one here did.

And yet the idea was appealing. To have someone in his corner who was prepared to listen even if they couldn't begin to understand.

To have someone to hold at night...

Whoa! Where the hell had that come from?

Luke could manage being alone. He had to. Just as well he'd learned to bury the kind of emotional involvement that could make reality too hard to deal with. He might be back in a very different reality now but the ability to remain detached at some level was just as important. More important, maybe, given that he felt the despair of a meaningless existence pressing in on him from all sides.

He was looking into a future that had only one bright spot. His work. And Anna was trying to undermine it. Something like fear made him straighten and defend himself by attacking.

'Are you suggesting I'm physically incapable of doing my job?' He had her pinned with his gaze. 'Hoping that it might prove too much and I'll quietly go away and let you take over again?'

He saw her eyes widen and felt a flash of remorse at being so harsh. He also heard the swift intake of her breath but he didn't give her time to speak. He couldn't afford to back down. Admitting defeat wasn't something Luke Davenport did willingly.

'This is my home,' he continued. 'Where I live and where I work. Where my future is. I'm back and I have no desire to go anywhere else.'

Which one of them was he trying to convince here?

'I wasn't suggesting anything.' Anna's tone was clipped and very cool. 'Maybe I was hoping there might be a satisfactory explanation for what happened in Theatre this morning. For your slow response to a significant bleed.'

A moment's silence hung heavily between them. Not that Luke had any intention of denying the accusation or trying to excuse himself.

'I lost focus,' he admitted simply. 'It won't happen again.'

He saw the way her features softened at his honesty. She wanted to believe him. But he could also see confusion in the depths of those astonishing green eyes. What had he been thinking, attacking her for asking what had been a perfectly reasonable question? No wonder she felt torn.

'Are you intending to report the incident?'

She held his gaze. She had courage, this woman.

'Would you?'

'Yes,' Luke responded without hesitation. 'Sloppy performance is never acceptable.'

Anna tilted her head in agreement but said nothing. They left the meeting room in silence. There seemed to be nothing more to be said.

So that was that. The subject was out in the

open and he'd all but told her he expected it to be reported. All he had to do now was wait until someone, presumably Albert White or one of the other hospital administrators, came to have a little chat with him.

It didn't happen the next day.

If anything, Luke got the impression that Anna hadn't said anything at all about him that wasn't complimentary, judging by comments made in the departmental meeting the next morning.

More than one member of the cardiology and cardiothoracic surgical staff said admiring things about Colin Herbert's surgery. The congratulatory buzz when Roger's case came up during the discussion on revised theatre lists was actually embarrassing.

Luke cut it short. 'I had some very able assistance from Dr Bartlett,' he told the group briskly. 'And she's the one with the real work to do with his CABG today.'

That coronary artery bypass grafting was well under way by the time Luke left his administrative tasks and headed for the theatre suite. He didn't don a gown or mask and enter

the theatre. Instead, he slipped quietly into
the observation deck and sat, probably unnoticed, in the far corner. You could see what
was going on and hear what was being said
and, if you wanted, you could focus on one
person and make judgments about their ability. Their personality even. That was why he
had requested that the space be closed during
his surgery yesterday. An unusual case would
have attracted as many people as could have
squeezed in here and, on some level, he would
have been aware of it.

Anna wasn't aware of him. He could watch
every movement and hear every comment.
He could feel the time and care she took with
every meticulous stitch as she took the veins
harvested from Roger's legs and used them
to make new conduits to take blood to where
it was needed in the heart muscle. Her voice
was as calm as her movements. She was polite
in her requests and prepared to discuss anything with the anaesthetist or bypass machine
technicians. She spoke frequently to her registrar as well, asking questions and explaining
her own decisions. A natural teacher, then.

With a voice that he couldn't imagine getting tired of listening to. Not when it was coupled with a brain that was clearly as focused but as flexible as her hands were. An impressive mix.

He stayed where he was only until the blood flow in the new coronary arteries was deemed acceptable and Roger was successfully taken off bypass. He would see Anna again today and maybe she would let him know who she had decided to speak to. He couldn't pre-empt her by speaking to someone himself because that would make it a bigger issue than it actually was. It wasn't going to happen again because he was in control now. Of every waking moment, at least.

But nothing more was said about it despite their paths crossing frequently when they shared a busy outpatient clinic and more than once during ward rounds and departmental meetings. By Friday, both Colin and Roger were on the ward and recuperating well and finally, late that afternoon, Luke got a call to the office of St Piran's chief executive officer.

'Luke.' Albert White shook one hand and gripped Luke's other shoulder at the same time. 'I'm so sorry this has taken so long.

It's been a hectic week that included a day or two in London. Welcome back. It's good to see you.'

'It's good to see you too.' And it was, except that he could feel the distance between them. He'd been on another planet since he had last worked here. But Albert was a familiar face. Part of the anchor that Luke hoped to use to stabilise his life.

'How's the family?'

'All well when I last heard any news.'

'I was astonished to hear that your parents had taken off to New Zealand, of all places. I hear they're living on a military base in North Island?'

'They are indeed. Dad's taken an administrative position. He calls it a semi-retirement but I can't see him ever not being full-time army.'

'No. And your older brother?'

'Currently in Australia. Helping train their SAS.'

Albert shook his head. 'Army family through and through. At least we've got one of the Davenport boys back again.'

'Yes.' The word was clipped. Luke didn't

want to discuss the 'Davenport boy' who would never make it back.

There was a moment's silence, which seemed appropriate, and when Albert spoke again his tone was more serious, acknowledging so many things that were not going to be said.

'How's the leg?'

'Oh, you know. Still attached. Still works. I'm not complaining.'

Albert chuckled. 'Works pretty well from what I've been hearing. What's with the commando techniques in the canteen? Leaping tall buildings on the agenda, too?'

Luke summoned a smile. 'I don't think so.'

'Well done, anyway. I hear the chap's doing really well.'

'He is. Dr Bartlett did a quadruple bypass on him. She's an excellent surgeon.'

'She is indeed.' The glance Luke received held a hint of relief. Any awkward subjects were being left well behind. 'So things are working out, then? You two going to be able to work as a team?'

Luke couldn't detect even a hint that the CEO might be fishing for any confessions regarding a bumpy start. Maybe he should say something about it himself but if Anna had chosen not to, perhaps he should respect her decision. Albert didn't seem to notice that his silence was covering a moment of confusion.

'Not that I expected any problems, but it was good to hear Anna singing your praises the other day. A pericardectomy, I hear?'

'Um…yes. First case. What did she say?'

'That you did the entire procedure off by-pass. That she was delighted to have the opportunity to learn something new.'

About the procedure? Or about him?

This meeting was nothing more than touching base. A welcome home.

'Come and have dinner some time soon. Joan would love to catch up.'

'Sure. Maybe when I've had time to find my feet properly.' Luke hoped his vague acceptance would not seem rude but he wasn't ready to get drawn into a segment of the St Piran's community that knew his family so well. He wasn't here because of the family connection. He was here because he'd had nowhere else to go.

Besides, he was getting into a routine now.

An icy swim in the ocean at daybreak to chase away the night's demons. As many hours as possible focused entirely on his job and then exercise and work-related reading until he was hopefully exhausted enough to sleep for more than a few hours. He didn't want to tamper with what seemed to be working. Or remind himself of the past, which would only emphasise too clearly how different life was now. Control was paramount.

Control could be undermined by confusion, however. Anna had had a whole week to decide how to present her concerns about his skills but she hadn't done so.

Why not?

Not that Luke wasn't grateful but he was definitely puzzled. She'd agreed that the matter should be reported. That sloppy performance wasn't acceptable. And yet she had apparently accepted his.

Why?

He would have spoken to her about it before leaving work that day but it was late and she had already gone. It wasn't hard to use his influence to find her contact details but Luke discovered that she was living well along the windy coast road that led to Penhally.

A phone call to thank her for making his first week back smoother than it might have otherwise been seemed too impersonal. What he said might even be taken the wrong way— tacit approval for not reporting the incident perhaps. Taking a fifteen- or twenty-minute drive to what was quite possibly only a small collection of dwellings and knocking on her door after dark was a long way too far towards the other end of the spectrum, however. Far too personal. Why was he even considering it?

It didn't seem nearly as inappropriate on Saturday morning. Especially as the world in general seemed a brighter place. Days and days of grey skies and intermittent rain had been blown inland by a stiff sea breeze and the sun was making a determined effort to raise the temperature by at least a degree or two. The surf had been high enough that morning to make his swim an adrenaline rush, and his leg hadn't collapsed under him when he'd attempted a slow jog on the softer sand.

Yes. For the first time since arriving back, Luke felt that things were a little less bleak. Some time out on a day like this to drive up to Penhally and revisit old haunts was an attractive idea. He might have intended to wait until Monday to give Anna the excellent article on restrictive cardiomyopathy he'd come across in one of the journals he'd been reading until the early hours of that morning but if it was in the car, he'd have the perfect excuse to drop in at her house on his way past if he chose to.

He did choose to.

Maybe because the signpost to the lane she lived on was so easy to spot. Or perhaps because the house he found at her address was so unlike what he might have expected. Not even a house. More like a cottage with its latticed windows and some kind of evergreen creeper scrambling along the faded shingles of its roof. The small garden was overgrown and…it had a picket fence, for heaven's sake!

If someone had asked him where he thought Dr Bartlett would be living, he would have imagined a modern apartment. Streamlined and minimalist. Devoid of personality—hers or its own. This cottage probably had tourists stopping to take its picture and a name somewhere under the tangled, prickly branches obscuring half the fence. Bay View Cottage perhaps, given the glorious sweep of Penhally Bay on display. It was only a short walk down the hill to get to a beach and, given the rocky coves he had noticed just before turning off the main road, the coastline was due to provide one of those gems that surfers searched for.

Sure enough, when he left the car and went a little further uphill towards the front door of the cottage, he could see a stretch of white sand beyond the boulders. This cottage might be rundown but it was sitting on valuable land. Any closer to Penhally or St Piran and it would be worth an absolute fortune. Was that why Anna had chosen it? As an investment?

That made far more sense than a desire to inhabit what had to feel like an alien space. Having come to terms with the apparent contradiction, Luke was now hesitant in knocking on her door. Had he passed a letterbox?

He could leave the article in there and then explain it on Monday.

He might have done exactly that if it hadn't been for the sudden loud noise from inside the cottage. A crashing sound not dissimilar to the one he'd heard in the canteen earlier in the week.

No scream followed the sound but he could hear the dismay in Anna's voice.

'Oh…no!'

CHAPTER FOUR

'Anna?' Luke didn't bother knocking. He tried the doorhandle and found it turned, so he shoved the door open. 'Are you all right?'

There was no response. Cautiously, Luke advanced along the narrow hallway. He could hear Anna's voice again. It was much quieter now. Soft and soothing.

'It's all right,' she was saying. 'Poor baby, you gave yourself a big fright that time, didn't you?'

Maybe he was in the wrong house.

'Anna?'

'Who's there?'

'Me,' Luke said as he stepped into a doorway on his right.

'Luke? Good grief! What on earth are you doing here?'

She sounded surprised. No, more like appalled. Luke opened his mouth but no words emerged. This was Anna?

She was sprawled on the floor, her arms around a large dog that was virtually in her lap and making enthusiastic attempts to lick her face. There were newspapers spread around them both, a collection of paintpots and an aluminium stepladder lying on its side.

'I was just on my way to Penhally. I heard the crash.'

'From the road?'

'No...I...er...had an article I wanted to give you.' It was weirdly hard to string a coherent sentence together so Luke gave up. He stared at Anna instead, trying to take in the faded, ripped denim jeans she was wearing. The paint-stained jumper. The soft waves of her loose hair that reached her shoulders. Those amazing green eyes that were staring at him in utter bewilderment right now.

Luke dropped his gaze. The dog was staring at him too. Warily. Pressing itself further into Anna's arms and visibly shaking.

'What's wrong with the dog?'

'He's scared.'

'Of what?'

'You.'

She should probably be scared herself, Anna thought. A large man she hardly knew had just come into her house uninvited. Into her bedroom. Well, it would be her bedroom again when she'd finished renovating it. Right now it was just a mess.

Like her head.

Luke was wearing some jeans that were probably as old as her own. He had a black woollen jumper on with the sleeves pushed up to reveal bare forearms. His hair looked windswept and there was a tension about him that suggested he could leap into action at any moment. To save a life or rescue a damsel in distress.

He'd thought she was in distress.

He'd come into her house to rescue her.

And here he was, looking rugged and grim and…and…gorgeous.

Thank goodness she had her arms full of warm, shivery puppy. She hugged him more closely.

'He's a rescue puppy,' she told Luke. 'I've only had him a couple of weeks. My neighbours, Doug and June Gallagher, own a farm and they found him in the creek. In a sack. They would have kept him but they've already got a lot of dogs and he was terrified of Doug. June reckons he's been badly treated by a man.'

'So you took him? You're going to keep him?'

He sounded as though she'd just informed him that she intended to fly to the moon. Anna almost laughed but she felt absurdly close to tears. This wasn't supposed to happen and the earth had just tilted beneath her feet.

Dr Bartlett didn't do feminine or personal. She didn't do attraction to her colleagues.

Mr Davenport wasn't supposed to meet Anna. And there were no rules about Anna feeling attracted to a man. There hadn't needed to be for too long to remember.

This was threatening to do her head in completely so she dragged her gaze away from the towering figure by the doorway and buried her face in the expanse of woolly hair in her arms.

'You're all right,' she soothed. 'He's not

going to hurt you.' The reassurance seemed to bounce back at her and it sounded good. The warmth and smell of her dog was good too. Comforting. Anna raised her head to find that Luke was closer. He had dropped to a crouch and he was looking at the puppy.

'What is he, exactly?'

'We're not sure. The vet thinks he's about four months old. She reckons he's part poodle because of the wispy hair. Or maybe there's some wolfhound in there. A designer dog gone wrong, we decided, and that's why nobody wanted him.'

'A poodle and a wolfhound?' Luke seemed to be making a valiant attempt to imagine such an unlikely combination.

He looked intrigued and, with his focus so completely on the puppy, Anna got the chance to look at him.

He looked so different. Was it the casual clothing or the fact that he was here, in her home? No. It was more than that. The grimness she was getting accustomed to in his face had lightened. The puppy had distracted him and caught his interest. Was it possible it might even amuse him? Make him smile?

Anna really wanted to see Luke smile.

'It could be possible,' she said, her tone deadpan. 'As long as they'd had a staircase handy.'

Luke's gaze flicked up. He gave a huff of sound that could have passed for laughter but there was no matching curl to his lips. Instead, there was an incredulous expression in those amazingly blue eyes. As though he was seeing someone he didn't recognise at all.

Because she'd cracked a fairly pathetic joke?

Or because of the reference to parentage? Canine sex.

Sex…

Oh, Lord! Anna closed her eyes. She couldn't hold the puppy any more tightly because she could feel his ribs too well already. Poor thing, he'd had a hard time in his short life so far. At least he'd stopped shaking, though.

'What's his name?'

'I can't decide. Every time I come up with one, I try using it but it doesn't feel right. Herbert was my last effort.' To her dismay, Anna realised that Luke would make the connection. That the surname of his first surgical case had seemed like a good name for her pet. How unprofessional would that seem?

Probably not as bad as talking about dogs mating on the stairs.

And did it really matter? This wasn't work. It was home. Different.

Confusing.

'He's got big feet.'

'Mmm. He's growing fast, too. I think that's why he's so clumsy. He got underneath my ladder and tried to turn around and that's how it tipped over.'

Luke was silent for a moment but then he looked at Anna and she saw that the grim lines were still missing from his face. There was a hint of amusement there but it was lapped by a sadness she could feel all the way to her bones.

'I knew someone once,' he said quietly. 'He grew too fast and looked a bit goofy, with his hands and feet always looking a bit too big for him, and he was such a clumsy kid we all called him "Crash". He grew up, though. Into the strongest, bravest guy I knew.'

He was talking about someone important. A fellow soldier, maybe? Someone he had loved who had died? Why was he telling her something so personal?

'I heard a crash,' Luke added. 'That's why I came inside.'

Anna swallowed. Luke's lips were moving. Slowly but surely they were curling into a smile. A real smile. One that changed his whole face, deepening those furrows to his nose but adding a sparkle to his eyes that made him seem so much more…alive.

It faded all too quickly and instinct told Anna that she had been given a glimpse of something normally well hidden. The real Luke? A letting down of some guard that not many people got to see, anyway. A real smile and he had chosen to bestow it on her.

Something deep inside her was captured. Something huge and warm and wonderful. Anna knew she would remember this moment for ever.

'It's a great name,' she said softly. 'Crash?'

The big pup wriggled in her arms and looked up at her. He tried to prick up his ears but they were too heavy and stuck out sideways. Liquid brown eyes were full of trust and a long tail gave a thump of approval.

'Crash it is,' Anna announced. She smiled up at Luke. 'Hey, thanks.'

'No problem.' But the smile had well and truly vanished from Luke's face and he stood up.

He was leaving. Something oddly like panic made Anna's heart skip a beat.

'Would…um…would you like a coffee or something?'

'No. You're busy and I'm on my way to Penhally. I'll leave the journal.' He dropped it onto a chest of drawers by the door. 'There's a good review of restrictive pericarditis in there. I thought you'd be interested.'

The reminder of work was timely. She had to work with Luke. Work and home couldn't mix. Professional and personal couldn't mix. What had she been thinking, blathering on about her rescue puppy? She scrambled to her feet.

'Thank you.' There wasn't a thing Anna could do about what she was wearing or what her home looked like, but she could summon as much as she could of Dr Bartlett. Lifting her chin, she could feel the shell of professionalism beginning to enclose her. Protect her.

'That was thoughtful of you. I did do as much research as possible when Colin was admitted but it might well be something I didn't come across.' She looked pointedly at the door. 'I'll see you out, shall I?'

'No need.' Luke turned to leave but then paused. 'Actually, there was something else.'

'What?'

The hesitation was almost imperceptible. 'You don't seem to have reported that incident from Colin Herbert's surgery. Or not that I've heard about.'

'No. I decided not to.'

'Why not?'

'Because you said it wouldn't happen again.' *And I believe you*, Anna added silently, looking away so that he wouldn't see any crack in her newly formed shell. *I trust you.*

Luke didn't say anything. After a long moment he broke the eye contact and gave a single nod.

'Thank you,' he said, the words somewhat curt.

And with that he was gone.

Anna stood very still. She listened to the

sound of her front door closing. And then the sound of a car engine starting up and a vehicle moving away.

Even then she didn't move. Standing like this, she could feel that shell cracking and falling away, exposing something tender. She could almost feel Luke's presence still in the room. She could still see that amazing smile.

And, heaven help her, but she wanted to hang onto it for just a little longer.

The sound pierced his eardrums, his body rocking from the force of the impact. Through the painful buzzing that came in the wake of the explosion he could hear the cursing of his companions. The screaming.

'Get out!'

'Get down!'

The ping of bullets ricocheting off the metal of their armoured vehicle came faster. An unearthly shriek from someone who had been struck ripped through the sounds of chaos.

Of panic.

He could feel the heat now. Not just the normal strength-sapping attack of the desert sun but the kind of heat that could sear flesh.

A lick of flames that could bring death with far more suffering than a bullet.

The dust was thick. Getting thicker. The chop-chop-chop of a nearby helicopter was stirring the ground. Bringing assistance, but it was going to be too late. It was getting hard to breathe. He could smell the dust. Taste it. Dust mixed with blood to become a suffocating soup.

His companions needed help. The driver was slumped over the wheel, others bleeding. The young paramedic was crying. Facing death and terrified.

He could feel that terror reach out and invade his own mind. He was frozen. Becoming aware of the pain in his own leg. Terrible, unimaginable pain. He couldn't breathe. Couldn't move...

They were his brothers, these men. All of them. And he was going to watch them die.

He was about to die himself. He could see the enemy emerging from the clouds of dust, their bodies shrouded with the clothing of the desert, their faces disguised by heavy, dark beards. He could see the cruel muzzles of the weapons they were pointing at him but he couldn't move.

Couldn't even breathe…

The sound of his own scream was as choked as the air around him.

Arghhh!

The desperate, strangled sound that finally escaped his throat was, mercifully, enough to wake him. Even as his eyes snapped open, Luke was throwing back the covers on his bed, swinging his legs over the edge so that it was a continuous, flowing movement that had him sitting, hunched on the side of his bed, his head in his hands as he struggled to drag in a breath.

The feeling of suffocation—of imminent death—was still there.

He couldn't afford to stay still. He knew what he had to do.

The warm, fleecy trackpants were draped over the end of his bed. His shoes were right there to shove his feet into. Running shoes.

It wasn't real, he reminded himself as he pulled the laces tight. It hadn't even happened that way. He had never seen the enemy. He had been able to move. To drag his companions to shelter behind the vehicle as the helicopter hovered overhead. He had staunched the flow of blood and kept airways patent. None of them had died.

But the nightmare was always the same.

He was watching his own brother die. Feeling the fear. Unable to help.

Matthew. Mattie. The clumsy kid with the happy grin who'd had to tag along with his older brothers and do everything they did. Crash.

Oh…God! What on earth had possessed him to suggest that Anna Bartlett use that precious nickname for that skinny, ridiculous-looking dog?

What was she doing with a dog in the first place? How could she keep a pet that needed so much time and love with the kind of hours he already knew she put into her career? She did love it. He had seen that in the way she held it and soothed it. The way her face had brightened with joy at finding a name she really liked.

He had now pulled on the coat hanging by the door. Within seconds he was lurching down the rough track that led to the beach. It didn't matter that it was the middle of the night. His night vision was better than most people's and he was getting very familiar with this route.

Maybe it didn't matter that he'd given his brother's name away to a dog. It wasn't as though he was planning to visit that unlikely little cottage again and they were hardly likely to be chatting about it at work because they never talked about anything remotely personal.

In fact, he was having enormous difficulty reconciling the woman who was his assistant head of department with the person he'd found on the floor of that room cuddling... Crash.

Sea air so fresh that it bit into his lungs and numbed his face barely penetrated his awareness. He could feel the shifting of sand beneath his feet and hear the sound of the surf crashing in right beside him but his mind had fastened onto that picture of Anna on the floor.

With her hair in a soft tumble of curls. Her arms holding a vulnerable creature. Comforting it. Protecting it. He had felt the love. That was what had hit him in such a poignant place. What had reminded him of the kid brother who had never come home.

He'd reached the end of the beach now. Turned to go home again. He might even manage another couple of hours' sleep before daylight came. Usually, by the time he had done this punishing circuit, the nightmare had faded.

And it was only then that Luke realised he hadn't had to fight the remnants of that terrible dream the way he always did. From even before he'd left his house, all he'd been thinking about was Anna.

Or rather the two Annas.

Now that he'd seen her at home, he'd be able to recognise what he'd missed at work so far, surely? Some signs that hidden beneath that power-dressing, uber-professional, calm, cool and collected surgeon was...the most compelling woman he'd ever met in his life.

He was watching her. And he was puzzled.

Anna could feel the unasked questions hanging in the air between them.

Had it been real? Had he really found her wearing scruffy clothes, with her hair in an untidy mop, living in a shambolic house with a rather large and definitely unhygienic animal? Did she really have a sense of humour?

It was easy to emanate denial because that wasn't who she was at work. She'd also had years of practice in deflecting any line of communication that threatened to become personal. Patients could be so useful.

Like first thing on Monday morning when the anticipation of seeing Luke for the first time since he'd been in her house was making Anna feel more nervous than she had since her junior years as a doctor when she'd had to perform in front of some eminent consultant.

Luke hadn't looked any different.

'Good morning, Anna. How are you?'

'Very good.' She wasn't going to return the query. Luke wasn't one of her patients.

'How's—?'

Crash? She knew that was coming next and she had to stamp on that topic of conversation before it could start. The temptation to talk about her puppy was too strong. She wanted to tell Luke that Crash had learned to sit. That he had stepped on an overturned lid of a paint tin and made a giant pawprint on her wooden floor and it had been such a perfect signature she'd been reluctant to clean it off. Would that make him smile again? She couldn't afford to find out.

'Mrs Melton?' She interrupted smoothly. 'Finally getting to Theatre, thank goodness. I know it's your slot this morning but I'm more than happy to do the surgery. Or assist.'

'It's a long time since I did a CABG.' He knew exactly what she'd done in changing the subject. She could see him taking it on board that her private life was not up for discussion. Could see the focus as he let it go. 'Might be a good idea if you assisted.'

Was this a challenge? To see if she did trust him to operate safely on his own? A sideways glance as Luke fell into step beside her made her notice that his hair was damp. Just out of the shower? That image was disturbing. Anna dragged in a breath, only to catch a whiff of something fresh and clean. Like a sea breeze. Good heavens, she could almost imagine Luke had just been for a dip in the ocean. In the middle of winter? Who would be that crazy?

Her senses were threatening to override her train of thought. What had he asked? Oh, yes… Was he offering her the opportunity to observe and judge his capabilities in Theatre or might he want her company for an entirely different reason?

'I can't imagine that you'll have any problems,' she said calmly. 'But I am a little concerned about the quality of her saphenous veins. I'm wondering about harvesting the lesser saphenous or possibly upper extremity veins, in which case I could probably be more helpful than a registrar.'

Your choice, she threw at him silently. I'm available.

He simply nodded. 'Excellent. Have we got time to review her films? I'd like to have a word with her as well and introduce myself.'

'Sure. I'm heading to the ward right now.'

Mrs Melton was thrilled to hear that the head of department would be doing her surgery. She beamed at Luke.

And he smiled back. Anna was watching

and she could see that it was a purely professional sort of smile. It still softened his face
and reminded her of when he'd smiled at her
but it wasn't anything like the same. It didn't
make his face come alive. It didn't come anywhere near his eyes.

She found herself watching him just as intently as she suspected he was watching her.
She saw him smile in greeting colleagues. She
saw him smile in satisfaction when he was informed of how well a patient was doing. He
even smiled directly at her on one occasion.
All mechanical gestures. Done because it was
expected and it would be impolite not to.

Anna wanted to know what those shadows in his eyes were from and why they
were dense enough to smother real smiles.
She wanted to know who the real 'Crash' had
been and why talking about him had cracked
open the armour Luke wore.

For that was what it was. Anna could recognise it because she had her own. By the end
of their second week of working together, she
had the weirdest sensation that they were like
actors. Playing their part on stage but with
each of them knowing perfectly well that the

role the other was playing was not the real person.

Even more disturbing, Anna was becoming obsessed with wondering about the real Luke. The man that had really smiled at her. Why did he come to work each day with his hair damp and smelling of the sea? The temptation to ask was becoming unbearable. Or maybe it was the desire to touch his hair...to press her face against it and see if that was where the impression of the outdoors and punishing exercise came from.

She wanted to know why he refused to admit that his leg hurt even when it was obvious it did. When there were lines of pain in his face at the end of a long day that she could feel herself. She could smooth those lines away. With her fingers. Or her lips. If he let her.

If she let herself...

The intrigue refused to go away. The pull became stronger but Anna was fighting it. Anyone seeing Mr Davenport and Dr Bartlett together would see nothing more than a purely professional association. Reserved but respectful. Discussions might be animated but they were only about their patients. Their work. Current research. New technologies. Endless topics to talk about.

A seemingly endlessly fascinating man to talk to.

If it wasn't for the puzzle that Anna represented, Luke might have been tempted to admit defeat.

Every day was the same. Enclosed within the walls of an institution that sometimes felt like it was filled with people who had created their own illnesses. Heavy smokers who seemed surprised that they'd had heart attacks because of their damaged blood vessels. Morbidly obese people who still expected lifesaving surgery.

What for? So they could carry on with their meaningless lives? Lie in bed and keep eating junk food?

'I'm not going to operate on Walter Robson,' he informed Anna after a ward round late that week. 'I refuse to spend my time patching someone up just to give them longer to indulge in slow suicide by their appalling lifestyle choices.'

If he'd hoped to get under her skin with such a terse and controversial statement, he was disappointed.

'I agree he's a poor candidate for surgery,' she said calmly. 'Maybe that will be enough of an incentive for him to stop smoking and lose some weight. If we can reduce his level of heart failure and get his type-two diabetes and cellulitis under control, it will reduce the surgical risk.'

Luke almost exploded. Thumped the wall beside them or walked away from his colleague. Told Anna what he was really thinking.

That she knew nothing about risk. Real risk—the kind that young, healthy people took for the benefit of their brothers-in-arms, if not for the much bigger human-rights issues. That patching them up was the kind of lifesaving surgery that had some meaning.

But that would open floodgates that had to remain shut. It would take Anna into a life that didn't exist for him any more except in his nightmares, and winning freedom from those nightmares was the hurdle he had to get through to survive.

He had discovered a new way of dealing with both the terrors of the night and the feeling of suffocation he could get ambushed by at work. He could distract himself by thinking about Anna. Just for a few seconds. Like a shot of some calm-inducing drug.

Her voice became a background hum as she talked about dealing with Walter Robson's anaemia and whether his chronic lung problems would improve if he carried through his vow to quit smoking.

Luke let his gaze stroke the sleek hair on top of Anna's head and then rest on the tight knot nestled at the nape of her neck. That clip thing would be easy enough to remove. The hair might still be twisted and squashed but he could bury his fingers in it and fluff it out until it bounced onto her shoulders.

His breath came out in a sigh. It was enough...the feeling of desperation was fading again.

'Luke?' Anna had caught the sigh. Fortunately, she misinterpreted it. 'The decision has to be on medical grounds, not moral ones.'

'Of course.'

This wasn't the place to discuss the ethics

of what represented a significant part of their careers. Much of the workload was genuine and worthwhile. He knew that. He used to get more than enough satisfaction from it.

Why did everything have to be so different now? So difficult?

And why couldn't he see what he knew was there—hiding behind the person Anna was within these walls?

She wouldn't let him. That was why. The boundaries had been marked and were being reinforced every time she changed the subject if he tried to talk about something personal, like the puppy he had named for her. Or had she even kept the name?

No wonder James had sounded puzzled back on his first day when they had been scrubbing in together. As though he had no idea of what Anna was like out of work hours.

Maybe Luke was the only person here who'd had a glimpse of that side of Anna.

He liked that notion.

He liked it a lot.

CHAPTER FIVE

'I'M HAPPY to cover Christmas Day.'

'So am I.' Luke's nod was matter-of-fact. 'Thanks, Anna. That's the holiday roster issues sorted, then. Let's get on with the rest of the agenda.'

Anna couldn't help but notice the look that passed between James and Charlotte Alexander, who were sitting together in this departmental meeting. No mistaking the look of relief. Joy even at the prospect of spending a special day together with no danger of being called in to work.

The movement of Charlotte's hand was probably unconscious. She seemed to be listening carefully to Luke as he introduced a new grading system for cardiac patients.

'It's hoped that this will be brought in nationwide to try and standardise criteria and address the increasing numbers of people that are dying while on waiting lists for surgery. We've been asked to implement this at St Piran's as of the first of January as part of a multi-centre trial, so your feedback is going to be important.'

Anna was listening, too, but she'd already read the proposal and she and Luke had discussed it at length. It was hardly surprising that she caught that movement from Charlotte in her peripheral vision. A hand that gently smoothed the loose fabric of her top, gathering it up as it came to rest cupping her lower belly. There really was no doubt now that she was pregnant. It would be a special Christmas for them, wouldn't it, with the extra joy and dreams that came with knowing they were about to become a family?

'As far as degree of valvar dysfunction goes, we're staying with the New York Heart Association functional classes. As you can see, mild is class one and scores two. Severe is class three and scores fourteen. If there is coronary artery disease present as well, it puts it into class four and we can add ten to the overall score.'

Luke had the score sheets projected onto the wall. He was going to cover all the non-coronary revascularisation type of patients like valve replacements and then he'd run through the more complex scoring system for patients who had arterial disease. He was being clear and methodical and making sure everyone understood. People were nodding approvingly. A system like this could make prioritising people on the waiting lists much more straightforward.

Charlotte was one of those nodding. As though she would be only too happy to be filling in the score sheets on her patients and adding her comments to the feedback that would be required. But how long would she be around to be doing that?

It was all very well having secrets but it was also annoying. When were they planning to share the information and allow arrangements to be made for Charlotte's absence for maternity leave? For James to be covered at the time of the baby's arrival? For a new member of staff to be advertised for, if necessary?

No wonder there was such prejudice against

women in top positions. Imagine if she was pregnant herself? Even if she worked up to the last possible moment and then took minimal maternity leave, the disruption to the department would still be huge.

Unthinkable. It always had been.

So why was she watching Charlotte surreptitiously right now instead of focusing on the information Luke was presenting? Wondering what her colleague was thinking and how she'd come to the conclusion that having a baby was more important than her career. What it might be like to feel a new life growing and moving within your own body. To face the enormous responsibility of caring for that baby when it was born.

The disturbing niggle was annoyance, not envy. Luke needed to know. He had quite enough on his plate settling back into running such a busy department and working the kind of hours he did with the extra stress of recovering from a major physical injury. Maybe it wasn't her place but Anna wanted to warn Luke. She could help him put arrangements into place to make sure they could cope with the inevitable disruptions.

Her gaze was on the head of department now. He was talking about the Canadian Cardiovascular Society's criteria for grading angina.

'The class is assigned after appropriate treatment, not at the time of admission or diagnosis.'

Luke stood tall but relaxed and his voice was clear and authoritative. What was the X factor in the way he presented himself that got people on side so easily? Anna found herself biting back a smile. It certainly wasn't his warm and friendly countenance. He was always so serious, often looking grim, and he could be downright impatient with staff who couldn't get up to speed quickly enough. He was utterly closed off on a personal level and yet he drew everyone in.

Already this department felt more cohesive than it had under her own leadership. There was enthusiasm for all sorts of projects that might otherwise have been seen simply as more paperwork and stress. In the space of just a few short weeks they had a new rostering system in place, had been chosen for this pilot centre for an important national initiative and several new research projects had been kicked off.

Maybe that X factor was because of the sense that Luke was driven, despite—or perhaps because of—the physical challenges it now incorporated. Anyone could see how hard it was for him to be on his feet all day and keep up with such a demanding schedule. This job was his life and he was going to do it so well that anyone who chose to get on board would have an unexpectedly satisfying ride.

And she was one of them. Funny how the resentment she'd felt at Luke returning to take his leading role in the department had faded so quickly. Perhaps it had been pushed away completely because she'd been watching him so carefully and the more she saw, the more compelling this man was becoming. Had she really thought she wouldn't learn from him? It wasn't just his technical excellence in Theatre. Apart from that momentary wobble on his first day back, Anna hadn't seen anything that would have undermined her opinion that he was one of the best in his field. It was rare for someone so good on the practical side to be so competent at administration, but Luke really seemed to enjoy the challenge of running a large department effectively.

Yes. The closer she could stay and work with Luke the more she could benefit. She wanted them to be a close team.

How close?

The odd question came from a part of her brain that was normally closed off at work. The kind of disruptive thought that had never been a problem in the past but, curiously, had started to plague her out-of-work hours lately. She couldn't distract herself easily right now either. She was trapped, motionless, and she had already been distracted by the people around her.

'Scores for the ability to work or give care are a little more subjective,' Luke was saying. 'Especially the middle category when it's threatened but not immediately.'

Anna's concentration was certainly threatened. She didn't need a sideways glance at the Alexanders to remind her of married couples amongst her colleagues. It happened all the time. Didn't they say that you were most likely to meet the person you were going to marry amongst the people you worked with?

It wasn't going to happen to her. The desire for a husband and family—if it had ever been there—had been dismissed long ago. About the time she'd discovered the passion she had for surgery and it had become obvious that if she was going to have any chance of getting to where she wanted to be, it had to be the only thing that mattered in her life.

Adopting a puppy had been extraordinary enough. A substitute baby? No. You couldn't leave a baby in the house for a helpful neighbour to collect and care for while you were at work. Or leave a pile of newspaper on the floor so you didn't have to get up in the middle of the night to deal with toileting issues. She still had to factor in collecting Crash every day from the yard he shared with June and Doug's dogs. To take him for a walk on the beach and spend time training and playing with him. To listen to the snuffles and odd whimpers in the night from his bed in the corner of his room. All in all, it was a major upheaval in her life. Not that she wasn't getting a lot of pleasure from it. And if it was a substitute child it was as close as she ever wanted to get, that was for sure.

No family, then. And what was the point of a husband if you weren't planning on having a family?

A partner was something different, however.

A lover.

At this point in the meeting Anna very uncharacteristically stopped listening to anything being said around her. She was watching Luke's hands as he shaped the size of whatever it was he was talking about. Strong, tanned, capable hands.

She couldn't stop herself imagining them running down the length of her spine. It would be no effort to fit the curve of her bottom into their grip and he would be able to pull her against his own body with no more than the slightest pressure. It would feel lean and hard, like his face.

And he would have turned that blinding focus onto her. Those incredible blue eyes would be on her face. On her lips as he dipped his head…slowly…to kiss her.

Oh…dear Lord… With a huge effort, Anna managed to tune back into her surroundings just as the meeting was wrapping up. People were closing diaries and starting to chat. Charlotte pushed back her chair and stood up.

'Just before you all go...'

The buzz of conversation died. Here we go, thought Anna, but the announcement wasn't what she expected.

'I've been involved in organising the staff Christmas function,' Charlotte said with a smile. 'It's in the canteen on the twenty-second, seven p.m., in case you haven't seen the flyers. There's going to be lots of nice food and plenty of non-alcoholic drinks if you're unlucky enough to be on duty. It's a chance for everybody to get together in the spirit of the season, so I hope you can all make it. Partners and families are welcome. There's going to be a Secret Santa. Bring a small gift and put it under the tree and then you'll get one yourself at the end of the night. Or just bring one for any children that might be there and if they're not needed they can go to the children's ward.'

Anna looked away from Charlotte. Towards Luke. Their senior cardiology registrar should be talking about her upcoming maternity leave, not a Christmas party. Luke had an odd expression on his face. As if he couldn't believe that something so trivial was being announced in a departmental meeting.

As though a party or celebrating Christmas was absolutely the last possible thing he would have any desire to do.

Did he ever relax? Let his guard down and enjoy something social?

Something intimate?

She gathered up her folder of papers and stepped around the table. Towards Luke. She couldn't stop herself. The wanderings of her mind during the meeting might be under control now, thank goodness, but they'd left an odd kind of physical yearning and it was like a magnet, pulling her towards Luke. She did her best to disguise it. Her professional mask was quite intact, on the outside at least.

'Good presentation,' she offered. 'I think we'll have full co-operation in the trial period.'

'Yes.' Luke was shutting down the program in his laptop. 'I'm hoping so.'

Anna's thoughts were tripping over each other. She had a strong urge to engineer a way to spend some time with Luke and it would be easy enough if she asked to discuss something professional, like the planned research project she was taking on to analyse post-operative infection rates in cardiac patients.

But something new and rather disturbing was happening. She could actually feel the war going on between her head and her heart. She didn't want a professional kind of inter-action. She wanted...

Oh, help... Was she actually thinking of asking him for some kind of a date?

No, of course not. She didn't do work rela-tionships. Of any kind. This was Anna getting rebellious, trying to claw her way through Dr Bartlett's armour. It simply wouldn't do.

Her thoughts might be running with the speed of light but she had been standing there for a shade too long judging by the quizzical set of Luke's eyebrows when he glanced up at her.

Anna was aware of the final staff members exiting the meeting room, including Char-lotte. She hoped her smile was offhand.

'You planning to go to the Christmas party?'

'No. Are you?'

Anna couldn't look away. Her mouth wasn't going to wait for her brain to mull over what seemed to be a perfect compromise between professional and personal. It just widened its smile and opened to say something extraordinary.

'I will if you will.'

Something flickered in Luke's eyes. Astonishment? Interest?

'I don't like parties,' he said.

'Neither do I,' Anna agreed. She could have left it there. What was wrong with her today? 'But this is a staff function. It's polite to put in an appearance. Especially for HODs.'

Luke was frowning now. 'You think I should go?'

'I think there must be a lot of people in St Piran's who would enjoy the chance to welcome you back. Good relations both within and between departments are useful.'

Luke grunted. He looked up as the meeting door swung shut behind the last person. 'Did you know Charlotte Alexander's pregnant?'

Was he trying to change the subject? 'I guessed. How did you know?'

'She told me. We need to look at possible

replacements amongst the registrars we have available. Or get in a locum.'

'Yes. How much time have we got?'

'We should look at getting it sorted next month.'

'It's going to be a busy start for the New Year. Which reminds me...' The rebellious part of Anna had finally been quelled. Maybe it was just as well Luke was so good at sticking to professional. 'I wanted to have a chat to you about the parameters for this infection study. How retrospective do you think we should make it? I've got my registrar primed to start digging through records.'

'Let's have a look at our diaries. We should be able to squeeze in a meeting. You can bring anyone else you want involved along as well.'

'I will.'

Not that it was likely to help, Anna thought, her heart sinking. If she was capable of having totally inappropriate thoughts about her boss when there were a dozen or more members of the department around her, what hope did she have by flanking herself with a couple of junior doctors?

She needed to escape. To get home and

get a grip. Heading purposefully away from work, Anna barely registered the huge Christmas tree in the hospital foyer with its twinkling, coloured lights but she thought of it again as she turned her car towards her cottage.

This was the silly season, she reminded herself. Everything would settle down, including whatever it was that making her feel so…unsettled.

The Christmas party was well under way by the time Anna managed to get there.

The canteen was noisy and crowded, warm with the inviting aroma of hot, savoury food and people determined to enjoy themselves. There were bright balloons and streamers and huge, shiny silver stars hanging from light fittings. There were flashes of even brighter colours as well. Where on earth had people found their accessories?

A trio of nurses wore headbands with big yellow plastic stars that flashed on and off. Steffie, the staff nurse from the cardiology ward, had earrings and a matching necklace that had red and green twinkling lights. Anna

spotted a set of glowing reindeer horns and
Santa hats made of shiny red sequins. She
passed a registrar who wore a large badge.
Rudolph's nose was flashing and a tinny version of a Christmas song could be heard competing with the background carol music in the
room. More than one person rolled their eyes
as the owner of the badge reached to push the
nose as the song finished.

'Not again, Peter. Please.'

A very young-looking nurse was dressed
in a naughty Santa costume, the rim of white
fluff on the bottom of her dress barely reaching her thighs. Anna groaned inwardly. This
really wasn't her scene at all. She knew she
must look as out of place as she felt. Prim, in
her skirt and jacket. It was getting harder to
respond to the smiles and greetings of people
when she was completely sober and they were
clearly making the most of the party drinks
available to those not on duty.

She felt like an island. A rather barren,
rocky one, moving through a sea of festiv-
ity. She had to be the only person there who
didn't have at least a string of tinsel tied on
to signal that they belonged.

And then she spotted Luke.

Another island. Even rockier, given the tight body language and an almost desperate look on his face as Anna edged through the partygoers to join the group of familiar faces.

'Anna. Merry Christmas!'

'Thanks, Ben. Hi, Lucy.' Anna smiled at Ben's wife, her gaze dropping to the bundle snuggled against the front of her body with a sling. 'I heard you'd had another baby. Congratulations.'

'Thanks. Yes, this is Kitty. She's ten weeks old now.'

A small girl was peeping out from behind Lucy's legs.

'This must be Annabel.' Anna searched her memory. 'It's her birthday soon, isn't it?'

'Christmas Eve.'

'Just as well she's a party animal.' Ben grinned. 'She's loving it.' He was holding Annabel's little brother, Josh, but he reached down to touch his daughter. 'Tell Dr Anna how old you're going to be on your birthday, darling.'

'Free,' Annabel said shyly. Ben tickled her head and made her giggle.

Who could help smiling at the joyous sound? Glancing up, Anna saw Luke's lips curve and it was, almost, the kind of smile he'd given her that day. Poignant. Real.

But not happy. The sound of laughter around them was virtually constant and Anna wanted to hear Luke laugh. To see and hear him forget himself in a moment of happiness. The feeling that he might never do that was heartbreaking. She tore her gaze away swiftly. Towards another smiling face.

But Josh O'Hara's smile looked forced and the petite, blonde woman standing beside him wasn't smiling at all. She was draining a glass of wine.

The A and E consultant noticed the direction of her gaze. 'Anna? You won't have met my wife. This is Rebecca.'

Charlotte and James Alexander joined the group, along with another man whom Anna recognised as Nick Tremayne, head of the Penhally medical centre.

'Has anyone seen Kate? I told her to pop in while I was upstairs visiting my patient but I can't find her anywhere in this crowd.'

'Nick!' Ben stepped closer to the newcomers. 'So you got in to see Mrs Jennings?'

'Yes. The surgery went well. She should be up and about with her new hip in no time. Home for the new year.'

'How's Jem?' Anna asked. 'He was the talk of the hospital there for quite a while.'

'He's great. Started senior school in September and seems to be loving it. Still gets a bit tired but it's been a big year for all of us.'

'Sure has.' Charlotte smiled. 'It's going to be a special Christmas this year. Your first together as a new family.'

'It's going to be wonderful. If I can find my wife, that is. Excuse me. Carry on enjoying yourselves. Oops!' Nick almost collided with a waiter bearing a tray of brimming champagne glasses.

Anna caught Luke's gaze and there was a moment of connection there. Neither of them was enjoying themselves in this setting.

It might be better somewhere else, Anna's response of a smile suggested. Somewhere without any of this crowd and noise. Somewhere they could be alone. Together. It had to be her imagination but Luke seemed to be silently in agreement. If nothing else, he certainly recognised the connection.

'Drink, Anna?' someone asked.

'No, thanks. I've still got patients I want to check on before I head home.'

'Definitely not for me,' Charlotte said happily.

'Or me,' James chimed in valiantly. 'I've climbed on the wagon with my wife.'

'Oh?' Ben's smile broadened. 'For how long, might I ask? Seven or eight months, perhaps?'

'Um…actually, there's something we probably should have told everyone quite a while ago now.'

The tray was still within reach and Josh's wife swapped her empty glass for a full one. Anna caught the expression on Josh's face. He's embarrassed, she thought in surprise. He doesn't want her drinking any more. No. The tension was deeper than that. It was hard not to get the impression that he wasn't comfortable having his wife there at all.

She took another glance at the woman she'd never met before. Rebecca had the kind of grooming that came, in her experience, with women who had plenty of money and too much time to spend on how they looked. Flawless make-up. Shoulder-length hair that was beautifully cut and exquisitely high-lighted. Her nails sported a perfect French polish and her figure might be curvy but it looked well toned.

Rebecca had also caught the look from her husband. 'What?' she snapped. 'You think I've had enough?' A tiny snort suggested that an unhappy exchange was nothing new to this couple.

It was Anna's turn to feel embarrassed. She looked away to where Lucy was giving Charlotte a one-armed hug that wouldn't disturb the sleeping baby in the sling. Ben and Luke were both offering their congratulations to James and they all seemed unaware of the sudden atmosphere Anna was separating them from.

'Maybe I have had enough,' Rebecca said, too loudly. 'Of everything.'

'I'll order a taxi for you,' Josh said. 'I've still got some work I need to do tonight.'

'Of course you do.' Rebecca's laugh was brittle.

'Let's go.'

'When I've finished my drink. It's not as if I have any reason not to, is it?'

Josh's voice was too low for anyone but Anna to hear. 'I think we should go now. This isn't the place.'

'But it never is, is it, Josh?' Rebecca raised her glass but, to her dismay, Anna saw that the woman's lips were trembling too much for her to take a sip and tears were filling her eyes. Debating whether she should say something when it was obviously none of her business, Anna was relieved to see Rebecca blinking hard. Making a determined effort to control herself.

But then she shifted her gaze to where Lucy was standing with her tiny baby and Charlotte had pulled her top tight to show off her rounded belly, and Rebecca's face just crumpled. She pushed her glass at Josh and turned, tears streaming down her face as she fled. The others all turned in surprise.

'Oh…God,' Josh groaned. 'Sorry about that. I need to… Would you…?'

'Give it to me.' Anna took the champagne

glass and Josh elbowed his way through the throng in pursuit of his wife.

'What was that all about?' Lucy looked worried.

'What happened?' Charlotte looked bemused.

'Josh and his wife. They didn't look very happy.'

Oh, no. Was this social occasion about to become the kind of gossip session Anna refused to engage in?

'Not everyone appreciates Christmas,' Luke said levelly.

'That's true.' Ben nodded and went along with making the subject about generalities. 'Look at the increase we see in A and E for things like self-harm.'

'The hype doesn't help.' Anna was more than happy to direct conversation away from colleagues and their probable marriage woes. She gave Luke a grateful glance and then waved her hand to encompass the party and all the decorations. 'There's this huge expectation put out that it's going to be the happiest day of the year. Brimming with fun, family times and the best of everything. No wonder it just serves to underline what some people aren't lucky enough to have.'

There was a moment's silence and Anna could have kicked herself. Had she been responsible for the atmosphere in this group going from joy at James and Charlotte's news to entirely unnecessary gloom? She bit her lip.

'I'm just hungry,' she said apologetically. 'Take no notice. I might go and find a sausage roll or something.'

'And I'd better take these guys home,' Lucy said. 'We need to pace ourselves to get through all the parties lined up for the rest of this week.'

'And I...' Luke was obviously trying to think of a reason to excuse himself as well.

No surprises there. The noise level around them was increasing. Music had been turned up to compete with the laughter and happily raised voices, and there was a new sound mixed in with the general hubbub. A sharp cracking. People cheered and then there were more muted bangs. Someone was handing out Christmas crackers and people were pulling them with gusto.

The sound was not unlike distant gunfire.

Anna's gaze flicked back to Luke. He didn't like parties anyway. How much worse would this be when it couldn't fail to remind him of being in a war zone? She could see his tension escalating. Instinctively, she found herself moving closer. Wanting to protect him. He looked straight at her and she had never seen him look so grim.

James was handed a cracker. 'Here we go.' He laughed, holding it out to Charlotte.

This bang was much louder. Charlotte squeaked in surprise, Annabel buried her face in her father's shoulder and little Josh burst into tears.

But Anna was still watching Luke. She saw the exact moment he stopped seeing her. When his face took on the same expression it had had in Theatre that first day. One of horror.

'Luke.' Anna put her hand on his arm and she could feel muscles as unyielding as steel beneath her fingers.

'Luke.' Her tone was more urgent now. She had to get through to him. Snap him out of this flashback before anyone else noticed.

But he didn't seem to feel her touch. Or

hear her. He started moving away and seemed unaware of the people in his path. Someone got jostled and spilled their drink.

'Hey! Watch where you're going.'

Ben and James were watching where Luke was going. Anna caught the glance the two men exchanged. Frowning, Ben opened his mouth to say something but Anna shook her head.

'I'll go,' was all she said.

It was quite easy to follow Luke. People were stepping aside like a wave as they saw him coming. Smiles faded from faces to be replaced with dropping jaws. Anna didn't catch up with him until he was well past the doors of the canteen. She barely noticed Josh coming in the opposite direction. Good grief, this party wasn't proving very enjoyable for more than one person.

Finally, she got close enough to catch hold of Luke's hand but he didn't stop. He towed her along until he reached the end of the corridor. The noise from the canteen was muted now, like the lighting in this junction that contained the lifts. Two big pot plants on either side of a bench seat had some tinsel draped over their leaves.

Luke stopped and his head turned swiftly from one side to the other. At some level he was making a decision on what direction to take next. He still felt just as tense. Just as distant.

Anna had to distract him. Bring him back to the present. She stepped in front of him and reached up to hold his face with both hands.

'Luke…' She tilted his face, forcing him to look down at her. 'It's me. Anna.'

He was still caught somewhere else. A long way away in time and place. Somewhere dark.

Anna had to do something. Without thinking, she stood on tiptoe, still holding Luke's face.

And then she kissed him.

CHAPTER SIX

LUKE knew that Anna was kissing him.

Just as he'd known that she had followed him from the canteen and had caught his hand. He'd heard the urgency in her voice.

But it had all been on another level of his consciousness. Maybe that was what it was like for people in a coma. Or coming out of one, anyway. They could hear the voices and feel the touch but there was a transition period before they were able to enter the same reality.

Something had snapped inside him with the sound of that cracker and he'd known he was getting sucked into a flashback. He'd tried to fight it off as he'd stormed out of the canteen. Tried to shut down the even louder cracks of the real gunfire he could hear. The explosions of landmines. The screams of dying men. But the pull had been huge. Even the smell of sa-

voury food became acrid. Like smoke. Rusty.
Like blood.

By the time he was in the corridor all Luke
had been aware of had been the need to escape. To find somewhere he could be alone
and bury his head in his hands until, somehow, he could wrestle the monster into sub-
mission and regain control. And then he'd felt
Anna's grip on his hand and heard her voice
calling his name.

He tried to clear his head. Tried so hard. He
wanted to get back to her. He was caught in
the horror of a battlefield and she was there
but not there. If he could just reach her, everything would be all right. Couldn't she hear
him shouting? That he was trying, dammit.
Doing his utmost to get to her.

Maybe she had heard. Maybe that was why
she was holding his head and pulling it down.
Pressing her lips against his with such intensity.

God…he recognised this form of escape.
Distraction. Release. An affirmation of life.
Passionate sex that carried no strings because
if you got involved you only risked more of
exactly what you were using it to escape from.

How did Anna know?

It didn't matter.

Luke could feel the force that had taken over his mind receding. He was in control again but instead of pulling away his lips moved over hers and his arms went around her body. He drew them both into the shadowy area between the bench and the giant pot plant.

He let his hands shape her body. Feeling the trim curve of her waist and the neat rounds of her buttocks and then up, beneath the layer of the tailored jacket. Up to the solid anchor of her shoulder blades and then around to the softness of her breasts. He cupped them and brushed his thumbs across the nipples that he could feel like tiny pebbles beneath the silky fabric of her blouse.

And all the time his lips moved over hers. Encouraged when they parted beneath his. Excited when his tongue made contact with hers. Aroused beyond belief when she responded, her tongue dancing with his and her hands touching his body.

This was Anna, for heaven's sake! At work. The place where she had no personality or, at least, no personal life anyone was allowed to encroach on. Had she been drinking? No. She'd refused alcohol at the party because she had work she still needed to do. They were both sober. Sober enough to realise that this was totally inappropriate.

How long had they been standing here, locked in each other's arms, lost in a flash of physical release that had exploded like a cork from a champagne bottle?

Too long. Not nearly long enough.

Had anyone seen them?

He had to stop but it was too hard not to taste her for just a moment longer. To hold her against the length of his body and imprint the feel of her into his brain. He would need that memory and it was too important not to make sure that it stuck.

He was kissing her back.

Anna had only intended to distract him. A brief, hard kiss that was supposed to have the same kind of shock effect that a slap on the face might provide to someone in the grip of hysteria.

But after that first stunned beat of time he

had kissed her back. His lips had softened and moved beneath hers and his hands had touched her body and something inside Anna had simply melted.

He hadn't seemed to hear her voice or know she was there as she'd followed him. Maybe he didn't actually know who he was kissing. She could be anybody so she didn't have to be Dr Bartlett, did she?

She could just be Anna.

An old version of herself, even. One that had been lost too many years ago to count. The young girl who had dreamed of finding true love. A prince who was going to think she was the most wonderful person on earth. Who would love her for being exactly who she was. For ever.

And layered on top of that dreaming girl were flashes of everything she'd discovered about herself later. The yearning for a soul mate. The ability to give love and the need to receive it. Wild things like a need for physical release. All the things that had had to be buried so that they couldn't become a torment.

For just a few seconds Anna let herself sink into this astonishing kiss because she knew she would never experience anything like this ever again and she wanted to remember it, but the insanity began to fade and maybe she transmitted a tension that had nothing to do with desire. Something changed, anyway. She couldn't have said who actually broke the kiss and pulled away.

Maybe they both did.

For a long, long moment they stood there, still close enough to touch but not doing so. Staring at each other. Anna could see it was Luke looking down at her, not a tormented soul who was caught in a different reality. He knew who he was. Where he was.

And who he had been kissing.

Oh…Lord…

Anna swallowed hard. How on earth was she supposed to handle this? And not just the kiss. She'd witnessed another flashback incident. He'd said it wasn't going to happen again but it had. OK, so he wasn't in the middle of surgery and it hadn't endangered anyone, but there was no way her conscience would allow her to make excuses or ignore the implications of this.

She had a professional responsibility here

and she had just complicated it to the nth degree by not thinking and by doing something
as outrageous as kissing her new boss.

Then again…maybe that gave her a way in.
An opening to talk about what had happened
and what they were going to do about it.

She took a deep breath.

'Feeling better?'

She knew.

Too much.

Luke could feel himself closing off. Slamming mental doors in an effort to protect himself. To protect her?

'Maybe I should ask you the same thing,'
he said coolly.

'Sorry?'

'You kissed me.' He managed to sound offhand, as though it hadn't blown him away.
Like it hadn't meant anything at all.

He could see the way her eyes widened in
shock as though he'd physically slapped her.
The way she collected herself and looked
away.

'You needed distraction.'

She couldn't know. Not everything. Not

that she was already a distraction that he held onto every single night. That she represented a kind of rope that he could use to haul himself back to where he needed to be. A link that he had now tied firmly into the horrors of the past but one that led back to the present. To the future. A rope that he just needed to run his hand along to save his sanity. He would get where he intended to go eventually, as long as he could feel it running beside him.

The rope had been formed largely due to the intrigue that the contrast between what this woman was like at home and at work had sparked. Appreciating the fact that she was an attractive woman had woven another strand into it. But this...this blinding demonstration of what physical passion she was capable of did more than thicken the rope. It had come alive. It was warm and soft and he could stay glued to it with no effort at all. He didn't even need to touch it because a part of his mind could see it. Glowing.

'It was the Christmas crackers, wasn't it?' Anna asked. 'That sound like gunfire. You had some kind of flashback, like you did that day in surgery.'

'Nonsense.' It was. It had to be because if it wasn't, it would mean he would lose his job and that was all he had to fill his future.

And if he lost his job, he would lose Anna.

'I didn't like the noise,' he admitted stiffly. 'I told you I didn't like parties. I left because I'd had enough. The noise of the crackers was just the last straw.'

'Do you actually remember leaving the canteen?'

'Of course I do.' And he did, in a vague, dream-like way. A background that had faded rapidly as he'd got sucked into the flashback. He remembered that Anna had been following him and... 'I...bumped someone,' he said aloud. 'They spilled their drink.'

That surprised her. 'You didn't look like you were aware of what you were doing.'

'I was...angry.'

'Why?'

'The party. The noise. All that food and drink and the silly costumes. It's all such a waste of time and money.'

She wasn't convinced. 'You didn't stop, Luke. You didn't hear me calling you. I kissed you because I couldn't think of anything else that might shock you enough to get you off whatever planet you were on.'

'And I hope you plan to include that little gem in whatever report you're obviously intending to make.'

A spark flashed in Anna's eyes. 'For God's sake, Luke. This isn't about reports or jobs or whether someone gets embarrassed. This is about the fact that if there's any chance of you "losing focus" or having a flashback or whatever the hell that was really all about that you're obviously not prepared to talk about, then you can't operate on people.'

Luke watched the play of expression on Anna's face. Her distress was all too easy to see in the frown lines framing her eyes. In the way her lips trembled.

'I'm not out to get you,' she said fiercely. 'I want to help you.'

It was more than that, Anna realised as the words left her mouth. Had it been growing within her all the time she'd been watching Luke so carefully? Hoping to see him smile? Thinking so often about that short space of time when they'd been alone in her house and tumbling ever further into the confusion of her response to him. She could see the shadows that clouded his life and his eyes. There were things that haunted him and closed him off but she'd had a glimpse of the man he'd once been. Or could be.

She wanted, more than anything, to dispel those shadows. To get close enough to be allowed to help him.

She cared about him, Anna realised with something like dismay. She couldn't pinpoint when it had happened. Maybe the evidence had been there for days and days. A sum of everything she had seen or imagined. Elements that had floated in an uncoordinated fashion until the fear she had felt in seeing Luke virtually run from the canteen.

Something else had been added in when she had felt him respond to her kiss. A confused medley of caring and attraction. Not something she wanted to try and analyse and she certainly couldn't possibly tell him about any of it. Not when it was beyond the realms of possibility that he could feel anything like the same connection. Or that someone like him would want help from someone like her. He was more qualified than she was in so many ways. He was older. More skilled. He had seen and done things she would never want to do.

No wonder he was looking at her in a stony silence that took a little too long to be broken.

'Help me?' The words were bitten out scathingly. 'How do you propose doing that, exactly, Anna? By spreading a rumour that I might be unfit to do my job?'

'No.' Anna tried to catch his gaze but Luke was looking at the blasted potted tree they were standing beside. 'I think if you have the time, you'll get on top of whatever it is or find the help you need from someone a lot more qualified than I am.'

The snort of sound was incredulous. 'A shrink, you mean? Cheers, Anna.'

She ignored the rejection. She'd be angry, too, if someone suggested she couldn't handle her own issues. 'What I was going to suggest is that you don't operate unless I'm assisting you. For the protection of everybody involved.'

'You think I need supervising? By you?'

Anna flinched, biting back the observation that he had needed her during Colin Herbert's surgery. Something told her that Luke was trying to turn this into a confrontation he could feel justified in dismissing. She had to find a way to rescue this discussion or she would lose him. For ever.

The lift suddenly pinged into life close by. The doors slid open.

'Oops, wrong floor,' a masculine voice said. 'Hey…sounds like there's a party going on.'

'Yeah. Staff do, mate. Doctors and nurses. Security wasn't invited.'

'Shame. Wanna crash it?'

'Nah. More than our jobs are worth. Come on. Push the damn button.'

The doors slid shut again but a single word of the exchange lingered in Anna's ears.

Crash.

The kiss seemed a very long time ago. Hard to believe it had happened, even. But it had and for a brief time Anna had felt the same kind of connection she had that day he'd told her about his friend 'Crash'. It was possible to find a chink in the armour he wore.

'Actually,' she told Luke quietly, 'I was

thinking of it more in terms of it being beneficial to both of us.'

'So I get a supervisor. What do you get?'

'A mentor,' Anna said. 'The chance to learn from someone whose work I already respect.' She managed a smile as Luke finally made eye contact again. Had she also managed to placate him? 'Think about it. I'm going to go back to that party for a bit. I need some food.'

Going back into the canteen was the last thing Luke wanted to do but he found himself following Anna after a brief hesitation. He needed to prove he could. To Anna and to anyone else who might have raised their eyebrows at the manner in which he'd left. Most of all, he needed to prove it to himself.

He could see Anna walking well ahead of him.

He didn't need a babysitter. Or help.

He didn't need somebody kissing him because they thought he was on 'another planet' either. Because they felt sorry for him?

No. Anna had said she could learn from him. That she respected his work. That didn't suggest she felt sorry for him. That kiss hadn't held any hint of unwillingness. Quite the opposite.

She'd kissed him because she'd wanted to kiss him. And what's more she'd wanted to keep on kissing him. It wouldn't have been difficult to pull away as soon as he'd responded. What she was saying was at odds with her behaviour. As much of a contradiction as her smart suits and paint-splattered old clothes. It was a puzzle and Luke liked that. He liked having Anna to think about. To ponder over. He was like a boat being tossed on a stormy ocean and Anna was his anchor. Maybe he could get to his future without her but it would be hard.

Lonely.

Luke was walking slowly. He could see the brightly lit interior of the canteen now, beyond the doors that were propped open by chairs. Anna had vanished into the crowd.

A couple stood on the shadowy side of the doors, partly screened because one of the chairs had shifted. A man and a woman. He wouldn't have taken any particular notice of them except that he could feel the atmosphere as he got closer.

A palpable tension. Maybe he recognised it because the air had the same charged feeling as it had had in those stunned moments after kissing Anna.

Sexual tension.

The man raised a hand to shove his fingers through his hair and then rub his forehead with the palm of his hand.

It was Josh O'Hara, Luke realised with astonishment. The A and E consultant he'd met the day he'd accompanied Roger into the emergency department after his cardiac arrest. The man last seen going after his distressed wife when she'd fled the Christmas party.

This woman was definitely not his wife.

She was quite tall and very beautiful, with long dark brown hair tied loosely into a ponytail.

'I saw her leave,' the woman was saying. 'She looked dreadful, Josh. You should go home. Talk to her.'

'I know. I will. But she had gone by the time I got outside and I just had to... Oh, God, Megan...'

It was only a snatch of conversation that he

overheard and Luke wished he hadn't. There was something going on and he didn't need to know about it. It was none of his business how difficult or miserable other people were making their lives.

He had more than enough to deal with in his own.

Something made him turn his head again, however, as he pushed himself back into the party.

He saw Josh move his head. Tilting it further into the space behind the door that no one in here could see. Luke could sense the intent. Josh was planning to kiss this Megan. But almost at the same moment his head jerked backwards and he saw the shadowy figure ducking from reach as she emerged. She was shaking her head and she walked away without a backward glance.

Almost ran away, in fact.

That's what he should have done when Anna had gone to kiss him. Ducked the gesture and gone.

So why did he feel relieved that he hadn't even thought of doing so at the time?

* * *

Sleep proved elusive for Anna that night.

She couldn't close her eyes without thinking about that kiss and thinking about it brought it unerringly back to life.

She could still feel it.

The way his lips had moved over hers. Exploring them. Claiming them.

The strength in his hands. Their sure grip when he had pulled her close.

That incredibly gentle touch of his thumbs on her breasts.

And every time she relived that particular moment, her nipples tingled and a shaft of desire pierced her belly. And every time it got stronger. Feeding on itself. Taking on a life of its own. Becoming so intense it was physically painful.

With a groan, Anna shifted her body, turning over in her bed yet again. She had to stop thinking about it before day broke and she found herself on duty having had no rest.

Becoming aware of an odd thumping sound a moment later, she dragged her eyes open to find another set of eyes disturbingly close to her own. A long, wet tongue emerged to lick her face and the thumping accelerated when

Anna laughed and wiped her face on her pillow to dry it.

'You're supposed to be asleep, Crash. On your bed.'

The puppy wriggled with delight at hearing her voice. He obviously had no objection to being awake in the middle of the night.

'It's all right for you.' Anna pulled her hand out from under her pillow and reached to stroke the dog. 'You can sleep whenever you want to in the daytime. I need to sleep now and I can't.'

Crash leaned against the side of the bed, his chin tilting up against the mattress.

'He made out it was all my idea,' Anna informed Crash indignantly. 'And maybe it was, to start with, but you know what?'

Big ears twitched into their endearing sideways position and Anna smiled as she stroked them.

'He liked it as much as I did, that's what. He could have backed off and he didn't. He kissed me back.'

And how!

Anna let her breath out in a long sigh. A release that was partly pure pleasure at the memory but it also held a good whisper of frustration and more than a hint of anxiety about the implications of it all.

Silence gathered around them both as Anna's thoughts drifted on the breeze of that sigh. Her hand stilled and finally Crash heaved a sigh of his own, folding himself into a lumpy shape on the floor. He didn't go back to his own bed. He was still there, right beside her, prepared to share any vigil.

But Anna's eyes had drifted shut. One thing was certain. That kiss couldn't be undone and it put her and Luke on new ground. Unexplored, potentially dangerous but undeniably exciting territory.

Was Luke awake right now?

Would he remember that kiss?

Oh, yes. Anna was as certain of that as she was about the fact that the kiss couldn't be undone. Curiously, the knowledge was comforting and sleep finally came, but it didn't quite erase the tiny smile curling her lips.

CHAPTER SEVEN

IF LOOKS could kill…

Anna had to bite back an ironic smile as she pressed her foot on the control to start the water flowing and reached for the small, soap-impregnated scrubbing brush.

She'd probably been glaring at Luke in a very similar fashion that first day they'd been in Theatre together. Resenting his presence. Resenting him. Knowing that she was perfectly capable of doing the job without him being there. Feeling demoted in some way.

Now it was his turn. This was his first theatre slot following that little talk they'd had after she'd chased after him out of the staff Christmas party. The issue had been ignored for the day or two since then. In fact, Anna had had the impression that Luke had been avoiding her and that had been fine because any embarrassment lingering from the kiss had been somehow watered down until it didn't exist any more. Maybe he was hoping she would also forget her intention of scrubbing in with him for the safety of everyone involved but she hadn't forgotten. She hadn't waited for an invitation either, she had simply arrived.

Luke was apparently focused on scrubbing his hands and forearms with commendable thoroughness. Under his nails and between his fingers. Carefully angling the water flow so that it chased soap from the wrists up to his elbows and then dropping his hands to rinse from the wrists to his fingertips.

He muttered something under his breath as he reached for a sterile towel to dry his hands. It sounded like, 'Blackmail'.

'Sorry?'

'Nothing,' Luke growled. He stepped towards a theatre nurse waiting to help him don his gown and tie it. He cleared his throat and raised his voice. 'Good that you had the time to join us this morning, Anna.'

'Wouldn't have wanted to miss it,' she responded calmly. 'Pretty complicated case. I'm sure I'm going to learn a lot.'

The nurse made an approving sound. 'We all are,' she said admiringly. 'The gallery's a very popular place today. Full house.'

Anna looked up and smiled at Luke.

See? the smile said. Nobody's going to blink an eye at me being in Theatre with you. We are the only two people who know the real reason I have to be here and we both know why it has to be this way. Her smile faded but she held his gaze. Get used to it, she advised silently. You don't have to like it but you do have to deal with it.

Not that she expected him to deal with it in quite the way he did. By making her the lead surgeon. Talking her through the more complex aspects but only taking over for a few minutes at a time. It was a long and complicated surgery. The middle-aged female patient had a tumour in one lung that had spread to send tentacles around the major vessels that returned blood to the heart. The diagnosis had not been made until the reduction in blood flow due to the compression had given her heart failure. Swollen ankles and shortness of breath had finally made her seek medical help.

Fortunately, they found no cardiac involvement, but the dissection needed to remove as much of the tumour as possible was tricky. The patient was on bypass for nearly five hours as Anna and Luke worked to free the blood vessels and remove a lobe of her lung. By the end of the procedure Anna was exhausted. It wasn't until their patient was off bypass and her heart was beating again effectively that she could relax at all and it was then that she realised how Luke had 'dealt' with what he'd taken to be her supervision. He'd made her do the work and put so much pressure on her that she hadn't had time to even think about how focused he had been.

If that was how he wanted to play this, it was fine by her. Brilliant, in fact. In order to watch her and challenge her to improve her own skills, he was having to focus just as intently as he would if he was doing the procedure alone. More so, in some ways, because he had to think ahead in several directions so that he could troubleshoot if she wasn't on exactly the same wavelength.

Not that any major discrepancies in thinking had occurred. They had been amazingly in tune. So much so that Anna would have noticed instantly if Luke had lost focus. He hadn't. She had been challenged. She'd learnt a lot. To outward appearances they had worked as a close, harmonious team. The initiative had been a huge success as far as Anna was concerned and not only from a personal perspective. The patient's quality of life had been improved immensely and, if she was lucky, the length of it might be well beyond current expectations.

While Luke might not be prepared to recognise it yet, there had also been an additional, albeit secret bonus. He had done more than save face. Nobody watching—and there had been plenty of them—would have thought there were any undercurrents. They would have seen a head of department using exceptional skills in both surgery and teaching. His kudos had probably been raised by several degrees.

She might be exhausted now but she was also delighted. This could work.

And maybe it was a good thing that Luke

was grumpy about it. Anna found she was frequently the recipient of glares over the next few days. Surprisingly often, and not just when she might have expected to cross paths with her senior colleague on ward rounds or in meetings.

It was getting so that she could sense that brooding, intense look from a considerable distance. From the end of a corridor, for instance, when she got out of a lift. Or from across the canteen when she joined a lunchtime queue. He seemed to be everywhere. All the time. It didn't matter how late she stayed at work to catch up on paperwork or how early she arrived to get ahead with whatever her day held. He was always there. Or was it just that she was so much more aware of it?

Too aware.

So, yes, it was good that he was grumpy. It meant that he wasn't thinking about that ill-advised distraction of kissing him. Or, if he did think about it, it didn't make him happy. Either way, he wasn't going to want a repetition of anything like that and that was exactly what Anna needed to push herself forward.

To get over it and get on with her career and her life.

It was good.

It was. And if she reminded herself of that often enough, it would be true.

It should have been a relief to get Christmas and the start of the new year over with.

To get back to business as usual and away from all the forced cheerfulness of so many people trying to spread the joy of the season. Even patients were wishing him a happy new year, and there'd been far too many invitations to social events to find plausible excuses to avoid. So many smiles to produce.

Theatre had been the best place to be, of course. No tinsel allowed in there and nurses had to remove any silly seasonal earrings. He didn't tolerate small talk either so he didn't have to hear people talking about how excited their children had been as they had counted down the sleeps or what people were planning to do to see in the new year.

The only downside of being in Theatre had been that Anna had followed through her threat of supervising him. His response had been a form of attack in a way. If she wanted it to be like this and pretend she was there to improve her knowledge and skills then she could jolly well put the hard yards in instead of watching.

To his surprise, Anna had embraced the perspective and anyone in the gallery would have been convinced that that was the only reason she was in Theatre with him. Even more surprising was how much he enjoyed teaching her. At some point during that first operation on the woman with that nasty tumour threatening her cardiac function, Luke had stopped watching like a hawk to catalogue things he could be doing better than Anna and, instead, began channelling his knowledge and watching how quickly she understood what he was saying and how deftly the information was put into use.

He not only enjoyed the session, if he was really honest with himself, it had also been a relief to have her there.

Just in case.

Having watched Anna so closely during that surgery, Luke found himself continuing to watch her. He justified the scrutiny by telling himself he was watching her to see whether she was watching him. He watched her on ward rounds and in meetings. Even in the canteen. It was easy to create any number of opportunities to watch his assistant. He could find patients in the intensive care unit whose condition needed review. Departmental issues to discuss. Research projects to plan and monitor.

He discovered that Anna spent almost as much time in the hospital as he did. Way too many hours to have any kind of life away from a career. How did she find time to work on renovating that small cottage she lived in or to give her pet the attention it needed? Not that it was any of his business.

Or was it? At one point, he had to wonder if Anna's willingness to put in so much extra time was purely due to her dedication to her career or whether it had something to do with him still being in some kind of probationary period. Was he just aware of it because he was trying to keep one step ahead of her?

Or…was he watching for a signal of some kind that she remembered that kiss?

That she might find herself thinking about

it as often as he did? Sometimes he would catch her gaze and he'd feel an odd buzz. A hint that she might remember.

That she might be wondering if it would be as extraordinary if it happened again.

Wanting it to happen again...

On one of the first days of the new year, Anna was with Luke and one of her registrars in his office. They were discussing one of the new research projects due to get under way.

'The main causes of prolonged hospital stay, morbidity and mortality following cardiac surgery are haemorrhage and infection,' Luke was reminding the young doctor present. 'And, quite often, infection is one of the sequelae of haemorrhage.'

Anna was listening quietly. This was an occasion when she was in Luke's company but his attention was on someone else. Even when he involved her in the discussion, he would forget to glare at her and the simmering undercurrent that she was waiting on for further evidence that Luke was unfit for the position of responsibility he held vanished. She could interact with—and enjoy—the company of an intelligent and stimulating colleague.

Bask in it even.

The registrar was nodding. 'Is that because they're more susceptible to infection due to a low cardiac output?'

'That's one of the parameters we need to keep in mind. There's also the issue of how long the chest has been open, whether they've been on bypass or whether hypothermia has been employed. There's a lot of stuff that's been written on aspects of this in other studies. What we're aiming to do is possibly challenge their findings with more current information or testing methods and/or add in any other significant parameters. Here, I've printed off some of the articles for you.'

The registrar's eyes widened. So did Anna's.

How long had Luke been in here already today to search out and print off this stack of material? And this was supposed to be a day off for him. Didn't he have other places he wanted to be? Or other people he wanted to be with?

And why was the thought that he'd rather be here, having a meeting with her, a cause for a rather pleasant internal glow? Not that Anna was going to analyse her reaction. She didn't get a chance to, anyway, because her pager sounded.

The disruption earned her a sharp look from Luke and Anna sighed inwardly. 'Can I use your phone?'

'Of course.'

She found Ben Carter on the other end of the line and listened intently.

'I'm on my way,' she said a short time later. 'Luke's here as well. We'll both come.'

'What's going on?' Luke demanded as she put the phone down.

'Helicopter's due to land any minute bringing in a thirteen-year-old boy. He's hypothermic and unstable. Ectopic activity increasing so he could arrest at any time. Ben wants us on standby in case rewarming via bypass is necessary. He's put a theatre on standby as well and called in a technician.'

'You're the one on call. I'm not even supposed to be here today.'

Anna was at the door already. She turned to see the registrar looking slack-jawed at the po-

tential case and Luke looking…good grief…
wary? Or hopeful? Why?

She didn't have time to consider any personal issues. There was a child's life at stake
here and if it came to trying to rewarm him
by using cardiopulmonary bypass it was new
territory for her. She'd read about it but never
even seen it done. A flicker of something like
panic had to be crushed.

She held Luke's gaze for a heartbeat despite—or perhaps because of—knowing he
could probably see that flash of fear.

'But you are here,' she said quietly. The
presence of the registrar in the room ceased
to matter. 'And I need you, Luke.'

They both followed her but it was Luke's
tall form striding beside her that gave Anna
confidence. They moved fast enough for him
to be limping by the time they reached the
emergency department but they were still side
by side.

A team.

The main resuscitation area in Emergency
was crowded. Helicopter paramedics in their
bright overalls and helmets were there with
the medical staff, transferring their patient

with great care. There was a bustle of activity and a buzz of urgent instructions.

'Gently! Don't bump him. Cardiac function is fragile.'

'Is the Bair Hugger on?'

'Dextrose, not saline. Get some more in the microwave to get warmed.'

'Make sure that oxygen is warmed and humidified.'

'Get some more dots on. We need a twelve-lead ECG.'

'What's his temperature now?'

'Nineteen point five degrees Celsius.'

Luke whistled silently.

'The lowest ever temperature that someone's survived without neurological impairment was around thirteen degrees, wasn't it?' Anna kept her voice low. The boy's mother was on the other side of the room, looking terrified.

Ben Carter was leading the resus team and he wasn't happy with the oxygen saturation level of the boy's blood.

'I'm going to intubate,' he decided. 'Anyone who's not directly involved step back a bit, please. It's critical we do this with minimal movement.'

One of the paramedics stepped well back, close to where Anna and Luke were watching. Standing by.

'What happened?' Anna asked.

'Kid got ice-skates for Christmas,' the paramedic said quietly. 'They live on a farm up north a bit and there's a dam. He and his brother went skating and he hit some thin ice and went through. Took his brother about thirty minutes to find a branch big enough to get him out and another half an hour to run home and raise the alarm. Probably ninety minutes before we arrived on scene and the wind chill was significant. First temperature we got was eighteen degrees.'

'Cardiac rhythm?' Luke was watching Ben and his team securing the boy's airway but he was listening to Anna's conversation with the paramedic.

'Slow atrial fibrillation. Marked J waves.'

Anything below a core temperature of thirty degrees was enough to put someone at risk of cardiac arrhythmias and arrest. This boy was dangerously cold but there was still hope. Anna remembered a lecturer at medical school talking about hypothermia.

'You're not dead until you're warm and dead,' he'd said.

The Bair Hugger was a blanket designed to force a current of hot air over the patient's skin. Intravenous fluids were warmed to try and raise blood temperature but these methods might be too slow to help someone with such severe hypothermia.

'Luke.' Ben had finally stepped back from the initial flurry of making sure their patient was as stable as possible. 'Didn't think you were on today.'

'I'm not.' Luke flicked a sideways glance at Anna and there was a hint of a smile on his lips. He was here because she wanted him to be but it seemed like he wanted her to know he was happy to be here.

'Well, I'm glad you're here. Both of you.'

'What's the plan?'

Ben looked grim. 'External exogenous rewarming is only going to achieve a rate of about a two point five degree increase per hour. He's too cold to wait that long. With full cardiopulmonary bypass we could get a rewarming rate of seven point five degrees an hour.'

'We can't justify something as invasive as bypass unless he's arrested. What about pleural lavage?'

The cardiothoracic registrar was looking bemused. Anna leaned closer. 'That's using an inter-costal catheter to pour large volumes of warmed water into the chest cavity.'

'Still pretty invasive,' Ben was saying. 'And possibly less effective. Right now we'll keep ventilator support going and monitor his rhythm. We should get results on the bloods we've drawn soon. I want to see what his acid-base status is. At least slow A fib isn't a malignant rhythm.'

'We need an arterial blood gas as well,' Anna put in. She stepped forward to retrieve the sheet of paper emerging from the twelve-lead ECG machine but she didn't get time to analyse the trace. An alarm sounded on one of the monitors at the head of the bed.

'He's in V tach,' someone warned. 'I can't find a pulse.'

'V fib now.'

'Start CPR,' Ben ordered, moving to the

side of the bed. He looked back at Luke, who gave a terse nod.

'One shock. If that doesn't work, bring him up to Theatre under CPR.'

'Theatre 3's on standby. Bypass technician was paged when I called Anna.'

'Charging,' someone announced. 'Stand clear.'

Luke gave another nod and touched Anna's arm. 'Let's go. Better if we're scrubbed and ready by the time they come up if we're going to be needed.'

A cold, still heart.

This lad was technically dead and here they were thinking they could play God and bring him back to life.

Luke could see the lines of strain around Anna's eyes. He knew that her lips beneath that mask would be pressed tightly together. And, despite how subtle it was, he saw the way she flinched when her hands touched the chilled flesh in the small chest they had just opened.

'We need to work fast,' he reminded her quietly. 'Standard bypass. Arterial cannula in the ascending aorta. Right atrial cannulation with a single, two-stage cannula.'

Anna nodded. She was already placing a purse-string suture around the major vessel that took blood from the heart to the rest of the body.

Within minutes, with both surgeons working together in a tense atmosphere, the cannulae had been positioned and the boy's blood was now being circulated through the heart-lung bypass machine instead of his frail-looking body. Circulated and being carefully warmed.

There was nothing more they needed to do surgically until it was time to take him off bypass and repair the vessels currently holding the thick tubes. Then they would—hopefully—restart his heart, close his chest and wait to see if he woke up. Wait to see whether his brain function had survived this terrible insult.

Hours later, Luke found Anna in her office. She had been pacing back and forth between the intensive care unit and the wards. Between the canteen, where she'd eaten nothing at all, and the ICU. Between her office and the ICU.

'It's taking too long,' she said when Luke appeared through the door.

'He's in a good rhythm. Body temperature is within a normal range. The hyperglycaemia has been corrected. Renal function is looking good.'

'I know, I know.' But Anna was still pacing, her arms wrapped around her body as if for comfort. 'Blood gases are fine, too, and I'm happy with cardiac pressures. But what about possible complications like thromboembolism? Or disseminated intravascular coagulation?' She dragged in a breath. 'Have you met his mum, Janet? Did you know his big brother is six years older and that she had two late miscarriages before Jamie came along? What…what if he doesn't wake up?'

'Anna…' Luke stepped in front of her, forcing her to stand still. He gripped her upper arms. She was so wrapped up in this case, so desperate for them to have succeeded, she was losing her perspective. He'd never seen her like this.

So involved.

Caring so much.

'The sedation is only being lightened slowly. It'll take time for him to start breathing on his own and he's not going to wake up before then.'

'But what if—?'

'Stop,' Luke commanded.

He was still holding her. Looking down at Anna's pale face. Those astonishing green eyes were locked on his. Hanging onto his words of reassurance. Believing what he was telling her. And then his gaze dropped to her mouth and he saw the tiny tremble of her lips and that undid something deep inside him.

'What you need, Dr Bartlett,' he said very softly, 'is distraction.'

She caught the meaning of his words as soon as he'd uttered them. Her gaze dropped to his mouth and he found himself running his tongue across his lower lip. Slowly. Deliberately.

Time came to a standstill.

'Mmm.'

The sound Anna made could have been agreement but it sounded more like need. Desire.

It was all the permission Luke needed. His hands left her arms. He used one to cradle the back of her head and with the other he cupped her chin. Then he bent his head.

He was initiating this kiss. He was in control and he intended to make sure Anna was aware of nothing but the sensations he was going to provide with his lips. And his tongue.

This was going to be a kiss that Anna would have no chance of forgetting. Ever.

Anna kept her arms wrapped around her body even after that first touch of Luke's lips.

She'd needed to keep hold of herself in those seconds leading up to that kiss. Feeling the way his fingers splayed and claimed control of her head and her chin. Sensing the intent of this being far more significant than the last time they'd kissed.

She'd kept her eyes open as she watched his face dipping to meet hers. So slowly. And she'd held herself even more tightly with her own arms then because she'd been sure she was falling.

Desire had sucked her into some kind of

vortex and she was spinning wildly. Totally out of control.

And then his lips had touched hers and moved over her mouth. Questing. Claiming. Giving. Demanding her involvement and response.

Sensations rippled through Anna and unlocked the awful tension that had been building from the moment she'd touched Jamie's small, cold heart. Her skin tingled and seemed to melt and then her muscles gave up conscious control. Her arms let go of her own body and, instead, moved to hold Luke's. She could feel the strength of his muscles and the steady thump of his heart and all the time his mouth was doing such amazing things to hers. Her bones were melting now. He could just scoop her into his arms and lay her down on the floor of this office and she'd willingly—

Luke pulled away and for a dazed moment all Anna could think of was holding on more tightly. Pulling him back.

'Phone's ringing,' he said gently.

'Oh…' Anna put her hand to her mouth and took in a shaky breath. 'I—I'd better answer it, hadn't I?'

Luke was smiling at her.

Really smiling. His eyes were crinkled and the corners of his mouth had disappeared into those deep furrows beneath his cheeks.

'Yes.' He nodded. 'I think you had.'

She actually stumbled moving towards her desk. Heaven only knew what the intensive care consultant on the other end of the line thought of her initial stammered response but the content of the call was more than enough to bring her back to the present and reality. She put the phone down a moment later.

'Jamie's breathing on his own,' she told Luke. 'He squeezed his mum's hand.'

To her horror, Anna felt tears gather in her eyes. She never cried. She most certainly never cried in front of a male colleague.

But Luke didn't seem to mind. He reached out and pulled her into his arms. Not to kiss her this time but simply to hold her. For long enough to be more than a celebratory hug. Long enough for Anna to know that he understood exactly how she was feeling. Long enough for her to take several deep breaths and get her brain working properly again.

'If we get up there soon, we might see him

wake up and then we'll get an idea of what kind of neurological impairment he might be left with.'

An hour later they were part of the group around Jamie's bed in the intensive care unit as the young boy's eyes flickered open. His father and older brother were there now, too, but it was his mother who was closest. The first person Jamie saw.

He blinked a few times. Opened his mouth and moved his lips but his brow furrowed as though he couldn't find a way to make his mouth do what he wanted it to do. He stared blankly at the woman leaning so close to him, with tears running down her face.

Everybody present was holding their breath.

Luke and Anna were standing side by side. So closely their shoulders were pressed together. Unseen by anyone else in the cubicle, Luke's hand moved just enough for his fingers to tangle with Anna's.

Jamie tried again.

'Mum?' The word was croaky but clear. 'What's the matter?'

Anna felt her hand gripped so tightly it was painful but all she moved was her head. Just far enough to meet Luke's gaze.

To see the triumph at the back of his eyes.

He let go of her hand before anyone could notice but that didn't break the link. It was still there in his gaze. A connection that had taken them way beyond being merely colleagues.

He would come home with her tonight. Or she would go home with him. It didn't matter. It wasn't even a decision that needed to be discussed because it had already been made. Back in her office. Or maybe well before that but neither of them had taken that step forward.

Now they had taken that step and they both knew there was no going back.

CHAPTER EIGHT

CRASH stayed at the farm up the road from Anna's cottage.

'He often does,' she assured Luke. 'That way I don't disturb the Turners by collecting him if I have to work late. June loves him to bits. She would have kept him except that Doug put his foot down.'

She was talking quickly, Luke noticed, as the glow of realising she had kept the name he'd suggested for her puppy wore off. Was she nervous? Unsure she was making the right choice here, a passenger in his car as they drove away from St Piran's hospital that evening?

He was feeling a bit uptight himself. Sex in an army camp was a lot easier than this. You got attracted or desperate for distraction and a tent or somewhere private was never far enough away to allow for second thoughts. No awkwardness. No pressure. No strings afterwards.

This was different.

There was danger here. For the peace of mind he was struggling to achieve. For the relationship with an important colleague that could get damaged. And for Anna…because she might get hurt. She might want something that he couldn't give her.

Like commitment.

Curious that the prospect of hurting Anna outweighed the more personal ramifications this step could represent. He wanted to protect her. To turn his vehicle round and take her back to the hospital. Let Anna drive home to her small cottage. Alone.

Luke flicked a sideways glance at his passenger as he turned onto the road that led to his beachside house. She'd pulled out whatever it was she used to restrain her hair and it tumbled to her shoulders. Her hands were clasped in her lap and she was still wearing her power-dressing clothes.

Not for long, though. Luke found he had to lick suddenly dry lips. There was still time, he told himself. He could turn round. Tell her that he'd changed his mind and maybe this wasn't such a good idea after all, given how closely they needed to keep working together.

But Anna seemed to sense that quick glance and she turned her head as well. Her eyes seemed huge in a pale face as they drove under a streetlamp. Her lips were parted a little and maybe she was experiencing the same kind of dry mouth he was because she mirrored his own action and licked her lips. The action rendered Luke helpless to act on any good intentions. Almost ashamed of himself, he cleared his throat and it came out in a kind of growl.

Anna sighed, assuming the sound was related to the conversation she was using to fill the awkward journey.

'I know, I was crazy to take on a puppy with the kind of hours I have to work but when I am at home he's wonderful company.'

Oh, God…was she lonely?

The urge to protect this woman from being hurt morphed into something very different. He might not be able to offer commitment or any kind of a future but he could step, temporarily at least, into that void in her life and give her some companionship. The kind of closeness that would make her feel like she wasn't alone in the world. That someone cared enough to give her pleasure.

That someone cared at all.

She wasn't the only one here who needed that.

Anna was pleased that Luke didn't draw the curtains in the bedroom he led her into. His house was almost on a beach. Not one of the rocky, dangerous coves that dotted this coast but a sandy stretch with enough width for smooth waves. The kind of gem tucked amongst the rocky ones that surfers loved to try and keep secret. She could see it because it was a clear, cold night and there was enough moonlight to not only show her the view but to mean that harsh electric lighting was unnecessary inside. That pleased her, too.

She had already declined an offer for any food or drink. That could come later. Or not. They were there for one reason and that was to continue the kiss that had begun in her office. To finish what had been started.

Standing here was different, however. Anna was too nervous to look at the bed so she stood in front of the big window that had the view of the beach and stared out. Luke came to stand very close behind her. His hands brushed her arms. A slow stroke from her elbows to her shoulders and back again and there his hands lingered.

'Are you sure about this, Anna?' he asked quietly. 'It's OK if you want to change your mind.'

She turned and it was suddenly very easy. As though his body warmth was an irresistible magnet. Her breast brushed his hand as she moved and the sensation blitzed any final nerves.

'I don't want to change my mind,' she said softly. 'Do you?'

By way of response, Luke bent his head and his lips touched hers. The chill of the evening outside was coming through the uncovered glass beside them and the pale light of the moon offered no pretence of warmth, but Anna had never felt heat like this.

Scorching her lips as Luke claimed her mouth. Trickling over her body with the touch of his hands as he undid the buttons of her blouse and undressed her. Building inside as she watched him strip and stand there, bathed in moonlight. Tall and lean and powerful. Magnificently male.

She wanted him to catch her in his arms and throw her onto the bed but, instead, he came to stand in front of her. Skin to skin. Her breasts pressed into the hardness of his chest and she could feel his arousal against her belly. He wanted her. As much as she wanted him. His arms came around her then and their lips met. In a kind of slow dance, moving as one person, they somehow made their way from the window to the bed and then they were lying together. A tangle of limbs and passionate kisses and a consuming need that brooked no delay other than Luke fishing in a bedside drawer for protection.

The few seconds of watching him was like being suspended in time and space for Anna. The piercing anticipation had to be the most delicious sensation she had ever experienced and she clung to it, knowing that it would end very soon. Wanting it to end so that she could feel Luke inside her. Touching parts of her body that had never felt so hollow. Reaching places that weren't even physical.

She just knew he would be able to touch her soul.

Passion so intense had to explode and burn out in a dramatic climax and if that had been the end of it, it would have been incredibly satisfying on a physical level. Even better was that Luke smiled at Anna when they finally caught their breath.

'Now we can really get to know each other,' he promised.

And they did. A slow exploration of each other's bodies. A shaping of muscles on Anna's part with a compliment on how fit he must be. A tracing of Anna's breast with a single finger that ran across the flatness of her stomach to her belly button.

'You are beautiful,' Luke told her.

She found the scars on Luke's leg and he tried to move her hand but she resisted.

'They're part of you, Luke,' she said gently. 'Don't hide. Please.'

He went very still as she touched the mis-shapen muscle of his thigh and the lumpy ridges of the scars.

'Ugly, isn't it?' he ground out finally.

'No. They tell me that you have courage. That you're different.' Anna propped herself up on one elbow to look down at Luke. Even in this half-light she could see the shadows in his eyes that were part of the scars she had just been touching. What she could feel on his leg was nothing compared to the scars that had to be still hidden.

'Special,' she added in a whisper, leaning down to kiss him. She tried to put what she couldn't put into words into that kiss. To tell him that she accepted him for who he was. With scars. That she had courage too. That she could be trusted.

They made love again and this time it was slow and sweet and, in its wake, Anna fell asleep in Luke's arms, drifting off in a cloud of utter contentment. Of promise. Of a hope so compelling it was safer to go to sleep than contemplate the notion that it might be un-justified.

She woke some time later to find herself alone in a strange bed. She lay there, listening, but the house had that peculiar kind of silence that told her she was alone within these walls. Turning her head, she caught the glow of a digital, bedside clock. It was 3 a.m. Where on earth was Luke?

Taking the rumpled sheet with her to wrap around her body, Anna climbed from the bed. Instinct took her straight to the window and she stared out, the way she had when she'd first entered this room. For a long minute it was too dark to see anything. Then the moon emerged from thick cloud and she saw him. On the beach.

Running.

How could he be doing that? Not just because it was the middle of the night and it had to be well below zero out there, but how hard would it have to be to do that, in soft sand, on a leg that was damaged enough to make him limp at a fast walking pace or put him in noticeable pain when he had to stand for any length of time?

He was more driven than Anna had suspected and it was disturbing. Maybe he wasn't driving himself towards something. Maybe he was trying to run away.

He came back to the bed a while later, warm and fresh from a hot shower, and when

he reached for Anna, she was happy to sac-
rifice further sleep to make love yet again.
This time, however, there was an edge that
hadn't been there before. Concern for Luke.
The knowledge that she was with a deeply
troubled man.

When daylight broke, Luke was absent
from the bed again but Anna knew where
to look. He wasn't running on the beach this
time. She could see the dark shape striding
into the surf. Diving into a breaking wave
further out and then surfacing to swim, with
a strong, steady stroke, parallel to the sand.

She had showered and dressed by the time
Luke returned to the house. She saw him
coming up the path in his wetsuit, carrying
dripping flippers in one hand. His face registered surprise.

'You're not going to stay for breakfast?'

'I'd better not. I need to collect Crash and
I've got a huge list of things I want to get
done on my day off. If I can finish the painting and get the windowsills sanded and var-
nished, I can put my bedroom back together
properly tonight.'

'Shall I come over after work and give you a hand?'

Anna hesitated. She could decline the offer and send a signal that she wanted to slow down whatever was happening between them. If she accepted, it would take them to a new level. The start of a relationship instead of a one-night stand.

Luke was pulling the zipper on his wetsuit. Peeling it away to reveal his bare torso, and Anna's body instantly reminded her of exactly what it had felt like to have those hands peeling away her own clothing. The sound of the nearby surf reminded her of watching him in the night, punishing his body by pounding over the sand. Enduring the pain in his leg because he was driven. And courageous.

And she…loved him for it?

Oh, help!

'I—I'd love a hand,' she heard herself say aloud. Good grief, what was she doing? She couldn't stop herself. 'I'll cook you some dinner. Do you realise we totally forgot to eat last night?'

Luke looked more surprised than he had on finding her dressed and ready to leave.

And then he smiled. 'Sometimes food can be overrated. I had everything I needed.'

Anna actually blushed as she smiled back. 'Me, too.'

A day at home was important for Anna.

By throwing herself into the renovations of her cottage and spending time playing with Crash, she could banish Dr Bartlett and let her recharge her professional batteries. Usually the door between work and home was firmly closed but today there was a wedge preventing that. She found herself wondering where Luke might be and what he might be doing.

He wouldn't be in Theatre. Although the tacit agreement that they would act as a team for surgery was still new, it was working and Anna trusted Luke not to break it. If something extraordinary happened, like Jamie's case had presented yesterday, he would call her in.

How was Jamie today? Anna peeled off her gloves and discarded the sandpaper she had been using, intending to make a call, but the phone rang as she walked towards it.

'I thought you might like an update on

Jamie,' Luke said. 'We're transferring him to the ward this afternoon. He's bouncing back from his surgery remarkably well and I think we'll find he'll end up showing little effect from being virtually frozen to death.'

Anna listened to Luke's voice and absorbed the welcome news. The call ended, she went back to varnishing her windowsill. Thoughts of Luke were there as pervasively as the smell of polyurethane. Catching sight of Crash ripping her sandpaper to shreds with his tail thumping, she made a mental note to get to the supermarket so that she had something to feed Luke for dinner tonight. What did he like to eat? What would he like to do when they'd finished eating?

Oh, Lord. She could only hope that Luke wasn't in his office, struggling to concentrate on important paperwork, getting ambushed by memories of their astonishing night together. On the other hand, maybe she hoped he was. This was all as confusing as it was wonderful.

She put a roast of beef in the oven to cook slowly and fill her cottage with a welcoming aroma. She wanted Luke to feel welcome. She purchased wine, too. She wanted him to relax and feel comfortable. This was another new step. A chance to get to know each other better on more than a physical level. A chance to talk about things other than work. A chance to test these newborn feelings she was experiencing. To see if there was a chance of finding ground that might nurture them or whether they needed to be ruthlessly weeded out.

Except that turned out to be harder than Anna had anticipated. Luke seemed happy to be in her home and he clearly appreciated the meal, though he declined any alcohol. He was polite but unforthcoming when it came to any personal conversation.

'What was it like?' Anna asked at one stage. 'Working in a field hospital?'

'Basic. Fast and bloody.' His tone was detached enough to signal a lack of desire to go into details. 'These Yorkshire puddings are fantastic,' he said into the moment's silence that fell then. 'Where did you learn to cook like this?'

'My mother was adamant that a girl had to be able to cook. So was my father, come to that.'

'And you weren't.'

It was a statement, rather than a question. Delivered with a quizzical edge that made Anna think he could see right into places in her heart that even she didn't peer into too deeply any more.

'Things that boys were allowed to do were more important. I jumped through the girl hoops but it wasn't enough.' Anna looked down at her plate. 'My father wanted a son that he never got.'

She heard Luke's fork clatter as he put it down. Then she felt him touch her hand. 'He got something better, then, didn't he? They must be very proud of you.'

Anna shrugged. 'Surprised might be closer to the mark. Disappointed, maybe, that I didn't become a teacher or a nurse and shower them with grandchildren. Grandsons,' she amended with an attempt to lighten the revelation with a smile. 'What was your family like, Luke? You weren't an only child, were you?'

'No. All boys in my family but if there had been a girl she would have been expected to do the boy things. She wouldn't have had a choice, really, being dragged from one military post to another. I was the one to break the family tradition and become a doctor instead of a soldier. Even then, I was expected to aim for a career as an army medic. I rebelled.'

'You went in the end. I'm sure your parents are proud.'

'They're in New Zealand,' Luke said, as though that answered the unspoken question. And then he steered the conversation away from himself again. 'What's the next project you've got lined up for the cottage?'

He helped her clean up after the meal and then he helped her move the bedroom furniture back into place. And then, as Anna had hoped he would, he took her into her own bed and made love to her. He wouldn't stay the night, however.

'I've got so much reading to catch up on,' he excused himself in the early hours. 'You've got no idea how out of date you can get by taking a year or two off. I've got to keep up my exercise program, too, and I can't miss my early swim.'

Too many good reasons not to stay.

'Don't you ever sleep, Luke?'

'Sleep's overrated.' He bent to kiss Anna again as he took his leave. 'Life's too short to waste it.'

Maybe sleep wasn't so overrated.

Fatigue was like a form of anger. Something that simmered and bubbled occasionally to splash in unexpected directions.

'That is a surgical mask, not a damned bib. Don't come into this theatre unless you're going to wear it properly.'

The junior theatre nurse went pale and fled. Luke looked away as Anna glanced up from the meticulous stitches she was placing in preparation for a mitral valve replacement. He knew there had been no real reason to snap at the nurse. She'd been delivering some new IV fluid supplies, not planning to come and lean over the operating table.

'I've got all the anular sutures placed and tagged,' Anna said.

'Let's get the valve seated, then, and tie them off.'

'OK,' Anna said as the procedure continued. 'I'll have the aortic needle vent now, thanks.'

Luke watched as she removed more air and then restarted the heart.

'Can you elevate the apex of the left ventricle?' she asked him. 'If those adhesions are too dense, I'll go for clamping the aorta. I'd like to follow up with an echocardiograph to check.'

Would she say something when this was over? Reprimand him in some way for his irritation with the junior nurse? He probably deserved it, given that this wasn't the first time.

Ripping off his mask and the disposable hat as he left Theatre, Luke pushed his fingers through his flattened hair. What was wrong with him?

It wasn't simply fatigue. Insomnia had been a part of his life for many months now and he had coped. Maybe the difference was that he was choosing to stay awake when he craved sleep. Night after night. It had been nearly a week now. He would hold Anna in his arms after they'd made love and feel the way her body softened and her breathing slowed. The blissful temptation of sleep would pull at him in those moments, too.

Taunt him.

When he needed sleep and was ready for it, it wouldn't come. If offered itself at times like this, when he couldn't accept. He just couldn't go there because he had no control over what his sleeping mind chose to do. While it could be the saving of him to have Anna to hold close in the wake of a nightmare, he had to spare her from sharing that part of his life, because then he'd have to talk about it and he wasn't going to do that with anybody.

If he could bury it, it would go away.

Eventually.

Luke fell asleep the next night Anna stayed at his house.

Maybe that was what had woken her— the change in how he was holding her. It was more like she was holding him right now. With a careful tilt of her head, she could see his face and it looked so different she was shocked. He looked so much younger. Unguarded.

Vulnerable.

Those piercing, intense eyes were shuttered. His lips were soft and slightly parted and she could hear his soft, even breaths.

Even the furrows at the top of his nose had softened. Anna willed herself not to move. She didn't want to wake him. Heaven knew, he needed the sleep. Nobody could keep up the kind of pace Luke did without coming to physical harm. It was no wonder he snapped at the people around him occasionally.

So she stayed awake. Holding this man she was coming to feel more deeply for every day. Wanting to protect him and give him the healing rest that only sleep could provide. That was probably why she felt the moment the nightmare started. The way the muscles beneath her hands and arms became so tense. She could hear the way his breathing became shallow and rapid. His heart was pounding beneath his ribs and she could feel the rumble of his moan even before it reached his lips.

'No-o-o-o…'

'Luke. Wake up.' Anna held him more tightly. 'It's all right. It's just a bad dream.'

She couldn't hold him now. The strength in his body was frightening as he twisted and fought whatever demons had come in his sleep. Anna could see the sheen of sweat on his body. His breath came in choking gasps now—as though he was suffocating.

'Arghhh!' The sound was one of agony.

The covers were hurled back from the bed and Luke swung his legs over the side. He was almost crouching there and he covered his face with his hands.

Anna scrambled to her knees and across the bed. Kneeling behind Luke, she wrapped her arms around him.

'It's all right,' she said, hoping her voice wouldn't betray how shaky she was feeling. 'I'm here, Luke. You had a nightmare.' That's all, she wanted to add, but bit the words back. This wasn't something that should be belittled in any way.

His breathing was slowing now. For a moment he leaned back into Anna's embrace but then he lurched to his feet.

'I need some fresh air,' was all he said. He began dragging on clothes. Fleecy track pants. Running shoes.

She couldn't make him tell her anything about the nightmare if he didn't want to. Anna closed her eyes. Waiting. Hoping.

'You...' Luke paused as he got halfway

across the room but he didn't turn round. 'You weren't... I didn't want you to see that.'

'It was a nightmare, Luke. Don't go. You don't have to run away from it.'

The huff of sound from him was angry. She knew nothing. And he wanted it to stay that way.

'Would you rather I went home?'

'Up to you. I won't come back to bed. I've got some work I may as well do now that I'm awake. After my run.'

And with that he was gone.

Anna didn't want to wait. There was no moon tonight so she wouldn't be able to see him down on the beach. She didn't want to watch either. Luke had his own way of dealing with whatever was bothering him and it didn't include her.

What was she to him? With a sinking heart Anna found her clothes and then the keys to her car. Was this just about the sex?

Distraction?

When she arrived home to her cold cottage, Anna put an electric heater on and made a pot of tea. It was nearly 4 a.m. and she was far too wound up to go to sleep again. She missed Crash.

Opening her briefcase, she got her laptop out and connected to the internet. With no emails that caught her interest, she idly clicked on a search engine and stared at the flashing cursor.

'PTSD', she tapped in on impulse.

So many sites. She opened the one that had been given first place in the queue and within minutes she was totally engrossed.

Post traumatic stress disorder was a syndrome that could develop following any traumatic event. Things like natural disasters and car crashes, violent assaults or even medical procedures, especially for children. Top of the list, however, as she'd known quite well, was war.

Traumatic experience put the mind and body into a state of shock, she read, but most people could make some sense of what had happened, process the resulting emotions and come out of it eventually. In PTSD, the person remained in psychological shock. There was a disconnection between the memory of the event and how the victim felt about it.

Anna read on, almost feverishly, skipping a few paragraphs to the heading of 'Symptoms'.

Nightmares.

Flashbacks.

Difficulty falling or staying asleep.

Irritability or outbursts of anger.

She found herself nodding at that one. She hadn't said anything about the way Luke had snapped at that poor theatre nurse the other day but other people were talking about it. And about the way he had avoided all social invitations outside the hospital over the Christmas and New Year period. Some were keen to remember his odd behaviour at the one event he had attended and the way he'd stormed out of the canteen.

Her eyes drifted further down the list. Not that she needed any more information to confirm what she was already convinced of.

Depression was common. So was guilt. People often attempted to numb themselves through substance abuse. Luke obviously avoided drinking but wouldn't his exercise regime fit into the same category? How numb would you get, running or swimming in the middle of winter? And physical pain could override mental suffering.

The victim could also feel detached from others and emotionally numb. They would have a sense of a limited future and wouldn't expect to live a normal life span or get married and have a family. PTSD would harm relationships, the ability to function and their quality of life.

There were treatments suggested, of course, but they came with the background rider that the sufferer had to be willing to confront it and not see the admission as a sign of weakness. Luke had been brought up in a military family. Was it the kind of thing that didn't get mentioned? That he wouldn't be able to allow himself to admit? He'd denied having flashbacks. Pushed her away in the wake of that nightmare. He 'hadn't wanted her to see it'. Had he ever, in fact, gone to sleep before when she'd been in the same bed?

Maybe her intrusion into his personal life was making it worse. Removing opportunities he might have otherwise had to sleep. Putting stress on him by making him think he had to factor her into a future that might already seem too difficult.

It was so clear to her that Luke was suffering from PTSD. It was also very clear that the only way to conquer it was to confront it. Somehow he would have to learn to accept it as part of his past. Numbing it or pushing the memories away would only make it worse and it was more likely to emerge under stress.

The sound of a distant beeping finally intruded on Anna's thoughts and she realised her alarm clock was going off. Her huff of laughter was ironic. It was time to get up and get ready for work. With a heavy heart she went through the motions, but she couldn't stop thinking about the pieces that had finally fallen into place and created a picture so much darker than she had feared.

As far as she was concerned, she was a part of that picture. She was in far too deep to escape. She didn't want to.

For better or worse, she had fallen in love with Luke Davenport.

She wanted to help him.

But how?

CHAPTER NINE

'WHAT's this?' Anna had stooped to pick something up from the floor of Luke's office.

He glanced at the scalloped, gilt-edged card she was holding. Damn, he hadn't noticed he'd missed his aim.

'Nothing,' he said. 'It was supposed to go in the bin.'

'But…' Anna was reading the fancy calligraphy and then she looked up with a stunned expression on her face. 'Luke…this is an invitation to a medal ceremony, isn't it? Returning Heroes. With a ball to honour the recipients of the medals.'

'I'm not going. I hate parties.' Luke swivelled his desk chair so that he could drop a file into the cabinet behind him. 'Was there something you wanted to talk to me about?'

'Yes.'

Another file tab caught Luke's eye and he pulled it out. It took several seconds to register the silence. Anna wasn't going to talk to him until she was confident he was listening.

Fine. He swung the chair back around. 'What do you want to talk about?'

She was still holding the card and looked down at it again. 'This.'

'That's not why you came in here. You didn't know it existed.' He could feel his eyes narrowing as he sighed. 'What was the real reason you came in?'

'This isn't even an invitation. It says you're "required to attend". That sounds pretty official. Will you get into trouble if you don't go?'

Luke gave a huff of laughter. 'What can they do? Kick me out of the army? Give my medal to someone else? That's fine by me. I don't want the damn medal.'

'Why not?' Anna sank into the other chair in his office but her gaze was unwavering. Fixed on Luke. She wasn't going to let this one go.

He felt trapped. Angry. The way he had ever since he'd woken from that nightmare to find Anna in his bed. This was becoming a problem. OK, the sex was great. She was great. He loved seeing her like this, at work, in her neat clothes and with her hair all scraped back. Being completely professional in their interactions while all the time they both knew what it would be like after, away from work.

When the clothes came off and the communication came through touch and not words. When they could both escape to a place that promised only pleasure.

But maybe it had run its course. It wasn't going to work. Not long term.

She was already too close. Had seen too much. She didn't represent a rope that he could use to help him into his future any more. She was starting to resemble a roadway. With traffic in both directions. He didn't want to go back. He couldn't. Because if he did, he would be taking Anna with him and she would see who he really was and then she would be the one to go.

And that might finally destroy him.

Anna could see the play of emotion on Luke's face. The annoyance that she was pushing when he'd made it clear he wasn't interested in either going to this ceremony or talking about it. She knew perfectly well she was stepping over a boundary here. She could almost see him weighing up whether she was worth the trouble.

Would he tell her to get out? Push so hard she had no choice but to leave? He'd been holding her at a distance ever since that nightmare. They hadn't been to bed together for three days now. They hadn't even spent that much time together at work. He was avoiding her because he didn't want to talk about the nightmare. Probably didn't want to admit how often he had them. Or that they happened at all, like the flashbacks. Talking about this medal ceremony and what it had to remind him of might tip them over the edge and it would all be over, but it was a risk Anna had no choice but to take.

Maybe Luke needed a push himself to recognize that he had PTSD. He had to be willing to confront his past. She was quite prepared to help him and be with him through any rough patches but only if it was part of a healing process. Otherwise she would just be locking herself into a miserable cycle of watching the man she loved suffer. Getting pushed away and hurt herself and then crawling back for more of the same.

She wasn't going to do it. If she did, she would only be allowing Luke to stay locked in that dark space permanently and he was worth more than that.

'Why not, Luke?' she asked again. 'Why don't you want to get the recognition you deserve? It's your name that's right at the top of that list. Does your family know about this? Will they be there, hoping to be part of the honour?'

'I don't want the damned medal.' The words burst out in an angry rush as Luke leaned forward on his desk, both hands clenched into fists. 'I haven't told my family because I don't want to celebrate what happened. Or to glorify war. To pretty it up for the media with everyone in nice, clean uniforms and rows of shiny badges. Dancing, for God's sake! That's about as meaningless as everything else in civilian life.' He lowered his voice and it became rough. Totally compelling. 'War is about blood and guts and people. People who can be terrified they're not going to get back to the ones they love. Who can die, in agony, a thousand miles away from the people who love them.'

He tipped his head back, closing his eyes. 'Yes, I survived. But what about all the others?'

Slowly, he brought his gaze back to Anna's. His eyes were dark. So shadowed they were blank of emotion. Like the rest of his face. 'I don't want a prize for being one of the lucky ones.'

Anna swallowed. Hard. She was part of his civilian life. Meaningless.

The silence stretched on. Tense and horrible. She had to say something. To try and defuse this awful distance escalating between them.

'Yes, war is about people,' she said finally. 'That's how they generally start, isn't it? You have a group of people, including innocent children, who lose their lives or have their rights as human beings threatened or taken away. Most people have to try and close their minds to the atrocities that go on because it doesn't affect their lives and they can't do anything about it, anyway.' She drew in a breath, the words coming more easily now. 'But some people are brave enough to put their hands up and say, I'll help. I'll go into horrible places and endure terrible things. Not because I might end up getting a medal for it but because it might—eventually—help to make the world a better place.'

Was he listening? Anna couldn't tell. She was talking hard and fast now, barely forming the thoughts before the words tumbled from her mouth. Desperately trying to let Luke know, somehow, that it was all right to have this as part of his past. That she accepted it. And if she talked enough, maybe by some miracle she could say something that would get through to him. Stop him from shutting her out and pushing her out of his life.

'If enough people didn't avoid even thinking about wars, maybe something could change without people having to die,' she continued. 'And maybe the publicity that comes from something like this is what makes them take notice. It's the heroes that people can't help taking notice of. That they listen to.'

Luke was staring at her now but his face was still devoid of emotion.

'Maybe the people who take the most notice are the ones who've lost someone they love. Because they have to try and make sense of it all.'

Which was exactly what Luke needed to do himself, wasn't it?

'Or maybe it's the people who will feel lucky for the rest of their lives because someone they love has come home. Thanks to one of those heroes. I'll bet the families of all the soldiers you saved would love to give you a medal, Luke, but they don't have to, do they? The army is going to do it for them.'

Still no reaction. Anna felt a flicker of anger. 'How do you think they'll feel if you can't be bothered to show up?'

That did it. Luke's face finally moved but it was only to turn away from her. 'Are you finished?'

'No.' Anna's mouth had gone dry. This was it. She had failed. He wasn't going to let her into this part of his life. Her breath came out in a ragged sigh. She closed her eyes in defeat. 'The party wouldn't be so bad,' she said dryly.

'At least nobody would be wearing reindeer horns.'

Opening her eyes, she found Luke had turned back to face her. For a heartbeat her flippant comment hung in the air and then she saw a change in Luke's eyes. A lightening of those shadows. A vaguely incredulous expression that took her back to...

Oh, help. Back to that day when Luke had come to her cottage and discovered Anna instead of his colleague, Dr Bartlett. When she'd made that stupid joke about unlikely dogs using a staircase to become mates. So she was no good at cracking jokes? Did he have to look at her as though he was seeing someone he didn't even recognise?

Someone stupid, maybe, who said meaningless things that made him wonder why on earth he'd ever been attracted to her?

But Luke's lips were moving now.

Good grief! He was smiling. Virtually grinning.

'OK,' he said. 'I'll go. On one condition.'

'What's that?' The relief that he wasn't shouting at her or physically throwing her out of his office was enormous. It was making her feel light-headed. Ridiculously happy.

Hopeful, even.

'That you come with me.'

Anna's head cleared astonishingly quickly. An image of a military ball sprang into her head. Men in dress uniform. Luke in dress uniform. He would look impossibly gorgeous. And she would have to be dressed up and feminine. No way would she be on ground where she could feel like an equal. But they weren't equal, were they? Even here. Not on emotional grounds, anyway.

She would be so proud of him if she went. She would be getting herself in ever deeper.

But wasn't that what she wanted? Needed? Or was it that she knew she should fight it but just couldn't help herself?

Anna shook her head, trying to clear the confused jumble of her thoughts. Luke misinterpreted the gesture as reluctance.

'You think I should go,' he said. 'And you're probably correct.'

Another memory was niggling at Anna now. She'd persuaded Luke to attend the staff Christmas function by telling him that heads of departments would be expected to attend. Look what had happened there. How much more likely would a flashback be when he was surrounded by army uniforms and by people wanting to talk about why he was being honoured as a hero?

'I won't go unless you come with me,' Luke said quietly. 'Please, Anna. I…need you.'

Three little words. Possibly the only three she'd ever hear from Luke but maybe they were enough.

'All right,' she said with a catch in her voice. 'I'll come with you.'

Why had he been so determined not to attend this event?

So bad-tempered about having to put on his dress uniform 'Blues' and act like a soldier? Gritting his teeth as he'd accepted all the congratulations that came with the medal now pinned to his tunic.

Hating it all so much he'd barely spoken to Anna, even though he could see how much effort she'd put into this on his behalf. Buying a new dress and having her hair done in some fancy way. Putting up with his foul mood for the whole of their drive to London. All those long stretches when the only sound in the vehicle had been the windscreen wipers trying to cope with the sleet of the January evening.

He'd only asked her to dance because it was the last duty he had to perform tonight. The recipients of the medals and their partners had been invited to take the floor first and people were watching. Clapping.

One dance and then he could escape. Drive back to St Piran, apologise to Anna and then forget the whole excruciating business.

The lighting was softened as the orchestra began playing a waltz. Chandeliers still sparkled overhead and the reflection of the crowd present could be seen in the glass of the floor-to-ceiling windows that filled one wall and afforded a spectacular view of London beyond. Diamonds glistened on women and the buttons on dress uniforms gleamed on the men.

Holding out his hand to Anna, Luke had the sudden, awful thought that he hadn't bothered to find out if Anna knew how to dance something formal. He'd had lessons as a teenager, along with all his brothers, and the skill was automatic. Not that he'd had either the opportunity or the desire to use it for a very long time. But Anna took his hand and came into his arms willingly. The dark, emerald fabric of her long dress shimmered in this lighting and he gathered her into a formal dance hold. Stiffly at first, until the steps came more easily. It was only then that he noticed how light Anna was on her feet and how well she was able to follow his lead.

More couples came onto the dance floor but Luke didn't even notice. In his relief that he wasn't embarrassing Anna and making her evening even worse than he had already by assuming a skill she might not have, he relaxed a notch. Another notch or two got added when he remembered that the evening was almost over. He was going to get through it. And that was when he finally looked down and really noticed the woman in his arms.

Her hair had been scooped up in some clever fashion to make coils that sat sleekly against the back of her head. Little bits had been pulled free, however, so that tiny soft spirals framed her face and drew attention to the lovely length of her neck. The style was formal and precise—like Anna was at work—but it was those free tendrils that Luke really liked. They reminded him of the way Anna was when she wasn't at work. Softer. Surprising.

Pure woman.

The fabric of her dress was silky under his hands. Almost as delicious as he knew her bare skin to be. The colour was sheer brilliance. How had it taken him this long to notice how it was a shade or two darker than her eyes and made them so...luminous.

So extraordinarily beautiful.

Mesmerising.

The music altered tempo as the orchestra started something less classical. Something moody and sweet. It was the perfect opportunity to make an exit from the dance floor but Luke had lost any desire to do so. Instead, he drew Anna closer. He wasn't following any routine steps now, just moving to the music that surrounded them. Holding an amazingly beautiful woman who followed every move he made so easily it was like holding an extension to his own body.

She looked and felt so lovely. She even

smelled so wonderful that Luke bent his head to get closer. Was that perfume coming from her hair or her skin? Or was it just Anna? It was hypnotising. A new space. An escape that was better than sleep. Better than sex, even, because he could keep this up for ever.

He certainly wasn't going to be the one to suggest stopping any time soon.

Anna had been very close to tears by the time Luke asked her to dance.

Wishing she'd never agreed to accompany him. A million miles away from this would have been too close. She'd tried so hard to look the part and he'd been so closed off and angry from the moment he'd arrived at her door to collect her.

The drive had been awful. Full of silences during which she had nothing to think about except the distance between them. That she was no closer to imagining a way out of this for Luke that could offer the promise of a happy future for him.

For them both.

Watching him during the ceremonial part of the evening had been even more grim. He looked just as gorgeous as she'd expected in the crisp, dark blue uniform with its braid and insignia, but she'd been able to see how much he'd been hating it. Tension so great it seemed like he could simply snap at any moment. Luke hadn't wanted to be a part of any of this. He hadn't wanted any of it to be a part of his past.

Could no one else see what she could see? That the event that had led to him being here tonight was what had scarred him so deeply. That he was determined to escape the memories and he couldn't see that the only way to stop them haunting him to the point of ruining his life was to turn round and confront them.

The tension had been contagious. All Anna had wanted was for the evening to end. To get through that long drive home somehow and then…what?

Admit defeat and see what she could do about putting her life back together the way it had been before Luke had come back to St Piran?

It had been the thought of trying to move

on without him that had been what nearly brought her to tears in public. But then Luke had held out his hand when the medal recipients had been invited to take the dance floor first. It had been the first time he'd touched her in what felt like a very, very long time, and as soon as Anna had felt that contact she'd known exactly where she really wanted to be.

Not a million miles away at all.

Right here.

In Luke's arms.

He could dance. When the initial awkwardness wore off, Anna was astonished to find he could actually dance beautifully. The music was soothing and the rhythm of the waltz easy to follow even from long-ago lessons. Glancing up, she found Luke's face still grim and turned away. He was going through the motions here, but in reality he was hunting for an escape route.

Dropping her gaze, Anna stared at the medal pinned to his tunic, awarded for an act of outstanding bravery during active operations against an enemy. It was a beautiful silver cross mounted on a wreath of laurel leaves with a crown in its centre. The ribbon had narrow stripes of dark blue on each edge and a central stripe of crimson. What would he do with it when he got home? Shut it away in its box and hide it along with the memories of why it had been bestowed?

Looking up again, Anna was startled to find Luke's gaze on her face. An intense gaze but one she was getting used to. As though he was seeing her properly for the first time. Looking…amazed.

The waltz ended and Anna knew this would be when Luke suggested they sit down or go to supper perhaps. Or just go home.

Instead, he drew her closer and she could feel some of that terrible tension leaving his body. They were so close. She could feel the length of his body against hers. Leading her. So powerful and yet it felt gentle, probably because she was so willing to follow.

And then she felt his cheek against her hair and Anna closed her eyes, sinking into the delicious knowledge that Luke wasn't just dancing now.

He was dancing with her.

Another medley of tunes began. And then another, but Luke made no move to take her away from the dance floor and Anna certainly wasn't going to be the one to break this connection.

She wanted it to last for ever.

The start of the fireworks display startled all the guests. The wall of windows provided a great view of the city lights on the other side of the Thames but nobody had noticed the grassy bank-side area until the impressive display got under way.

It began with a sound like a cannon firing. A huge silver rocket shot up into the blackness of the sky and then exploded into a shower of tiny silver spheres that drifted down slowly.

Not that Anna was watching them. At the first sound Luke had stiffened so abruptly that she had tripped on his foot. Then he moved again, so sharply Anna could swear she felt him snap. He dropped his arms from her body and turned swiftly, weaving between couples who had also stopped dancing to see what was happening. They began to move towards the windows.

Anna moved in the opposite direction. Following Luke. All the way out of the ballroom. Through the area where a buffet supper was being served. Through the vast foyer where staff were now stacking all the chairs that had been used for the initial ceremony. Down a wide flight of steps. She could feel the sting of sleet on her skin. Gathering up the folds of her dress, she raced after Luke. Around the corner of the building. As far away as he could get from where the fireworks were happening.

And there he stopped. When Anna came around the corner she saw him, his head on his arm, leaning against the stone wall. She could hear him gasping for breath in the same way he had when he'd been having that nightmare.

'Luke!'

'Go, Anna.' The plea was hoarse. 'Get out. While you can.'

She came up to be right beside him. 'I'm not going anywhere. Talk to me.'

'I can't.'

At least part of him was there and aware

of her. He'd been like that in the canteen too, hadn't he? Having a flashback he couldn't control but still aware of things around him, like bumping into someone and spilling their drink. Maybe, if she tried hard enough, she could get through to him.

'Why not?' she begged. 'Why can't you talk to me, Luke?'

'My problem. If I told you, it would become your problem.' The words were staccato. Agonised. 'I won't do that to you.'

'It's already my problem.'

'No. You can go. I want you to go.'

'I can't do that, Luke.'

'Why the hell not?' His head turned and the expression on his face broke her heart.

'Because…because I love you, that's why.'

Luke buried his head again and he groaned. It was a sound of such distress but was it due to her confession or because of whatever still had him in its grip?

Fireworks were still going off, muted a little by the vast building between them but still loud. Possibly loud enough that he hadn't heard what she'd just said. Or maybe he had chosen not to hear it because he already had too much to deal with.

'It's the noise, isn't it?' She had to touch Luke. To get closer. 'Where are you, Luke? What do you see?'

A moment's silence and then Luke spoke in a low, desperate voice she barely recognised.

'We're under fire. We're on our way to a village. There's children hurt by a landmine but we don't get there.' The words were rushing out so fast it was hard to hear them clearly. 'It's an ambush. Another mine. And artillery. The truck's tipped over. Everybody's hurt. I…I felt my leg snap.'

He dragged in a breath. 'We need to get out. Danny's unconscious. His airway's blocked. There's a chopper coming. I can smell the smoke and the blood. The guys are screaming. I'm trapped. I'm trying to get them out and I can't move. I can't breathe…'

Anna was gripping his arm. 'Yes, you can, Luke. You did get them out. All of them. That's why you got the medal tonight. You saved everybody in that truck. You saved their lives.'

'But I didn't...' Luke groaned again. Or was it a sob? 'Not the life I wanted to save.' Yes, it was definitely a sob now. Torn from somewhere deep inside. 'I couldn't save Crash, Anna. I...wanted to...so much...and I...couldn't...'

Racking sobs took hold of Luke's body now. All Anna could do was to hold him as hard as she could and be there. Saying nothing. Letting him hold her so tightly it was impossible to take a deep breath and letting him rock her as he rocked himself.

And eventually, as she became aware of how damp and cold they were both going to be, Luke quietened.

'Let's go home,' she said.

Luke waited outside while she collected their coats and the car keys.

'I can drive if you'd like.'

'No. I'm all right.' Luke's voice was sombre. 'Better if I'm doing something. I'm sorry about that.'

'I'm not,' Anna said, but Luke didn't hear her. He was striding ahead to where the car was parked.

Sleet was still falling and got thicker as

they left the outskirts of London but the road was still clear enough. Anna listened to the windscreen wipers. They sounded different now. Maybe because the atmosphere inside the car wasn't as charged as it had been coming in the opposite direction. The tension was gone. Luke seemed tired but calm.

'Who was Crash?' Anna asked softly. 'A friend?'

'My brother. His real name was Matthew. Mattie.'

'Oh…'

Anna was searching her memory. She'd known that name had come from something special. A kid who'd grown too fast, he'd said, and looked a bit goofy with big feet. So clumsy he'd earned the nickname of Crash. He grown into…what had Luke said? Oh, yes. The strongest, bravest guy he knew.

And then he'd given her that first smile. The one that had melted her heart.

'He was younger than you?' The question was tentative. It seemed too good to believe that Luke was finally talking to her.

Letting her in.

'Yeah.' Luke's gaze was fixed on the road

ahead. He was driving a little below the speed limit. Taking it carefully.

Anna felt safe with him but did he feel the same way?

'There's an older brother, too,' Luke said after a moment. 'The Davenport boys, we were called. A collective troop. A mini-platoon. Nobody questioned that we would do anything but take after our dad and join the army.'

'It must have been hard for you, then.'

'Yeah.' The word was heartfelt. 'I felt guilty. Especially after Crash joined up. I'd always tried to look out for him, you know? In the end, though, he was looking out for me. He was the only one who understood why I wanted to be a civilian. A doctor.'

Anna couldn't ask the obvious question but it was hanging there and Luke could sense it.

'He got killed in action in Iraq,' he said very softly. 'And it just broke me up. I owed him so much. I missed him so badly. In the end, the answer seemed easy. I joined up to honour his memory. To do what I should have done all along. I thought it would make me feel less guilty. That it would somehow help fill the horrible, empty, useless feeling I had.'

A long silence this time and then Luke sighed. 'All I really achieved was to screw up the rest of my life. I'm not fit to do my job any more. I'm not a viable proposition to be in any kind of a meaningful relationship. I meant what I said, Anna. You should get out. Relatively unscathed. While you still can.'

'And I meant what I said,' Anna whispered. She wasn't going to tell him again that she loved him. It was enough to know she had said it aloud and it was true. Instinct told her he wasn't ready to hear those particular words but she could remind him of something else she'd said. 'I'm not going anywhere. We all need courage to face the future,' she added carefully. 'It's not a sign of weakness if you have to ask for help sometimes.'

Maybe she could remind him of something he'd said, too. 'You're the strongest, bravest man I know,' she said, deliberately using the words he'd used to describe his brother. 'You'll make it.'

This wasn't the time to talk about finding the help Luke needed or how to find it. They'd made enough of a breakthrough tonight. All Anna wanted now was to get home and go to bed. With Luke.

And sleep. She was so tired. The windscreen wipers flicked in a steady rhythm. Swirls of tiny white flakes zoomed towards them in a hypnotic pattern. Anna could feel her eyes drifting closed.

She was sound asleep, Luke noticed, as they finally left the main roads behind. The snow began falling more thickly and he slowed their pace. He didn't like the deteriorating conditions but he could take his time getting them home. Funny, but he felt like he had all the time he needed now. For anything. He couldn't remember when he'd last felt this... peaceful? Maybe he never had.

He stole another glance at Anna. He would get her home safely. He knew the road and he could cope with the weather.

What he couldn't control was the other traffic on the road that night. Especially when he had no warning of what was coming around the corner. The driver of the big truck probably didn't realise how far his wheels were over the centre line of the coastal road because the snow was starting to settle in patches and the road markings were fading.

The jolt of leaving the smooth road surface and then hitting a fence post woke Anna and all Luke could hear as he fought desperately to prevent the car tipping into a roll was her scream of fear.

CHAPTER TEN

ANNA'S scream was cut off abruptly with the first impact of the rolling vehicle but the sound of metal shearing and scraping on rock was another kind of scream. Airbags deployed with a blast and shockwave that was indistinguishable from gunfire.

Luke was inside his nightmare but he knew he was awake and that made it so much worse. So confusing. His mind was being rocked and jolted as viciously as his body. One moment hanging in the straps of his safety belt, the next jarring on solid ground. A maelstrom of fear and desperation. The past, the present and things that had never been real, and never would be, existing only in his imagination.

He was in an army vehicle again but not the one in which he'd met the end of his time at war. In one that he'd never actually seen or touched. Just imagined. The one his brother, Matthew, had been driving. And each time they hit solid ground, they were hitting the mine that had destroyed the person he loved most in the world. Once, twice…three hits and he was still alive and awake.

This time, he had to save him.

Or he would die himself.

The violent churning of the landscape, vehicle and people probably lasted no more than thirty seconds but it felt like for ever. And then there was silence. A broken headlamp flickered for a second or two and then died.

It was pitch black and utterly silent.

Luke had been convinced that the worst sound he could ever hear were the screams of frightened and dying men, any one of whom could be his brother. Even the terrified sound Anna had made had become the last breath Crash had expelled.

In that instant, however, he knew the real truth.

That silence was far worse.

Crash.

Blindly, Luke reached out. His fingers caught in the limp, metallic folds of airbags that had erupted from the steering-wheel, the centre console and the dashboard.

'Can you hear me?'

A tiny sound in the silence as he strained to listen. An indrawn breath. Tentative and ragged.

'Y-yes.'

It wasn't Crash. It was Anna.

Of course it was. He'd known that all along. Hadn't he?

And she was alive, thank God. 'Are you hurt?'

'I...I'm not sure...'

He had to move. To find a source of light and then check Anna out. He had to get her out of this and make sure she would be all right. Any other course of action or result was unthinkable.

But his head swam when he tried to move. Impossible to tell which way was supposed to be up. Had the car ended up on its roof instead of its wheels? Was it really Anna?

Luke found the catch of his safety belt and released it. His body didn't start falling so he wasn't upside down. His head started to clear.

'Take a deep breath,' he told Anna. 'As deep as you can.'

He listened to her comply with his request.

'Is it difficult? Does anything hurt?'

'N-no...'

'Can you move your arms? God, it's so dark. I can't see anything. Does your neck hurt? Don't move your head if it does.'

He could hear Anna shift position. Could see a change of shape in the darkness.

'I...I can move.'

So could Luke. He turned and began to lean sideways so that his hands could reach Anna's huddled figure on the far side of the vehicle. She was lower than he was. The car was on some kind of slope.

And then he froze.

It wasn't his head swimming this time. It was the car that was moving.

Rocking gently.

There was a scratching, scraping sound coming from somewhere beneath them. Metal on rock. And Luke became aware of another sound. He hadn't noticed it before because it could have been the rush of his own blood pulsing in his head.

Somewhere, far below, waves were rolling onto rocks.

They had been on a coastal road that often came close to clifftop. There had been a fence of some kind. A farmer's field or a barrier that was there to prevent anyone getting too close to a dangerous place? Like one that had a sheer drop to rocks that would not be survivable?

Perhaps it was just as well it was too dark to see anything outside.

Cold, damp air was coming in with the sounds of the night. Luke's door seemed to be missing or crumpled to leave an open space. Survival instinct was trying to kick in. The upward ground was on his side and he had an escape route. Even if the car was teetering on the top of a cliff, he could make a dive for it and roll free.

But that would change the weight distribution dramatically and that might be all that was needed to tip the vehicle and send it plunging over the edge.

With Anna still inside.

He would rather die himself.

The car was still rocking. Scraping.

'Luke?' Anna's whisper was terrified. 'What's...happening?'

'Don't move,' he said softly. 'Give me a sec. I need to think.'

Fear was clawing at him now. A dense cloud that contained a kaleidoscope of images and emotions that paralysed Luke for a moment. Sucking him into the place he couldn't allow himself to go.

No.

He couldn't smell blood. Or smoke. Or dust. Nobody was screaming.

They were in a car, not an armoured vehicle. This was Anna. Not Crash.

So why was it just as important that she was going to be all right? Crash was the person he had loved with all his heart. The one he would have given his own life to save.

It had taken a split second for Luke to understand the truth that silence could be more dreadful than any scream.

The truth he now learned arrived with similar, blinding clarity.

He had only been confused about the person he needed to save because of an emotion he hadn't allowed himself to entertain.

He loved Anna.

A different kind of love than he'd had for Crash but it was just as powerful. More so, even. He'd been kidding himself thinking of her as his rope. Or anchor. Or any other kind of tool to help him find his own future.

She was that future.

From that first moment when he'd found himself under her resentful glare she had entered his consciousness. His mind and—slipping somehow under a defensive radar—his heart.

'Luke…' Anna was crying. 'Talk to me. Are you hurt?'

'I'm fine.' He moved his hand carefully, just far enough to grip hers. 'As long as you are.'

'What happened?'

'We've had an accident. There was a truck. It came around a corner on the wrong side of the road. I had to swerve and… Oh, God, I'm sorry, Anna.'

The grip on his hand tightened. 'That doesn't matter. We just need to get out.'

'We have to be careful. I'm not sure how stable the car is and I don't want it to move.'

'I'm scared.'

'I know. I am too but we'll get through this, Anna. Together.'

'Are you sure you're all right? It's not... I mean... You know...like a flashback thing?'

Oh, yes. The flashbacks he'd never admitted to. He couldn't admit to loving Anna either, could he? What did he have to offer her? He was broken.

'I want to get out. I want to get home.'

'I know. We will. I'll get you out, Anna. I'll take care of you.'

There was a light outside now. Coming closer. A powerful torch that filled the interior of this battered car in a sweeping motion. For a heartbeat Luke could see Anna's face clearly. The way she was looking at him.

She wasn't going anywhere, she'd said— way back before the accident had happened. She'd said she loved him.

He could see that love in her eyes. He could fall into it. Return it? How much courage would that take? What if he failed her, as he had failed his brother? If he lost her...

'Anna...I—'

The light got brighter. Steadier. A man's

voice called out. 'Whatever you do in there, don't move. I've got a chain in the truck and I'm going to get it onto the back of your car. Help's on the way.'

Luke didn't want to move. Neither, it seemed, did Anna. The grip on his hand was tight enough to impair circulation.

'Don't let go of me,' she begged. 'Please. Not yet.'

'I won't,' he vowed. I can't, he added silently, because I love you.

The nearest hospital was St Piran's.

Ben Carter was astonished to find Anna and Luke turning up in the emergency department, dressed up to the nines, in the early hours of the morning but he was more amazed to be able to give them a medical all-clear not long afterwards.

'You're both incredibly lucky. A few bumps and bruises but nothing that a good sleep won't help.'

Anna caught Luke's wry glance. As if a good sleep was remotely likely for him even when he hadn't been through such a traumatic

few hours. It was a private exchange. Ben
didn't see it because he was shaking his head.

'I can't imagine what it must have felt like,
seeing your car going over that cliff when the
chain broke. The rescue guys are going to be
talking about their good timing for years to
come.'

'So will we,' Anna said. She smiled at
Luke. 'Let's go and see if that taxi's here yet.'

They went to Luke's house because it was
closer and Anna was still worried about the
effects the accident might have had on Luke
that no X-ray or examination would have
picked up.

To have had this happen today, of all days,
when he had been starting to open up to her
about the past that haunted him so badly. No
wonder he was so quiet now. And why he
made no move to make love to her when they
went straight to bed. They were both utterly
exhausted but Anna was determined to stay
awake. To be ready to hold Luke when he
had the nightmare she was sure would come.

At some point, however, she fell asleep
because it was impossible not to. When she
awoke to find winter sunlight warming the

room, she gasped in horror. Had she slept through Luke waking? Going to outrun his demons on the beach or dispel them with an arctic swim? He never missed his dawn swim.

But he was still there. Beside her. One arm draped over her body. Her gasp must have woken him because his eyes were open.

'You OK?'

Anna nodded. 'I'm sorry...'

'What for?'

'I must have slept through you getting up. I didn't mean to. I wanted...'

Luke was staring at her with an odd expression.

'What?' she breathed. 'What's wrong?'

'I didn't get up,' he said slowly. 'I didn't even wake up.'

'You slept through the whole night?'

'What was left of it, anyway.' He blinked at her, disbelief still etched on his features. 'That's hours. Hours and hours and hours.'

Anna's lips trembled as they stretched into a smile. 'How do you feel?'

'Different...' Luke's gaze dropped to Anna's lips and then dropped further. 'Hungry.'

'You want breakfast?'

'No.' He looked up again and smiled. 'I want…you.'

Anna snuggled closer, raising her face to meet Luke's kiss. 'I want you, too.'

'You're not too sore or anything?'

'A bit stiff and achy. Nothing that a walk on the beach in some sunshine won't cure.'

'Soon.' Luke's lips brushed hers gently and then came back as he sighed. 'Or maybe not that soon.'

His mouth claimed hers this time and Anna surrendered willingly. The walk could wait.

The last day of January found them walking on the beach.

A dawn walk that had become a firm habit now. Crash was with them, loping around on his big, puppy feet with a stick of driftwood clamped between his teeth.

'You're supposed to bring it back,' Luke called.

'He wants you to chase him.'

'That won't help his retrieving training.'

'No.' Besides, Anna didn't want to let go of Luke's hand. She loved this time of day with him. In the soft light and breathing the fresh, cold air. Walking so close they often leaned on each other as well as holding hands. And sometimes, as they did right now, they would stop and watch the waves rolling in for a minute or two.

'You haven't been for a swim since the accident.'

'No. I don't need to any more.'

Anna gave Luke a questioning glance but he was still staring at the waves.

'When I came back from Iraq,' he said a moment later, 'it seemed like I had no connection here any more. Or anywhere. Part of me was still over there. Caught up in the frenetic battle to save lives. To stay alive. Civilian life seemed empty. Meaningless.'

Still Anna said nothing. She couldn't. She remembered Luke saying something about that and she hadn't forgotten thinking that she had been included in the things that had no meaning. She knew that wasn't true. Maybe Luke hadn't told her as such but he was showing her. Every day. In so many ways.

'It made me numb, swimming in a freezing sea and getting tossed around by the surf,' Luke continued quietly. 'And it helped…then.

I don't need to be numb now. I don't want to be, even for a moment.' He turned his head and looked down at Anna.

'Because even if it was just for the length of time it took to have that swim, it would be too long to feel numb. I don't want to give up a second of the most amazing feeling I could ever have.'

Anna's breath caught. She knew the answer but had to ask the question. To hear the words spoken aloud. 'What is it...that feeling?'

'My love for you.'

His kiss tasted of the sea and it was slow and exquisitely tender. Anna stood on tiptoe and wrapped her arms around his neck. It took the impatient bark of a large puppy to bring them back to the present moment. Luke laughed, stooped to pick up the stick that had been placed right beside his feet and threw it again. Then he took Anna's hand in his and they began walking again, a triumphant Crash making wide circles around them with the stick back in his jaws.

'I love you, Anna,' Luke said. 'You are the reason I want to get up in the mornings and the reason I can't wait to get to bed at night. I hope I never have to have a night or day without you to share it with but…' He took a deep breath and let it out in a sigh. 'I'm not going to ask you to marry me. I can't.'

Anna's feet stopped without any such instruction from her brain. Her hand tugged at Luke's a heartbeat later and he had to stop, too. She stared at him. The shadows in his eyes had begun to lift in the last week or so but the sadness she could still see in his face was heartbreaking.

'I can't offer you anything,' Luke said. 'I've lost my job.'

Anna gave her head a slow shake. 'You didn't lose it. You had the courage to go and talk to Mr White about everything and he had the good sense to persuade you to go onto the board of directors for St Piran's. You're going to be a brilliant administrator, Luke, and it's not as if you're not going to be part of the department for teaching—'

'Your department now,' Luke interrupted.

Anna looked away. It was so weird to think she had wanted to hang onto that position so badly that she would have preferred Luke to have never come back to St Piran's.

'I have PTSD,' Luke said into the silence. 'An official diagnosis from a qualified shrink.'

'An eminent psychiatrist who specialises in cognitive-behavioural therapy,' Anna corrected with a smile. 'Someone who thinks you're making amazing progress already.'

She watched a wave roll in. And then another. And then she turned to face Luke again.

'All you ever need to offer me is your love, Luke.'

He was watching her face with that intent gaze of his. Listening carefully. Waiting to hear what she would say next.

'And I don't want you to ask me to marry you,' she said.

She saw him swallow hard. Saw a flicker of doubt—fear, almost—in his eyes.

Anna smiled. 'Because I'm going to ask you.'

She took a deep breath. This shouldn't be so hard, should it? She'd been competing in a man's world for long enough to be able to tackle anything.

'I love you, Luke Davenport. With all my heart. I don't want to have a single night or day without you in it either. Will you marry me?'

He was still staring at her. One of those looks—as if he was seeing her for the very first time.

'Um… Please?' she added.

His arms came around her with such speed that Anna squeaked as she felt herself grabbed and lifted. She was being whirled round and round and the world was spinning.

'Yes,' Luke said. 'Yes.'

He stopped whirling her but was still holding her well off the ground, his hands around her waist. Her hands were on his shoulders as he slowly lowered her enough for their lips to touch.

A new wave came in, leading the incoming tide further up the beach, and it reached far enough to swirl around Luke's ankles and splash Anna's legs with pure ice.

Luke dropped one arm to catch Anna behind her knees. He scooped her into his arms and carried her through the still foaming wave to dry sand but he didn't put her down. Crash followed as they left the beach to go home and get ready for their new day. And still Luke hadn't put Anna down.

And that was just fine by her.

She was exactly where she wanted to be. Moving into her future, cradled in the arms of the man she would always love.

* * * * *

His eyes reflected a dark forest today as they searched hers.

Her heartbeat erratic, Alexa was unsure of his intentions, uncertain if she could allow herself elation at his appearance. But oh, how she wanted to dash into his arms. To make everything right between them again.

"Graeme. . ." Her lips spoke his name in a breathy whisper. "Why are you here?"

A sad smile lifted one corner of his mouth, but he said nothing. Probably as unsure as she was about what to say. Was there anything left between them?

"Why did you leave that day?" Alexa finally voiced the question that had burned inside ever since he'd walked away without listening to her explanation, without looking at her.

"You've heard the old saying, 'If you love something, let it go. If it's yours, it will come back to you'?"

"Yes." *That had better not be your excuse.*

"Because I knew you were at a crossroad. I had to give you the space you needed to decide what you really want in life. I couldn't stand in the way of that. I knew if I looked at you, then it was all over for me, because believe me, Alexa, I wanted to fight with everything in me to keep you."

ELIZABETH GODDARD is a seventh-generation Texan who recently spent five years in beautiful southern Oregon, which serves as a setting for some of her novels. She is now back in East Texas, living near her family. When she's not writing, she's busy homeschooling her four children. Beth is the author of several novels and novellas. She's actively involved in several writing organizations including American Christian Fiction Writers (ACFW) and loves to mentor new writers.

Sheltering Love

Elizabeth Goddard

Heartsong Presents

Dedicated to my grandmother, who loved and encouraged me all the days of my life until she passed away in late 2010. Her sheltering love will be greatly missed.

Special thanks goes to Kevin Lindenmuth of Kevin Lindenmuth Productions/ Brimstone Media Productions for his assistance in my questions about documentaries. Any mistakes are mine alone. Thanks to Ellen Tarver and Nancy Toback for their editing expertise, and to my faithful critique partner, Shannon McNear.

A note from the Author:
I love to hear from my readers! You may correspond with me by writing:
> **Elizabeth Goddard**
> **Author Relations**
> **P.O. Box 9048**
> **Buffalo, NY 14240-9048**

ISBN-13: 978-0-373-48604-5

SHELTERING LOVE

This edition issued by special arrangement with Barbour Publishing, Inc., 1810 Barbour Drive, Uhrichsville, Ohio, U.S.A.

Scripture taken from the Holy Bible, New International Version®. NIV®. Copyright © 1973, 1978, 1984, 2011 by Biblica, Inc.™ Used by permission. All rights reserved worldwide.

one

Siberia couldn't be worse.

Or at least Alexa Westover felt like she'd been exiled. Traveling from New York to the West Coast to work on a documentary, she was returning to the place where she'd spent her childhood. Northern California and the redwoods would ignite memories, and most of them she wouldn't welcome.

She jiggled the key in the lock of the pinkish, paint-chipped door to her room at the Redwood Motor Inn. Swinging it open, she threw her luggage on the double bed covered with a floral spread and breathed in the heavy scent of cheap lavender air freshener.

Barry Seymour, her cameraman, handed off her forgotten toiletry bag and her briefcase holding her laptop.

"Is that everything?" she asked.

He grunted and took one step over to the door to his room.

She slammed hers. A few seconds later, she heard his door slam as well. Barry hadn't said a word on the hour-and-a-half drive up the coast to the state park. She plopped on the bed and kicked off her heels. A prima donna couldn't have been more ungrateful than Alexa at that moment.

Shame hovered near her conscience, threatening to temper her exasperation. Landing a job shortly after getting her degree at Columbia University had been really, *really* lucky, even for her. A million people dreamed of creating a successful documentary, but only 1 percent were actually given the chance to see their ideas produced in a professional and lucrative manner. Alexa was one of the few, thanks to a keen-eyed professor at Columbia who'd seen something in her worth recommending to his friend at Simon Productions.

Clive Gates quickly assessed her talents and hired her. But soon Alexa found herself in deep with this powerful man in the filmmaking industry. She'd been his special project—someone he planned to groom in the business—and now she was not only heartbroken, but exiled because she'd dared to speak her mind, challenging him in front of others.

Who was she kidding? He'd lost interest in her months ago, personally and professionally, and the respect she'd initially garnered from her peers was nowhere to be found. All her ideas and suggestions were continually shot down, placing her business acumen and creativity into question by everyone at Simon.

She exhaled, long and slow.

I don't even know who I am anymore.

Nor did she care at the moment. The only thing she wanted was a hot shower. She stumbled from the bed into the small, sixties-styled bathroom and flipped on the shower to get things steaming while she put in a call to Clive. She'd spent the awkward drive up the coast formulating her words.

Looking at her smartphone, realization dawned. No signal. *What?* She'd forgotten that little detail—but then again, she would have thought by now more cell towers would be installed.

Her chance to write, direct, and produce her first documentary and make a favorable impression in this close-knit film community was quickly fading, taking her hopes and dreams with it. Funny that should happen in the very place where she'd grown up.

Alexa stomped into the bathroom. No steam clouded the mirror. No hot water. No cell signal. What about Internet?

And in the end, there would probably be no interview with Graeme Hawthorne either. Where had she gone wrong? Alexa replayed this morning's events in her mind.

Heels clicking and armed with nothing but an outline of her script, Alexa strode down the university halls of Humboldt University in Northern California, mentally preparing herself to interview the leading expert in redwood forest biology for her documentary. *Changing World, Changing Forests*—a film about the effects of climate change on forest ecosystems—hadn't been her first choice, but she told herself she'd make it shine.

Professor Peter Bryant had readily agreed to the interview, and she'd sent him the questions a week ago to help him prepare.

Barry strolled next to her, taking one step to her every two. Stocky and dressed like a lumberjack, he preferred to wear casual attire and didn't look like he belonged at the university. But he'd definitely fit in with their final destination. As they neared the end of the hall, monarchs took flight in her stomach. Alexa thumbed through various release forms and looked over her notes as she walked. "Don't forget to catch the light in his eyes, okay, Barry? And let's make sure his office is quiet enough for good sound—"

"I know what I'm doing." Barry's cold tone left no doubt about his thoughts.

He had years of experience as a cameraman, and Alexa would do well to use that to her advantage rather than alienating the guy. She knew he'd not wanted to accompany her. Somehow she'd have to fire up his enthusiasm for the project as well as her own if she had any hope of creating an award-winning documentary—something she would need if she was going to take charge of her career again.

The door to Professor Bryant's office stood open, allowing Alexa entrance into a small reception area accented in soft earth tones and decorated with diplomas and award certificates. A woman with short, graying hair smiled up at her from a neat, document-laden desk. A nameplate rested next to a bonsai tree, engraved Trish Thompson.

Her best professional smile in place, Alexa thrust her hand forward. "Alexa Westover with Simon Productions. We have an appointment with Professor Bryant."

Trish slowly stood as her jaw slid open. "Oh, I'm terribly

sorry." She came around the desk. "Didn't you get my message?"

The monarchs in Alexa's stomach dive-bombed. "Message?" she asked and waited—her hopes tied up in the receptionist's answer.

"Professor Bryant was in a car accident this morning and is in the hospital. I hoped to catch you before you left, but I must have missed you. Still, your office should have informed you at some point. I'm sorry for your trouble."

Distress battled with compassion. "I'm sorry to hear that. I hope he's going to be all right."

Alexa waited for Trish's response, counting on a hopeful outcome.

"Thank you for your sympathies. I'll be sure to let him know."

"Could we see him and let him know in person?" Alexa cringed at the way her question sounded. Was she overstepping?

"I'm afraid that wouldn't be possible." Trish eased forward and edged her hand under Alexa's elbow, slowly escorting her to the door. "He won't be available for quite some time."

With quick efficiency, Alexa removed her elbow from Trish's grip. "Isn't there anyone else we can see while we're here? This documentary is time-sensitive and very important."

Trish seemed to consider her request but said nothing.

"Please, we've come a long way."

"There is someone who might be able to help." Trish scribbled on a piece of paper and handed it to Alexa. "But I'll give you fair warning. He won't be easy to find, nor will it be easy to garner his cooperation."

Alexa glanced at the paper. Graeme Hawthorne. "No phone number?"

"I don't have his number, and if I did, I'm sure it wouldn't do you any good."

What did she mean by that? "Then how do I find him?"

"He's conducting his research in the coastal redwoods near Jedediah Smith State Park. Find a place to hang out with the locals. He'll turn up sooner or later."

"That's very. . ." *Strange.*

Trish merely shrugged and mouthed a voiceless 'I know' as though she'd heard Alexa's thoughts.

❧

Graeme Hawthorne took aim with his high-powered compound bow and shot the fishing-line-threaded arrow. The projectile soared toward the canopy and lobbed over one of the lower branches almost twenty-five feet high.

The call from a local naturalist came early this morning, informing Graeme there might be a tree taller than Hyperion, the redwood tree believed to be the world's tallest living thing at just over 379 feet.

Seventy feet taller than the Statue of Liberty.

Climbing the towering evergreen and dropping a tape measure was the only way to be sure. After a five-mile hike in search of the tree while wearing his pack heavy with climbing equipment, Graeme refocused his energy. He still had an hour and a half or more of ascending the trunk to reach the crown, or the top of the tree. He tied a nylon cord to the fishing line and dragged it over the branch, then did the same thing with the main rope he would use to climb.

In becoming a forest canopy scientist, he'd learned his tree-climbing skills from the best climbers at Humboldt University. With more than three hundred feet of rope hanging in a U shape over the branch, Graeme assembled his gear, which included a safety harness, a helmet, and soft-soled boots, and hoisted himself up the tree using a complex assembly of rope and carabiners.

Sequoia sempervirens. Latin for "forever living." The rest of the world called the massive trunk of immense height a giant redwood, and Graeme was embarking on an attempt to determine its height. Of all the redwoods in Northern California, the coastal redwoods were the tallest.

If only you could see me now, Summer. Graeme missed his golden-haired, environmental activist fiancée. Almost a year now since her ill-timed discovery had gotten her killed, and

Graeme hated that he was beginning to forget her voice, her face. A few months ago, he began to notice the mental picture he kept locked away in his heart slowly fading. Sure, he had photos of them together and a few videos, but the little details that he loved—the laugh lines around her eyes and mouth, the way she looked at him when she wanted him to kiss her, or the way she laughed when he said something funny—had begun to fade.

Regret swam in his stomach and his hand slipped on the rope, jerking his attention back to the present. A fall could be lethal.

Hanging in midair as he maneuvered his way up the tree, all he could see from this height—almost a hundred feet up—was tree trunk, which, oddly enough, smelled lemony. He ran his hand over the wrinkled bark before continuing his climb.

In this way, Graeme was witness to a lost world. A mass of giant ferns, weighing tons when drenched with rainwater, came into view and protruded from the trunk in front of him—one of innumerable hanging gardens. Teeming with plant and animal life, including new and undiscovered species, the mysterious forest canopy left much to be explored, as though it were a new frontier.

"You doing okay up there?" Randy, his associate and fellow tree climber, squawked over the two-way radio.

Graeme paused, secure in his saddle harness.

"Never been better," he said, responding into his radio.

And it was true—throwing all his focus into the redwood canopy biology had saved his life in more ways than one. In the trees, he could maneuver vertically or horizontally. He was Spiderman. In the trees, he could hide from the demons that chased him, both real and imagined.

"I think I'm almost at the one-hundred-foot mark," Graeme said. "Get ready."

Graeme preferred working alone if possible, but Randy Starr had been eager to join Graeme once he and Peter received funding for the project, and, invaluable for his keen research eye, Randy had proven his worth as an assistant while he worked toward his degree.

Graeme positioned the marker in the tree then dropped the weighted end of the measuring tape, which fell in a straight line all the way to the ground.

Fifteen seconds passed.

"Ninety-five feet." Randy's voice squawked over the radio again, disrupting the peaceful forest.

Graeme's stomach growled. He could seriously use Sally's greasy cheeseburger and fries right now.

"Time for a snack," he said.

Randy understood his need for fuel and would probably take the opportunity to do the same. Graeme climbed onto a nearby branch and slid a protein bar from his pocket. While he chewed, he studied the canopy, then gazed up to the sky, though from this position, all he could see were branches and needles. At least another hour of tree climbing awaited him before he could reach the top. The tree hugger who'd called him might be right—this could be the tallest tree, the tallest living thing, and Graeme would be the one to document it, the first to climb the titan.

Voices bounced off the tree trunks, emanating from somewhere in the distance and increasing in volume, indicating the hikers were heading his way. Graeme froze. He and Randy were deep in the forest, far from any groomed trail. Graeme's paranoia clawed out from the neatly hidden box in the corner of his mind, and he prayed the hikers would pass the small two-man research team without noticing.

Randy knew the drill.

two

The next day, Alexa sat on the bank of the Smith River that snaked through Jedediah Smith State Park watching clear water—a remarkable Caribbean blue in places—tumble over rocks then smooth out until it became a mirror reflecting redwoods and a partly cloudy blue sky. She tossed a pebble into the water, sending ripples across the glass.

Losing Professor Bryant's interview had seriously thrown Alexa's schedule off. This documentary wasn't meant to be a voice-over while the camera panned a three sixty of the forest canopy.

Interviews. She needed interviews.

Regardless, she and Barry had their work cut out for them while she attempted to replace Professor Bryant with the elusive Graeme Hawthorne. She'd spent the rest of last evening reworking the outline of her script—good thing she preferred to work off a loose outline and could afford flexibility—and she and Barry discussed exploring the park to capture images today, preferably the most unique and amazing. From her personal experience, she knew that would be easy.

The difficult part lay within Alexa. She must be the only person alive who dreaded exploring these ancient woods. She needed to face the forest of her childhood on her own to dispel her emotions. That's why, in the end, she told Barry they would make better time looking for Hawthorne by splitting up.

If they couldn't find the botanist today. . .

She couldn't consider failure. There had to be a local biologist she could interview who was knowledgeable enough to discuss the climate's change on the redwoods. If they didn't locate Hawthorne today, she'd give Trish at the university another call and beg for her help or plead for another name. And if she did find Graeme Hawthorne, considering the man was apparently skittish, she'd play her hand very close. He might be her last chance.

A snap resounded from across the river. High in the trees, a few branches shook.

Alexa slowly stood to her feet and waited.

A bear?

No, she didn't think a bear would climb that high. She glanced behind her, wishing that Barry would happen upon her, camera in tow. Probably it was nothing more than a broken limb plummeting to the forest floor.

Curious, Alexa jogged down the riverbank to the narrow plank bridge built by prison inmates and hurried across the river. The trailhead opened up to a three-pronged fork in the path. Alexa took the right prong and hurried along the canopy-darkened trail. Children laughed in the distance, reminding her of when she and her sisters, Camille and Sela, were growing up with the redwoods as their backyard.

The trail veered left away from the river.

No, no, no. She cringed at the thought of keeping parallel to the river. That would mean leaving the plainly groomed path, though she had no clue if she'd find anything of interest worth her efforts. A familiar dread gripped her throat at the thought of going off-trail, of going too deep in the woods. But as long as she kept the bridge and the river within her sights, she'd explore, if only a little. After all, if she was going to film this documentary, she would have to get over her anxiety. She had to start right now.

Stepping off the trail, she made her way through thick undergrowth of giant ferns and vines, pausing when she heard rustling noises.

Wildlife—a squirrel, raccoon, chipmunk, or. . .a much larger animal. . .a bear or a mountain lion—hiding in the brush. Alexa hoped for the former and was continuing forward when her hiking boot snagged.

She stumbled but managed to catch herself against the trunk of a tree, stopping her fall. With a glance down at her ankle, she spotted the culprit.

Fishing line? It was then Alexa also spotted the crossbow resting against the tree and a long rope hanging. After untangling the fishing line from her boot, Alexa stepped away from the massive trunk to gaze upward.

Her gaze followed the rope, which disappeared in the limbs and greenery, but wait—

Booted feet dangled in the air then swung horizontally.

A tree climber? She'd heard of them but had never actually seen anyone climbing in the redwoods, and she'd grown up here. This fellow might have heard of Graeme Hawthorne.

Wondering how to draw the climber's attention, she looked around. Tugging on the rope might work. She wrapped her hand around the thick nylon fibers and then thought better of it. She could very well cause the person to fall.

Alexa cupped her hands and yelled. "Hello up there."

A full thirty seconds ticked by in which she wondered if the climber heard her or if he was simply ignoring her, though it might be a woman. She was just about to call up again when the rope jerked.

She stepped forward and looked up again. A body dropped slowly, like someone rappelling down a cliff. Definitely masculine.

He popped down in front of her like a spider on a web. Alexa yelped, then covered her mouth.

The man removed a hard hat from his head, and she found herself being appraised by intelligent but suspicious eyes— misty green eyes in a handsome face hidden behind a week's worth of stubble.

Those eyes stared into hers. The hint of a frown tugged at the man's lips, and he shoved his hand through wavy brown hair. His gaze roamed the length of her then settled back on her face.

"Was there something you needed?" He began disassembling his contraption.

"Yes, actually. My name is Alexa Westover."

She thrust out her hand, wishing she'd taken a softer approach—her professional I'm-every-woman approach might scare him off and she needed information.

He stared at her hand, appearing to consider if shaking it would harm him. Then he slowly took it in his. Electricity charged up her arm.

He quickly released her hand, making her wonder if he'd felt it, too.

"Graeme."

As in Graeme Hawthorne? Alexa could hardly contain her excitement.

Easy, girl. Everything about him screamed wild stallion. Any second he would bolt if she didn't move slowly.

"Is that what you wanted? To introduce yourself? You're lucky I was on my way down the tree or you'd be waiting here for over an hour."

"Actually, I wanted to find out if you would take me up."

Incredulity spread over his demeanor, and he swiped his brow. "You can't be serious."

Alexa wasn't exactly sure she wanted to climb the tree, but she couldn't think of anything else to get him talking. "Dead serious."

He paused from packing his gear and suspicion crept back into his gaze. "You're telling me you came here to ask me if I would take you up. How did you know that I climb trees?"

🜢

He had her there.

The striking, blue-eyed brunette was up to something. And Graeme was on his guard. He'd spent yesterday climbing and measuring what he hoped would be the tallest redwood, but it turned out to measure only 370 feet—just nine feet less than Hyperion.

Today he was back to collecting data for research when

he'd come close to falling—something he'd never done before. His stupidity and curiosity had left him careless when he'd spotted the woman sitting on the riverbank. From his perch in the tree, he'd watched her, feeling like a stalker, and now he'd drawn her attention. He'd never acted like such an idiot.

Grabbing her length of silky hair, she pulled it behind her head and tied it in a knot. "That's just it. I didn't know. I happened upon you and now I want to climb." With an impish grin, she shrugged and made her way to the trunk, where she jammed her hands into her form-fitting jeans and leaned against it.

The trees seemed to sway around him. What was happening? No woman had stirred him since Summer—until now. His heart sank a little. His gut told him this woman was anything but tenderhearted—beauty was only skin deep, as the saying went.

One could hope.

"I don't believe in recreational climbing. If you have an important scientific question to answer, then you have to evaluate if it's worth it to disturb the trees and the plant and animal life growing there."

When she didn't respond, Graeme finished zipping his pack and glanced at her. "So do you have a scientific reason for climbing the tree?" he asked. And when she answered in the negative, he was done. Good riddance.

"Do *you*?" she asked.

Graeme had just begun lifting the hefty pack, but at her words, he let it drop. "Excuse me?"

"Do you have a scientific question to answer?" she asked.

Where do I begin? If only he could ignore her. But she wasn't going away without his response, and he couldn't exactly call the police because she was disturbing his peace.

Sweat slid down his back. His muscles were beginning to feel the exhaustion that came with climbing a tree that rivaled the tallest skyscrapers, and though he was in the shape of his life even at thirty-two, his body screamed for nourishment.

"I'm a scientist. I ask questions all the time." Graeme took a breath then hefted the weighty pack over his back. "But right now I'm hungry."

He trudged through the undergrowth, taking care to leave it as undisturbed as possible, unsurprised that Alexa followed. Once he made it back to the trail, he stopped and glanced at her then quickly looked away. If he wasn't careful, he could end up drowning in those baby blues.

"Okay, I guess this is it. It was nice to meet you, Alexa." He marched forward.

She had to take several steps to keep up with him. "What? You're just going to leave me here?"

What did she want from him? Already her gaze made him uncomfortable, and she'd disturbed his day in the trees.

He rocked his head back and stared at the canopy then back at her striking eyes. "I'm sure you can find your way from here."

three

Alexa headed back to her motel room to regroup. Hawthorne had just left her standing there.

Of all the. . .

She needed a plan. Finding him hadn't been the difficult part, after all. He'd flat out rejected her.

That was a response she was unaccustomed to. She rolled her shoulders, hoping to shove her frustrations aside. She hadn't exactly explained about making a documentary, but the guy was a little wary, and the fact that Trish hadn't even had a phone number to offer signaled just how much he didn't want to be found.

Understanding him better would help her secure what she needed from him, but Alexa had to work smart. And she had to work fast.

But she'd made a mistake—he might not be so easy to locate next time. He wasn't exactly a phone call away, but then, neither was Clive these days.

Right now, she needed to try Clive's number again. Scrolling through the contacts on her smartphone, Alexa located his cell number. She lifted the handset of the cream-colored in-room phone and, following instructions, pressed the 9, allowing her to dial out of the room. She tapped the complimentary pen against the pine veneer of the small bedside table and listened to the phone ring one, two, three times then forward to voice mail.

Clive's smooth voice offered his apology for being unavailable. Dutifully, Alexa left a short message asking him to return her call. She ended the call and leaned back, wanting to say so much more and wondering if she should have.

What happened to us? Why did you give me this project? Don't you miss me? All questions she knew she could never ask Clive. The last thing she needed was to fuel his ego. Besides, she knew the answer to the first two.

The last one surprised her—she didn't actually care whether he missed her, and the idea left her with a new awareness—freedom. When it came to Clive, she'd given up much of her independence. Maybe she didn't need him as much as she'd once thought.

Then it hit her. In her message, she'd failed to leave him information about where they were staying and how to reach them. Hopefully he caught the number from which she'd called from caller ID, though that didn't always work. She rolled her head back and stared at the ceiling but decided she'd save counting the tiles for tonight when she needed help getting to sleep.

Alexa changed into her Jimmy Choos. She loved these high-heeled sandals, and the hiking boots were giving her blisters. She'd grown up wearing hiking shoes, but left them behind when she'd moved to New York. It was then she'd started her love affair with fashion, specifically high heels. Though she might look out of place wearing these here, they kept her anchored to her life in New York like nothing else, and right now she felt like she was being sucked into the life she'd left in the redwoods.

She grabbed her bag and left the room, took two steps to the room next door, and knocked. The television blared inside the room, telling her Barry had finished exploring. They'd agreed to meet back at the motel around lunchtime.

After no response she knocked again. "Barry, it's me."

Ten seconds later Barry opened the door. "Yes?"

"Want to grab some lunch?"

"What did you have in mind?"

"Funny." Her gaze shot to the diner attached to the motel. They'd eaten at Sally's Burgers and Fries last night. "It's not like we have a lot of choice unless we drive to town, and

I want to stay close for now."

"That's fine. But we need to hit town at some point this afternoon." Barry grabbed his baseball cap and wallet and shut the door.

They strolled across the parking lot to Sally's, a hamburger joint decorated like a fifties diner. An old Righteous Brothers tune resounded from the jukebox across the room. A sign informed them they should seat themselves, and Alexa chose the same booth in the corner where they'd sat last night. She slipped in on the far side so she could watch the ten or so other diners.

Soon enough a waitress wearing jeans and a denim button-down shirt blocked her view. "What'll it be?"

"I'll have a cheeseburger, side of fries, and a Diet Coke." Alexa cringed inside. Too much of this fare and she'd grow out of her clothes before they were done here.

"Make that a double," Barry said.

"A double?" The waitress glared. She wasn't as friendly as the woman from last night.

"A double cheeseburger, large fries, and supersize the Coke."

The woman quirked a brow. "This isn't Burger King, but I'll see what I can do."

When she returned with their order, which included two Cokes for Barry, Alexa contained her laugh until the waitress walked off. "Looks like you made a new friend."

Barry ignored her. Probably too focused on his food. Alexa bit into her cheeseburger, chewed, and nodded. "Not bad." Though she'd grown up a half hour down the road, she couldn't recall Sally's. Barry wolfed down his burger and fries, dragged a napkin across his mouth, then shoved back his cap and crossed his arms. "I told Clive about what happened and where we're staying."

Alexa dipped a fry in ketchup, not wanting to reveal her relief that at least Clive knew how to get ahold of her. Then again, Barry had probably painted the loss of their first and most important interview in a negative way. She would have put a positive spin on it.

She blew out a breath. Who was she kidding? Barry probably hoped Clive would demand they return to New York.

"Thanks. What did he say?" Alexa almost wished she hadn't asked because it made her look weak. She held her breath and painted with the ketchup.

When Barry chuckled, she caught a glimpse of his wry grin. He was watching her paint.

"Lucky for you he told me to support you in every way," he said.

Alexa's heart almost jumped from her chest, and she worked to suppress her surprised elation. Relief didn't come close to expressing how she felt at that moment. But why the change of heart? Clive had always been her biggest supporter, but that was in the beginning—when she'd been his pet project. Before she'd questioned his extracurricular activities.

"If you botch this film, he doesn't want you to be able to point the finger at me, but wants the fault to lie with you alone."

Pain squeezed her chest. If only she could bring her gaze to meet Barry's and show him she wasn't in the least intimidated, that his cruel words hadn't devastated her. She had always held power over men and knew how to use it. But lately, her stores in the self-confidence department had drained.

Barry leaned forward and kept his voice low. "Look, I won't lie to you. If I'd wanted to work on the same project for weeks on end, practically living in the jungle, or the redwoods, take your pick, I'd work for National Geographic. Simon isn't paying me enough. I doubt they're paying you enough. But I'll do my time, give it everything I've got so I can earn my get-out-of-jail-free card. By that I mean an award for this film, a star in the concrete. Whatever. But you get what I'm saying." Barry slid from the booth and stretched, revealing his small paunch. He glanced around the diner, then back to Alexa. "What's on the schedule this afternoon?"

Alexa pressed her back against the seat and refocused her thoughts. Barry hadn't spoken that many words in one breath since she'd known him. "Let's review the script I've rewritten; then you can show me what you caught on film this morning while exploring."

"Did you find anything?"

"I'm not sure yet." She hadn't told him about her encounter with the botanist, and she wouldn't—not until she had something to tell.

"See you back at the motel." He apparently wasn't willing to linger while she finished her last fry. Fine with her. She needed a moment to herself anyway and forced down one last greasy fry then drew in a long, slow breath and sat up tall.

Winning Barry's favor would go a long way in making this project the best it could be. The only way to do that was for Alexa to make a complete about-face of her own attitude. Being served the proverbial humble pie at every turn was wearing on her. But what men like Clive and Barry didn't seem to understand was that women who wanted to make it in the business world had to be tougher than their male counterparts. That had left Alexa with a few enemies— jealous coworkers looking for every opportunity to bring her down. Fighting for her career was like fighting for her very survival, and Alexa was getting tired.

She checked her phone for cell reception in the restaurant as if things had changed since yesterday. Still no signal. The forest around the hotel and diner was closing in on her. Memories wouldn't stay locked away if she remained in the redwoods very long. The time necessary to take an overdone documentary topic and create something unique would not equal the amount of time she wanted to spend here.

To do this project right, she needed forty-five hours of

footage to create a three-hour video that would win awards at film festivals. Alexa pressed her face in her hands.

Forty-five hours. The clock was ticking, and she needed to convince Graeme Hawthorne to give her an interview.

Alexa strolled to the exit, and as she glanced out the windows at the front of the restaurant, she spotted the botanist with his back to her, standing in the parking lot, at least what looked like his back. She'd certainly got a good look at that side of him when he walked away from her earlier.

She shoved through the door and strolled on the sidewalk to catch up with him. The tip of her heel caught. It snapped as her momentum continued forward. Hawthorne stood in the direct path of her fall. She grabbed what she could and squeezed.

The sinewy muscles beneath his T-shirt kept her from slamming into the asphalt. They rippled beneath her acrylic French manicure as though reacting to her tiger claws. She'd almost regained her footing when he turned and grabbed her arms to steady her.

"Uh. . .I'm so sorry." Could the day get any worse?

This close to him, he smelled of earth and evergreen needles—like he'd been living in the forest.

And. . .she hadn't smelled that in a very long time.

❧

Graeme maintained his controlled response to the pain this woman had inflicted on him with her fingernails. Were those things real? Sheer reflex had caused him to grab her arms and secure her unsteady, slender form.

He kept his hold on her wrists as he studied the abject humiliation in her striking baby blues. Reaching down, she tugged off her shoe and held it up for him to see. "My heel broke off. These sandals have never let me down before."

"Well, I've never been stabbed with nails before." He chuckled. "There's a first time for everything."

"No, I mean, my Jimmy Choos. They're reliable. They cost

a fortune, by the way, even though I bought them on sale." She frowned and looked down, then back up at him. "I'm sorry. You don't need to hear about that."

She scrunched her face as though she didn't know what to make of his lack of response. But she was right—he didn't want to hear about her shoes.

Jimmy Choos, huh?

Why was she here? Was she going to follow him everywhere?

"You want to hear my scientific question? All right. I've got one. How does climate change affect the redwood forest?"

Graeme studied her. What was she up to? He needed to test her merit. If she passed, then she might be worthy of his time. "Meet me at the tree where you found me. Tomorrow morning. Ten o'clock."

She blasted him with a thousand-watt smile and it twisted his insides—unfortunately, in a pleasant way.

"I'll be there." She marched off ahead of him, and he stood there, watching her sashay away barefooted, faded jeans hugging her long, slender legs.

He released a lengthy exhale. He honestly thought he'd seen the last of her today. To think, when she'd asked him to take her up in the tree, his heart had jumped at the thought—but it was a moment of weakness.

He watched her until she entered her room. Was it too far-fetched to think that someone could have sent her to find him and report back? Yes, it was. He was too suspicious for his own good.

four

While Barry drove them the twenty minutes to Crescent City, the nearest town where they could get a few groceries, a cell signal, and Internet, Alexa stared out the window of the compact rental car, watching as they left the thick redwoods behind. The countryside flattened and the trees seemed to shrink in size, if only a little. She cracked the window to breathe in the salty scent of the Pacific, the coast only a few miles away.

She smiled to herself, recalling her first encounter with Hawthorne earlier today. He wanted to know how she knew he climbed trees. He was the absent-minded-professor type, an idiot or an introvert suffering from paranoid delusions. He'd asked the question like he'd suspected her of doing a background check on him, and he demanded to know why, when clearly, anyone standing under the tree could see him hanging from the branches. To be fair, though, scientists and creative people alike were often concerned there was a thief after cerebral content lurking around every corner.

In a way, she *was* after intellectual property, or at least his knowledge on her topic, but not for the reasons he might suspect—they were on the same side of this environmental battle. Once she explained things, she hoped he'd be willing to share information freely.

If he suspected her of wanting to steal something, he might not show per their agreement, and that idea irritated her like a sliver in the back of her neck, just at the base of her head. If she could have gotten his contact information without him bucking, she would have.

All she had to go on was their meeting time and place, and now that she'd located him, she and Barry could potentially

move to a motel in town. They'd stayed in the heart of the
redwoods like Trish suggested in order to find the scientist.
But then again, the best documentaries were created when
cinematographers took up residency on location, so to speak.
If there was anything Alexa needed now, it was a stellar,
Sundance Film Festival award-winning documentary.

Changing World, Changing Forests was for the good of the
world and the good of the uninformed and unaware. And the
good of Alexa Westover's future in film. She jostled that truth
behind other thoughts cluttering her mind, like her breakup
with Clive. Why hadn't he contacted her yet? That was just
good business, wasn't it, despite personal feelings? Or had he
already shoved this project beneath the commercial-grade
carpet of his office along with her, believing the documentary
and Alexa would go nowhere fast?

A glance at her cell brought a rush of adrenaline. "A signal!"

Barry looked at his phone and began dialing. Alexa
pressed her hand against his wrist. "You're driving. I think
it's against—" The road sign informing that cell usage while
driving was illegal came into view. "See? Against the law."

"I got that." Barry continued his dialing.

But Alexa was simply a passenger. Though she'd called her
voice mail via the landline in her motel room, Clive hadn't
left a message, and to add insult to her pain and frustration,
her smartphone indicated she had no messages. Like the
device with which she accessed voice mail would make a
difference.

But Barry didn't need to know she'd been ignored. So she
dialed voice mail just to make sure there were no messages,
then called Clive directly. He didn't answer. She would e-mail
him on her progress.

Why had she held on to hope that Clive would change his
mind about her doing this project in the redwoods? He'd sent
her away like a child banished to the corner for a time-out.

Alexa had been on the verge of quitting, but she couldn't—
that would mean failure. If anything, she'd take what he'd

given her and make it brilliant. She just didn't know how.

Not yet.

Something in her—call it instinct or a sixth sense—told her that Graeme Hawthorne would play a key role in this documentary. It was almost as if Providence had led her to his place in the trees. The thought left her. . .well. . . uncomfortable.

One of three sisters raised by a single mother, Alexa had not left any portion of her life to divine intervention since clawing her way out of her poverty-stricken home to attend Columbia University on a scholarship. Then while she was away, her mother died. She wasn't sure how she felt about her lack of control over her life at the moment, but it was time to take charge once again.

She and Barry spent the rest of the day checking and responding to e-mails at an Internet café in town, gathering a few forgotten toiletries, bottled water, protein and snack bars for hiking in the woods, and mosquito repellent. Barry wanted seafood for supper, and Alexa, hating the smell much less the taste, ate the dried-out chicken breast instead at the overpriced restaurant. Still, compared to Manhattan prices, they were getting a steal.

Back in her bed that night, she tossed on the hard mattress, chewing on the fact that tomorrow was day three and all they had was limited footage of the redwoods. But these things took time.

Part of Alexa's success in life lay with her persistence, her unwillingness to give up. Scheduling interviews was a top priority when filming a documentary, but hanging this project's success on one rain forest scientist was maddening. For all she knew, Hawthorne wouldn't be any good on camera, and good on camera was essential.

She punched the pillow, trying again for a comfortable position.

With her initial impression of him, she'd seen a vibrant, charismatic personality folded into a sinewy form. His square, rugged jaw and woodsy eyes were welcome accents to his intellect. For the first time in days, maybe even weeks, Alexa smiled as she drifted to sleep.

ze

Graeme sat in the recliner and watched the ten o'clock news in the living room of his little one-bedroom log cabin. A fire crackled in the potbellied stove, giving the place a warm and cozy feel and making it difficult for him to keep his eyes open.

Yesterday, when he and Randy had climbed the tree to measure its height, and the group of hikers had almost stumbled upon them, he'd feared that he'd been found. That dread had burdened him for so long it had almost become second nature. At the same time, he was beginning to think he was borrowing worry—no one was watching him from the shadows anymore.

Nor were they looking for him, and if they were, they'd never find him here.

Still, he couldn't imagine any place he'd rather be—since he was a tree climber at heart, the redwoods were the main reason he'd gone into botany in the first place. If only he wasn't beginning to feel like he'd let Summer down when he fled Costa Rica.

Graeme squeezed the bridge of his nose. He'd been desperate to hold on to his love for her, despite the fact that death separated them, but time hadn't taken long to steal those feelings from him.

The woman he'd met today in the forest and who had fallen into him in Sally's parking lot magnified his inner struggles, forcing him to see clearly things he'd rather ignore.

He tugged off his old hiking boots and headed for a shower. He needed a shave. The only thing he inherited from his father was this pair of hiking boots, and with each passing day, he was beginning to understand the wisdom in that. He never allowed himself to count on anyone or anything. No expectations. No disappointments.

If he hadn't just looked into the most stunning blue eyes he'd ever seen, he wouldn't have found himself in need, wouldn't have to face how empty his life had become. But he couldn't afford for this woman to sashay into his life and sweep away all he had left of Summer. He simply wasn't prepared for that sort of complication. He had too many secrets to keep buried.

The television blared out a story that snapped him from his thoughts, and he rushed back into the living room.

The news anchor continued, "The university professor who was critically injured in a car accident early yesterday morning is still in critical condition."

❧

"He'll be here, don't worry." Alexa swatted at a mosquito, wondering if the repellent had been made with sugar, and hating that doubt swarmed her as well. The scientist hadn't a clue she was filming a documentary. At the very least, she'd need his signature on a release form before they captured him on film.

Hawthorne wasn't expecting her to show up with a cameraman, and though at the time, bombarding him with the truth hadn't been an option, now she wondered how she'd convince him to cooperate. At first he seemed to warm to her, but he'd quickly replaced his friendly demeanor with a back-off-or-I'll-bite attitude.

Barry waved his hand, shooing the obnoxious, carnivorous insects buzzing around his stocky form. Alexa almost laughed—Barry seemed to attract the little monsters and most were after his blood and not hers.

"The lighting is no good. The forest is too dark. I'll catch a few shots of him in the tree, but for the guts of the interview we need to see him somewhere else," he said.

Another fail. She hadn't told Barry that Hawthorne wasn't expecting lights, camera, and action. Nor had she ushered Barry over to her side of the equation. He still didn't like her. But if he were any kind of professional, he'd do his job right.

They'd both have this documentary on their records even though Barry might think he would lay any failure at her feet. Defeat was not an option.

As she waited and hoped that Hawthorne would show, the quiet forest enveloped her in a mist-laden fantasy sort of way. She'd shoved her childhood memories so far away she was hard-pressed—at that moment—to come up with the reasons she'd wanted to leave this place.

Ah yes, there they were, just at the edge of her mind, where they would stay. A twig snapped in the distance, and Alexa searched the woods for the cause.

Graeme Hawthorne stood about forty feet away, looking trim and rugged and melding into the forest like he'd always been there between the giant ferns and massive redwood trunks. The orange-barked, smooth branch of a madrone tree hovered inches from his face, almost hiding his expression, but Alexa could still read him.

He was the spirited steed again, edgy and preparing to buck.

&

Graeme's legs refused to move, stuck in the quicksand of his mind.

He'd spent earlier this morning attempting to uncover the details about Peter's car accident, wanting to ignore the tendrils of fear that the same person who'd caused Summer's deadly accident—the one in which Graeme had barely escaped with his life—was responsible and getting closer. How could he entertain such an idea? It was a stretch. Logic had failed him and fear had taken hold.

Graeme might, just might, be going crazy.

He'd discovered that Peter had been the cause of the accident, no one else. Regardless, he wasn't in the state of mind to keep his meeting with the gorgeous brunette named Alexa and had toyed with being a no-show. But if she was genuine, how could he as a scientist ignore answering her question? By all appearances, Alexa Westover was the complete opposite of

Summer, and with that, he shouldn't be vulnerable. *Shouldn't* being the operative word.

But right now, as he stared at her and the friend she'd brought—a stout man who hadn't yet noticed Graeme—he was beginning to question her sincerity. Again, his suspicions screamed in his mind—what was she up to? He liked his privacy and this party had suddenly become too crowded.

Graeme considered slipping back into the forest and disappearing—it wasn't like she could find him unless he allowed her to. She'd discovered him yesterday because of his momentary slip—nothing more.

He gazed on, more indecisive than he'd ever been, staring at her slender figure and captivating but tenuous smile. Since first spotting him, she'd become a porcelain statuette, as though she sensed his edginess and feared movement would scare him off like the forest wildlife.

Did she know how close to the truth she was? For reasons unknown to him, Graeme forced his legs from the quicksand and took the remaining steps to Alexa, watching her visibly relax and her soft smile turn brilliant again, lighting the forest canopy and Graeme's heart.

Danger, danger, Will Robinson. But her smile drew Graeme to her—she was an enchantress and he had no power to resist. He stood only three feet from her now and the man leaning against the tree stood erect, revealing he was a little taller than Graeme had expected.

"I was beginning to doubt you would show." Alexa tugged her lustrous hair over one shoulder. Was that a little quirk of hers, or some form of enticement she practiced in the mirror to get it just right? Regardless, Graeme could hardly pull his eyes from her long mane, appalled that he couldn't disarm this woman's power over him with his analytical mind.

"I'm a little late, I admit, but I honestly didn't believe you'd be here. And you brought a friend."

"Yes, this is Barry."

Graeme nodded at Barry and spotted the camera. Not just

any camera. An expensive, high-quality, digital mini-DV camera, the type used to make movies. Documentaries. "What's going on here?" Graeme hated his defensive tone. He'd been an idiot. Now he was that proverbial deer caught in the headlights. He took a step back.

Alexa took two steps forward, sending a light floral scent—not of the forest—his way. "You were going to answer my question, remember? What are the effects of climate change you see on the redwoods?"

Graeme glanced at Barry, who lifted his camera. "Could we get a shot of you in the trees today and do the interview in your office?"

Realization finally grabbed hold—the woman had turned his brain to mush because he'd taken this long to comprehend what was happening. "Why didn't you tell me you're filming a documentary?"

five

And obviously, she expected him to be part of it. She sent her cameraman a look that told Graeme the guy was filming.

Rage exploded in Graeme's head, and he stalked toward Barry and pressed his hand against the lens, forcing the camera down.

"Watch it, man. You'll damage the camera!" Barry shuffled away from Graeme and held the camera out of reach then inspected it.

"There is no way I can allow you to do that." Graeme couldn't believe the force of his words. "I haven't signed anything giving you permission."

"I thought you said you'd lined up the interview, Alexa." Barry had joined forces with Graeme now? What was going on?

"Look, I'm a scientist who studies the trees. You're disrupting my work." *I'll sue if you put me on film.* There was no way he could explain the reasons for his needing obscurity.

"Barry, could you give us a moment, please?" Alexa never took her crystal blue eyes—eyes that had now turned dark—from Graeme.

Was she going to keep him here with a look? To Graeme's chagrin, it was working.

The cameraman stalked off in the direction of the groomed path, loaded with an attitude that left Graeme wondering if he'd come back.

Alexa finally broke eye contact, releasing Graeme to draw a breath and grasp that he'd been holding it. She tugged her hair behind her ears, making her look on the young side of seventeen rather than twentysomething.

When she looked up at him again, it seemed as though

she were transparent, allowing Graeme to look right through her, and he liked what he saw. It wasn't like he could be transparent with her in return. Little did she know that her innocent involvement with him could potentially put her in danger, especially if he allowed her to film him. Being on a film sent out to who knew where, Graeme might as well call the murderers and tell them where he was.

"Look, I know I made a mistake by not being up front with you. Yes, I'm filming a documentary, but it's on an important topic. I would think you'd welcome the opportunity to explain to the world what's happening to the forest in terms of change."

Graeme stared at a redwood burl the size of a refrigerator—a misshapen, round growth on the trunk—and scratched his head. He was invisible in the trees until she showed up. "I don't do documentaries. I have too much work and too little time."

He finally turned his back on her and stomped away, hating the way his heart raced at the confrontation, hating the way he'd rather acquiesce to her request, and hating even more the reason why—he wanted to spend time with her.

She stalked behind him, but he hadn't expected anything less. "Who else, then? Just give me a name and you'll never see me again."

Her words stopped him in his tracks. Deep inside his gut, he admitted that wasn't what he wanted. She'd stirred something in him. His better judgment told him she would complicate his life in ways he couldn't imagine.

"Originally, I had scheduled to interview Professor Bryant at Humboldt University." Her voice caught in her throat.

"You know about his accident, then."

"Yes."

Great, just great. It wasn't her business. Any words that left his mouth would be too many and too much information if spoken to this woman.

Graeme kept his head down, staring at the burnt-orange evergreen needles on the forest floor. He heaved a sigh, sensing how important this was to her. When he inhaled, an earthy scent wafted around his head.

"There are a few others you could interview. I'm surprised you didn't call them first rather than tracking me down," he said. She'd been lucky at that or she had special skills she hadn't shared with him.

"I didn't plan for my interview with Bryant to fall through. I expected him to point me to others as we progressed, if needed. Yours was the only name that his assistant gave. There must be a reason for that." Alexa's voice was soft now, almost calming Graeme's troubled thoughts.

Almost.

Graeme and Peter were laboring together on research, but Graeme was the silent partner, needing to remain behind the scenes. Maybe his name would show up in the credits once their research was complete, but if he needed to, he could be long gone should someone try to track him down here. But agreeing to Alexa's documentary was pushing it.

Finally, he lifted his gaze, daring to look at this woman who held power over him, hoping she hadn't yet figured that out.

"I'll get you names and contact information by this evening," he said.

She cocked a well-defined brow. "Do you know how to find me?"

"You're staying in the motel connected with Sally's, right?"

"You're good. But I'm at a disadvantage. I don't have a clue how to contact you." Angling her head, she smiled. "Will you give me your number? E-mail? Anything?"

"I think you've managed well enough without it." With his statement, he was shooting for a little closure and weaved his way through the ferns and brush to the main trail.

He swept past Barry, who waited on the trail. The guy barely managed to hide his scowl—what a friendly guy. Then he headed off in the opposite direction from the trailhead. He had a five-mile hike ahead of him until he met up with Randy, who should be waiting with their gear. He hadn't lied to Alexa when he said he had a lot of work—collecting data in the treetops required much more than brainpower when one was required to climb the skyscrapers of the forest.

As he disappeared into the thickening woods, he felt Alexa and the cameraman's curious stares on his back. He'd get her those names soon enough. Scrawl them on a sheet of paper and leave them in an envelope stuck under her cheap motel-room door. Then maybe she would leave him alone and eventually leave his forest.

Still, somehow he knew he'd not seen the last of her.

And that made him smile, despite igniting a war between his better judgment and his desire to see her again.

❧

Alexa could almost feel Barry's hackles rise as together they watched the gun-shy botanist slip into the wilds of the redwoods. She bristled, fully expecting Barry to point a mouthful of buckshot her direction.

She started away from the trailhead, planning to hike deeper into the redwoods, but unlike Hawthorne, she remained on the trail. Barry stayed rooted where he stood.

"Wait a minute. Where do you think you're going?" he asked.

"We need some footage."

"No, you don't. You're not making me follow you around while you act like you know what you're doing. You tricked me, Alexa. You lied to both of us. That man wasn't expecting an interview. Nor was he willing to give it. Wait until Clive hears about this."

Alexa pivoted on her heel to face Barry. She was only a few yards from him and saw that he was breathing hard and not as a result of being out of shape. If Hawthorne were a stallion, Barry was a wild boar ready to charge, nostrils flaring.

Bring it.

"Riveting, Barry. Is that why you're here, really? So you can spy on me and report back all my failures? Well, I'll let you in on a secret. The camera-shy botanist is getting me names. Lots and lots of names. That means interviews."

Alexa pressed her hands on her hips. Hawthorne's reaction to the camera had piqued her curiosity—not the outcome he'd wanted, she was sure. Adrenaline shoved excitement through her veins. She welcomed the challenge Hawthorne had given her. "And we're not finished with this guy yet either. You can take that to the bank or to Clive, whichever you think you can trust more."

Oh yeah, now she was feeling more like herself. And now she had him thinking. Barry appeared to stand taller and closed the distance between them, a look of respect on his face. Alexa thought she just might have pulled him halfway over to her team.

&

After an invigorating afternoon spent in the woods, Alexa wanted to cut the filming short to make sure she was in her room and available when Hawthorne showed up with names. She showered and freshened up, wanting to shed her body of the sweaty, woodsy smell, although now that she looked at her squeaky clean skin in the mirror, she wondered if the man might prefer that scent.

Brushing her tangled wet strands, she scowled at her reflection. Why was she even thinking about what scent he preferred?

Graeme Hawthorne was the first man—and she wasn't counting Clive on this pie chart—who didn't seem to respond to her beauty. She'd used that asset on more occasions than she cared to admit, and without even giving it a second thought.

But now, for some reason, the very idea turned her insides. What kind of a person was she to count on her looks to pave the way for her? It wasn't like she didn't have any brains or talent. Clive had certainly wanted the whole package that she offered.

Alexa stared at herself, devoid of makeup, hair in lumpy tangles hanging from her scalp, her eyes a little red from lack of sleep. She was a mess—but this was who she was without all the fluff. Was there someone out there who could love the real Alexa Westover?

And who was she? Again, she wasn't sure anymore. The person she was in New York, the person who'd made every effort to live on the other side of the country from where she'd grown up, was not the girl she'd been in rural Northern California. At some point, someone would see through her façade. Maybe if they did, they could show her who they saw. She'd never looked back since leaving here and wasn't sure she wanted to look back now.

Loathing the unbidden thoughts—they couldn't come at a worse time—Alexa swept her tangled thoughts away as she brushed.

Dressed in a clean T-shirt and jeans, she stared at her laptop and the footage captured so far, logging a description of each segment and where to find it. In the end, an organized written record of where to find everything would make the process go smoothly when it was time to edit interviews and create transitions. She and Barry would share this responsibility.

Looking at the images Barry had filmed, Alexa saw now that he'd caught a few images of her, more than she'd suspected, on film. Not fair. But what she saw surprised her. A small half grin slipped onto her face and into her heart.

She appeared to be enjoying herself and looked genuinely happy. In one image, and she remembered him filming this, she climbed onto a bridge where the bases of the giants had fused together when they were just little tykes, hundreds of years before.

This afternoon had been filled with exploration, and her creative juices were flowing like they'd not done in weeks. Slowly she'd gone deeper into the woods and managed to keep her fear-laced memories and regrets safely contained in the back of her mind. Was it possible she could finally put everything behind her? That what Clive had meant for punishment had actually benefited her?

What was meant for bad, God is using for good?

Alexa shook away the memory verse along with the deep, melancholy thoughts and stood up, tugging her hair into a knot at the base of her neck. What was with all these serious thoughts? She glanced at her watch.

Seven thirty already? Where was Hawthorne? Disappointment engulfed her. She'd trusted him to provide what she needed. Without those names, she was all but done here, and the confident words she'd slung at Barry earlier today fell flat.

Alexa stomped to the door and yanked it open to the crisp scent of earth and mossy wilderness lurking across the street from the motel.

Though Alexa needed those names, and expected him to show with them, she'd wanted to see the distrusting and edgy botanist again—his woodland smell and handsome face, those mysterious forest-green eyes that stared at her in that unnerving, searching way.

Alexa pressed her fist to her chest. Did she dare admit what she was feeling, even to herself? She wanted Graeme Hawthorne to discover who she was, to see the real Alexa. Why, she wasn't sure. She didn't even know the man. The forest was having a strange effect on her emotions.

Where was he?

Should she go into the woods to look for him again?

To her credit, she'd braved the woods so far, but no way— no way!—could she step foot into the redwoods with a setting sun. Alexa glanced down, and that's when she saw a wrinkled envelope. She picked it up, seeing her name scribbled across the front.

Regret pricked her heart. He'd already come and gone, and somehow Alexa had missed him. Maybe when she'd taken the shower to freshen up, just for him, he'd knocked on the door. Maybe when she'd been staring at herself in the mirror, evaluating her appearance, he'd knocked. Or maybe he hadn't knocked at all, planning to leave the envelope without so much as a hello.

six

Graeme stumbled through the creaky door of the little church where he'd become comfortable visiting these last few months. Empty pews and an old musty smell greeted him as he entered the Church in the Redwoods tucked away in the heart of the forest not far from where he studied his trees.

His trees? Their massive size—in both height and girth—had fascinated him since he was a boy, and they were now the focus of his research, the center of his universe. But they belonged to God, not Graeme.

As did Summer.

He found himself sitting on the faded red cushion of the pew in the front of the sanctuary, though if there'd been anyone inside, he would have resigned himself to the back row for a quick escape or not entered at all.

With his head bowed, he struggled to disengage from today's distractions so he could pray. The stunning Alexa had almost undone him with one look when he spotted her waiting there as they'd agreed, but then his momentary willingness to open up and allow another human being into his world had been shredded when he discovered she was filming a documentary.

And he was glad for it. He'd not been thinking clearly or he wouldn't have agreed to meet her to begin with. Unwilling to face her again, he'd paid a boy to stuff the envelope containing the names of a few others who might work for her documentary under her door.

Considering she'd gone out of her way to trick him into showing up, she'd known he wouldn't agree. The truth was, he wished he could. He wished he was free to pursue those opportunities, but he was a captive in a prison of his own making. Never again would someone be hurt because of him or his research. That included Alexa Westover. Beautiful filmmaker extraordinaire.

Footfalls resounded—heavy on the left foot—and approached from the back of the church along the center aisle. Graeme squeezed his eyes, unsure if he needed to disengage the sharp-eyed pastor before he saw too much. Didn't the man have anything else to do? Graeme reined in his bitter attitude—he'd had the privilege on countless occasions to watch Jacob Emory carve his life-sized creations out of redwood burl. But who was Graeme kidding? He'd needed Jacob to find him here or else he never would have come.

The pastor stood behind Graeme and squeezed his shoulder. "You've been on my heart. Glad God brought you down from the trees long enough to come see me."

Graeme huffed a laugh. Just like Jacob to think that God had sent him for a visit.

"What's troubling you, son?" He limped around Graeme to sit next to him on the pew.

The way Graeme understood the story, Jacob had been injured in a logging accident long before God had called him to pastor this little church. Dressed in his work clothes—a flannel shirt and jeans—Jacob stared at the pulpit like he sensed Graeme didn't want to be studied.

And he was right. Graeme knew all too well what it meant to analyze something or someone, and he couldn't stand the thought of being on the receiving end.

What's troubling me? Nothing and everything. Where did he begin? Graeme heaved a long sigh, feeling some of his burden dissipate just for the effort he'd made in coming here.

"Something's happened," he said.

Jacob leaned forward and propped his elbows against his thighs, hanging his head. Patient enough to allow Graeme the time he needed, he said nothing.

The problem was, Graeme wasn't exactly sure what was disturbing him more—that Alexa had found him, that she was making a documentary, or that she'd awakened him from his slumber in the trees. Resigned to a life of obscurity and loneliness, he'd been content until Alexa had plowed her fingernails into him.

"You don't have to put words to it, son. The good Lord already knows the guilt that burdens you. When are you going to let it go?"

Leave it to Jacob to voice the thoughts Graeme had tried to ignore. But yes, Jacob was exactly right. Alexa had stirred up the guilt Graeme felt that Summer had died instead of him, that he'd fled because the murderers wanted them both dead, and that he had been hiding ever since.

What a mess he was in. He could never be free to leave until the situation was resolved, nor could he love again until he forgave himself and let Summer go.

"I don't know how you do it, Jacob, but you always manage to open my eyes without even knowing what's going on." Graeme stood and swiped his sweaty palms against his jeans.

"That's because truth is always light that shines in the darkness." Jacob stood and met Graeme's gaze; then he thrust out his hand to shake Graeme's. "And the truth will set you free, son."

In his Jeep, Graeme bounced along the dirt drive that curved between the trees until it reached the lone cabin he'd rented from Peter. Funny that he'd finally been given an opportunity to study the redwoods—a lifelong dream—but the dream had twisted into a nightmare, the kind where you run down a long, dark hallway with someone chasing you, but you can't seem to go anywhere.

The truth will set you free. . . .

&

"I would have to say. . .um. . .I guess?" Caldwell Chambers, a pale, skinny guy in his midthirties, scratched his head then shuffled papers around on his desk. "Look, this isn't the sort of thing I do."

"I understand," Alexa said.

"I spend most of my time on research."

And not much time with people, Alexa thought.

Did the botanist know the answer or not? She'd sent him the interview questions ahead of time after locating him per Hawthorne's instructions. Two days later, she and Barry were in the plant-lined office of the scientist's conservative, eco-friendly, solar-powered home just off the Avenue of the Giants located two hours south of where they'd first met Hawthorne.

The extra lighting Barry had assembled for the interview flickered, and he lowered the camera as the three of them glanced around the room as one, like they were expecting something more.

"Was that a seismic. . ."

"Event? An earthquake?" Chambers chuckled and cleared his throat. "No, it's just a glitch in my solar-powered system. I was tinkering around last night. Either that or more likely it doesn't deliver enough wattage to power that extra light you brought. Here, let me turn a few things off." He powered down his computer and switched off the desk lamp.

Why couldn't he speak smoothly like that when answering Alexa's questions?

"Okay, let's try this again. Remember, you've already explained your background and your research. Now all you have to do is tell us if you've seen any effects of climate change on the forests and what they are."

"Talk about a loaded question. Um. . .the answer is complicated."

Please stop with the "ums."

"Just take your time," Barry said and held the camera steady.

She'd have a ton of editing if she could even use this guy. Some people's personalities worked well on camera; others, not so much. Alexa doubted that she would be impressed when she viewed the film.

Alexa caught Barry's glimpse in her direction from behind

the camera, and if she was reading him right, he agreed. Chambers would not work on camera and it was doubtful they could use his interview at all.

She stood and paced the little office, taking in all the greenery—Boston ferns, peace plants, various palms—all meant to clean the air. It looked like a jungle inside. "Caldwell, just tell us about your house. You've obviously put a lot of time and energy into creating a green home. Why solar power?" she asked.

Barry lowered the camera and stared at Alexa, but she motioned for him to continue filming. Maybe at the end of the day Caldwell would say something they could use in the overall documentary. Or at some point, she might consider filming a documentary about green homes and what it takes to make one. One never knew what the future would bring. She had the strange sense that her future working for Clive was shaky at best, though, so maybe she should credit common sense or logic rather than instinct.

Shaking off the demoralizing thoughts, she focused again on Chambers.

He became animated and informative when speaking about the eco-friendly modifications he'd applied to his home until, finally, Alexa had to rein him in. He offered them a tour of the home, and they complied because he'd been kind enough to give them the interview.

When their visit was over, Alexa stood on the front porch and shook Chambers's hand. "Thank you for agreeing to see us."

"You're welcome. Call me if you need anything else."

He tossed her a big smile, clearly pleased with himself, especially since he'd spent half an hour speaking flawlessly about what really mattered to him. Funny, she would have thought going green and a changing climate's effect on the forest would go hand in hand. But maybe it was a matter of the difference between work and play.

After Barry stowed the camera and light, he and Alexa waved again as they climbed into the car and crawled out of the shaded driveway. At the end of the drive, Barry stopped to look both ways, his gaze settling on Alexa.

"What was that?" he asked.

"I know you didn't like that I indulged him in his obvious hobby."

Barry turned right onto the Avenue of the Giants—a scenic drive that paralleled the freeway. "Have you got anyone else lined up, Alexa? Because if not, I'm ready to head back to my apartment in New York."

Alexa stared out the window, watching the giant redwoods called sequoias—thicker trunks than their taller cousins along the coast—and drew in a long breath, not caring if Barry sensed her uncertainty. "This was the only guy on the list Hawthorne gave me that I could get ahold of for this week."

"What about the professor at Humboldt—maybe he's out of the hospital now and ready to see us."

Alexa shook her head. "Nope. I thought of that, too, so I talked to Trish, his assistant. He's on medical leave. And she told me that if I found Hawthorne, I struck gold. So we check out of our hotel and head back to the Redwood Motor Inn at Jedediah Smith State Park."

"For what? Striking gold is one thing; mining it, getting it out of the ground, is another. You know you won't be able to find Hawthorne again—he'll be watching for you. That guy has a serious aversion to people."

Despite her best efforts, Alexa hadn't been able to shake Graeme Hawthorne from the forefront of her thoughts. She shifted in the passenger seat. "Look, Barry. A good documentary is about the writing, planning, and scheduling, but it's also about going with your gut. And my gut tells me that Hawthorne is key to this story. Stick with me, will you? Give me another week."

A little niggling said he was important to her heart as well, but she shoved aside the fleeting thought. Another week to convince Hawthorne to give her an interview, and she wasn't even sure she could locate him in that time. She couldn't blame Barry if he was less than enthusiastic.

He didn't respond and glanced her way intermittently while driving, as though considering his answer. The slight frown on his face was tempered with a light in his eyes that encouraged Alexa.

"I've got to hand it to you. You're one of the most driven people I've ever met." Then a smile replaced his frown. "But honestly? Clive will have my hide if I don't give you what you need to make the best film you can, and I can't have anything but the best on my résumé. Call me selfish."

"Yes!" Alexa sat straighter and laughed and stared out the window. Tears were forming in her eyes. When she knew her voice wouldn't shake, she turned to Barry again. "I've always wanted to navigate a car through one of those drive-through redwood trees. Can we do that before heading north?"

seven

Muscles burning, Graeme dropped the pack bearing his climbing equipment at his feet and gazed upward at the canopy, where he spent most of his life these days. He drew in the scent of unadulterated, old-growth forest—earth and moss—and the woodsy scent of redwood needles carpeting the woodland floor. Being back in the forest he loved, preparing to enter the canopy, invigorated him like nothing else.

He was a little breathless after his week in Seattle conferring with Matt Horne regarding some of his data gathered from the Olympic National Park wilderness. Funny how it only took one week away from a hike in the woods for Graeme to feel out of shape. He had put off the trip long enough and thought staying away from his usual hangout for a week was a good way to lose Alexa Westover just in case she hadn't taken the detour he'd given her all the way to Humboldt Redwoods State Park—a good two or more hours south.

Randy threw his pack to the ground next to him. "So you think you lost your shadow?"

Graeme shoved his hand through his hair before securing his hard hat, giving himself time to think about his answer. "I hope so."

The fact that he had to think about his reply was a little irritating. He'd not been able to get the woman out of his thoughts while gone, and if he was honest with himself, there was a small part of him that wanted to see her again. He thought a week away would help him forget about their brief encounter. But that had been deluded, if not hopeful, thinking on his part.

47

Using the crossbow, Randy shot the fishing line over the branch; then he turned to look at Graeme. Randy's scrutiny made him a little uncomfortable.

"What?" Graeme asked.

Randy chuckled and looked away, his gaze following the trunk of the tree all the way to the branch they'd harnessed. "You like her, don't you?"

Graeme couldn't believe what he was hearing. "Are you insane? What makes you say that?"

"You haven't been the same since the day you met her." Randy began the task of attaching the rope and tugging it over the branch.

"You know why, and it has nothing to do with me liking some woman I just met and barely know. It makes me uncomfortable that someone found me, and I certainly don't want to be in a documentary."

An hour and a half later, they'd collected leaves from the top of the tree to study hydrostatic tension, or gravitational pressure that reduced the amount of water available in the tree crowns, and were on their way down.

"I hear Peter's health is improving." Randy rappelled down a quarter of the trunk's width away from Graeme.

"Yeah." Graeme was more than relieved that his professional colleague and longtime friend—the guy who'd given him a purpose and a place to hide after he fled tragedy—was recovering, though slowly. Graeme had kept his distance, though, not wanting to draw unwanted attention to himself or Peter just in case Summer's killer was looking for him.

"Maybe you could send your girl back his way," Randy persisted.

"I'm not sure he'd agree to it at this point, but I'll ask him. And on Alexa?" Why wouldn't Randy leave it alone? "She's not my girl. Why do you keep bringing her up anyway? She's long gone." Graeme's research assistant was getting on his nerves, to say the least. He realized that he was frowning at the thought of Alexa being long gone.

"Okay, I wasn't going to tell you, but I have a feeling you're going to find out sooner rather than later," Randy said.

Graeme froze, hanging in midair. Had something happened to Alexa and her cameraman? Heart racing, his thoughts and fears escaped the feeble control he held.

No. Randy would have told him if something serious had happened.

"Are you going to tell me, or what?"

"I saw her with the camera guy this morning."

Graeme's insides tensed. "What? Where?"

"Heading into the woods along the trail, filming away."

"Still filming? How long does it take to make a documentary?"

Graeme continued down the tree, not wanting to confirm to his cohort that he did, in fact, like Alexa, and he wasn't sure if he was frustrated or happy that she'd returned. How did he avoid her now?

Boots finally touching ground on the mat of needles, Graeme detached himself from the gear. Randy trudged around from the other side of the massive trunk and began stuffing their equipment in the packs. "I guess the question now is do you keep hiding, or face this problem head-on?"

Graeme stared at Randy, struggling to comprehend which situation the man was referring to. Struggling with the way the words slammed him, he inhaled as his mind filled with images of Costa Rica.

"You okay?" Randy straightened and looked Graeme in the eyes.

Shaking off the momentary lapse, Graeme took off his helmet. "Sure, I'm fine. I'll just take things as they come."

What choice did he have?

Two hours later, he and Randy hiked out from the wilds and onto a path well traveled, drawing near enough to civilization that the sounds of cars driving along Highway 199 could be heard through the trees. Alexa and her cameraman stood directly in Graeme's path.

His earlier words rushed back to him. *"I'll just take things as they come. . ."*

He glanced Randy's way and saw his attempt at hiding a wry grin. Graeme almost grinned himself, because no matter what his head told him, his heart was glad to see her, glad for another chance to watch her graceful walk, her stunning eyes, and that long mane of gorgeous hair.

When Graeme was within a few feet, he stopped and attempted an irritable, standoffish demeanor, but an unbidden smile caught him off guard. There was something different about her.

A little less makeup maybe? He wasn't sure, but she looked more like she belonged in his world this time. And he liked that a little too much for comfort.

❧

Had it been her imagination, or had the guy with Hawthorne gone out of his way to make sure their paths collided today? She'd caught him watching her earlier in the day and then he'd smiled and tipped his hat. But there was no way she would believe Hawthorne had known she was back; otherwise she wouldn't be looking at him now, because he would have gone into hiding.

She needed him in this documentary. Somehow she had to win him over. Angling her head, she studied him. He'd neglected to shave again, but the rugged look—at least on Hawthorne—appealed to her. Now that was new.

And. . .he studied her back. Warmth slid over her shoulders and up her neck—a reaction she hadn't experienced in far too long. She managed to keep from turning away in heated embarrassment only because she enjoyed the appreciative look in his eyes too much. Not what she'd expected at all, but then. . .he did the unexpected.

He brushed past her on the trail as if to ignore her, but a trace of a smile remained on his lips.

"Aren't you glad to see me?" She hiked next to him, though he wasn't making it easy. She had to take three steps to his one.

Suddenly he stopped and turned to face her, ready to tell her to get lost, she was sure. Shrugging, he held up his hands. "I can't help you. I don't know what else you want from me. You're like one of those ten o'clock news reporters getting in someone's face. Namely mine."

Now *that* stung. Alexa's mouth dropped open, and when he continued along the trail without her, she remained behind, staring at a blur of trees and ferns. Shaking off his nasty tone, she caught up with him.

"Is that how you view me? You couldn't be further from the truth."

He continued walking, and this time Alexa let him go without following. "Dr. Hawthorne," she said softly, remembering the Bible verse about a word softly spoken. Where had that come from? "Graeme."

She'd not spoken his first name until that point. Would he bristle in reaction?

Pausing, he hesitated before facing her again. She couldn't believe it worked. At his questioning gaze and softened expression, Alexa closed the distance between them. Something in his eyes told her this was her moment—it was now or never. She had to reel him in.

"I think we got off on the wrong foot. That's not who I am at all. In fact, I bet you didn't know I grew up here, did you?" Alexa was careful to keep her voice gentle and nonconfrontational. Putting him on the defensive would only backfire. "I have a sister who lives a few miles up the road, and another a couple hours away."

That got his attention, and he cocked his left brow. He said nothing and instead, held her gaze longer than any man should, that is, unless he had a personal interest.

Alexa's breath caught in her throat. The meaning of her next words was quickly morphing into something she'd not planned.

"Have dinner with me? My sister would love to meet you. And I'd love to get to know you better." Her heart fluttered as though she'd asked him on a date rather than a friendly business dinner.

Oh Sela, I hope you're not going to kill me. Alexa hadn't even contacted her sister to let her know she was in the area. But she had her reasons.

Regret flickered in his eyes—Alexa could easily read it because that was part of her training. His reaction quickly zapped much of her remaining drive. Had she lost this battle?

He shook his head and tore his gaze from hers to stare at the ground instead like he was ashamed. "I appreciate your invitation, but. . .I just. . .can't."

Alexa found her disappointment magnified by the fact that she'd wanted the dinner with him for far more than business reasons. She wanted to know this mysterious tree climbing, extremely attractive botanist. In the presence of his raw masculinity, Clive and whatever was left of their relationship, if anything, slipped even further from her thoughts.

Graeme Hawthorne marched away from her. His buddy trailed along behind him, lugging a massive backpack, then glanced back at her and offered an apologetic shrug.

Barry nudged her. "You ready?"

"Not yet." Alexa rushed down the path until she was a few yards behind Hawthorne. "Think about it, and if you change your mind, meet me outside my room tonight at six."

And on that statement, Alexa nailed the rest of her hopes. When she whirled around, Barry saluted her. Only when the two men disappeared from sight did Alexa and Barry start down the path, trudging back to the motel.

"I can see what Clive saw in you," he said.

Why'd he have to bring up Clive?

"So you think he'll show?" Barry asked.

"Are you a betting man, Barry?"

"Only when it's a sure thing, but I honestly believe there's a chance the guy might show."

Alexa smiled to herself, liking Barry's newfound belief in

her. It went a long way in refueling her depleted stores of self-confidence.

"Yeah?" she asked, glimpsing his way. He was breathing hard as he hiked next to her on the paved path back to what represented culture in this remote area.

"He likes you, Alexa. But then, you probably already know that."

"Well, whether or not he shows is the least of my problems at the moment. I've got to call my sister, who doesn't even know I'm here, and tell her I'm bringing a business date to her house for dinner tonight."

eight

Alexa puffed at a dark strand of hair that had strayed into her eyes from her loosely styled updo—hair tucked in a bun at the base of her head, with soft tendrils framing her face. Silver hoops hung from her ears, and she tried to clasp the matching silver necklace behind her neck.

Would the man even show? Was she crazy to wear this black, clingy dress? She always traveled with clothes that were versatile—that she could wear for business or a date— but here in the redwoods, maybe this was a bit too much.

She frowned at the mirror, unable to rein in the nervous excitement coursing through her at the prospect of seeing Hawthorne tonight. She couldn't remember the last time she'd been this jazzed about a dinner date. This wasn't a date, she reminded herself—she didn't even think of him by his first name—but the image in the mirror belied her intentions. And if it wasn't a date, then why hadn't she invited Barry?

The clasp slipped from her fingers. No matter how hard she tried, she couldn't put the necklace on, at least not without help. The clock on the bedside table declared it was 5:59. If he'd changed his mind and decided to go to dinner with her, he would be here any second now.

Alexa's palms began sweating profusely, and she rushed to the little bathroom to wipe them on a hand towel then sprayed lime-basil body spritz in the air and walked through the mist. She peered at the mirror while pressing another dab of mauve lipstick on her lips and rubbed them together, then smeared a little smoky eyeliner in the corner of her eyes.

From the mirror, she could see the clock on the table in reverse—it was now two minutes after six. A little pang zinged through her heart.

He wasn't going to show. She sagged, peering at her reflection and thinking what an idiot she'd been to put all this effort into dressing up for a business dinner when she was only going to her sister's. How insane she was to think for a minute it was anything more. He certainly wasn't going to think of her as anything other than a nuisance.

Admit it. Her interest in him went deeper than the interview. But all undertakings were a lost cause. No business dinner. No date. No interview. It wasn't often she lost at this game, at least not so early on, and her insides twisted.

Alexa began tugging out the earrings—it wasn't like there was any place upscale enough around here for her to go dressed like this. Sela wouldn't mind if she was in jeans, but she'd definitely mind if Alexa didn't show up for the dinner. To be fair, Sela had been a gem on the phone, understanding about Alexa's work schedule and believing the excuses Alexa had given for not stopping over to see her sooner.

Leave it to Sela's generous nature. She'd been the one to invite Alexa over for dinner. Then Alexa had asked if she could include a friend. Everything had worked out like a dream.

A knock resounded on the door. Alexa froze, her pulse accelerating and moisture spreading over her palms again. She quickly stuck the earrings back in.

Wait. . .

That was probably just Barry wanting to console her with a burger at Sally's because Hawthorne hadn't come.

She crept to the door for a glance through the peephole.

Graeme Hawthorne. Her mouth went dry. He'd actually shown up.

Drawing in a long breath and standing tall, Alexa gathered her composure and told herself this was strictly business. She needed that interview.

He knocked again.

Placing her sweaty palm on the knob, she turned it then

swung open the door and flashed a dazzling smile. "Glad you could make it."

Hawthorne appeared a little dumbstruck, if Alexa had to guess, as his gaze shimmered with appreciation. She hadn't dressed up for nothing, then, but she also had to pause and catch her breath as she took in the man before her—was it really him? Dressed in a tweed sports coat over a cream-colored shirt, he'd shaved and his cologne enveloped her.

He'd gone to a lot of trouble for her, too. This *was* a date. . .whether either of them wanted to admit it or not.

"You look. . .wow. . ." He ran his hand over his face like he wasn't accustomed to the smooth texture. A nervous chuckle escaped. "Sorry, I can't think of what to say."

Alexa laughed. "Wow is good. You look wow, too, if I may be so bold." Yeah, he cleaned up really nice.

"Are you ready to go?" he asked. "Wherever it is that we're going."

"Wait right here while I grab my purse."

Alexa slammed the door and dashed back into the room. Why had she just closed the door in his face? She wasn't thinking clearly, that's why. She searched the room for the little black bag that went with the dress. There, on the dresser. Grabbing it, she stuffed in her cell phone and lipstick and driver's license and the slip of paper with Sela's directions in case she forgot. Better stuff in a credit card, too, just in case. Oh, and some cash. Why hadn't she done this before? The silver necklace lay where she'd put it. She slung the purse over her shoulder and lifted the necklace.

Alexa opened the door, feeling breathless. "Sorry about that. Listen, can you help me put this on? I wasn't able to get that clasp to work. Maybe you can do better."

He took the necklace she offered. She eased the motel door shut and turned her back to him. Graeme lifted the necklace over her head then around her neck. She could have done that part.

His warm breath caressed the back of her neck. His fingers,

brushing her skin as he worked to clasp the necklace, sent electric currents through her.

❧

Graeme focused on the clasp that kept slipping from his fingers. Why was he having so much trouble with this? He exhaled slowly and a few strands of her shiny mane, rolled into a silky ball at the base of her swanlike neck, reacted to his breath. His mouth became an arid desert, parched, cracked, and thirsty.

He shouldn't have accepted her invitation, even though it was supposedly to discuss the documentary, and a way for her to present her case. That he'd even given this a second thought should have been a warning sign. He shouldn't be here now, but all afternoon, after she'd put the proverbial ball in his court as though he'd agreed to the game, he'd not been able to think of anything else except the way Alexa had said his name.

Graeme. . . He closed his eyes now, hearing the sound of it on her lips.

The clasp closed on the tiny hoop. Finally. "There," he said, bringing his thoughts back to the moment.

She adjusted the necklace and turned to face him, lifting her eyes to meet his, an enticing smile on her soft, pink lips. Graeme realized she'd caught him staring at her mouth. When he lifted his gaze to hers again, it was as if they each took a moment to assess the other—the beginning of a familiar dance and one he wasn't ready for. But he couldn't help himself.

He smiled. "We're meeting your sister for dinner, right?"

"At her house, yes. I hope that's all right."

Her silvery blue eyes reminded him a little of an albino redwood in the moonlight—a rare and beautiful thing. He should have known the first time he looked into them, documentary or not, he was in deep trouble. This seemingly unshakable thing he had for this woman was a serious complication.

Afraid his voice would betray his thoughts, Graeme shrugged and gestured to his wreck of a Jeep. He wished he'd had time to wash and wax the thing, but at least he'd cleaned himself up, and considering her look of approval, he'd given himself away.

Graeme opened the door for her and assisted her as she climbed into the vehicle, a little high for a lady in heels and a sleek little black dress. Her attire gave him pause about what to expect at her sister's, but he'd worn the best he had at the moment. She slipped into the passenger seat, her tan legs smooth and taut. Graeme closed the door on the image.

He climbed in and started the Jeep, having to give it a few tries before it complied. The thing needed a tune-up, but he'd bought it with the cash he had on hand when he'd returned to the States and it would do until he moved on. Putting on her seat belt, Alexa discovered an old bag of Cheetos stuck down in the crack between the seat and the console.

Graeme snatched the bag out of her hand, crackling it, and hating the embarrassment flooding him. To his surprise she snatched it back, laughing.

He backed out while she opened the bag and looked inside. "These are stale. I can't believe this is what you consider food."

"A guy's gotta eat."

"How do you stay in such great shape, eating like this?"

"I need directions." He idled in the parking lot before turning onto 199.

"Oh, right." She tugged a piece of paper from her purse and held it up. "Take 199 toward Crescent City; then at Elk Road take a right. Go five miles and then turn left."

"Left onto what street?"

"No, left into her place. She lives next to the burl shop that she owns."

Graeme followed the instructions and they headed down the highway. If he had any sense at all, he would turn back around and tell her he was sorry, that he'd made a big mistake. But no, Graeme Hawthorne was a fool of a man, falling under Alexa's spell.

"Listen, thanks for letting us take your car. I wouldn't want to leave Barry without transportation."

Why hadn't she invited Barry? But he didn't need to ask. He knew. He glanced over at the woman watching the redwoods rush past through the passenger side window. This wouldn't be the first time he'd walked into an ambush with his eyes wide open.

nine

Alexa had never experienced claustrophobia, but if the anxiety that squeezed her chest right now was any indication of that fear, she felt sorry for those poor souls with any sort of clinical phobia. This business dinner. . .date. . .with Hawthorne—whatever it was—and seeing Sela for the first time in a long while taxed her nerves. She was definitely losing her knack, considering that not long ago, throwing the two spicy situations together in the same bowl wouldn't have fazed her in the least.

Hawthorne turned his Jeep in need of shocks to the left and into the driveway of Sela's gift shop, the rustic log cabin where she'd lived with her husband before he died, situated to the right and back a few yards from the store. Very much aware of Hawthorne's masculinity and rugged good looks, Alexa drew in a breath and smiled at the attractive tree hugger next to her as he shut off the ignition. They'd shared small talk on the drive over, unwilling to delve into deeper issues until the pleasantries were spent, and yet, Alexa had never felt such a strong connection with anyone.

"Here we are." She sounded like an idiot, but the man had cracked her smooth and polished veneer.

She didn't wait for his assistance but opened the door, planning to hop out, escaping the close quarters of his Jeep— but Hawthorne met her, having rushed around, and gently circled her waist and lifted her down.

Alexa enjoyed his proximity entirely too much and the thought made her uncomfortable—an unusual response— but maybe that was because she was no longer the one in control of the game. He released her but didn't move, his athletic figure blocking her.

"Why did you change your mind about tonight?" she asked.

Something skated across his features, but it disappeared before she could read him.

"Let's just say you intrigue me—you got me asking questions." With a cockeyed grin, he took a step back, freeing her to flee captivity—but Alexa remained where she stood.

"And as a scientist, you couldn't resist?"

"I wasn't talking about science."

Hawthorne had just turned up the heat on this experiment and it infused her cheeks. The guy was loaded with as many twists and turns as a good novel—she certainly hadn't expected that from him. "We should go. Sela will be waiting."

Alexa strolled clumsily on the gravel drive, her heels catching between every rock, it seemed, reminding her of when her heel had snagged in a crack and she'd fallen against Hawthorne.

He chuckled. "Why do you torture yourself by wearing those things? They're completely impractical."

"Like I could wear hiking boots with this dress." She wanted to glance back at him but thought better of it and concentrated on the path to the house in back, Hawthorne not far behind her. "I suppose you're going to tell me I shouldn't have worn the dress."

"If we continue this conversation, I'll end up on a slippery slope where I'll inevitably say something that you'll take the wrong way."

"I was so hoping you'd take the bait." *And say how much you liked the dress.* Still, she'd already gotten a wow out of him.

"Not a chance."

"You're great." Laughing, she stopped walking and turned to face him. "That's why I like you, Hawthorne."

He took her hand and weaved his fingers with hers, surprising her and sending warmth streaming all the way to her extremities. "Call me Graeme," he said.

Maybe Barry should have joined them, after all. "All right.

Graeme," she said softly, though she had used it once before.

She liked the way he looked at her when she said his name.

He relinquished her hand, and they walked the remaining length of the drive until they stood on the small porch, though Alexa couldn't stop thinking about the way he'd taken her hand. She knocked twice and the door swept open to reveal her beautiful redheaded sister, Sela. She smiled with the warmth only Sela could give.

"Hello, you two. I saw you in the driveway but didn't want to interrupt." She widened the door and motioned for them to enter.

Alexa hugged her sister, regretting that they lived so far apart and that she'd stayed away for so long. She'd fled Northern California to find a new life, but at times like these, what she left behind crashed down on her heart. She scrunched her face, willing the tears away, knowing she should have come to see Sela when she'd first arrived.

Stepping away from her sister, she placed her hand on Graeme's sturdy arm. "This is Graeme Hawthorne, a local botanist who studies the treetops."

"And I'm Sela." She smiled at Graeme, and his face lit up in response.

"A pleasure to meet you," he said.

A sliver of jealousy coursed through Alexa—would Sela steal his interest? There had always been something about Alexa's older sister—an inner beauty—that snagged men. But Sela had only had eyes for one man.

"Have a seat in the den while I finish dinner. I hope you like smoked salmon."

Alexa didn't mention her aversion to seafood and was surprised that Sela had forgotten. Her sister led them from the foyer through a wide opening into a cozy room where a plush sage sofa and loveseat faced a small wide-screen television. A local news station was on. Photographs and custom-made guitars lined the darkly stained paneled walls except where one wall boasted a large panoramic window showcasing the backyard view—a few redwoods and the Smith River.

Beautiful. Sela had been blessed beyond measure to marry a man who owned such a property. Every frame contained photographs of her looking happy in David's arms, their golden retriever at their feet. But Alexa worried how long Sela would keep the memories of her deceased husband on the wall. "I'll help you, sis," Alexa offered. "Sit down, Haw—Graeme."

"You sure there's nothing I can do?" he asked, looking like he felt out of place.

Alexa smiled. "No. You're good."

Graeme seemed content to watch the news when Alexa left him behind to assist Sela in the kitchen.

"You can get the rolls from the oven," Sela said.

Alexa grabbed a pot holder. "Smells good."

"He's quite a looker. How on earth did you meet him?"

"It's not like that, Sela. We're. . .not together." Alexa dumped the rolls into a bread basket, unsure how to explain her relationship with Graeme. "I'm here to film a documentary and I want to interview him."

"So you asked him to dinner, and you're wearing that dress?" Sela asked, tasting a bit of salmon, a mischievous smile on her face. "Come on, there's something between you two. I saw you in the drive."

Alexa leaned on the counter, considering her response.

"What about Clive? That's gotta be tough." Sela gasped. "Are you still working for him?"

Graeme stepped into the kitchen, his expression unreadable. "I noticed all the photographs. Is your husband joining us for dinner?"

A slight frown creased Sela's forehead. "My husband is deceased."

She lifted the plate of smoked salmon and glided past Graeme, a soft smile on her lips.

Pain swept across his face as he followed Sela. "I'm sorry.

I lost someone, too, so I understand how you feel."

His words hung in the air, pressing heavily on Alexa while she lingered in the kitchen. Graeme was nothing like Clive. He was caring, kind, and considerate.

"Please don't apologize—you couldn't have known." Sela's soft voice drifted from the dining room into the kitchen where Alexa remained.

Great. Alexa hated the thoughts bombarding her, but now Graeme and Sela had something to draw them together.

⁂

After dinner, Sela invited Graeme and Alexa to sit outside. The deck behind Sela's cabin was well made but needed repairs. He considered offering to help since she didn't live that far from him. Mosquito-repelling candles glowed every few feet, or else they probably would have chosen to remain indoors. Either way, when Graeme's day had started this morning, he never could have imagined it would end like this, in the presence of two beautiful and amazing women.

Alexa had seemed more subdued during dinner, though Graeme didn't know her well enough to be sure. For all he knew, she wound down like this at the end of every day. Or maybe it was a matter of being with her sister that effected the change. Often people behaved differently with family. But no, he sensed that something was bothering her.

Though Sela had asked questions about his research during dinner, she'd been gracious enough not to press him on his limited responses. The conversation remained light and upbeat, and he'd found it interesting, especially when Alexa shared about her school days and film degree, and then working for the film production company. Though she hadn't confessed she'd been romantically involved with her boss, a man named Clive, Graeme had his suspicions.

As the sun dipped lower and sunset drew near, Graeme found himself mesmerized, listening to the two women talk about their childhood, and he enjoyed their laughter. Had

Alexa known she'd disarm him simply by including him for a sisters' reunion?

She stared at him from across the deck where she lounged in a wicker chair. She'd finally given up the heels, trading them for a pair of Sela's flip-flops. "What?" she asked.

He sent her a questioning look.

"You were staring at me. What were you thinking?"

Sela yawned in an obviously exaggerated way and stretched her arms. "You two stay out here and enjoy the rest of the evening. But I'm going to hit the sack."

Graeme and Alexa both stood at the same time, protesting. Sela took a couple of steps toward him and squeezed his hand. "I'm so glad to meet you, and I hope to see you again. Please, stay for the rest of the evening if you like. Besides, I know you and Alexa have things to discuss."

"Thank you," Graeme said. It was all he could manage.

Sela crossed the deck to Alexa and hugged her.

"Night, sis," Alexa said. "I'll try not to wake you when I grab my purse and shoes."

When Sela closed the french doors at the back of the cabin, Graeme looked to Alexa, wondering what she planned for them next. Would she end their evening together now? Graeme wasn't ready for it to be over.

"You have an amazing sister," he said.

Alexa smiled, but Graeme noticed the slight crease between her brows. He moved next to her on the deck, the wicker chair squeaking when he sat.

"Sela's available, you know," she said.

So that's what was bothering her? Graeme stared at the decking, wanting to hide his unbidden pleasure at her jealousy. "I don't know. I think she's still in love with her husband."

"I'm worried about her. He's been gone for over two years and she still hasn't let go." Her words sliced through him—she couldn't have known, any more than he could have known about Sela's husband when he asked, so he would temper his words, that is, if he could find them.

"That was insensitive of me." Alexa released the bun from the back of her head, and her long, beautiful hair splayed over her shoulders. "Do you still love the woman you were engaged to?"

He'd shared a little about his relationship with Summer during dinner. "Everyone is different, I suppose. But I think it might take loving someone else to make you forget."

His own words sounded foreign to him, so shocking were they. He'd never thought the day would come. He peered at Alexa now—long and hard—and she finally lifted her striking eyes to meet his gaze. A knot swelled in his throat and he cleared it.

"You know, this isn't why you invited me. You're supposed to try to convince me to give you an interview for your documentary."

He loved the soft smile that spread across her face. Something in her entire demeanor had changed; he'd noticed that when he'd seen her on the trail today. Had the redwoods transformed the person he'd first met into someone more approachable? But why did he care? He wasn't looking to meet someone to love—in fact, far from it.

"Are you saying you're not convinced already?" She laughed softly.

Now, *that* he could get accustomed to. Plus, she wasn't hammering him with her I'm-a-professional-and-I-always-get-what-I-want attitude. "Oh, I'm convinced. But I just can't deliver."

Her entire expression seemed to crumple, but he simply couldn't comply, nor could he explain. If his paranoid fear turned out to be valid, he could be putting her in danger.

"But I'll do what I can to help. You can interview Randy and I'll fill in the gaps. Can you live with that?" Would that be enough to spare her involvement in his predicament? Or had he just crossed a precarious line?

She jumped from the chair. "Yes!"

He rose to join her and laughed at her complete, childlike exuberance, astounded to see this side of her. Despite his unease at agreeing to this small thing, pleasure suffused his heart—it had been far too long since he'd made someone happy or felt the joy in return.

She laughed. "You have no idea how happy you've made me."

Then she popped up on her toes and gave him a peck on his cheek. "Thank you," she whispered.

With that, she could have pushed him over with her little finger. Her light fragrance wrapped around him, mesmerizing him. Staring straight ahead at the river, listening to the soothing rush of water, he finally realized that it had grown completely dark.

When he glanced at his surroundings, Alexa was gone. "Alexa?"

At the back door of the house, Alexa dangled her little black bag and crazy heels in one hand and softly shut the door with the other. She glanced his way then began to slip her shoes on.

Graeme crossed the yard to meet her. She pressed her hand against the wall to support herself while she tugged on her heels. Soft lighting from a nearby lamp lit her features. Shoes on, Alexa leaned against the wall of the log cabin and gazed into his eyes.

The mane that she'd released minutes before hung to one side, over her right shoulder. Longing to touch it, Graeme did the unthinkable and lifted a dark, silky strand and rubbed it between his fingers. He released the tendril of her gorgeous hair and moved his hand to the soft, smooth skin of her cheek. She closed her eyes and—had she shuddered? An ache coursed through him.

Alexa's eyes remained closed, and Graeme drew in the scent of her, closing the space that separated his lips from hers.

Suddenly a dog barked nearby. He jumped, startled. The french doors opened, and Sela stepped outside.

"Graeme, Alexa? Is that you?" She took another step and spotted them, looking every bit like she'd been asleep. "I'm sorry—oh, I'm sorry, guys."

"No, it's fine. We were just leaving." Graeme took Alexa's hand in his. "Thank you for dinner."

On the drive back to Alexa's motel, he kept her hand solidly in his, resting on the console between them, though he wasn't sure why. He couldn't make any sense out of what he was doing. Neither of them spoke but rather languished in a comfortable silence.

This was going much too fast for his comfort. As a scientist, he spent weeks, months, and years collecting data, which he studied before making an opinion—his credibility relied on analyzing the data correctly.

He had the vague sensation that his lack of objectivity regarding Alexa would end up putting them both in jeopardy—either physical danger or danger involving matters of the heart—and either way, he was in trouble.

ten

Alexa had been given a new lease on life since Graeme agreed to help her. Sure-footed and lighthearted, she followed him, along with Barry and Randy, through the redwoods, off-trail, trekking around the sword ferns, waist-high and taller, and the ancient-looking mutant trees. Funny, they were hiking in the Valley of the Lost Groves. Memories from the dark, lonely night she'd spent lost in the woods attempted to swallow her alive, but she couldn't blow this opportunity. She was stronger than that now, and put one foot in front of the other.

Graeme knew what he was doing and where he was. It wasn't likely he'd get them lost; the confidence he exuded as he led them deeper reassured her. Besides, she couldn't imagine any place she'd rather be than trudging behind him in the wilderness. What had gotten into her?

The fresh air and inspiring setting—despite her disturbing memories—or was it Graeme? She enjoyed traipsing through this valley where redwoods resembled prehistoric temple ruins that nature had taken back, and it was so quiet she could hear God's voice if she tried.

The thought sent a pang through her heart. She paused, pressing her hands against her chest. It had been a very long time since she'd even tried. . . . She'd prayed that night she'd gotten lost in the woods, but God hadn't listened. If He had, she wouldn't have gotten lost.

But here she was, alive and well. Maybe He had listened after all. *God, help me to find You again.*

Barry nudged her from behind. "You okay?"

Alexa nodded and pushed forward again, following Graeme. Carrying his backpack, he led the group as he explained the changing climate's effect on the redwoods and said that most of the research was ongoing. A giant had fallen across a deep gully, creating a natural bridge. Graeme crossed first, then Randy.

When Alexa's turn came, she stepped onto the trunk, wet and slick with moss. Her left foot slipped, but she quickly regained her balance.

"Wait." Graeme inched his way forward on the log toward her then held out his hand.

"I can do this," she said, but accepted his offer anyway.

"I know you can." His hand was sure and strong in hers, backing up the confidence in his words. He ushered her across the massive trunk, and together they scrambled up the bank of the gully, which was higher on that side.

"Thanks." Alexa looked up in his face, mere inches from hers. Her hand remained in his. His proximity reminded her of the near kiss last night. Or had she just imagined it? She'd been hard-pressed to focus on much else after that.

Aware they had onlookers, though in her peripheral vision she could see Randy staring skyward and Barry still making his way forward on the trunk, she inched back, putting some space between them.

"You're welcome," he said, smiling down, then released her hand and marched forward.

Having crossed the log bridge, Barry was breathless and wiped the sweat from his forehead. "How much farther?"

No one responded to his question. Randy looked at his compass and map, conferring with Graeme a few yards ahead of Alexa and Barry.

"Why not use GPS?" Barry asked, clearly disgruntled with the long hike.

Having to refer to a map didn't exactly mean they were lost, but a familiar anxiety coiled inside Alexa.

"I brought it, but the woods are too dense here and I can't get a signal. Hence, the compass and map." Randy held up the map for Graeme to examine. "We know where we're going, though—don't worry."

Barry sent Alexa a mocking expression, meaning he didn't believe the guy. This could take awhile.

Water gurgled nearby and Alexa, making certain Graeme remained in sight, searched the area for the brook she heard trickling. Finding it, she relaxed on a mossy rock, resting her legs.

Barry found a boulder to lean against. "Is it necessary for us to hike so far?" he asked, keeping his voice low.

"He's helping us now, Barry. Let's just go with it. Who knows what he'll show us?" Alexa took a swig from her bottled water.

"You mean he's helping *you*." Barry leaned over and picked up a sliver of bark. "You work fast, by the way."

Alexa took her time and another gulp, considering Barry's tone. "What are you getting at?"

"Meaning you and the scientist are an item already. Nice work."

She glared at him. "You're misreading things. I'm not using him."

"Fine by me, but what about Clive?"

Alexa glanced Graeme's way and found him still discussing something with Randy. She hoped it had nothing to do with location—if there was a time for them to get lost, it *would* be when she was with him.

"Clive and I are history. You know that." She reworked her hair, securing it tighter in the ponytail, then tugged the baseball cap in place again.

Barry took a drink of water and watched her, a strange, knowing look in his eyes. But what?

"Unless you know something I don't," she said and watched him, gauging his reaction.

"I might. But what do you want me to tell Clive?"

Alexa stood from the rock. "Nothing. He hasn't had the common courtesy to speak to me since I got here. Unprofessional, if you ask me. If he wants an update on this project, you direct him to me. Understood?"

"Look, Alexa. I'm in a bad position here. Surely you can see that."

She stuck a finger into the brook, watching the water skirt around it. "I know. And I'm sorry about the hike this morning. I just want to capture as much as I can while we're here."

"Don't worry. I think we're going to have plenty of footage. But listen to what you're saying. We're going to finish at some point and then we'll leave this forest behind, along with the scientist in the trees."

Graeme pushed through a fern to stand next to Alexa. Disappointment flashed in his eyes; then it was gone. Had he heard what Barry said?

The emotions Graeme stirred in her had been unexpected, and so far she'd been able to ignore the niggling reminder that she wasn't here to stay. What did she and Graeme have together, really? For certain, they would not have enough time to see things through, to discover if they had a future together. A crazy notion to begin with. He wasn't her type.

"You really shouldn't wander off. There are bears and cougars here, not to mention you could get lost."

❧

Graeme stepped into obvious tension between Alexa and her cameraman, and he didn't like it. Although Graeme hadn't known Barry that long, he hadn't trusted him since the moment they met. But then, he hadn't trusted Alexa at first. His attraction to her had clouded his judgment, no doubt there. But he had no desire to overcome it, Summer's face quickly slipping into the shadow of memories in the light of Alexa's smile.

She stared at him, a dark reflection in her eyes. What had happened to her bright demeanor? "How often do people get lost in these woods?" she asked.

"This valley is off the trails, off the grid, and anyone who finds it stumbles upon it, or knows about it like I do. But if you're asking how often people get lost in any redwood state park, I guess that depends on what you mean by lost. If you mean lost for a day or two, or forever, not very often, but it happens."

As she tore her gaze from him, grief flitted across her features; then she shoved by him and strolled to Randy about ten yards away, appearing ready to continue with the hike.

Barry shoved from the rock. "Where exactly are we going?"

The cameraman was a funny guy. How could he not be swept up in the beauty of this place? Graeme pushed aside his concerns for Alexa and his frustration with Barry and smiled, hoping to restore the earlier friendly camaraderie of the hike. "It's not far now."

Suddenly she was at his side. "Are we lost, Graeme, or have you been taking us in circles on purpose?"

Graeme didn't respond, appreciating that she'd noticed.

"I recognize this little brook from a half hour ago." She cocked a brow and acted tough and challenging, but Graeme didn't miss the shard of alarm in her eyes.

"I know where I'm going—don't worry. I don't want you to remember how to find where I'm taking you."

"As if." At least she gave him a teasing smile.

"I discovered a tree that I named King Solomon, one of the largest trees in the coastal redwoods. Only a few people, botanists like me, know where to find it. I'm just trying to keep the location a secret in case you ever happen to wander here on your own. By the way, you can't put the location or even mention the Valley of the Lost Groves in your documentary."

"Fair enough," she said. An engaging smile returned to her lips and her eyes shone again.

Graeme's heart staggered at the breadth of his feelings for her. How had it happened so fast?

"Why keep it a secret? Shouldn't people be allowed to see this important discovery?" Barry strung his camera across the other shoulder. That had to be uncomfortable for the length of their hike.

"Recreational climbers, adventurers, and sightseers would destroy this unadulterated forest if the world knew where to find it. I'm protecting the environment. You can put *that* in your film, only referring to Randy. Right, Randy?"

He grinned. "Yeah, sure. What he said."

Graeme led the hikers again, and this time Alexa hiked next to him. Being able to show her this exotic forest exhilarated him. A few minutes later they stood at the base of the colossal redwood, and Graeme said nothing because words were not enough.

He watched Alexa's soft lips edge open as her gaze spanned the length and girth of the giant. "Wow."

"Can I film now?" Barry asked.

Graeme knew that Barry was eager to get this done with, but even he appeared impressed.

"Randy, share about the tree. Alexa, you can do a voice-over later, but I want you to know what you're looking at now."

"Sure thing." Randy dropped his pack. "King Solomon is one of the largest coastal redwoods, at least that we've discovered. We measured it at 365 feet, containing 45,000 cubic feet of wood. That's how scientists measure and compare the size of a tree—by how much timber they contain. Height is only one comparison."

Randy rubbed his hand along the rough, reddish bark. "What's really impressive about this tree is that the girth, which is twenty feet around, is nearly the same all the way to the top. There are fifty extra trunks shooting from the main trunk, and six fire caves."

Barry shut off the camera. "Excuse me, fire caves?"

"An opening where the tree is hollowed out by a fire or some other damage," Randy said. "Three of the caves are big enough for a person or two to walk inside."

While Randy continued to answer Barry's questions, Graeme made his way around the tree to where Alexa had disappeared to. He found her running her palm down the trunk like she was petting an animal.

He sidled next to her. "What do you think?"

Shaking her head, she pursed her lips. "How can anyone understand unless they can see it in person?"

Graeme frowned. He'd already explained why he didn't want people to see this.

Smiling, she glanced at him. "I don't mean it that way. I understand the public would destroy it, and there are so few things left untouched anymore."

Alexa reached up and pressed her hand against Graeme's cheek, forcing him to admit he'd longed for her touch all day. He lost himself in her silvery-blue eyes.

"I realize you took a risk by bringing us here. Thank you for that."

She slid her hand down his face, and he felt her plucking every tightly strung chord in him. Finally, she let her hand drop, but he caught her wrist, unwilling to relinquish the electric charge she gave him. He might be a scientist, but this woman could reduce his brains to mush, and for some insane reason, he liked that.

"Remember the first time I saw you in the tree and what I asked you?"

"You asked if I would take you climbing."

Alexa yelped and yanked off the baseball cap. She shook out her hair. "I think I have something crawling around in there. Do you see something?"

Graeme wanted to run his fingers through her long mane. "Nope, you're good."

Alexa reworked her hair back into the ponytail, but she left the cap off. Good, he could see her hair and her eyes better now.

"Well?"

"It's dangerous. One wrong move and you could be seriously injured." *If not killed.* He swallowed to push down the growing knot.

"I trust you."

The problem was, Graeme couldn't trust himself to make a good decision when anywhere near Alexa.

eleven

Alexa glanced down at the needle-carpeted ground from where she hovered 120 feet above.

Good thing she wasn't afraid of heights, but then, if she were, she never would have pressed Graeme to take her up. She'd done some rock climbing in the past, but tree climbing was nothing like it. The method Graeme used to move around in the trees was called an arborist style of climbing, only modified for climbing trees like the redwoods.

Yesterday, after they'd returned from the long jaunt through the Valley of the Lost Groves, Barry had been tired and grumbled that he wanted to rest. The hike had exhilarated Alexa, especially when Graeme agreed to consider taking her up in the trees, depending on how easily she picked up the tree-climbing lessons. They'd taken a couple of hours to break, shower, and eat, and then Graeme had given her a crash course on tree climbing.

Alexa had given it everything she had, and she'd been rewarded with a look of admiration on Graeme's face. Satisfied she could climb with him, they'd gone their separate ways to rest up for the big climb the next day when they would return to King Solomon.

She could hardly believe that she was climbing a giant redwood with a tree canopy scientist, though Graeme had refused to allow Barry to film any part of their climb. The cameraman had appeared relieved, and he'd not come with them on the hike to the tree.

At the moment, she had secured an anchor point with the rope and hung next to Graeme, who looked adorable in his helmet.

"It's like a different world up here, a different planet," she said. "I feel like I'm a child again, sitting in a swing."

He jerked his head around to look at her. "Is that all?"

Her cheeks grew warm. "Well, it's much different, but you know what I mean. I've been to the top of the Statue of Liberty, and of course the Empire State Building. Neither of those compare to this. There's nothing like it."

"I'm glad I was able to bring you up and show you my world." He grinned beneath his helmet and swung his rope over another branch, another anchor point. "Now, are you good to hang here for a minute? I want to saw off a dead branch. Our ropes twitching around can knock that loose. We call that a widow-maker, by the way."

He grinned and winked, which did crazy things to Alexa's insides, then pulled a small hacksaw from his pack.

"Are we going any higher?" she asked. "We're not even halfway up."

"We've still got plenty to explore, even at this height." He studied her, making her feel bashful, which was a rarity for her. "I don't want to press our luck."

"You don't believe in luck, do you?"

"No. Just stay here. I'll be right back." He disappeared around one of the many trunks that sprang from the main tree, which they'd been climbing in for the last half hour.

Sitting in her harness, Alexa held on to the rope and enjoyed the quiet of the forest. Her radio squawked. "You still there?"

"Where else would I be?"

"I'm still cutting. I'll be there in a few minutes. Stay where you are."

Ten more minutes passed and the first shivers of concern crawled over her. If she contacted Graeme, she feared she could cause him injury if he were in the middle of cutting the rotten branch.

A crack resounded through the forest, sending shards of panic through her. She clung to her rope, hoping none of the rotten branches above were going to fall. Was Graeme all right?

Then it hit her: there were more dangers in the trees than height alone.

"Alexa?" Graeme's voice squawked over the radio again.

"I'm here." She didn't like that he seemed miles away even though he was in the same tree.

"The branch fell away, only it's blocking my path. I want you to climb around to the brook side of the tree. I'll meet you there. Can you do that?"

Alexa looked to her right. "Yes."

She was secured to the tree by the main rope. All she had to do was attach alternate ends for an anchor point, and she could move around like Spiderwoman. She grinned, loving the freedom she felt. No wonder Graeme spent most of his time in the trees.

After connecting a new anchor point, she began climbing toward the direction of the brook. The way the branches crossed each other on this side they became a tangled mess, and before long, she found herself surrounded by pillars of rotten wood.

I can't make it through here. Things were beginning to get a little tricky. Maybe a less complicated tree would have been better. What had Graeme told her again? There were fifty extra trunks shooting from the main trunk—if she hadn't seen the lofty system of trunks towering to the sky herself, the image would have been mind-boggling and impossible to imagine.

She had no choice but to go back. Graeme would be disappointed in her, and Alexa was unaccustomed to disappointing people. She hated that. But more than that, she hated letting Graeme down. How strange that she cared so much about what he thought of her.

Alexa prepared to reposition her anchor point, but then. . .where had she come from? She searched the section of ten or so trunks she'd just weaved her way through, but nothing looked familiar. What was worse, everything around her appeared decayed, and she didn't want to secure herself to rotten wood that could snap and fall, taking her with it.

Not good.

Anxiety coiled in her chest, and her hands slipped on the rope. Memories lashed at her like branches. She was a child again, running through the woods that were growing dark long before the sun even set.

No matter which way she ran, she couldn't find her father, who'd taken her hiking that day. Why had she wanted to follow the rabbit? Why hadn't she listened to her father?

She'd called out for him as she ran and ran. Finally exhausted, she'd slumped against a fallen trunk, terrified of the dark forest.

Alexa snapped her thoughts from the vision-like memory. "No. . ." She fumbled with the rope, feeling it slipping through her sweaty palms.

Graeme's words washed over her. *"Panic will get you killed."*

But she couldn't help it. She'd never considered she could actually get lost among the tree trunks in a redwood.

She squeezed her eyes shut and pressed her forehead against the branch nearest her, feeling the rough bark against her skin.

I will not panic. She drew in a calming breath and turned her thoughts toward God. "I'm lost again, God. I swore I'd never come back here. Please help me."

"Alexa?"

The radio almost slid from her grasp as she yanked it free from the strap. "Graeme."

"Where are you?"

A knot choked off her words.

"Can you hear me? Where are you?"

"Graeme," she said. "I'm so sorry. . ."

"What's wrong?" Concern threaded his voice.

"I can't believe I'm going to say this, but. . . I'm lost."

"Stay where you are. I'll find you."

Alexa rested her head against the rope, loving the reassurance she heard in his voice. There was definitely something special about this man. Every so often she glanced at her watch as she tried to forget the night she'd gotten lost as a child. But every minute that ticked past was a painful reminder of the hours she'd waited to be discovered.

"Alexa." Graeme's voice was strong and confident.

She realized that he wasn't speaking over the radio. She searched for him and spotted him on the other side of the trunk nearest her.

"You must be disappointed in me," she said.

He was closer now, making his way over to her. "How could you think that? Of course not. I never should have left you. But let's save this conversation for later and get out of here."

Alexa followed Graeme, anchor point to anchor point, out of the nest of rotten branches and trunks—all of which grew from King Solomon.

An hour later, when she planted her feet on the soft ground, she sighed and slid all the way down, sitting with her back against the massive trunk. She was exhausted. How was she going to walk out of here?

Graeme threw the ropes and equipment down by his pack to organize. His face looked drawn, like he'd aged. He tossed the last rope over and then strolled her way, plopping down next to her, and took her hand.

"You okay?"

She smiled, hoping to push aside his concerns. "Sure. That was an experience I'll never forget."

He chuckled, sounding anything but happy.

Leaning her head against the trunk, and catching her breath mentally and physically, she turned to him. "I mean that in a good way."

❧

Sitting close to her now, Graeme studied her, realizing too late how much he'd wanted her to experience and enjoy this. It meant the world to him. But he'd put her at risk. Because he'd wanted to connect with her in this so desperately, he'd not used good judgment. When he'd called her on the radio, he could hardly bear to hear the trembling in her voice.

Hearing her say she was lost had shaken him.

"You seemed pretty rattled when I found you." He looked away from her and rubbed his forehead. "I never should have left you. Never should have taken you up to begin with."

Graeme pushed up and stood over her, hating the guilt weighing on him. Was he destined to care about someone, only to lead them into danger? He began winding the ropes and bundling them, putting his focus where it belonged.

Alexa approached and pressed her hand gently against his side. He stiffened, unsure how to react to the heat of her touch. She found his hand.

She weaved her fingers through his. "Look at me."

He faced her.

"I would do it all over again." A soft smile lifted her lips, her face inches from his. "There was nothing like it in the world. Not even the top of the Statue of Liberty could compare."

At her words, hope corded around his heart. He searched her eyes, admiring the way the silver mingled with the blue, casting an unusual light and making them look like cut topaz. "You mean that?"

What am I? Sixteen?

Her smile grew and it seemed she was holding back. "And I think there's no one like you in the world."

Graeme's heart hammered in his ears. Her words floated to him on a whisper and tugged him toward her and downward. He pressed his lips against hers, feeling their softness, and sensing her response, he wrapped his arms around her, drawing her closer. Alexa slid her hands up and around his neck.

Powerful sensations coursed through him. But that wasn't all. Part of him shouted that he was betraying Summer's memory, that he was being unfaithful. But that was only because his heart had failed to let her go. With Alexa in his arms, he knew his heart was finally ready.

The scent of Alexa's shampoo mingled with the outdoors and swirled around him, wrapping him in a warm cocoon. He knew when the kiss ended that he would never be the same.

Too soon, Alexa loosened her hands from behind his neck and eased her lips from his, but she lingered then kissed him lightly. "Are you ready to head back to civilization?"

Keeping her in his arms, he chuckled. "Do we have to?"

She pressed her head against his chest, and he held her close. Having this amazing woman in his arms, having just taken her into the giant he'd discovered and named, was like a dream.

Graeme had never been a dreamer, and he feared this wasn't real.

twelve

As Alexa stood at the door to her motel room, staring up at Graeme after their day in the trees, she grinned, feeling like this was their second date, if she could call it that. "Thanks for today, Graeme. You transported me to an incredible new world."

He leaned against the doorframe, smiling down at her. "I'm glad you enjoyed it, and I'm a little surprised, considering. . ."

"Considering what?"

"The second time I saw you, you were upset because you'd broken a heel." He grinned. "What did you call it again? A Jimmy Choo?"

He remembers that? "Maybe being here so close to nature has been good for me."

The look in his eyes said he agreed, and it did things to her insides, reminding her of their kiss. She leaned in and he met her halfway, only he didn't wrap her in his arms but instead pressed his lips gently against hers. He lingered there, hesitant, as though contemplating his next move.

"I have to go," he whispered, his breath warm against her face, then stepped back. When he headed to his Jeep, disappointment skirted her heart. But she knew they each had things to do.

She needed to shower.

"Graeme?"

He paused next to the vehicle, the door open. Alexa walked over to him. "Seeing that tree, climbing in it, changed me. Don't you think the rest of the world needs to see and experience that? Please consider allowing us to film you climbing in King Solomon. It would mean the world—"

"No." He cut her off and shuttered away the earlier

warmth and passion in his gaze before sliding into his vehicle. "I'm sorry."

Alexa took a step back as he shut the door and watched him drive from the parking lot. He'd thrown up his wall again, looking like the same man who'd stonewalled her before as though they hadn't shared the experience today. . .or the kiss.

What was with him? She should have waited for the right time and place to ask, but she thought they were past that.

She trudged to her door, feeling the aches and pains of a day spent hiking and climbing; then she spotted Barry leaving Sally's diner and waited. As he strolled her way, Barry gnawed on a toothpick, looking like a man who'd enjoyed his meal.

When he stood in front of his door, he grinned. "You look a little worn, but no worse for the wear."

"I'm not sure if that's a compliment or an insult." She laughed and unlocked her door. "I'm tired to the bone, but it was well worth it."

"It was a compliment. You're a different woman than when we came here, Alexa."

"Now that sounds suspiciously like there's an insult buried in there somewhere, but I'm too tired to take issue with it."

Barry leaned against the wall, crossing his arms. "You're not as uptight now as you were when we arrived. There. It's out."

Alexa wasn't sure if Barry wanted to pick a fight with her, and she especially didn't want to spoil the end to what was almost a perfect day. Had she not gotten lost in the tree, which sounded incredible to her now, it could have been the perfect day.

She shoved her door open. "Good night, Barry."

"Before you go. . ."

Alexa paused in the doorway, eager for a long, hot shower. "What is it?"

"You've gotten everything you need now?"

Tension squeezed her shoulders. "I'm trying to talk Graeme into letting us film him climbing in the trees."

"Look, I think you've been brilliant, but I don't think even you are going to make that happen."

Alexa sagged a little, hating to admit defeat. "Give me two more days. We'll show Graeme what we have and get voiceovers where needed, see what else he can suggest. You okay with that?"

"You've never asked me my opinion before." Barry grinned.

❧

Two days later Alexa stood with Barry at the front door of Graeme's home and knocked. He'd given meticulous directions; otherwise they never would have found the secluded log cabin located a half mile's drive from the main highway on an unpaved, well-hidden path. Alexa had shuddered when she'd first stepped from the rental, wondering how he could stand to be so alone. It was a far cry from Manhattan.

Graeme opened the door and grinned, though Alexa detected something had changed. "You found me."

"Barely," she said and waited for him to invite them in.

He extended his arm to gesture them inside, and Alexa stepped in first. She took in the quaint living room, accented with a huge circular rug, a couple of sofas, and a rocking chair. A woodstove burned in the corner.

"Thank you for agreeing to this, Graeme. I know you like your privacy."

"Do you?" He lifted a glass of water to his lips.

Alexa couldn't read his expression, but asking him if they could film him climbing in King Solomon had definitely changed his attitude. She was surprised he agreed to see her this morning at his house. She was thankful that at some point during their time together he'd shared his phone number, with the stipulation that no one else knew, or she wouldn't have been able to contact him.

She cleared her throat. "Yes. And as we discussed on the

phone, we'd like to show you what we've done so far and get your thoughts. Barry and I worked late into the night editing as much as we could."

Graeme nodded. "Can I get you coffee? Orange juice? Water?"

"I'm good. I'm going to retrieve the equipment from the car," Barry said.

When he disappeared, tears stabbed behind Alexa's eyes, surprising her. She took a step toward Graeme, hating that her feelings were melting away her professionalism. But she feared Graeme believed she was simply using him to get her film.

"Look, I'm sorry that my question offended you." *Please open back up to me.*

Graeme turned his back on her then strolled into the kitchen and set his glass on the counter. He released a heavy sigh then turned around and leaned against the counter. "Come here."

Relief melted her heart, and she moved to Graeme, hoping she'd gotten through to him. He pulled her into his arms and Alexa held on.

"I'm sorry for acting like a jerk. I wish you could film me, film the tree. I wish I could make you understand."

When she heard the car door slam outside, she knew Barry was headed back inside. Alexa stepped out of Graeme's arms and resumed her professional posture. Still, she gave him a light peck on his cheek. "I do understand, and thank you," she whispered. She understood why it was important to keep the tree hidden, but she didn't understand why Graeme was afraid to appear on camera himself. What was behind that?

❧

For the next two and a half hours, Graeme stared at Alexa's computer screen and the roughly edited portions of her film and offered information and his suggestions for improvement. Alexa handed him a rough draft of what he was to read into a mic, serving as a narrator to the film.

Though he was hesitant, he ended up agreeing. He helped polish the draft by adding his own words where necessary. Alexa's appearance in his forest to film his trees seemed to shine a light down on him, revealing that he'd chosen to run, and that he'd been hiding for months now.

Her bravery and tenacity in climbing King Solomon, and in getting the footage she needed for her film, amplified his cowardice in hiding.

The real clincher? He wasn't even sure hiding was necessary anymore, if it ever was.

"I have to say, I'm impressed with what you've done so far."

"Really?" Alexa flashed him a warm and brilliant smile, lighting his heart. He was glad he could make her smile like that.

Barry packed away the mic and recording equipment. "If this is it, we'll be heading back to New York in a couple of days. Won't we, Alexa?"

Alexa scowled at Barry then turned to Graeme, blinking back tears.

"Already?" Graeme had known this was coming. Then why did the news shock him? What if he offered them King Solomon after all? No, what was he thinking?

"But there's still this swimming hole I spotted in the Smith River that I want to jump in before we head out." Barry opened the door and walked to the car.

Alexa slipped her laptop into its case slowly. When she finished, she glanced at Graeme, her lips trembling with a sad smile.

"From New York, we'll travel to Costa Rica to film in the rain forest, adding to the documentary. You wouldn't happen to know someone there I could talk to about the trees, would you?" She sniffled and laughed, wiping at something in her eye.

Costa Rica? Graeme stared at her in stunned silence. Was this some kind of joke?

"Graeme?" Alexa touched his shoulder. "Are you okay?"

He turned his back to her and pressed his hands on the

table, staring at the floor. "No. There's no one in Costa Rica. You shouldn't go there."

"What do you mean? There's a project for reforestation there. It's the perfect place. Surely you—"

"Don't go."

"Are you telling me not to go to Costa Rica? Or are you telling me not to go to New York? Help me to understand what you're saying."

Suddenly the scene exploded in his mind. Summer telling him she'd come across incriminating information at Jarvis, the big construction company that would build the dam, and then the pickup truck appearing in his rearview mirror, coming up on them fast. The truck slammed into the back of their compact car. Graeme tried to correct his course and maneuver away from the truck. But the driver was intent on forcing them off the bridge. His stomach dropped with the vehicle as Summer screamed, the water from below coming at them fast as they dove into the estuary.

Alexa placed her hand over his, causing the present to rush back. Graeme gasped, dragging in air. Slowly he drew his gaze up to meet hers and thought he saw his own anguish reflected in her eyes.

"Graeme," she whispered. "What's going on?"

"Nothing." He shook his head to clear the images and headed for the kitchen to grab his glass of water. Alexa followed.

"Don't tell me nothing. Something is wrong."

"I can't tell you." How could he? Besides, the less she knew, the safer she was. Graeme slammed the water down then turned the faucet on and splashed his face. "Now, you have to go, and that's for the best."

"Don't shut me out like this, Graeme. Please. We've come a long way, you and me, since that first day we met. I thought you trusted me by now. But then last night and now today, you're closing me off like there's nothing between us."

Graeme swung his gaze to hers. "What is there between

us, Alexa? Tell me. You're going home to New York. You never planned to stay. Both of us knew that. You used me. Maybe I used you a little, too."

The hurt pooling in her eyes was unbearable. Graeme looked away and listened to the sound of her footsteps as she walked out the front door.

thirteen

When Alexa's vehicle had driven out of sight, lost somewhere along the wooded path out, Graeme shoved away from the kitchen counter where he'd been leaning and moved to the sofa, dropping like he carried a heavy burden. Resting his elbows on his knees, he hung his head.

To think that Alexa could be working for Jarvis and this was all a charade to drag Graeme back down to Costa Rica was beyond paranoid.

Why go to that much trouble? But then, why kill someone in the first place?

In his line of work, crossing paths with someone creating a documentary was to be expected. If he hadn't fallen a little too hard for the beautiful filmmaker, and she hadn't just shared that she was headed to the same place where he'd lost someone, and had fled for his life, maybe he wouldn't think he was going crazy right now.

Either way, he was at risk of being exposed. Either way, he couldn't stand the thought of Alexa going to Costa Rica. Somehow he had to stop her.

Graeme picked up the phone and called Peter—the man had been one of his closest friends when Graeme had returned from Costa Rica. Maybe he could help Graeme to see clearly what should be his next step, if he needed to pack up and move on. Would his life ever consist of something more than fleeing or hiding?

While Graeme waited for an answer to the ring, someone knocked on the door. He jerked around to face the windows, feeling on edge. Through the window he saw Pastor Jacob, another of his closest friends, and he definitely needed someone to talk to right now.

Thank You, Lord.

If only Jacob's advice didn't border on cryptic.

Graeme hung up the phone, deciding to call Peter later. He opened the door to a smiling Jacob, though concern shone in his eyes.

"I hope you don't mind me paying you a visit. I haven't seen you in a few days and wanted to check on you."

"You're welcome here anytime. Come in." Graeme swung the door wide.

"I saw a couple of visitors pulling from your drive onto the main road. Is that what has you looking like a buck that can't decide whether to fight or run?"

Graeme chuckled. "That depends on what I'm up against. Care for some coffee?"

"Sounds good." Jacob followed him to the kitchen. "What are you up against, son?"

"As a scientist, I have to say that all the data isn't in yet, but I think I've just been nudged out of my comfort zone."

"God will do that to us every time."

"How can you think this is God?"

Jacob's boisterous laughter resounded through the cabin. "God never lets those He's called stay comfortable, or hidden, for long."

Slamming his cup down a little too hard, Graeme studied Jacob. "Who said anything about God calling me?"

"Because, Graeme, He's entrusted you with the truth, and you're keeping it hidden. What did I tell you last time we spoke?"

" 'The truth shall set you free.' But honestly, that's a bit obscure. You could be referring to anything."

"We both know I'm referring to why you fled and why you're here."

Graeme crossed his arms, thinking on Jacob's words. "I'm here because this is where I've always wanted to be. I love it here. Things just worked out this way. So what if the canopy keeps me hidden?"

Jacob tossed his head back, finishing the last of his coffee; then he set the cup down. "Well, looks like you still have some wrangling to do. So I'll leave you to it."

He turned to make his way to the door, leaving Graeme more frustrated and disappointed than he'd been when Jacob arrived.

"Wait," Graeme said.

Jacob paused and turned around. "What is it, son?"

"There's someone else involved now. I'm afraid she could be heading into danger." Alexa would talk to people in Costa Rica about the film, and someone would find out she knew Graeme and where to find him.

"You have always had the power to stop this. It's in your hands."

੧

In Crescent City, Alexa sat in the rental while Barry picked up a few items at a local drugstore.

She decided to enjoy the weather, so she climbed from the car and leaned against the hood, her phone to her ear. As soon as they'd come out of the dead zone on the drive from the redwood park, Alexa's phone had pinged, letting her know she had several messages. To her astonishment, one of them was from Clive, asking her to return his call. She'd fumed inwardly, not wanting Barry to know the extent of her frustrations and then report back to Clive. She strongly suspected the only reason Clive had called now was because Barry had informed him of the nature of her relationship with Graeme.

A relationship that had nowhere to go.

Clive's voice mail came on. *Figures.* Alexa left a quick message and informed him she would be back in the dead zone within the hour. He could call her at the motel.

Just as well. She was in no frame of mind to talk to the man. Graeme and her dilemma with him had occupied her mind, sweeping Clive out of any remaining closets.

Though she didn't blame Graeme for speaking the truth— shining the light on what they had both ignored—his words had wounded her, and the pain still lingered.

"You have to go. It's for the best."

The most frustrating part? She was no longer certain she wanted to leave Northern California.

Coming back here, she admitted that her ties to this place ran far deeper than she realized. After getting lost—the trauma hadn't ended there. Her mother had blamed her father for letting her out of his sight on their hike that day. Before any of them realized what was happening, the blame escalated and her father left her mother, left them all.

Alexa had never stopped blaming herself. In New York it had been easy for her to forget the life she'd left behind. Perhaps that's why Clive had sent her here—to remind her where she'd come from and what he could do for her, keeping her in line. She never should have confided in him.

Did any of that even matter now? Graeme had somehow changed her perspective. She wasn't certain she wanted to leave him. They'd shared a kiss or two, but in her world one or two kisses didn't make a commitment. Still, Alexa knew that things with Graeme went much deeper—they were connected in a way she couldn't define, and she didn't want to lose that connection.

Why had she allowed herself to be carried away with him? What did she expect him to do? Ask her to marry him? They were opposites and, in fact, lived on opposite sides of the country.

She couldn't get out of her head how upset Graeme had been about her leaving. If only she knew whether his reaction was about her leaving for New York or her plans to travel to Costa Rica.

She glanced behind her at the drugstore. Barry was still inside, giving her an opportunity to do an Internet search on her smartphone.

"Okay, Graeme. What connections do you have in Costa Rica?"

A call came through. Alexa glanced at the number.

Clive. Her palms grew slick and her pulse raced. He had far too much power over her.

"Hello, Clive, it's good to hear from you." She plastered a smile on her face, knowing he couldn't see it, but maybe it would come through her voice.

"Finally. I hate that you've been unreachable for the better part of three weeks."

She stifled her sarcastic response. "Yes, well, just working on this project. I think you'll be more than pleased."

"Right, on that project. The sponsor is waffling, so I need you back in New York as soon as possible. No sense wasting any more money."

"We're almost done, Clive. What's the problem?"

"There are already plenty of documentaries about the redwoods, don't you think?"

Acid burned in her throat. He'd sent her to do this, and now he was changing his mind? Alexa closed her eyes and drew in a breath, picturing Graeme and his love for the trees. "No, Clive. There aren't any like the footage we have, or the information and sources." But Alexa couldn't publish Graeme's name.

"Source? You mean like your Dr. Hawthorne. Barry's told me about him."

Is that why you're calling, Clive? You're jealous? "Oh, so you've been communicating with Barry and not me? Well, I haven't a clue what Barry told you, but Graeme Hawthorne is brilliant. There is no one else like him."

"But you can't use him on the film, can you? I already know about that, too."

She wanted to wring Barry's neck. "Hold your judgment until you've seen the film. I have a new slant on this, and it includes a trip to Costa Rica before it's done." Alexa held her breath.

Clive went silent for a few seconds. Alexa almost thought she'd lost her connection.

Barry climbed into the car behind her, throwing a bag into the backseat.

"Alexa," Clive said, his voice gentle this time, and holding a note of longing. Perhaps he was trying to stir old feelings in her. "You never would have come to work for us if I didn't believe in you, see your uncanny ability to capture a story on film. The truth is, I miss you."

He misses me. But it was too late. She knew, too, that he was waiting to hear those same words from her.

Why couldn't she be strong when it came to Clive? If only he didn't have the ability to make or break her career, she was certain she would walk.

"Look, Clive." She sighed. "I'll be. . ." *Home?* "Back in a few days."

She ended the call and frowned. Manhattan seemed like another planet, far from home. And Clive was the last person on her mind lately. He was brilliant but arrogant. Graeme was brilliant and humble. If only he weren't hiding something. Clive had hidden something from her, too.

fourteen

"Don't splash me!" Alexa wiped the droplets from her face. "I mean it."

Sitting on the rock ledge, she watched Barry, along with ten others, enjoy the beautiful Smith River–fed swimming hole. He laughed then dived down, swimming deeper into the clear water. Given her conflicted state of mind, Alexa couldn't bring herself to join Barry in his need to experience the river.

Once he'd gotten this out of his system, they would pack up their things at the motel and head to the airport. They had an early flight in the morning. To think how much she loathed coming here to begin with, and now the thought of leaving ripped at her. But what choice did she have? She'd made her decision to leave years ago. Her time here was done.

It's over...

And that included the beginnings of whatever she'd started with Graeme. They'd both been foolish to give in to whatever had drawn them together. The last time she'd seen him was at his cabin. She continued to struggle with the look on his face, the hurt and realization in his eyes. The resolve in his voice when he told her that her leaving was for the best.

Alexa hung her head, unmoved by the beautiful scenery surrounding her. She thought she meant more to him than that, and had hoped beyond hope that he would contact her yesterday. She hadn't been given the chance to properly thank him or tell him good-bye.

More than likely, Graeme had disappeared into the forest and didn't plan to resurface until Alexa was long gone.

In a way, there was at least one good thing to come out of her time here. She knew now that God wouldn't leave her, even though Graeme would. Coming back to the redwoods, she'd had to face a torrent of memories. She thought God had left her alone that night long ago, and her trust in Him had faltered. Why? Why hadn't she realized He'd been there protecting her through the night?

"Thank You for sending someone to rescue me, Lord." She hadn't whispered the words, but she was sitting alone, and the swimmers made too much noise to hear her prayer.

Footfalls crunched behind her. Another swimmer on a beautiful day. Wanting to experience her last day, wishing for much more time here, she drew in a breath. *Now just help me to figure out what to do with my life.*

Boots appeared in her peripheral vision, standing next to her. "Alexa."

Graeme. Her heart leapt. Alexa squeezed her eyes shut, committing the sound of his voice to memory.

She lifted her face and was rewarded with the grin she loved as Graeme smiled down at her.

"I thought I'd find you here," he said. "But I'm sorry if I interrupted your prayer."

She smiled to herself and stared at the water. What did he think about that? "You heard?"

He scrambled down to sit next to her, hanging his legs over the edge like her. "I heard you the day we climbed King Solomon, too, when I had to find you in the tree." His voice was quiet and gentle. "I'm there with you, you know."

Her heart thrummed—he was on speaking terms with God. "No, I didn't realize that."

Alexa regretted her choice of words. To think that Graeme was a Christian, shared the same beliefs, was more than she could have asked. Yet he was still out of reach.

Graeme sighed. "That's because I don't do a very good job of living out my faith in a way that's visible to others."

Alexa frowned, knowing exactly what he meant. After all

these years, she was finding her way back to Him.

"Maybe it's not that. Maybe we just haven't had enough time together. And as for others, maybe you're not around people enough because you're isolated, always in the trees."

"Possibly." He flashed his roguish grin. "Why aren't you swimming?"

"Now there's a serious change of subject." Angling her head, she watched his expression. "I wasn't in the mood."

She wanted to ask him why he'd come—he'd spoken to her with such finality before. His appearance was only prolonging things between them. Things that could never be. Still. . .she was glad he was here.

"Are you in the mood for a walk on the beach?"

I would love that. Alexa blew out a breath. "Barry and I are leaving tonight to drive to Sacramento. Our flight's in the morning."

"I see."

An awkward silence grew between them, but it was enough that Graeme was here. If only she could share all her thoughts with him, make him understand.

"What did you have in mind, Graeme?"

"Can you change your flight?"

They spoke the questions simultaneously then laughed together.

"I have a friend whose sister runs a bed-and-breakfast on the Oregon coast. In Brookings. She has some rooms available for us, if you're interested. I thought we could spend the weekend exploring the beach and the tide pools."

Alexa's breath caught. "Wow. You're inviting me. . .really?"

"Separate rooms, that is. Just to clarify." He cleared his throat. "And you could invite your sister, too."

When Alexa didn't answer, he stood and offered his hand. She took it and allowed him to assist her. Graeme cupped her cheeks, sending her heart spinning, and she closed her eyes, savoring the moment.

"Graeme, we're only prolonging the inevitable," she whispered and looked at him. "Why did you come here today?"

"Because." His forest-green eyes searched hers. "I hated the way we ended things the other day. All we ever have is the moment, and we should never leave things undone or unsaid."

Words spoken by a person who has experienced losing someone he loved, Alexa thought. Someone who was preparing to face another loss.

❧

"Look! Here's one," Sela squealed. "This starfish is huge."

Graeme relinquished Alexa's hand as she bounded toward her sister. They'd hit the coast just right—a low tide had been waiting almost as soon as they'd arrived at Karen's Bed-and-Breakfast. She'd greeted the four of them and then helped them settle into their rooms.

Fortunately, he and Barry were given separate rooms, but Sela and Alexa opted to share. He supposed they'd stay up late and giggle like schoolgirls, catching up.

Graeme's sneakers squished into the moist sand as he approached the cluster of rocks where Alexa, Sela, and Barry hovered. A gust of wind whipped strands of Alexa's gorgeous hair from the clip and gave it a life of its own.

"Oh, Graeme. Thank you for convincing us to stay the weekend. I'd forgotten what it was like to walk on one of the most beautiful coasts in the world." Alexa's smile dazzled him.

He grinned and stared down at the pinkish ocean animal clinging to the rock, surrounded with anemones. A wave washed up around his ankles.

"You really should take your shoes off," she said.

"The water's too cold." Graeme ran his fingers over the hundreds of mussels gripping the sides of the boulder.

"You get used to it after a while." Sela, beautiful like her sister, with her shiny, flowing auburn hair, smiled at Graeme.

He caught Barry watching her. The guy was definitely enamored, but nothing would come of that relationship over the weekend. Other than being warm and friendly, Sela hadn't appeared to have any romantic notions on her mind, though if he were Barry, he would have felt awkward at best, watching Graeme and Alexa hold hands.

He'd hoped for more time with Alexa, and a chance to talk her out of going to Costa Rica, though he hadn't exactly formulated a plan. There were other places in the world where she could travel and study the changing climate's effect on the forest.

Alexa released her hair from the clip and shook it out, then fought with the wind to secure it again. He stifled a laugh at her efforts. Today wasn't even that windy for the coast.

His heart sighed. She was so beautiful. How was he going to let her go?

"A penny for your thoughts."

Graeme suddenly realized Alexa was staring. What would she say if he told her the truth?

I'm falling for you, Alexa. He might have a PhD, but he was no genius when it came to matters of the heart. "I'm glad for this weekend. Glad you guys could change your flight."

She moved to stand next to him, allowing her gaze to roam his face. "Me too."

"All right, you two," Sela interrupted. "None of that sappy stuff right now. Let's keep exploring."

Graeme laughed when Alexa shot Sela a sisterly scowl, to which Sela responded by tossing a sand bomb at her feet. Alexa reached down and grabbed a fist full of sand, forming a ball of her own.

"Oh, now, please. I was only kidding." Sela giggled and ran.

Alexa chased her down the beach and threw the bomb. Sela screamed as it hit her in the back and fell apart.

"Can you believe those girls are grown women?" Graeme trudged alongside Barry to catch up with the sisters.

Barry chuckled. "I wish I would have met her sister when we first arrived."

Graeme slowed down. "Oh? Why's that?" But he knew exactly what Barry was thinking.

Barry arched a brow. "Then maybe I could be holding hands with her this weekend, like you with Alexa."

I doubt that.

"I'm not sure what you hoped to accomplish this weekend, or then again, maybe I am," Barry said, the current of an innuendo in his tone.

The last thing Graeme wanted was to start an argument with Barry—that could ruin the rest of their time here—but the guy had crossed the line. "What are you, Alexa's brother?"

"Maybe."

"Alexa is an adult. She can make her own decision. But to set the record straight, I didn't invite her along this weekend for what you are suggesting."

"Then why? This can't go anywhere."

Incredulous, Graeme stopped and turned to face Barry. The girls were up ahead and strolling back to them. Countless others—families, couples, and children—roamed the beach, strolling around Graeme and Barry when necessary. A man wearing a Dodgers baseball cap and old green army jacket sat on a large, pale chunk of driftwood—by the size it had to be a redwood trunk—drawing in the sand. He glanced up at Graeme, making him aware that he and Barry were talking too loud.

This time Graeme lowered his voice. "Don't be so sure, not that it's any of your business."

Barry squinted as he looked west toward the sun, gazing at the ocean behind Graeme. "Then I think you should know. . .she already has a boyfriend."

Graeme didn't buy that Barry had shared the news because he was trying to be a friend. While he tried to decide whether to challenge Barry or act like it didn't matter to him, Alexa and Sela approached.

"So we're laughing and throwing sand and you guys are having a serious conversation?" Alexa grabbed Graeme's hand and, jogging forward, tugged him behind her, washing away his fears and doubts.

He tried to live in this moment. It was all they had, but his heart longed for much more. He hoped there might be a future for them together. But how?

Maybe he should have a little faith. . . .

&

That evening, Alexa lounged in a lawn chair, watching the fire flicker in an elegant fire pit situated behind Karen's B and B. Karen had created a warm yet stylish place for guests to take their dinner at a buffet and rest by the fire. Equally interesting to Alexa was the way Graeme became animated when talking. While she nibbled on tortilla chips dipped in guacamole, she watched him stand there holding his plate, talking to Barry and another man.

Graeme wasn't anything she had ever wanted in a man—he didn't wear designer suits, wasn't involved in a high-profile career, and preferred nature over city lights. She wasn't sure how, but he'd turned what she thought she wanted upside down. And if it were possible, the man had chipped away at the façade Alexa had created, helping her see the person she used to be. The person she'd tried to leave behind years ago still existed deep inside her heart.

If only she could sort through her confusing thoughts. If only she could figure out why it mattered, considering in two days she'd be on a flight back to New York.

I don't want to go back. It wasn't for her anymore, if it ever was. Not really.

Her energy spent from a pleasant afternoon on the beach and in the company of those close to her, Alexa closed her eyes and sighed, putting aside the confusing thoughts for now.

But she felt that uncanny sense that someone was watching her and wondered if it was Graeme. When she opened her eyes, she found him still caught up in his conversation.

She tugged her gaze from him and scanned the small, private gathering. Karen, the bed-and-breakfast owner herself, smiled over at Alexa from the buffet table; then, carrying a plate and a drink, she made her way around chairs and small tables and slid into the chair next to Alexa.

"Can I get you something else?" Karen's smile was beautiful, and her face delicate but strong, framed by short dark hair.

"No, thank you." Alexa almost wished Karen wouldn't have approached her so that she could enjoy the evening in peaceful reverie, but the woman seemed warm and friendly enough.

"I have to admit I was startled to hear from my brother, Peter, asking if I could host Graeme and a few of his friends. I didn't realize he had any." Her laughter was smooth and soft. "I'm so glad to meet you."

"It's nice to meet you, too. Thanks for letting us stay. You really have an A-class B and B here. But why do you say that about Graeme?" Alexa inclined her head, curious to know what Karen could tell her about this mysterious man who'd burrowed into her heart.

"Oh, I guess I shouldn't have said that. He's one of Peter's friends. I'm just surprised I haven't seen more of him, that's all." Karen set her plate on the round table between the two chairs. "At one time, I had hoped he would notice me. I had a crush on him. We grew up in the same small town."

"Really?"

"Yes. He and Peter were friends then. They went off to college, going their separate ways, but apparently their studies led them along the same path. The last I heard, Graeme was engaged. But. . ."

Alexa sat up taller in the chair. "No, don't stop. I want to hear more."

"No, I've said enough. I know that he's only got eyes for you now and seems very happy. It wasn't my place to bring up his past, and I'm sorry for that. I talk too much sometimes."

"We should never leave things unsaid or undone." Alexa recalled Graeme's melancholy words. "What happened to her?"

Alexa followed Karen's somber gaze to Graeme, who stopped talking in midsentence. He excused himself and strolled to where they sat. "I hope I'm not interrupting anything."

"Not at all," Karen said. She rose from the chair. "I was getting to know your friend. She's lovely, Graeme. I'll leave you two to enjoy your evening while I see to the other guests."

Graeme nodded and smiled, but concern flared behind his eyes as he took a seat next to Alexa.

"Are you having a good time?" He lifted his icy drink to his lips and took a sip.

"Of course. Karen's wonderful, by the way. Why didn't you ever date her?"

Graeme choked, and after a fit of coughing, finally regained his composure. "What did she say to you?"

Alexa smiled, enjoying making him squirm a little. "Oh, nothing much. That she had a crush on you at one time but you didn't return the interest, and the last thing she knew you were engaged, and now you're here with me."

His brows crinkled as he stared into his glass. "She said that?"

Alexa had thought to tease him, but his dark expression quickly caused her to regret it. "I'm sorry, Graeme. It's none of my business."

Fearing she would lose the pleasant friendship they'd shared today, she reached for his hand and he accepted, squeezing hers in return.

Somehow she sensed the desperation in his touch.

"You mean like it's none of my business that you have a boyfriend back in New York?"

fifteen

This was not how he wanted this weekend to go. Why did either of them need to dredge up the past, or in her case, the present? He waited patiently for Alexa's reply, knowing that her reaction would determine the rest of their time together. Then again, maybe he shouldn't have asked the question. Tension knotted his shoulders.

"And you believe that I have a boyfriend in New York?" Alexa ran the tip of her finger around the top of her glass.

"No." Graeme slugged the last of his tea, feeling uncomfortable with the direction of their conversation.

Barry had simply been trying to stir things up. Graeme had known that, but the thought of her in another man's arms did crazy things to his head. The thought that she would kiss him, when she cared for someone else, disturbed him. In response, he refused to succumb to the unwarranted jealousy that image aroused. Maybe Barry had told him that because he was envious. Maybe Barry lost his chance with Alexa, and never had one with Sela. Who knew?

But what Graeme did know was that he didn't want to go into details about what happened to Summer. He rose from the chair. "Can I get you something more to drink?"

"Sure, if you're going." She held up her glass and he took it. Their fingers brushed, making him wish they had time alone.

But that probably wasn't a good idea, and he should be thankful for the people around them. He headed for the end of the buffet table where he found an offering of tea, lemonade, and coffee.

Sela brushed up against him. "You seem like a really nice guy, Graeme."

Pouring himself and Alexa another glass of tea, he smiled

and watched Sela empty the last of the coffee into a mug. Sela and Alexa were so much alike, and yet very different. He barely knew either of them; still, he could tell they were both special. Any man would be blessed to be in their company for a day, let alone a lifetime.

What was he thinking? He wasn't in a situation to even entertain such thoughts. *Lord in heaven, help me. . . .*

He lifted his now-filled glass of unsweetened tea to his lips. "Why do I get the feeling I have a lecture coming?"

She held up the steaming mug and paused. "See what I mean? You're a nice guy, and you already know what I'm going to say, so I won't need to lecture."

He huffed a laugh. "Not really, no. But I can guess. It has something to do with you not wanting to see your sister get hurt."

Pressing her lips together, she smiled then sipped the hot coffee. "You sell yourself short. You knew exactly what I was going to say."

Graeme studied his glass again. At this rate he'd know every nuance of the Asian image etched on the side before their evening ended.

"Alexa is more fragile than you think. I just want you to know that. She suffered terrible heartache as a child, and I'm not sure she's ever gotten over it. Be careful with her." With that, she smiled then left him to mull over her words.

He watched her float over to Alexa and hold out her arms. "Come on, sis. We've got so much catching up to do. Let's make an early night of it and have some girl talk."

Alexa glanced his way—a question in her eyes. Did he want her to go? Graeme simply drank from his glass, remaining noncommittal. Hurt flashed across her features before she turned a smile to Sela.

"Sure. I'd love that." Alexa gracefully untangled herself from the comfortable lounge chair and rose. "Good night, everyone. See you in the morning."

Graeme took a step forward, hoping to interject his

plans. "And since tomorrow is Sunday, I'm hoping we can leave early enough to attend the Church in the Redwoods. Everyone okay with that?"

Sela smiled first. "I'd love that. I've always wanted to visit there. Alexa?"

Alexa nodded. Barry frowned before finally agreeing. What choice did he have?

As Graeme watched her stroll next to Sela, heading along the walkway to their room in the house, he wondered what he'd been thinking to invite her here, to extend his torment. He'd forgotten how complicated a relationship could be.

He was playing with fire, and in his world in the trees, a fire could destroy everything.

But it could also birth something new. . . .

&

Once inside the small room decorated in a seaside theme, Alexa plopped on one of the two double beds, arranged similar to a motel room. Sela had excused herself to run an errand, and promised to return in five minutes.

The time alone was agonizing, considering Alexa couldn't pull her thoughts from Graeme. Shouldn't she be with him out there right now? Why hadn't he given her a sign that he wanted her to stay? What was with men these days? Or had he simply wanted her to decide for herself, and she had hurt him by leaving?

It was too much, these games that men and women played, and the game she played with him would soon be ending, with or without a winner. But neither one of them would win; they both knew that.

The door creaked open. "Okay," Sela said, entering the room. She shut the door behind her. "Sorry about that. But I had to grab some snacks. Karen had all sorts of goodies for us, including sodas and chips."

Sela giggled and spilled the contents of one of the sacks she carried out onto the bed next to Alexa. "I really like that woman. Think I've found myself a new friend."

Alexa rose up on her elbows and examined the items. "Do you seriously expect me to eat all that candy and fit into my clothes tomorrow?"

"Not candy. Chocolate."

"Chocolate *candy*. Hello?" Alexa laughed, almost grateful her sister had dragged her away from the growing tension between her and Graeme. She took one of the chocolates and unwrapped it then popped it into her mouth.

"Glad to see you smiling. I thought you were going to die from sorrow and dissolve into the grass when I dragged you away from him."

Searching the other sack for the sodas Sela had mentioned, Alexa found one and popped the top, washing down the chocolate.

The carbonation burned, and Alexa squeezed her eyes. "Why'd you do that anyway?"

"I think you know why." Sela frowned. "I'm really worried about you, sis."

"Nothing to worry about. I'm leaving in two days."

"Then why do this to yourself? Why do this to him?"

"What exactly, pray tell, am I doing?"

"Do you have to ask?" Sela leaned forward. "You're carrying on with him as though you have a future together."

Alexa placed the soda on a coaster and lay on the bed, tucking the pillow behind her head. "How do you figure?"

"Quit playing dumb with me. He cares deeply for you. I don't want to see either of you get hurt. If you're so bent on this career that keeps you anchored in New York, why string him along?"

"Those are fighting words, Sela. I am not stringing him along. I didn't mean for this to happen, and you don't know all of it." Alexa slurped on the soda, hating that Sela was vocalizing all the misgivings she herself had worked to ignore. "And what if. . ."

Sela sank into her own bed, resting her head against her arm.

"What if I decide to stay?"

"If that's even a remote consideration, you need to share that with him. For all you know, he's not ready to commit and is counting on you leaving."

"Boy, I love the way you put a positive spin on things," Alexa said, certain her sarcasm wasn't lost on Sela. "The truth is, we hardly know anything about each other."

"If you don't know him, then how can you really care for him?"

"Not everyone follows the same rules as you, Sela."

"What is it, then, that's between you? How would you define it?"

"I don't know, but you picked up on it the first time you met him, didn't you? What do you think?" Alexa turned her head to look at Sela, apprehensive about her answer and yet hopeful at the same time.

Sela picked at something on the pillowcase. "The first time I saw you two together, that night at my house, it was like you were each considering a dance with the other. By the end of the evening, clearly, you had engaged. But by tonight. . ."

Alexa swung her feet off the bed and sat on the edge. "What?"

"Alexa, you love him." Sela's eyes glistened with tears. "I'm sure he feels the same."

Covering her mouth, Alexa smiled. She closed her eyes then dropped back across the bed. *I knew it. . . .*

"But Alexa, people who love each other hurt each other all the time. Loving him doesn't give you an easy answer."

"Why do you always have to be the older, wiser sister?" Alexa grinned, feeling moisture at the corners of her eyes.

sixteen

Alexa stepped into the small sanctuary behind Graeme, his cologne wafting around her, wishing she hadn't agreed to attend church. They were all wearing casual attire, but Graeme assured her it would be fine.

He'd been distant this morning at breakfast. Perhaps it was as Sela said—the man didn't want to commit and decided he'd made a mistake by inviting her to spend the weekend with him on the beach.

She longed to reach out and grab his hand, put things back where they were, giving them at least this memory together, untainted by fear of a future that could never happen. From behind, Sela nudged her forward and farther into the old-time sanctuary. A small gathering was already seated in the pews, and a few stragglers continued to enter behind Alexa, Sela, and Barry.

Graeme had chosen a pew in the back and gestured for them to follow, but before he could sit, a man wearing a flannel shirt and jeans approached him and shook his hand. They spoke in soft tones and Graeme glanced at Alexa, indicating he wanted to introduce her.

She strolled toward him and he smiled like nothing was wrong, putting on a show for the man, whoever he was.

"Alexa, I'd like you to meet Pastor Jacob," Graeme said.

A pastor? He was dressed more like a lumberjack.

"Very nice to meet you. So glad you could join us today." Pastor Jacob thrust out his hand and took hers, his grip strong. Warm light emanated from his eyes.

Alexa instantly liked him, and at the same time, she felt exposed as though he could see everything wrong inside her soul. He reached out and shook hands with Sela and Barry.

"I live in the area," Sela said. "I've always wanted to visit but have been attending a church in Crescent City. This would be much closer."

"We'd love to have you, of course," Jacob said.

The pastor excused himself and made his way to the pulpit to start the service. After a pianist played a few hymns, leading the congregation in worship, Pastor Jacob started in on his sermon.

Sitting next to Graeme in the pew, Alexa found it difficult to concentrate on the words at first, but the pastor's voice was soothing and convicting at the same time. He delivered the Word of God in a way that pierced the soul, depositing hope deep inside her heart.

He spoke about redeeming the past and healing painful memories that have shaped a person. Alexa could hardly breathe. How could he have known?

"First Corinthians chapter 13, verse 11. 'When I was a child, I talked like a child, I thought like a child, I reasoned like a child. When I became a man, I put the ways of childhood behind me.' Paul is exhorting us to get free of those things that keep us bound and tied up, keeping us from spiritual maturity."

Alexa remained unmoving, thinking about the painful memories that had shaped her entire life. If she hadn't gotten lost, would her father have stayed? Would they have remained a loving family, and then would she never have sought to run away from this place? She wouldn't have found herself in New York, living the life she'd attained, only to realize that lifestyle wasn't a reflection of who she really was.

When Pastor Jacob closed with prayer, Alexa shut her eyes and prayed silently. *Lord, help me. Redeem the past. . . .*

"And never forget, the Truth will set you free." Pastor Jacob dismissed the gathering.

Alexa slipped from the pew first and exited the small church, wanting to keep private that she'd been emotionally and spiritually moved.

Once inside Graeme's Jeep, he invited them to lunch.

"Thank you, Graeme, but I need to get back to my business. You can drop me off on your way to lunch," Sela said. "And thank you again for the wonderful weekend."

Graeme glanced in his rearview mirror and smiled. "You're very welcome."

Despite Sela's talk of Graeme loving Alexa, she wondered if after she was out of the picture, Graeme and Sela would spend time together, becoming friends and possibly more.

"I need to pack the rest of my stuff." She sighed and looked out the window. "I can eat a protein bar."

"Thanks, Graeme," Barry said. "But Alexa is right. We should probably head to Sacramento this afternoon."

When they dropped Sela off, Alexa climbed from the Jeep to hug her sister good-bye.

"I'm so glad we had this time together, sis." Sela squeezed hard, unwilling to release her. "I know you have some decisions to make. I'll be praying for you."

Alexa stepped from Sela, fighting the emotions overwhelming her. "Thanks. And I'll try not to be such a stranger."

After she climbed back into the vehicle, Graeme drove them back to the motel. Barry thanked him for the weekend and carried his small bag to his room. Alexa hung back, uncertain if Graeme would remain distant.

He tugged her suitcase from the back of his Jeep and lugged it to her room for her, setting it on the floor.

There was so much Alexa wanted to voice—words both harsh and tender. Though accustomed to speaking her mind, she failed miserably. "Thank you for the weekend, and for. . .everything. For your assistance on the documentary."

Alexa couldn't look at him and set her purse on the dresser, forcing her thoughts on packing up the room, assuming that he would walk out the open door any minute.

"Look at me." Graeme reached for her, tugging her around to face him. "You know I care for you."

She stared into his forest-green eyes, wondering where his words would lead.

He brushed the back of his hand down her cheek, and she struggled to maintain her composure.

"This weekend didn't exactly turn out the way I wanted," he said.

"It started out wonderful. What happened?" Alexa believed he was as torn over their relationship as she was.

"Have lunch with me?"

She looked away. "Why should I? There's no point." If only she'd heeded those words instead of agreeing to the weekend on the coast.

"Because there was a reason I invited you to the coast. A reason besides wanting to be with you. There are things we need to discuss. I just. . .never found the chance. Please, Alexa. It's important."

"All right, but I need to tell Barry."

&

The Sunday lunch crowd made Sally's a little too packed for Graeme, especially considering what he planned to share with Alexa. He'd been an idiot not to simply pull her aside while at Karen's and tell her the truth. But things weren't that simple, and he'd been afraid the truth would ruin their weekend together. Yet it was another truth that had caused him to distance himself emotionally. From the start, Sela had gained his respect, and her well-chosen words had gone directly to the heart of the matter, forcing him to see what he'd ignored.

He tried to wrench his emotional connection from Alexa. But it was much too late. Holding a to-go bag of burgers and fries, Graeme steered Alexa back to the Jeep.

"Where are we going?" she asked.

"I know the perfect place. It should be less crowded."

She sighed. "I'd really prefer to stay near the motel so I can finish packing."

"It's not far. I just want to talk to you in private."

Sitting in the driver's seat, Alexa next to him, he maneuvered from the busy parking lot and drove a mile and a half up the road, turning into a deserted picnic area. He wondered how long it would stay that way. The three picnic tables were spread out, fortunately, in case others showed up.

Choosing the table nearest the Jeep, they unwrapped their lunch and ate while trying to keep the wrappers in place despite the breeze. Graeme could see she wasn't interested in lunch, and he wasn't either, really. He finished chewing the hamburger he usually loved, only today it was tasteless, and placed his hand over Alexa's.

Her beautiful mane hung around her shoulders, framing her face. A different kind of hunger coursed through him along with a strong sense of protectiveness. He had to keep her safe. The only way he could stop her from going to Costa Rica was to tell her the truth, and yet telling her could put her in danger as well.

She slipped her hand from his. "What was so important that you had to drag me here?"

"After New York, you still plan to head to Costa Rica to finish up the documentary?"

She placed her elbows on the table and tucked her hair behind her ears. "I'm not entirely sure. The sponsor might pull the funding for this project. All I can do is pray that Clive loves what I've done so far."

"He's the guy you work for, right? You told me a little about him when we had dinner at your sister's house."

"Yes. And the cofounder of the production company. He brought me on right out of college. I was lucky to have gotten his attention."

Jealousy stung him. "He's the boyfriend that Barry referred to, isn't he?"

"Very astute of you, but that's long over. Not that it matters."

Her words stabbed, but what did he have to offer her except the ugly truth of his situation? He hoped Jacob was right and that sharing the truth would set him free. He desperately wanted to make things right on all counts. But he knew to find the peace he was looking for, he'd have to go much further than simply telling Alexa.

A black sedan pulled into the picnic area, driving beyond the Jeep, and parked, reminding him he was running out of time.

Graeme searched for the words he needed to explain things. "There's a reason why I don't want you to go to Costa Rica."

She arched one of her well-defined brows. "I had planned to Google that information. See what your connection was. Regardless, I'm not sure how it could affect me."

A man climbed from the sedan and passed the picnic tables, walking up the trail leading from the picnic area. Graeme froze, recognizing him as someone he'd seen on the beach. Same Dodgers baseball cap, same army-green jacket.

"What's wrong?"

"Nothing." He finished his soda and chewed on the crushed ice left in the cup, watching the guy. Was he having a knee-jerk reaction just because he'd seen the same guy in two very different locations? This man wasn't the one he'd seen watching him in Costa Rica before he'd fled. Still, alarms resonated in his head. "I think we should go."

Alexa shook her head. "This is the end of the line for me. You know I need to pack. Now tell me what you have to say. Graeme, you're not even listening."

"No, you're not listening." Graeme stood and gathered the lunch sacks and wrappers.

From beneath the bill of his cap, the man's gaze locked on Graeme. Graeme's pulse kicked up a notch.

A silver minivan steered into the picnic area and parked. Had Graeme imagined the man's posture shrinking back? He made his way to one of the empty picnic tables as a family climbed out of the van. If Alexa wasn't with him, Graeme would stay and see if the guy approached him. Find out if his time in hiding was up. But that could put her in danger.

"We have to get out of here," he said and tossed the trash in the garbage. Alexa still hadn't moved from the table. As calmly as he could, he grabbed her arm, trying to act like nothing had set him off. "Please."

"You're scaring me."

"I have my reasons. Will you trust me?" Graeme held his breath, wishing he'd never gotten involved with Alexa. All this time he'd remained unnoticed; then Alexa barged into his life and now, if his worst fears were coming to pass, Summer's killers had found him.

Alexa slid from the picnic table. "Fine. You can take me to my—"

"Not yet." Graeme cut her off, not wanting the guy to hear that she was staying in a motel. He had to be careful.

He exhaled and urged her around the table and into the Jeep, hoping not to draw attention. What a ridiculous thought. It was far too late for that.

seventeen

Graeme hurriedly opened the passenger door, but Alexa hesitated. He gripped her shoulders. "I'll explain everything. Just get in."

Alexa studied him, believing she could trust him, but his sudden strange behavior made her question his judgment.

"Please, we don't have much time."

Shaking her head, she climbed into the Jeep. He rushed around to the other side and got in then started the vehicle and backed up. He peeled from the parking lot and headed north on Highway 199 toward the Oregon border.

"You're going the wrong way. My motel is the other direction. What's going on?"

"I need to see what that guy is going to do. If he's following me. And if he is, I don't want to lead him to your motel room."

He glanced in his rearview mirror and frowned then whipped the Jeep around the car in front of them. Alexa held on to the grip at the top of the cab. She leaned around to look behind them. Several cars followed, and at that moment, a black sedan—the same one at the picnic area—passed someone on a curve.

Alexa pressed her lips together and stared at Graeme. "I've seen my share of movies, but I can't believe you actually think someone is following us."

"It's my fault. I'm so sorry I dragged you into this."

Okay. She definitely didn't like the sound of his words and drew in an edgy breath to calm her nerves.

"Into what, Graeme?" Her voice shook, giving away her anxiety.

Without responding, he punched the gas and sped around

another car, swerving back into the right lane seconds ahead of an oncoming car.

Alexa screamed and the driver honked at them. "Graeme, I don't feel comfortable with you driving this fast."

She held on as he raced up the curvy two-lane highway then glanced out the passenger window. The road hedged the Smith River with its snakelike curves a hundred, sometimes two hundred or more feet above the ravine. "Why did you head this direction if you thought we were being followed? This is a dangerous drive even if you're going thirty-five."

"I can lose him this way. He's not right behind us, is he? That's because this is a dangerous road for him, too."

"Him? Who are you referring to exactly?" Alexa held back the full extent of her questions, her patience on the brink.

"Let me lose him first. I need to focus on the road."

"I won't argue with you there." Alexa took some pleasure that they were stuck behind a slow-moving, compact-car-towing RV. She could catch her breath with slower speeds.

"Thanks for that."

"I don't see him," she said, peering through the back window. "I don't think we can lose him on this road, though."

Graeme glanced in the mirror. "He's six cars behind."

"Only six?" Alexa allowed her gaze to roam the Smith River gorge to her right. Beautiful jagged rock formations rimmed the cliffs all the way to the river, which tumbled over large boulders.

Rock formations that could quickly turn deadly. She could have enjoyed the view under different circumstances.

But right now, she had a pressing question. "If he's following you, why didn't he approach you at the picnic area? He was there with us."

"When he got there, he looked up the trail at first. I think he was making sure we were alone. And I think he was about to approach me when the minivan pulled in, but he didn't. He needs me to go away quietly."

Go away quietly? Alexa swallowed. "What will he do if he catches us?"

Graeme sighed, and she whipped her head around to study him. His expression was grave. "Never mind. I don't think I want to know," she said.

It didn't look like he was close to offering an explanation, either. This was getting better by the minute. Still, Alexa struggled to comprehend that someone meant them harm and was following them. It was too much to take in.

"Then. . .why don't we pray?" she asked.

"I've been praying all along."

"I mean, out loud. Together."

"Go for it." Graeme swerved around another car at a bad place in the road.

Alexa feared the next time he did that, he might not be so lucky—there could easily be a car around the mountain cliff rimming the road, heading straight for them. "Lord Jesus, please protect us. Save us from our enemies; make a way out for us. Be our refuge." *And help Graeme, no matter what trouble he's in.* Alexa appreciated that praying was coming back to her so easily, and she realized how much she missed it, missed trusting in God. Somehow she needed to trust Him in this situation, too.

"Now, if I can make it far enough ahead, then turn off the road on a curve where he can't see I've turned, we'll have lost him. He won't discover we're off the road for a long while, and even then, he'll struggle to turn around. I know just the place up the road about four hundred yards. Pray we can make that."

Alexa clung to the grip on the ceiling, silently praying they could lose this guy. The mountain road grew steeper, and Graeme gunned the engine, speeding around another RV.

A car was heading straight for them and laid on the horn. Graeme floored the Jeep, stressing the engine to increase speed on the incline. He'd yet to pass the RV, which suddenly decided to accelerate.

"Graeme?" Alexa ground her teeth and pressed her feet into the floorboard like she could slow the car. Every muscle and nerve ending in her body grew tense.

She held her breath, dreading the impact. With the carved-out mountain to accommodate the road on their immediate left, and an RV to the right, there was no place for them to go.

Off road wasn't much better, considering the rocky drop.

Alexa covered her face and squeezed her eyes, her heart crying out to God. The Jeep whipped to the right. The honking car passed them to the left. She opened her eyes to see the Jeep driving off the road.

Alexa screamed.

&

The vehicle bounced over the dirt road that hugged the cliff face inside the gorge, winding down toward the river where people could fish off a rocky embankment. The entrance was hard to see from the highway, which made the secluded path their best chance at losing their pursuer.

At least they'd made the risky maneuver. Graeme steered the Jeep as far as he could down the road and parked behind a copse of trees. The man would have difficulty finding the road at all, and even if he did, Graeme would see him coming in plenty of time to take evasive action.

Still, he didn't plan to stay here for long, just long enough to make sure his pursuer hadn't followed yet. Blowing out a breath, he shut off the ignition then looked over at Alexa.

She stared out the window, her shoulders trembling. Graeme reached over and squeezed her hand. "Are you all right?"

"I won't know the answer to that until I hear what you have to say. What is going on?" Finally, she turned to face him.

Graeme pressed his head against the seatback and rubbed his forehead. "Look, I hate that I got you involved in this. That you were in the car with me when all this came down. But I didn't want the man to see where you were staying. Which means I need to get you back so that you can pack and leave this place as soon as possible. Get as far away from me as you can."

"I'm not leaving without answers."

Graeme sighed. "I'm sorry I didn't tell you sooner, but I hate thinking about it, much less talking about it. I had planned to tell you. Had wanted to tell you this weekend."

Alexa opened the door and stepped out.

"Wait, Alexa. . . ." He jumped out of the Jeep and trotted around the front. "Where are you going?"

"I need some fresh air and the sound of the river is soothing." She wrapped her arms around herself. "So finish what you were saying already."

Graeme sat on a large boulder and watched the river tumble over the rocks, creating white-water rapids. This close to the river, he wasn't sure he could hear if a vehicle was coming down the road, so he glanced back intermittently.

"I came to the redwoods because it was the perfect place. I could continue my research and I could hide."

"But why would you want to hide?" Alexa stepped closer to him now, concern in her eyes.

"I was working on a forest restoration project in Costa Rica."

Alexa rocked her head back like she was beginning to understand, but of course, she knew nothing yet.

"My fiancée, Summer, was a botanist, too, and was there working with me. One day she called me, frantic, and needed me to come pick her up. It was pouring down rain that day, and I found her standing in a back alley, soaked to the bone."

Graeme glanced back at the road and watched a truck park. A man and two children climbed out. The man grappled with fishing poles from the truck bed.

Alexa closed the distance between them and sat on the rock next to him. Her shoulder brushed his arm, reminding him of the attraction between them. She hung her head, her hair draping over her face like a curtain; then she tilted her face to gaze at him. "I'm listening."

"Summer had always been an activist, even in college." Graeme stood now, feeling the anger and emotion of that day. "I told her to leave it alone! We weren't in the land of the free, home of the brave. We weren't in the US of A." He swiped his hand down his face, gathering his composure.

He glanced at the road again. "We should go now."

"Not until you tell me everything."

"I'll keep talking, but you need to pack and leave. We should head back." Graeme trudged to his Jeep, Alexa not far behind.

They climbed in; then he started the ignition and pulled forward, praying silently.

"Summer found her way into a construction company that had won the bid for a hydroelectric project."

"You mean a dam."

"Yes. A huge project, worth millions to the company. She thought they would care about the damage caused to the environment."

Graeme crept forward in the Jeep as they neared the highway juncture. After looking both ways, he breathed a sigh and turned left when traffic allowed. With the traffic and the snakelike two-lane road, the man after him would probably cross the Oregon border before realizing Graeme was no longer ahead of him. Even then, it would take time to make his way back. Still, Graeme didn't want to waste any time getting Alexa safely back to her room.

"Okay, so your fiancée took on a big company. That's nothing new."

"You haven't heard everything. So I'm driving and Summer is shaking and in tears. She was so upset, I could hardly make out what she was saying."

In his rearview mirror, Graeme spotted a vehicle passing others on the road—not often done because of the danger. Thankfully, it wasn't his shadow. "I guess Summer was tired of being on the losing end of things, tired of letting companies destroy the environment. She went looking for trouble. While someone was out of his office, Summer rifled through papers and found some incriminating information."

"And that didn't make her happy?"

"No, she was scared to death. Someone walked in on her, and she made excuses and left."

"What could be so bad that she was afraid for her life?" Alexa whispered as if thinking out loud.

Graeme felt a large knot lodging in his throat. "Oh, she found what she was looking for, all right. Someone was going out of their way to hide the truth about environmental damage. And there was a file that included a reporter's picture—a man who'd died in an accident a few weeks before. Summer was scared the man had been killed for trying to expose the truth. She had more to tell me, but before she finished, someone ran us off the road."

Swiping the sweat from his brow, he peered in the rear-view mirror. "I was driving that day. We were on a bridge and went over the side into a river."

He glanced at Alexa. Her face had visibly paled. That they were hedging a river now and being chased by the same people—mostly likely—wasn't lost on her.

"My old run-down Honda Civic couldn't compete with the truck. We dropped into the San Juan River like a bag of bricks."

"Graeme, you don't have to tell me—"

"Yes, I do. You wanted to know, and I *need* to tell you all of it."

He squeezed the steering wheel as he spoke. "I tried to save her."

Images of Summer's terrified face accosted his mind, but he had to focus; he had to drive now. He had to keep Alexa from experiencing the same fate just by being in the car with him. "But Summer's seat belt was stuck. I couldn't find the knife. Nothing went right. I went up for air, and when I came back, she was. . .gone. I figured if I could somehow get her out, I could revive her. But it didn't happen that way."

Graeme finally turned into the motel parking lot. "I'm

going to park around the back so if the guy happens to pass, he won't see my car. When you get out, head to your room and pack. Tell Barry what's going on so he knows you need to leave and fast. It's the only way I know to keep you safe."

"Wait, Graeme. What happened next? Why are they still chasing you?"

"At first, I thought if I hid, they might think I was dead, too. But that would never work. I couldn't have people I know thinking I was dead. When the police showed up, and the car was pulled from the river, I told them someone ran us off the road."

"What? You didn't tell them that Summer discovered something incriminating?"

"Her method of discovery was illegal, and besides, it was a tall charge in a foreign country. Before I could gather my gear and leave, I realized I was being watched. They thought I knew something. I went directly to the airport and, once in the States, landed on Peter's doorstep. I've been here hiding, working quietly in the treetops ever since—that is, until you found me."

eighteen

Relieved to be off the road and out of the chase, Alexa stared out the window, unable to look at Graeme. His detailed account certainly explained a lot. Like why he didn't want to be on film.

But much about creating documentaries had to do with exposing injustice. Clive himself had garnered attention by exposing a pharmaceutical company's unethical practices, and yet here she'd fallen for a man who'd—

"So you just ran away?" Incredulous, her eyes burned with tears, but she wouldn't shed them. "How could you do that?"

"What should I have done?" Graeme raised his voice to equal the ire in hers.

"Find a way to expose these people for what they did to your fiancée. That's what."

"So I'm a coward. Is that what you're saying?"

Alexa squeezed her eyes shut, hating that Graeme might not be the man she thought. "Look. I represent exposing the truth. And—and you're hiding it."

"Exposing the truth is a noble ideal until your life is on the line, or the lives of those you love." Graeme's intense gaze breached the barriers of her heart. Pain—like nothing she'd seen—warred with affection. She'd hurt him, she knew.

"Graeme," she croaked. "I'm sorry. . . ."

"No need to be." He stepped from the Jeep, came around to her side, and opened the door. "You were being honest, and I needed to hear that. Now, you should pack and leave. Forget about me. Forget about Costa Rica. That path could be dangerous for you now."

Alexa slid from the vehicle and looked into Graeme's face. "So this is how it ends?"

"It would seem so." He shut the door and jammed his hands in his pockets. "You'd better go."

She strode away from him, heading toward her room at the far end of the motel, but before she'd stepped from the cover offered by the back of Sally's diner, Alexa whirled around. "I'm not sure I can let this go, you know."

"Is it worth your life, Alexa? Or Barry's? Or whoever else you get involved?"

Unsure how to answer, she frowned.

"You have to take into account that now they know you're involved with me, and I'm apparently a wanted man. This isn't the story for you, sweetheart."

Sweetheart?

He grinned. "Let it go for now, okay?"

In response, she felt a slight lifting at the corner of her mouth. "I'll take your advice under consideration."

She couldn't help herself and made her way toward him. She stood taller to reach his cheek and kissed it. "In the meantime, stay safe, okay?"

"I'll give it a try." He trotted around to the other side of his Jeep. "I'll wait here until I see you two leave. Then I'll know you're safe."

❧

Alexa hurried down the sidewalk under the awning, passing the motel rooms as she went. She hated that she was leaving him like this. Hated herself for her contrary thoughts about him running from the situation. Her heart was breaking. . . .

But more importantly, concern for his safety overwhelmed her. "Lord, please protect him. And show me what I need to do."

When she reached Barry's door, she knocked, uncertain how to explain the situation but knowing they needed to leave now. She glimpsed over at Graeme, still sitting in his Jeep, watching.

Anxiety squeezed her chest as she watched the road, hoping the black sedan wouldn't roll into the parking lot and spot her.

When Barry answered, she explained that she would be ready in fifteen minutes—which was a stretch—but she wanted Graeme gone before his stalker headed back this way.

In her room, she began tossing the remnants of her clothing into her luggage then stopped, plopping on the bed. How could she go back to New York?

There was too much at stake here—Graeme's life. How was he going to deal with this problem? Be rid of the situation once and for all? Would he just keep running? Would he contact the authorities to explain what happened?

A pain sliced through her heart—if he fled, she might not see him again. She wouldn't know where to look, and knowing him, he'd be sure to hide his tracks. But what if she simply called the police herself and told them everything? That should get the justice ball rolling, shouldn't it? Then Graeme would be safe to continue his research here.

A knock at the door drew her attention.

Barry. . . .

⋅⋅⋅

After watching Alexa and Barry pack up their rental car and drive from the parking lot, Graeme felt his tense shoulders relax, knowing Alexa would be out of harm's way. But she'd left him to face his demons from the past.

Graeme steered his ride along the path to his cabin, wondering if the man who'd followed him knew where it was.

He parked in front of the cabin that Peter had rented to him what seemed like ages ago and sat in the Jeep, studying the surrounding area. Nothing looked disturbed. Graeme got out, his sense of urgency weighed down by Alexa's opinion of him.

Unlocking the door, he entered the house and flipped on the lights. She was right.

I'm a coward to have run. But who was he to face powerful men in a third-world country where he was certain he would have ended up in the river, just like Summer, if he'd stayed?

He'd spent the last year existing practically off the grid, hoping that no one would actually come and look for him. What had tipped them off? Had they searched through Summer's belongings, much of which he'd left behind in his frantic flight from Costa Rica? The items she left behind with her death would have been shipped to her parents, if anywhere. Her folks couldn't know if anything was missing.

Maybe he'd made a mistake in coming to the redwoods to begin with. Regardless of how he'd been discovered, the game was up.

And what was it all for? Graeme swung at the lamp on the table and it crashed to the floor. When would this end?

He had no choice but to disappear again.

No. . . .

There was always a choice. He didn't want to leave. He loved Alexa.

But staying wouldn't bring him any closer to her. She had her own life and career, far from his in the wilderness. Alexa preferred the skyscrapers to the trees; she preferred to be surrounded by millions of people rather than enjoy the quiet of the forest. Otherwise, why would she have moved from her home here on the redwood coast to New York?

By all appearances, he and Alexa were not a good fit, and that's why he couldn't figure out what had drawn him to her. Why did she return his affection?

They were obviously completely different—she wanted to expose the wrongs in the world, and he wanted to hide from them. That she considered him a coward was devastating. She didn't respect him and so they had nothing between them.

Yet that wasn't at all true. As he tugged his duffel bag from the top of the closet and began stuffing clothes and necessities inside, the question plagued him.

Am I a coward for running from this threat again? Was he running from more than a Costa Rican hunter? Was he running from love?

He stared through the window at the view of the backwoods behind the cabin. He loved the redwoods, and he hadn't completed this project with Peter. Even if he had, there was always more research to be done.

No. He wasn't going to run this time, flee the place he called home. He would face the man and fight, if he had to. Though he wasn't exactly certain that he was willing to die to stay here, he hoped that wasn't a choice he would have to make. Before he took any action, Graeme needed to pray and ask for guidance.

He dropped into the chair next to the bed. "Lord, I lost Summer because of this situation. I lost freedom, and I've lived in fear. Now I'm about to lose a woman I love—if I haven't already lost her because of my weakness. But when I am weak, You are strong."

A sense of peace engulfed him, encouraging him. "Show me what to do. If I call the police, what do I say to convince them? What can they do since it happened in another country? Where can I be safe?"

The phone rang, startling him. Graeme didn't recognize the caller ID but snatched it up—it could be Alexa. "Yes?"

"You have already lost one loved one, yes?" The voice had a Spanish accent.

Frost crackled down Graeme's spine. "Who is this?"

"If you don't want another beautiful woman to die, then you will meet me."

"I don't know what you're talking about. Who is this?" *Idiot.* Pretending he wasn't who the man thought wouldn't work. What was he doing?

"Here's a reminder."

"Graeme, I'm so sorry." Alexa's voice quivered but then became stern. "But don't—ow, you jerk." Her defiance quickly turned to a whimper, and it sounded as if he'd yanked her away.

Pain at the sound of her fear, at the thought of her abducted, infused his anger and crushed Graeme's chest.

"Crosswood Trail. You know the place."

Graeme squeezed his eyes, picturing the trailhead. It was way off the beaten path. How did this guy know about it? There wasn't a chance anyone would stumble upon them in those woods. "No, I don't. Pick another trail."

"No, this one. I can see if you're alone. And you know what happens if you're not."

"You have to give me time to find it."

"You have twenty minutes."

"No, wait!"

But it was too late. The pursuer-turned-kidnapper hung up.

Graeme grabbed his jacket and rushed out the door, starting the Jeep and swerving from the driveway in what seemed like one fluid motion.

Was the man insane? Twenty minutes wasn't enough time to make it. Graeme didn't have time to consider what to do, much less contact the police and get put on hold then have to tell them about a kidnapping, nor did he have a cell signal here, so he couldn't call them while driving. But then, this man had planned on that.

What had happened? He'd watched Alexa drive off with Barry. Where was her cameraman? Acid singed his gut.

His past had finally caught up with him.

nineteen

Sweat dripped down Alexa's temple and into her eyes, making them sting. Bound and gagged and left in the trunk of a car, there wasn't a thing she could do about it.

Her mouth taped shut, she yelled in muffled frustration and kicked the trunk, hoping it would pop open. Her furious grunts were muted and pointless, but she had to make noise on the off chance someone might hear; otherwise she had no hope until Graeme arrived.

There wasn't a safety latch for her to escape.

She nearly lost her lunch as the car sped and swerved along what must have been the Smith River Ravine. At least she knew that much, because she had no clue where the trail at which he'd asked Graeme to meet them was located. From the long drive, and the sudden bumpy road, Alexa reasoned that he'd now driven off the main highway and was making his way toward the trail. He somehow knew he'd beat Graeme there if only by a few minutes.

But that was just it—would he come for her? Maybe Graeme would decide that Alexa was as good as dead and it was too late for him to save her.

Lord, please. . .help me. . . .

Trembling, she couldn't stop the fear that zapped her energy, her will, but. . . No! She had to be strong.

To fight, if she got the chance. Still, it was difficult when looking down the muzzle of a gun. And now she better understood what Graeme had meant. Her high ideals about dealing with injustice were somewhat tempered from this experience.

Suddenly the vehicle stopped. Alexa tensed, wondering what would happen next. Was she within seconds of death?

Perhaps he'd wanted to take her far away to kill her so she would never be found.

The trunk lifted. Bright light blinded her. Strong arms tugged her brusquely from the trunk and clumsily set her on the ground. Pebbles and rocks ate into her legs and backside. Dust tickled her nose.

Holding his firearm, the kidnapper nudged it under her chin, forcing her to look up at him. She squinted at the sunlight behind him, unable to fully see his features. But she'd already seen him and had memorized every inch of his face, which could be her death sentence.

"I would like to present you whole and unharmed, or else I fear my quarry will run. I'm going to remove the ties from your ankles. If you run, I won't kill you. You'll suffer much worse than that. Do you understand?"

Alexa nodded, imagining painful torture at the hands of this man. Her nose began to stuff up from the dusty ground or something in the trunk that had stirred her allergies. With her mouth covered, she struggled to breathe and leaned her head against the car bumper, trying to slow her need for oxygen.

He cut the plastic ties around her ankles. Alexa straightened her legs.

"I'm going to pull the tape from your mouth so you can breathe. If you cause trouble, I'll put more tape on, and you'll have to suffocate. Do you understand?"

Alexa nodded vehemently. To stretch her legs, to breathe—yesterday, she took these for granted. He ripped the tape from her mouth, a cruel grin on his face, causing Alexa to almost cry out, but she muffled it behind closed lips, wanting to keep the tape at bay.

"Good girl." He patted the top of her head. "You can stand up if you like, but remember, don't run or you'll pay."

He thrust his hand toward her. Alexa turned her face and moved her body to the side, avoiding his touch. She tried to stand on her own, but it was useless with her wrists tied behind her back. He laughed, then tugged her to her feet.

"Now all that remains is to wait and see if he comes for you."

Alexa wanted to ask the man if he would then release her. But she knew too much, had seen too much. Her knees trembled at the thought.

Then she saw a plume of dust in the distance. Was it Graeme, or some innocent person or family about to stumble into trouble? Thirty seconds later, the grill of Graeme's Jeep came into view and the vehicle bounced over the dusty road. Alexa remembered they were to meet at a trail and she glanced at her surroundings, noting the trailhead marker. Did the kidnapper plan to lead Graeme and Alexa along that trail to some remote, forgotten strip of earth?

Graeme stepped from the Jeep and stood frozen, his stance wide. Relief flooded her, though all it took was the stricken look on his face and all her doubts became certain.

No way would the kidnapper allow either one of them to live.

৯

One look at Alexa standing there, frazzled and helpless next to her abductor who held a gun, and it was all Graeme could do to keep his knees from buckling under him.

That's why he simply remained standing, bracing himself with a wide stance. Alexa stared at him. In her eyes he saw relief knotted with dread, and too quickly, the relief completely vanished. She'd held on to the hope that he would show up—and the thought that she would even question his appearance ripped his soul open.

But worse, he imagined that fear replaced her momentary relief because she knew, like Graeme, that it would take a miracle for them to escape alive and unscathed.

Lord in heaven, if I haven't prayed enough already, I'm asking You again—show us a way out! I'm sorry it had to come to this before I would step out with the truth.

"I'm here just like you asked. Now let her go." Graeme forced coolness into his voice as he made his way toward

Alexa and the kidnapper. He came here with every intention of negotiating for her life.

"Not so fast." The black-haired man grinned, revealing his confidence that he had the upper hand, and waved his gun. "I need for you to get into the car now."

Graeme held his hands out. "Look, I don't know why you're doing this. Who are you? What do you want?"

"I think you know why I've come. As to who I am, you can call me Ricardo if you have need to speak a name." He shoved the pistol under Alexa's chin, making Alexa gasp, her eyes wide with fear. "Now get in the car."

Not willing to press him, Graeme lifted his palms in surrender. "Okay. . .okay. Just don't hurt her."

Graeme walked over to the car and looked at Ricardo.

Ricardo waved the gun. "Get into the driver's seat."

Doing as he asked, Graeme glanced Alexa's way, trying to send her a message of hope. The look she gave Graeme told him she was counting on him to get them out of this. He slid into the driver's seat, pushing a small flask out of his way, and kept his hands on the steering wheel. In the rearview mirror, he watched Ricardo force Alexa into the backseat, the gun aimed at her head.

"Now you will start the car and continue down this road."

After turning the key in the ignition, Graeme hesitated. "But where does this road go? I'm not going to drive if you're not going to release her."

In the rearview mirror, Graeme looked into Ricardo's narrow eyes and his crooked-tooth grin as he cocked the gun, pressing it against Alexa's temple. "I think you will, my friend."

My friend? The term was like a hot poker down Graeme's throat. "Please, I don't know anything. You have no reason to do this."

"You know enough. Drive unless you want her to die."

Graeme pushed on the accelerator and the car lurched forward on the bumpy road. He'd only thought he'd been terrified—now he felt like he and Alexa were looking death in the face, and it went by the name of Ricardo. Why, oh why had he gotten involved with her? If he hadn't fallen for her amazing eyes and lustrous hair, for her inner strength and beautiful spirit, for her persistence and talent, she wouldn't be here right now with him, facing certain death.

But how could he have resisted beautiful Alexa Westover—especially when she so clearly returned the affection and attraction? "I'm so sorry, Alexa," he murmured.

His own safety aside, his first priority was to make sure Alexa survived this, and by the looks of things he would have to act soon. Unfortunately, negotiating had never been his forte. He would have to take physical action against Ricardo, but if he was going to die anyway, at least Alexa would have a chance this way. Either way, he had to formulate an escape plan and quickly.

"Where does this road go?" He pretended he didn't know this region, but he was well acquainted with the wilderness they were entering and knew the road would eventually dead-end. At one time the state park service had planned to complete the road through this wilderness, giving access to the coast. No doubt Ricardo had every intention of dumping them where they wouldn't be found for a very long time, if ever.

"You'll find out soon enough."

Graeme's pulse roared in his ears at the thought of the road ending. He drove slowly, thinking and praying. Images of that fateful rainy day when Summer died replayed in his head, as if foreshadowing his current predicament with another woman he loved.

This is my fault! I never should have fled. I should have stayed to fight.

He couldn't allow this to happen again. If nothing else, he should tell Alexa how much he loved her now, before it was too late to tell her—he'd left too much unsaid to Summer—although that might frighten Alexa even more. She might believe he'd given up on them surviving this. And that would be half true. He still held on to hope that Alexa would live, because he intended to take Ricardo with him to the next world.

He glanced in the mirror and caught her terrified gaze. "Alexa, I love you. If I had it to do over again, I'd give up the trees for you. I'd live with you in New York, or wherever you wanted to live—you've become important to me."

Again he glanced in the mirror and saw her eyes shimmering.

"Really, Graeme?" she asked, a tremor in her voice.

"Yes. I'm sorry it took Costa Rica coming back to bite me for me to tell you how I feel."

Ricardo responded with a malicious chuckle. "I knew you remembered why I had come for you, my friend. Have you told your new girlfriend everything? Like what happened to the last one?"

&

Alexa wanted to tell the jerk to shut up.

Graeme must be saying he loved her because he feared the end was near, and that terrified her, but at the same time. . .

Graeme loves me. . . .

Her throat constricted, but like Graeme, she was desperate to tell him everything. "I love you, too. I would give anything if we had more time together. Please. . ." She choked on the next words. "Tell me we'll have our time together."

"Pray, Alexa. I can't believe that God brought us together just to have this henchman end it all."

"That's enough. The both of you shut up before I shut you up!"

Graeme stopped the car when the road dead-ended. The fact that they were now stopping yanked away Alexa's moment of hope, and then with a look in the mirror, she noticed the sliver of a grin on Graeme's face. Why was he smiling under these circumstances?

Was it because she loved him? Unfortunately, love wouldn't be enough to save them.

twenty

Hearing Alexa say she loved him and ask him to tell her they would have time together ignited Graeme with determination. They *had* to survive this. And in that moment, it was as if the forest mist had lifted.

He saw things clearly now.

In Costa Rica, Graeme wasn't on his own turf and had nothing with which he could fight or save Summer from the trouble she'd stirred. But what Ricardo apparently hadn't taken into this equation was that the redwoods were Graeme's backyard. He was far more familiar with these woods than Ricardo was.

Graeme knew how to survive in the wilderness, and that flask could be of use. That is, if he could get them free.

The tricky part would be escaping without getting shot—and that's where a little muscle and a little faith—the size of a mustard seed—would come into play.

If we can just get away from him, he'll never catch us or find us.

Graeme drew in a breath, fearing that his next question might accelerate the man's deadly plans, when Graeme hadn't quite formulated his own.

Time. He needed time.

"Now. You can get out."

Slowly Graeme opened the door and climbed from the car, praying every second that God would provide an escape. By the time he stepped on the ground and got out, Ricardo was already standing next to Alexa, holding the muzzle of the gun in her back.

Graeme hoped for the chance to punch this man for his part in killing Summer. For terrifying Alexa. Graeme would do everything he could to make sure that was all Ricardo did to Alexa.

"Where are you taking us now?" he asked.

"We're going for a hike. This time no one is going to escape. The animals should take care of your bodies."

Alexa gasped and covered her mouth.

Graeme ground his teeth, hating that Ricardo had been so graphic in front of her. "You said you were going to let her go if I met you."

"I don't recall those exact words. But even if I said them, surely you didn't believe me."

"No."

"And yet you met me, willing to die with your girlfriend this time. I'm impressed."

Shame squeezed Graeme's insides. Ricardo thought him a coward as well, just like Alexa had. But maybe Graeme had survived to fight another day, and today was that day.

Using his gun, Ricardo motioned for them to start walking toward the edge of the woods. "Don't even think of trying anything, or you'll get to watch her suffer."

How could any man use a woman like that? Ricardo was a monster. He nudged Alexa forward and she stumbled.

&

Alexa righted herself quickly enough, avoiding Ricardo's expected rebuke. It would be tough hiking in her Jimmy Choos—the pair that she still had left—but better that than walking with her bare feet against the pebbles, sharp rocks, and all manner of insects and spiders, though that was the least of her worries. Not that Ricardo cared at all. She'd put them on anticipating the drive to the airport and the subsequent return to her life in New York. At the time, she hadn't known she'd be kidnapped!

Now it appeared she would never leave her childhood playground.

She thought about growing up here, about playing hide-and-seek in the redwoods, that is, before she got lost. After a night spent alone in the shadowy and dark forest, she wouldn't dream of hiding in the woods even to play a game.

Strange that life experiences could change a person's perspective. Now she'd give anything for the opportunity to hide in this forest—she welcomed the protection offered by the lofty trees in the wilderness looming ahead of them. But how could she escape into the shelter of the redwoods? It wasn't like Ricardo would stand by and watch her chase after a rabbit like she'd done as a child.

She stumbled again, finding it more difficult with each step to trudge along this overgrown trail. If she survived this, maybe she would film a historical documentary about the man who invented high heels and the reasons women wore them.

Ricardo was literally breathing down her neck now.

Suddenly she knew what to do. She watched Graeme's lithe form hiking ahead of her. What was he thinking? Was he also formulating a plan?

If she put her idea into action, would he cooperate? Follow her lead?

Besides the kidnapper, he was the only one standing in the way, and if he didn't understand what she had in mind, it wouldn't work. She needed his participation.

But time was running out. Minutes, maybe only a few seconds, remained of her life if she didn't act now.

Graeme walked ahead of her deeper into the woods as Ricardo jabbed her in the back with his gun. Did he have a specific spot he'd chosen to do his deed? How did she get away from him before it was too late? This was. . .insane.

Her heels snagged again and she stumbled. She hoped Ricardo didn't make her take them off because her plan wouldn't work if he did. Graeme whirled around to face her.

Ricardo immediately lifted the gun to her temple, pressing hard. Alexa couldn't help her breathy whimpers. If only she'd taken some sort of defensive fighting course, she'd know how to elbow the guy right where it counted. Still, she wasn't sure she would have the guts with a loaded gun pointed at her head.

"She can't walk in those," Graeme said, searching her eyes, a slight grin at the corner of his mouth.

Remnants of the same grin he'd had in the car. How could he smile at a time like this? Unless. . .

Unless he was trying to signal her. "Glad you didn't stab me in the back with your nails like you did before. Remember?"

Ricardo predictably jabbed the gun in her back.

From there, everything seemed to happen in slow motion.

Alexa stumbled forward again. She ground her heel into a rock. It snapped off, and she fell.

At lightning speed, Graeme shoved her out of the way midfall. He rammed into Ricardo.

"No!" she screamed. "Graeme!"

A deafening gunshot rang out. *Lord, help us!*

Graeme wrestled with Ricardo, pressing Ricardo's gun hand upward, and two more shots fired off rapidly. Alexa screamed and took cover, crouching behind a tree. Whatever happened next, she was going to have to run for it. She unfastened her sandals but held on to them. They represented her life in New York—a life she was hanging on to by a precarious thread. Running away from where she'd grown up had been her way of surviving.

And then Alexa knew. . .she was a survivor.

She would live through this. She and Graeme together.

Another shot rang out.

How many bullets did that leave? She had no idea about guns.

Was he trying to use all the bullets?

That would effectively put them on equal footing. The men fought and then fell to the ground together. Graeme got the upper hand and rolled onto Ricardo.

He knocked the gun from Ricardo and it slid a few feet away.

Graeme punched Ricardo in the gut and the face, appearing

to lose himself in pummeling the man.

Incapacitating that man works for me.

But the gun. . .she had to get the gun. It rested on the far side of where the two battled. From where she crouched, she rose and made her way to circle them and retrieve the weapon. With that in hand, she could end this.

They could take Ricardo to the police. Graeme could tell them everything about Costa Rica then.

Ricardo slammed a rock into Graeme's head. He went limp and fell over.

No. . . .Graeme! Alexa's heart wrenched. She wanted to rush to him. Had Ricardo killed him?

Ricardo eyed her, a wicked, yellow-toothed grin spreading over his face. They both glanced at the gun. She could never beat him. Her already-racing heart seemed to prepare for launch after countdown. *Three, two, one. . .*

Blastoff! In that instant, Ricardo scrambled toward the gun.

And. . .Alexa ran the other way.

❧

Pain sliced through Graeme's head. Momentarily stunned, he reoriented himself to the critical situation and hurriedly got to his feet. Ricardo was inches from the gun. Alexa sprinted by Graeme and grabbed his arm.

Together they ran as fast as they could, just making the trees.

A bullet whizzed by. Alexa froze and hunkered behind a large redwood.

"No." Graeme kept his voice low but forceful. "If we stay here, he'll find us. The trees only get thicker as we go. We have to keep moving."

He pulled her behind him, and they ran. Another bullet slammed the tree next to Alexa, splintering the bark. She ducked, but Graeme forced her to keep moving.

Considering the nine-millimeter, Graeme knew Ricardo had seven more shots left before he had to reload.

They kept moving, continuing through the redwoods,

which in this part of the forest grew thick with a variety of trees. Ricardo had chosen this rough country so that the authorities would never find Graeme and Alexa. By the same thinking, Graeme figured he could lose Ricardo.

Somehow he needed to face the man and end this—but not with Alexa's life at stake.

Breathing hard, she stopped and rested against a tree. "Is he still following us?"

"We have to keep going until we can be sure. Otherwise he can shoot us where we stand without any warning."

"But are we lost now, Graeme?" Her hands on her hips, she took long breaths. "I just. . .I can't get lost again."

Again? Graeme frowned. "With any luck, Ricardo will be the one who gets lost. Let's move and keep quiet."

Graeme gently urged her ahead of him as he glanced back. Keeping her in front of him now would be the best way to protect her from any more bullets if they even came. Ricardo couldn't know where he was if he'd followed them. Graeme hoped the man had given up, but he wasn't willing to take that chance.

The problem remained that Ricardo might be waiting for them if and when they made their way out of this wilderness. The thick woods grew dark, the hiking more difficult with the steeper incline. Graeme aimed to go higher so he could get a look at their surroundings and better determine which path would lead them to help. Help that he should have gotten long ago.

Finally, they stood on a precipice and looked over the vast wilderness around them.

Breathtaking. As far as the eye could see, the tallest trees in the world mingled with other species as they swelled, rising with the hazy Siskiyou Mountains and falling in the valleys and ravines. Graeme wished he could enjoy the moment.

He grabbed Alexa's hand and squeezed, unwilling to relinquish control of his emotions—everything flooding his thoughts. They'd both nearly lost their lives. They'd both confessed their love. His heart swelled with love for her now, but under the circumstances, he might overwhelm her.

From where they stood, the sound of metal crashing and twisting resonated through the forest. Alexa gasped. "What was that?"

"I think Ricardo has just taken care of the Jeep. He doesn't want to leave us a way out."

"How can you be sure?"

"That's what I would do if I were him."

"What are we going to do?" Alexa pulled her hand away.

"Look." Graeme pointed toward a plume of dust in the distance. "You can see him driving away in his car."

He caught a glimpse of the small car before it disappeared behind the trees. "Well, at least we don't have to worry about him chasing us now. But it's still too risky to hike back along the road. He'll expect us to try. Besides, it's probably a longer hike than the direct route."

They'd done it. Graeme heaved a long sigh. They'd actually survived this. For now.

"Thank You, Lord," he said. Now it was just him and Alexa in the wilderness, and *that* Graeme could handle.

"What happened, anyway? I watched you and Barry drive away."

Alexa dropped to the ground, sitting against a fallen trunk. "We stopped to get gas. I thought he was after you, not me. That I was safe. There wasn't anyone else around. I left my room in such a rush and I needed to use the restroom. It was one of those old around-the-side-of-the-building facilities."

She covered her face and her shoulders shook. "That's when the guy grabbed me. I have no idea what Barry thought when I never returned."

Graeme slid to the ground next to her and put his arm around her shoulders. "It's over, sweetheart. It's over."

If Barry knew anything of what happened, he would have called the police and someone was already searching for Alexa.

She looked up at him, her eyes wide. "What do you mean it's over? We're miles from civilization—too far to make it before it gets dark, and maybe too far to make it even in a few hours."

Hours? Try days.

twenty-one

"How will we survive? With no cell service, it's not like we can call anyone." Alexa watched Graeme's eyes, wishing she could find comfort in their forest-green depths, but it just wasn't working this time.

His signature cockeyed grin spread over his face.

"Why are you smiling?"

"Because you're so cute."

Alexa shook her head and looked away. *What are we going to do, Lord?* Graeme apparently wasn't willing to take their dire circumstances seriously. To think, moments before she'd wished for the chance to find safety in these woods, but now she realized she'd only traded one lethal situation for another.

"Am I the only sane person here?" she asked.

"Ever heard the term *survival skills?*"

She whipped her head around and stared. "Sure. I haven't got them. So I hope you're telling me that you do."

"If there's one thing I know how to do, it's how to survive in these woods." He chuckled. "What do you think? I spend all day working as far away from civilization as possible, and I wouldn't know how to survive in the wilderness?"

Alexa stood up and brushed off her jeans. "I still don't see how you can laugh about any of this."

Graeme remained sitting. He'd picked up a stick and drew in the dirt. "I hate seeing how distressed you are."

"Laughing the situation off isn't helping, if that's what you think." Alexa began pacing. Losing her way in the King Solomon giant redwood was one thing, but this was entirely different.

Not like this. Her legs quivered even more than they had when Ricardo had a gun pointed at her. But somehow, that

145

experience had been almost too surreal for her mind to accept.

But this. . .this she'd experienced before firsthand, and her mind knew very well what to expect. The difference between now and then? Someone had been looking for her the instant she'd gotten lost and they knew approximately where to look, and even then, she wasn't found until the next day.

He threw down the stick and stood up. "I only thought to lighten things up."

"Brilliant. Let's see some of those skills."

"All right." He gently lifted her hand. "Give me those shoes."

Graeme took the shoes from her and examined them.

"What—what are you doing?"

Taking the shoe that wasn't broken, he slammed the heel against rock.

"No!" Alexa yelled at him. "Not my Jimmy Choos! I was going to get the other one fixed."

"I'm glad to hear that. It means that deep down, you trust me to get you out of here." He lifted the other shoe and compared the bottom of them both. "You can still get them fixed if you think it's necessary, but right now, you need shoes."

Alexa took them from him, slipping them on her feet. "They feel funny."

"Now you're good to go. Follow me." Graeme took off, heading in the opposite direction from where they'd come.

Alexa followed, smiling a little to herself. "What's the rest of the plan?"

"Do you still have your cell on you?"

"If that mattered, the guy would have taken it from me. But sure, it's in my pocket."

Alexa reached into her jeans and pulled the phone out, fearing it had been crushed or broken.

"Crud, the screen is cracked. Don't you have one with you?"

"Mine is turned on. Yours might still work. Let me see this."

"I don't understand. If we can't get a signal, what's this all about?"

"At some point, someone will be looking for us. The authorities can still possibly get a ping on one of our phones. That's what we're going to hope and pray for as we hike back to civilization. Understand?"

Alexa sagged. "I'm sorry for giving you a hard time. You know what you're doing. I should never have doubted you."

"Got it." He grinned and held up her cell for her to see that it still worked. "But the battery is low."

He handed it back to her, and when she took it, their hands brushed. Finally, all the pent-up emotions erupted. "Oh, Graeme."

"Come here." He brought her into his embrace, his arms wrapping tightly around her, keeping her safe.

She pressed the side of her face against his sturdy chest and heard the strong beat of his heart. "I feel like my life is in your hands right now." And her heart. . .

God, why did You let me get lost again?

Please give me a sign that You're with us. That we're going to make it out alive. Forgive me for struggling to trust You.

Graeme brushed his hand down her hair. "We're going to be fine. But we need to get going. We need to find or make shelter for the night, preferably next to a water source."

"Find shelter? Are you expecting there to be a cabin out here?"

When Graeme released her, he kissed her lightly on the lips and smiled. "You'll see. Ready?"

"Yes." Alexa hiked behind him around the giant ferns and other plants she couldn't identify. When space allowed, she hiked next to him. This might be an interesting addition to her documentary. Or not.

"Tell me about your childhood, Graeme. We've got plenty of time; I'd like to know you much better."

He glanced her way and grinned. "Right now I think we'd better save our energy. We can talk once I figure things out."

That sounded a little too ominous for Alexa. He'd convinced her that all was well, but maybe he'd only been protecting her from the truth. She decided to let him focus on keeping them alive and walked quietly, following his lead and praying.

They spent the rest of the afternoon—what seemed like hours to her aching legs and feet—until the evening became chilled and the forest began to grow dark, which was long before the summer sun would set.

She hoped they'd find shelter soon.

❧

Full-on night would be upon them within the hour, and Graeme wanted to kick himself for not stopping earlier to set up a makeshift camp. The way Alexa clung to him now, she acted like a small child terrified of the dark.

A fire cave that looked big enough for the both of them waited just ahead. He heard the trickle of water near them. Relief swept through him, but he didn't let Alexa see that, wanting to keep her reassured. Fortunately, he'd slipped the flask out of the car with him. With the small container, he could boil the water. Otherwise, he'd have to collect dew, or they'd have to take their chances with giardia and other contaminants before drinking the water. Twenty years ago, he wouldn't have worried as much about drinking the water.

When Graeme finally stood next to the multitrunked redwood, he peered up a few feet into the fused trunks—a perfect nest for his little bird.

"What are you doing? Are we stopping here?" Alexa asked.

Graeme saw a scared little girl when he looked at her. Concern rippled through him, but then, maybe her reaction was normal. And he was simply one of a billion in the clueless male of the human species.

"Remember seeing the fire cave in King Solomon? There's an opening big enough for the both of us to stay tonight."

Alexa frowned, clearly not happy with his choice. "I thought you said there was a cabin around here somewhere."

Graeme sighed. "Don't worry. This will be perfect. I'm going to go up and check it out first, though, okay?"

"Don't take too long." Alexa nodded then pressed her back against the tree, looking out into the forest.

Graeme climbed up into the ample base of the trunk and looked inside the cave. It was warm and dry, which was good. He'd feared it would be too wet. He ran his hand around inside and brushed out the old webs, sending any spiders scurrying.

He descended the trunk then plopped on his feet. "Let me help you up."

Alexa hesitated.

"Come on. You can rest up there while I build a fire."

"What about food? Are you going to cook us dinner, too?" Finally, a smile brightened her face.

Graeme hadn't realized how much he missed seeing her smile. Making her smile. He hoped one day soon he could put that smile on her face every day.

But he was being far too expectant about a future with her.

"I can forage for edible plants and berries, kill a small animal. More than likely, we'll just eat bugs."

Even in the waning light, Alexa's face paled. "You're kidding, right? Because if you aren't, then I can just wait until we're rescued, or at least wait for those berries."

Graeme laughed. He reached into his shirt pocket. "While I'd love to show off my most excellent survival skills, for now we'll share this energy bar."

"You!" Alexa smacked him in the arm. "How can you joke at a time like this?"

"Take the whole thing. I've got a couple more."

"So you just happen to have that in your pocket?" She tore at the wrapper.

"Force of habit. I've always got something to eat in my pockets." He grinned. "But at some point, we might need to ration. Now, up with you."

He gave her a boost then followed her up to make sure she

got comfortable. He had no doubt she would instantly fall asleep once she was.

Alexa paused at the cave entrance and peered back at him. "I hate to sound like a wimp, but what about spiders?"

"I brushed it out for you. But you can just sit out here if you'd rather, while you wait for me to come back."

"Where are you going?"

"I won't be long. Don't worry."

❧

Alexa watched Graeme climb down and then hop to the ground. She nestled against the trunk just outside the fire cave, planning to keep a vigilant watch for anything that might approach. Elk, bear, mountain lion, raccoon, spider, snake, or. . .Ricardo. Of course, Ricardo wasn't coming for them now. Nor could she afford to waste energy thinking about the possibility that he might watch for their miraculous return to town. She had to survive this night. What exactly did she fear?

She'd made it out alive that night she'd been lost.

The ancient redwood boasted several trunks springing from one base and cradled Alexa, sheltering her from the darkness, from the woods, and. . .from the memories of that night long ago. Despite her resolve to watch for danger as she waited for Graeme, her eyes grew heavy.

Flickering light startled her. Alexa opened her eyes and shifted, trying to shake off the uncomfortable ache in her back.

Where am I? Her grogginess lifted and she remembered she was in the tree, waiting for Graeme. Apparently she was no good at keeping watch. Graeme was on the ground, stoking a small fire he'd surrounded with rocks.

She crawled to the edge of the trunk and watched his handsome face and athletic form in the flickering firelight. Why had she been so afraid? And why had she ever wanted to leave this place?

When he glanced up and grinned at her, the monarchs were back, fluttering inside again.

"You're awake." He stood from where he'd crouched next to the fire and made his way over to the tree.

"Why didn't you wake me?" Alexa hung her legs over the edge.

"Let me help you down." Graeme reached toward her.

"No, I'm good." She could do this, and wanted to show him her strong side.

"You sure?" His cockeyed grin sent her heart flipping.

On second thought, maybe she did want to feel his arms around her. "No, I'm not. Maybe a little help couldn't hurt."

Alexa climbed halfway and then Graeme's hands were on her waist. Once her feet were on the ground, he swept her into his arms. She buried her face in his chest, loving the feel of security.

When she looked at him again, his gaze roamed her face. "Are you. . .okay?"

She smiled. "Yes."

"You look better."

"Thanks, I guess."

"You thirsty?" He moved to the campfire and lifted a small flask. "I boiled the water and let it cool. It's safe to drink now."

Alexa took a long drink, quenching her thirst. When she finished, she handed it back to Graeme.

"There's something I want to show you." He held out his hand.

She placed her palm in his. It felt right. Good.

Graeme led her away from the fire, from their tree. Unease at leaving the cozy little camp he'd created tried to make her crazy again.

"How much farther?"

"Shh. It's just right there." Graeme pointed.

But he didn't need to. A tree glowed silvery-white in the moonlight. "What. . .is that?" Alexa took a step forward.

Graeme seemed to take her cue and led her deeper into the forest and away from their fire. "It's a rare sight, that's what. An albino redwood."

Alexa reached up and ran her hand over a few white fronds. "It's beautiful."

"There are only six that we've discovered in all the redwoods. Now, seven."

Taking her eyes from the striking tree, Alexa studied Graeme's face and his eyes as he admired the tree.

"I think it's a sign from God. I prayed He'd give me a sign that we were going to make it out alive," she said.

Pulling his gaze from the tree, Graeme focused on Alexa, but she saw the same admiration for the tree in his eyes now as he looked at her.

"I think you're right," he said.

Alexa snuggled against Graeme when he wrapped his arm around her waist. Together they looked on at one of nature's exotic mutations; or rather, one of God's striking creations.

"There's something I've wanted to tell you," she said.

twenty-two

Graeme released her, hearing the serious tone of her voice. "Let's go back to the fire. I don't like to leave it."

Her soft hand melted into his as he led her back to their simple camp. He dropped down at the base of the tree and invited her to sit next to him. He held his arm out, and Alexa leaned her head back, her warm body fitting perfectly into the crook of his arm. He ran his hand through her glossy dark hair—something he'd wanted to do from the first day he'd seen her.

He was glad she'd gotten some rest. She no longer seemed as timid about her surroundings. Now she was much more relaxed.

"What was it you wanted to tell me?"

She drew in a long breath. He could tell she was getting tired again.

"You want another energy bar?" he asked.

"No, thank you. But how many of those things did you bring with you?" She chuckled.

Graeme laughed. "Enough. Now, tell me."

"Remember when you mentioned people sometimes get lost in the woods?"

What was she getting at with this? "Yeah?"

"Well, I was one of those people."

Graeme held his breath.

"That's why. . .I left. That and the fact that the incident ended up tearing my family apart. I never wanted to come back here. And I especially never wanted to spend a night lost in the woods."

Tensing at her story, he relinquished his hold to face her more completely. "Oh, Alexa. I'm so sorry. I. . . Well, that explains why you acted so anxious earlier. But you know we're going to be fine, right? You said God gave you the tree as a sign."

"Yes. I know we're going to live. I survived the night all on my own as a child because I was finally rescued. But that night terrified me. It was hard to let that go. I think maybe God wanted me to be here again so I could get over it." A slight smile lifted her lips. "And I have you. God gave me you to help me through."

"I'm so sorry I brought you into this mess, Alexa. I hope you can forgive me."

"There's nothing to forgive."

"What made you come here to do the documentary, if you were that averse to it?"

"That's a long story."

"I'm not going anywhere." Graeme settled back against the tree and offered his arm to Alexa again. He was glad when she took him up on it and snuggled closer.

"This isn't anything I'm proud of, but I made the mistake of getting involved with the man I worked for. You already know that."

"Clive?"

"That's the one. People working at the production company didn't like me because they thought he showed me favoritism. I guess I did take advantage of the situation, but eventually I discovered that Clive was spending time with someone new and I called him on it. He denied it, of course, and when someone wanted to sponsor this documentary, Clive sent me to work on it, knowing how I felt about my home."

"I don't get it. Why didn't you just quit?"

Alexa yawned. "Believe me, I wanted to. But you don't just quit on Clive. If I want to work in this industry, I can't burn bridges, especially with him. Like I said, it was a mistake to get involved to begin with."

Graeme didn't like what he heard. "And do you still believe Clive was seeing someone else?"

"I'm not sure what to think anymore, whether I was overreacting and possessive, or he was cheating."

Alexa had unfinished business with this man in New York. And Graeme was even more unsettled about a future with her. "Well, I know what I think. I think you should climb up into the fire cave before you fall asleep. You're yawning every five seconds."

They stood and he assisted her in climbing the tree. Once in the crook of the trunk, she looked down at him. "Aren't you coming up?"

"I need to put out the fire first." And then he planned to sleep outside the fire cave unless Alexa grew chilled, and in that case, he would keep her warm.

Once he finished putting out the fire and making sure the embers were completely snuffed out, he allowed his eyes to adjust to the forest, thankful for the small glimmer of light from the full moon tonight.

Believing Alexa was already asleep inside the large fissure in the tree, Graeme settled himself against the opening of the fire cave.

"Graeme?" Her voice was soft. "Are you there?"

"Yep. I'm guarding the cave." He hoped she caught his teasing tone.

"Thank you."

Maybe not. He smiled at the idea that Alexa thought of him as watching over her. "You're welcome."

"Can I ask you something?"

Their exchange was beginning to remind him of the Walton ritual good night calls.

"Anything at all," he said, savoring this moment with her, lost in the forest. If they were not rescued tomorrow, the day would tax their energy and patience. Could their frail relationship survive that?

"Those words we spoke to each other when we thought we were going to die—were they real?"

He closed his eyes and listened to the night sounds. At least for his part, the words were true. But her question disturbed him. "Everything I said to you was true, Alexa. I love you."

"And I love you, too," she whispered.

Graeme wanted to crawl into the cave with her, but he knew better. Still, her question smacked him back to reality.

The better question is, will our words spoken to each other under harsh circumstances stand the test of the real world?

Once back in the real world, would Alexa return to her Clive?

≈

Pain broke into Alexa's dreams. She stirred awake and rolled to the side, her face pressing against soft mossy earth.

She gasped and sat up, remembering that she'd slept in the giant crack of a redwood trunk. Jerking around, she looked for Graeme. He wasn't inside the cave with her. She could have sworn he was there beside her, keeping her warm.

But maybe that had been a dream, and her cheeks grew hot. She was glad he wasn't outside the cave peeking in at that minute. She crawled out of the space and spotted Graeme on the ground next to the small fire he'd stoked. He was working hard for her. No doubt, if he were on his own, he would already be hiking toward civilization.

She scrambled out of the tree and dropped to her feet. Feeling a pang up her ankle, she reached down to rub it.

"Are you all right?" he asked.

"Yeah, I'm fine. How many days are we going to be at this, Graeme?" To think, last night she'd felt safe, and though she believed they were going to make it, she dreaded the thought of hiking for days.

He frowned but quickly recovered, replacing it with a grin. "I won't lie to you. The terrain slows us considerably. But remember, we're still hoping that the authorities will catch a ping from our phones."

Alexa yanked hers from her pocket. "No such luck. Mine's dead already."

"Why don't you get some nourishment before we head

out? I picked blackberries. I've got a few energy bars left, but I want to save them, just in case."

Alexa nodded and sat by the fire, feasting on Graeme's provisions and wanting nothing more than to take a hot shower, brush her teeth, and sleep on a soft mattress.

Suddenly a low roar caught her attention. "Do you hear that?"

Graeme looked up at the tree crowns. "It's a helicopter."

"They've found us!"

&

In her motel room, Alexa finished packing her things. She'd had to stay over for a couple of more days until the local authorities were done with their questions. Her flight out of Sacramento had been rescheduled again. She and Barry would drive back this evening and fly out tomorrow. She hoped beyond hope that Graeme would come see her off and say good-bye. Maybe they could discuss what they meant to each other, if there was a future for them.

They hadn't had that opportunity because they'd been rescued, though Alexa was grateful for that. Both were stunned to learn that Ricardo had been arrested. The gas station owner had gone to find the missing key for the men's restroom and had seen the man who'd taken the key throw a woman in the trunk of his car. Ricardo had parked in the back of the station, hoping to stay hidden.

The gas station owner had immediately called the police and given them the license plate number. When Alexa didn't return, Barry went inside the gas station, looking for her, and learned from the woman what happened. Once Ricardo was apprehended and taken in for questioning, they learned he was in the country with a bogus passport.

The news propelled Graeme forward in telling the truth about what happened in Costa Rica. They'd been quickly separated, each made to tell their side of the story and to give statements.

She assumed the authorities would look into working

with the Costa Rican government to investigate. But things took time. And right now, Alexa was running out of time. Someone knocked on the door. Alexa's insides warmed. *Oh, please let it be Graeme.*

"Barry." She smiled, hiding her disappointment. "I'm not ready yet."

"That's okay. I just wanted to check on you."

Alexa gave Barry a hug. "I can't thank you enough for what you did."

"There's nothing to thank. Take your time. You know where I live." He winked and gave her a strange smile, like he was keeping a secret. She was too tired to care.

She owed him for taking action when he did, calling the authorities and telling them what Alexa had told him about the situation when she disappeared, or else she might still be hiking.

Alexa closed the door, hating that she missed Graeme. Hating the growing fear that she might not see him before she left. Where was he?

Another knock came on the door, this time a different rhythm. *Graeme?*

Smiling, she swung the door open and frowned. "Clive?"

The man was handsome and took her breath away, especially dressed in a casual designer button-down shirt, the sleeves rolled to the elbow. His cologne wrapped around her, confusing her. Her reaction to his presence was all too familiar.

And unwelcome. *No. . . .*

The dark blue depths of Clive's eyes were haunted. "Baby, I've been so worried about you. As soon as I heard what happened, I took the next flight out."

"Really?" Alexa could hardly believe that he still cared. Or that it mattered. What was wrong with her?

She'd been hurt, terribly hurt, but never admitted it until that moment, because of her desperate need to be a career woman, strong and professional. Her desperate need to be loved by this man. But she'd given up on him weeks ago—

the first time she'd looked into the forest-green depths of Graeme's eyes.

He reached for her, tugging her into his arms. Clive worked out and took care of himself, but as he enveloped her, Alexa could feel the difference between his strength and Graeme's sturdy form.

It had been so long since he'd held her like this. So. . .long. *Why couldn't you have done this when I needed you to show me you cared?*

The room seemed to spin, making Alexa dizzy and weak. She wanted to step away from him. Why couldn't she. . .just. . .step. . .back?

He ran his hand down the back of her hair, reminding her of Graeme. Graeme's touch had conveyed love and tenderness, but Clive's conveyed ownership, much like she was a prize thoroughbred.

"I love you, baby. I'm sorry for all our troubles."

Alexa drew from her inner strength and fought the power Clive had held over her from the beginning. She freed herself from his arms. "It's too late, Clive."

He grinned in disbelief, holding his hands out. "I'm prepared to offer you the next big project, Alexa. You're going to love this one. It's everything you've ever wanted and more."

Her eyes grew moist as she listened to his words, but she killed the tears. He knew exactly how to work her, telling her he could give her everything she dreamed about. But those dreams had changed.

"There's nothing you have that I want." She could hardly believe her words, but they were true.

He chuckled, his half grin wavering. "You've been through a trauma. You're not making any sense."

Clive took a step forward, but Alexa stood her ground.

"Did you forget what we had together?" he asked.

Alexa shook her head. "I didn't forget. There were more bad times than good."

"I'm going to kiss you. Then let's hear what you have to say."

Alexa was almost as unsure as the overconfident Clive appeared to be. Would his kiss transport her back to the world she used to love? Would it change her heart, bring her love back to him? She feared the answer, and yet at the same time, her lack of response would convince him once and for all that she was serious about not wanting what he offered.

"Go ahead and kiss me, then."

Clive took another step forward, his face inches from hers. He slid one arm around her waist and weaved his other hand through the hair at the back of her head, then arched her backward, holding her in his arms—like some overdramatized romantic movie—and thoroughly kissed her.

Admittedly, her head began to swim, and she found herself trying to respond. If only she wanted to be lost in his world again, possibly she could get her career back on track. But what was she thinking? Her life had changed here. She had changed. No longer was she the same woman who would use her beauty, use this man, though she thought she had loved him, to get what she wanted.

Relief elated her. *It's over. . . .*

Finally, Clive ended the kiss and released his hold on her. Alexa smiled, but not for the reason Clive would expect. She was about to tell him when. . .

Graeme stood in the doorway, hurt in his eyes. He turned and trudged away.

twenty-three

No! Alexa dashed past Clive and out the door. "Graeme, wait!"

She grabbed his arm and tried to make him look at her, but he was intent on opening the door to his Jeep. "Listen to me, it's not what you think. I wanted to convince him that I didn't care anymore. He would only believe that if he kissed me."

Graeme opened the door, climbed in, and started the engine.

"Did you hear what I said? Why won't you listen to me?"

He backed the Jeep from the parking lot and drove away, never once looking at her.

What? Why didn't he believe her? Now what would she do? She'd just lost the man she loved while trying to convince another man she didn't love him. The world made no sense.

Alexa brushed by Clive, who stood there, hands in his pockets, watching the whole thing, she was sure. She plopped on the bed, refusing to cry in front of the man. He thought he had the upper hand now.

He shut the door behind him and sat in a chair. "I already know about your little infatuation with the scientist, and given my own indiscretions, I'm willing to let that slide. Now let's go home."

He stood and held his hand out to Alexa, fully expecting her to go back to New York with him. And what idiot wouldn't go back to their home and their job?

But her eyes had been opened to what she'd become in New York. She shook her head. "I'm not going with you."

Clive laughed. "But Alexa, you can't be serious."

Alexa stood and faced the man she'd believed she once

loved. "As of this moment, I'm officially resigning. I'll turn over all the work I've done on *Changing World, Changing Forests*, but I expect to be paid for that."

The irony? Her documentary was about how the changing world had changed the forest, but creating the film had the opposite effect on her.

The forest had changed her instead.

Clive frowned. "I don't believe this. You're serious, aren't you?"

Concern and tenderness glimmered behind his eyes, a rare thing. For an instant, she considered she'd made a mistake, but she blew out a breath. "Yes. Thank you for sending me here. It was a real eye-opener, as they say. This is my home, and I want to come back."

Clive paced the room, scratching his head. "I suppose we could move the offices to California."

He would do that for her? Did he really care that much? Was she making a mistake, giving him up? So much had happened in a short period of time, but now she knew the truth in her heart.

"No, you don't understand. I don't want to work for you anymore. I want you out of my life. We were never good for each other."

Clive said nothing and stared at her, looking like he'd suffered a great loss. She never would have believed that without seeing it.

She chuckled and looked at the floor then back up at him. "Besides, I have a great idea for a documentary. I'm going to start my own company, too."

To her surprise, he smiled. How she used to love that smile. "You're going to be my competition. I always figured that would happen one day."

He moved close to her and kissed her on the top of the head. "Good luck, Alexa. See you around."

Then Clive walked out the door, leaving her, too.

And Alexa dug her Jimmy Choos out of her luggage and tossed them, what was left of them, in the garbage.

❧

"What do you think about this?" Alexa's sister Camille held up an unusual black-and-white painting she'd created of a snowy winter scene. Sunbeams shined through the gray clouds across a mountain range and onto an iced-over lake. A reminder of an Ansel Adams photograph, only in oils.

Alexa gasped. "That's beautiful. I just. . .I think it might be too depressing, though."

While her husband, Romeo, attended a restaurant convention, Camille was staying with Alexa to help her decorate her rental home and set up the garage office for her new film company—Westover Productions.

Camille set the framed canvas on the floor against the wall. "Oh, sis, I'm sorry."

"I hope that doesn't hurt your feelings. The painting is amazing. Really. I feel special because my sister's paintings are in demand and I got one as a gift. Maybe put it in the living room?"

"Sure, I'll try it there."

Alexa stared out the window. From the small house situated on a hill, she could see the rocky beach and ocean. What a blessing.

Thank You, Lord.

But the skies were gray today, and between the muted coast and Camille's painting, Alexa could use a little color in her new office. In her life. She hadn't seen or spoken to Graeme in over a month.

Camille approached Alexa and rubbed her arm. "You really are in a bad place, aren't you?"

Alexa drew in a quick breath. "Not at all. I'm excited about being on my own. About being back in the redwoods and near my sisters. What could be better than that?"

Sympathy emanated from Camille's eyes before her smile replaced it.

"And I'm glad you're here, too." Camille gave Alexa a big hug. "Now I'm going to start working on dinner."

"Oh, don't bother. We'll get Chinese or something." Alexa didn't want to feel guilty for not helping Camille in the kitchen, but she needed to focus on her work.

"Nope. I'm cooking. You get busy working on your new company."

Camille left Alexa to herself, and she focused her thoughts on the new documentary. She had every intention of pursuing the injustice behind Graeme's fiancée's death, exposing the secrets Summer had discovered. Alexa had heard that the hydroelectric project had been delayed while authorities conducted an investigation. Someone had gone to great lengths to hide the truth about the environmental damage to the San Juan River and surrounding wetlands.

If she had any sense, she'd pursue another topic, because this one kept her thoughts on Graeme and she needed to let him go. Why was it so difficult? She hadn't known him that well—but he'd touched her soul, connecting with her, and she couldn't simply forget that.

Regardless of her failed relationship with Graeme, God had given her a second chance at being herself. He'd sent her back to the forest where her life had first changed for the worse, back to her roots and the quiet where she used to be on speaking terms with Him, and. . .

He'd healed her emotions. She felt whole now. If only she could have met Graeme after she'd found herself once again, after Clive was out of her life.

Alexa sighed and picked up the phone. Cameraman Garrett Kessler had expressed interest in working on this documentary with her and was prepared to travel to Costa Rica. Staring out the window at the big waves, whipped by a windy day, Alexa dialed Garrett's number.

A noise behind her drew her attention, and she turned to let Camille know she was on the phone.

Graeme—in all his handsome ruggedness—leaned against the doorframe, wearing a jacket the color of a worn-out green army fatigue. His eyes reflected a dark forest today as they searched hers.

Her heartbeat erratic, Alexa was unsure of his intentions, uncertain if she could allow herself elation at his appearance. But oh, how she wanted to dash into his arms. To make everything right between them again.

"Graeme. . ." Her lips spoke his name in a breathy whisper. "Why are you here?"

A sad smile lifted one corner of his mouth, but he said nothing. Probably as unsure as she was about what to say. Was there anything left between them?

"Why did you leave that day?" Alexa finally voiced the question that had burned inside ever since he'd walked away without listening to her explanation, without looking at her.

"You've heard the old saying, 'If you love something, let it go. If it's yours, it will come back to you'?"

"Yes." *That had better not be your excuse.*

"Because I knew you were at a crossroad. I had to give you the space you needed to decide what you really want in life. I couldn't stand in the way of that. I knew if I looked at you, then it was all over for me, because believe me, Alexa, I wanted to fight with everything in me to keep you."

"Then"—Alexa steadied her voice—"why didn't you?"

"Because where you are in your life right now was a decision you had to make on your own, without coercion from me. And look at you." His crooked grin made her dizzy again. "You've got your own company, set up in your own office. And you chose to live in the redwoods. You came home all on your own. I didn't want to be another Clive in your life, using you to get what I wanted."

Could he be any more selfless? Alexa could hardly comprehend all that he said. Graeme had looked into her eyes and saw who she really was inside. It took being with him for her to find herself again, for her to realize how much she missed her home in the redwoods.

"Besides, seeing you with him made me really angry." He took a step toward her, and in his eyes she could see the longing there. He'd missed her as much as she'd missed him.

৯

In an instant, Alexa was in his arms, kissing him. Her lips were soft, yet demanding more of him, and at the same time pouring everything from her heart and soul into him. He needed this woman for his very survival, and he would protect her with his life.

Without Alexa, Graeme had struggled to live and breathe. But now he knew beyond a doubt that they were meant to be together, though for the weeks since he'd last seen her, doubts had slammed him every day.

His passion rising, he tore his lips from hers and whispered in her ear. "Marry me, Alexa. I can't live another day without you in my arms. I want to fall asleep with you beside me every night and wake up with you every morning. I've waited long enough to find you again, and life is too short. We both know that."

He cupped her cheeks in his hands and gazed into her stunning eyes—the eyes that he'd lost his heart to the very first moment he'd looked into them.

Her eyes reminded him of the Smith River swimming hole, clear and glistening. "Yes, Graeme. There's nothing I want more."

"How quickly can you be ready?"

A laugh escaped her sweet lips. "I have plans to go to Costa Rica. I'll give them up for you, Graeme, if that's what you want."

"No, Alexa. I can't change who you are, nor do I want to. You're a woman bent on exposing injustices. A woman with a cause. I love that about you. You taught me to stop running, to stop hiding, and to stop fearing. We'll go together. After we get married, that is."

In reply, her brilliant smile brightened his heart and burned away any remaining doubts.

৯

Images of the last month and week ran through Alexa's head

at a dizzying speed. She couldn't believe how her life had changed in such a short period of time.

To think that one week ago, Graeme had come back to her and asked her to marry him. Within a week's time, they'd prepared all the necessary paperwork and arrangements were made for their small wedding.

Alexa and Graeme now stood side by side at the pulpit in the small Church in the Redwoods.

A light emanated from Pastor Jacob's eyes as he read the wedding vows, and Alexa listened to Graeme repeat the words with truth and passion. Camille and her husband, Romeo, Sela, and even Aunt Erin were attending, along with Sally from the diner, Graeme's research associates Randy and Peter, and Peter's sister, Karen.

In the forest that night long ago, Alexa had lost something precious; then she'd lost her father, her mother when she died, and finally, she'd lost herself, burying her pain in the city lights and skyscrapers of Manhattan. But she'd found her way back, thanks to God, thanks to His bringing Graeme into her life. And nothing she could have imagined could compete with the plans He'd made for her.

"I now pronounce you husband and wife. Ladies and gentlemen, I give you Mr. and Mrs. Graeme Hawthorne."

Alexa had planned to turn and face her smiling family, but Graeme tugged her into his arms again and kissed her with all the passion of a man who was tired of waiting. Her ears rang with his love and something in the distance. . .laughter and clapping.

epilogue

One year later. . .

Alexa brought the bowl of popcorn to Graeme and gently lowered herself on the sofa, which was becoming more difficult with each passing day. At eight and a half months pregnant, she felt like an elephant the way she lumbered around, and feared Graeme no longer thought her attractive, especially with the way he seemed to go overboard at convincing her that she was.

The baby kicked hard this time. "Oh, there was another one."

Graeme smiled and placed his hand on her huge belly. "I think I can actually feel Little Ricky's feet there," he said.

The commercial ended, returning the programming back to PBS and the documentary *Diminishing Returns*, about man's battle to protect nature while securing energy resources.

Alexa grabbed some popcorn and enjoyed the buttery flavor. She was relieved to be back in the redwoods, in their own home, expecting their first child. Filming the documentary had taxed her energies and creativity, and their relationship when she and Graeme learned she was pregnant—but she'd finished and quickly sold the film, creating a name for Westover-Hawthorne Productions.

For now, she decided, she was all Graeme's, her focus on her husband and her baby. She would follow God's leading to the next important documentary. After all, that plan had definitely been working for her.

She tilted her head sideways to watch her handsome husband as he leaned forward on his elbows, caught up in the story playing on the television. The scene was a particularly confrontational one in which Alexa and her cameraman had been threatened by Jarvis Construction.

Graeme exhaled next to her. "I hope you're done with this type of story for a while."

A deep, long ache sliced up her back. Surprise hit Alexa. She hadn't expected so much pain. "I just got my inspiration for our next story."

She tried to stifle her cry.

Eyes wide, Graeme turned his attention to her. "What's wrong?"

"I'm having a baby. It's time, Graeme. I think there's another contraction coming."

Graeme sprang to his feet. "Is that normal? I mean, isn't that a little fast?"

Alexa tried to breathe through the contraction the way she'd been taught, but instead she ended up holding her breath, concentrating on enduring the pain.

"I'll call the midwife."

Graeme tried to leave her side, but Alexa grabbed his wrist, squeezing with all her strength. "There's no time," she said between gritting her teeth.

"What do you mean?" His panic-stricken words seemed to magnify her pain.

Still gripping him, she worked to steady her voice. "You have to deliver the baby, Graeme."

"I can't—I can't. Let me call the midwife."

Alexa screamed. "The baby's coming *now*."

She wasn't sure how, but she had Graeme's hand again, and she burrowed her gaze into his, summoning all the strength to make him understand. "You. Can. Do. This. I know you can. You've climbed the redwoods; you've escaped a killer twice. You can deliver a baby."

Minutes later, Alexa was breathing easier and holding little Ricky—the nickname they'd given their little girl Raquel—in her arms, the cord still attached. Graeme insisted they wait until help arrived before cutting the umbilical cord. Sheryl, the midwife, was on her way, along with the ambulance Graeme had called. Dispatch had been able to talk him through the delivery.

He smiled down at her. "Ricky has your gorgeous eyes."

Alexa focused her gaze on the forest-green color of his. "You know their eyes change color, don't you?"

"She's keeping this color, and considering her impatience to be in this world the minute she decided it was time, she also has your strength of will."

Alexa could live with that. "You did it, Graeme. You delivered our baby."

"Sweetheart, you did all the work." Graeme leaned down and kissed her; then his gaze shifted from her to Ricky. The man was in love with their little girl.

"But I couldn't have done it without you." He'd been there for her since she'd met him. Kept her safe in the wilderness and protected her in Costa Rica. He never stifled her creativity and was her biggest supporter. And in him, Alexa had found home again. She knew who she was and who she wanted to be as long as she was resting in Graeme's sheltering love.

Dear Reader,

Growing up in Texas, I was always fascinated with the famous and mysterious redwood trees I saw in pictures and movies. They captivated me, and it was my dream to see them one day, but living far from Northern California, that idea seemed impossible. I couldn't have known that one day I would live in southern Oregon in a small town whose main highway was called Redwood Highway because it was the same highway that ran all the way into Northern California and the redwoods state park systems.

God blessed me beyond measure with this dream. Hiking in the redwoods with my family quickly became one of my favorite pastimes while living in Oregon for five years. Now I'm back in Texas, and I've returned to dreaming, but I've had the privilege to write Heartsong romance novels set in the redwoods.

In *Sheltering Love*, Alexa climbs a redwood tree with Graeme. In the real world, she would need to be an experienced tree climber in the arborist style, and then Graeme could teach her how to climb a redwood with a technique that's only been developed in recent years by a tree canopy scientist at Humboldt University. As you can imagine, one wrong move could be fatal. I took artistic license for the sake of the story and because I wanted you to experience climbing a redwood with Alexa.

Thank you for taking this journey with me.

Blessings,
Beth